Prais

"Rapier wit, goo____
eccentric characters make Daille's entry a first-class
romantic read."

—*RT Book Reviews* on *Family Matters*, 4.5 stars, Top Pick

"Daille crafts a beautiful love story with a steadfast
hero and a conflicted heroine who wants love on her
own terms. There's great relationship development in
this warm holiday read."

—*RT Book Reviews* on *The Lawman's Christmas Proposal*

"Daille has painted a wonderful story of two wounded
souls trying to find their way back to each other."

—*RT Book Reviews* on *The Rodeo Man's Daughter*

Praise for *USA TODAY* bestselling author Stella Bagwell

"A sweet story."

—*RT Book Reviews* on *Daddy's Double Duty*

"Her expressive narrative gives her seemingly ill-fated
couple substance and makes their love story palpable.
Talented storytelling keeps readers absorbed and
makes the first kiss unforgettable."

—*RT Book Reviews* on *Her Rugged Rancher*

"Inspiring and heartwarming."

—*RT Book Reviews* on *Her Texas Ranger*

"A wonderful read, rich in conflict and plenty of sparks.
Stella Bagwell will steal your heart."

—*RT Book Reviews* on *Just for Christmas*

HOME ON THE RANCH:
NEW MEXICO SECRETS

———— ⚒ ————

BARBARA WHITE DAILLE

USA TODAY Bestselling Author
STELLA BAGWELL

Previously published as *The Rodeo Man's Daughter*
and *His Texas Wildflower*

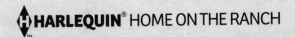

HARLEQUIN® HOME ON THE RANCH

ISBN-13: 978-1-335-50719-8

Home on the Ranch: New Mexico Secrets
Copyright © 2018 by Harlequin Books S.A.

First published as The Rodeo Man's Daughter
by Harlequin Books in 2012 and
His Texas Wildflower by Harlequin Books in 2011.

The publisher acknowledges the copyright
holders of the individual works as follows:

The Rodeo Man's Daughter
Copyright © 2012 by Barbara White-Rayczek

His Texas Wildflower
Copyright © 2011 by Stella Bagwell

PLEASE RECYCLE

THIS PRODUCT IS RECYCLABLE

Recycling programs
for this product may
not exist in your area.

HARLEQUIN®

Printed in U.S.A.

™ www.Harlequin.com

CONTENTS

The Rodeo Man's Daughter   7
by Barbara White Daille

His Texas Wildflower   241
by Stella Bagwell

Barbara White Daille and her husband still inhabit their own special corner of the wild, wild Southwest, where the summers are long and hot and the lizards and scorpions roam.

Barbara loves looking back at the short stories and two books she wrote in grade school and realizing that—except for the scorpions—she's doing exactly what she planned. She has now hit double digits with published novels and still has a file drawer full of stories to be written.

As always, Barbara hopes you will enjoy reading her books! She would love to have you drop by for a visit at her website, barbarawhitedaille.com.

Books by Barbara White Daille

Harlequin Western Romance

The Hitching Post Hotel

The Cowboy's Little Surprise
A Rancher of Her Own
The Lawman's Christmas Proposal
Cowboy in Charge
The Cowboy's Triple Surprise

Harlequin American Romance

The Sheriff's Son
Court Me, Cowboy
Family Matters
A Rancher's Pride
The Rodeo Man's Daughter
Honorable Rancher
Rancher at Risk

Visit the Author Profile page at Harlequin.com for more titles.

THE RODEO MAN'S DAUGHTER

BARBARA WHITE DAILLE

To my readers who love the town of Flagman's Folly, New Mexico.

I hope you enjoy this chance to visit there again!

And, as always, to Rich.

Chapter 1

A long memory made for bad company when a man had too much time on his hands. Especially when those hands held a sizable number of grudges.

Caleb Cantrell eased up on the gas pedal of the pickup truck he'd rented earlier that morning at the airport. He cut the engine and stepped down from the cab, his worn boots hitting the ground and raising a cloud of dust. First time in ten years he'd set foot in Flagman's Folly, New Mexico, and the layer of dirt that now marked him made it seem as if he'd never left.

Yet he'd come a hell of a long way since then.

Here on the outskirts of town, he stood and stared across the unpaved road at the place he'd once had to call home. After he'd left there, he'd slept in no-tell motels, lived out of tour buses and trucks and, eventually, spent time in luxury hotels. Didn't matter where you went, you could always tell the folks who took pride in ownership from the ones who didn't give a damn.

Even here, you could spot the evidence. Not a ritzy neighborhood, not a small community, just a collection of ramshackle houses and tar-paper shacks. A few had shiny windows and spindly flowers in terra-cotta pots. Some had no windowpanes at all. Here and there, he noted a metal-sided prefab home with too many coats of paint on it and weeds poking through the cinder blocks holding it up.

And somewhere, beyond all that, he knew he'd find a handful of sun-bleached trailers, their only decoration the cheap curtains hanging inside. The fabric blocked the view into the units through the rusty holes eaten into their sides.

Sometimes, the curtains blocked sights no kid should see, of mamas doing things no mama should do.

Swallowing hard, he retreated a pace, as if he'd felt the pull of one rust-corroded hulk in particular. It wouldn't still be there. It couldn't. But he had no intention of going over there to make sure.

Across the way, a gang of kids hung out near a sagging wire fence and a pile of cast-off truck tires. Still quiet, but soon their laughter and loud conversations would start, followed by the shouts from inside the houses. Some of the houses, anyway.

The rough edges of his ignition key bit into his palm.

In all the years he'd been gone from this town and with all the miles he'd logged, he should have shoved away everything that bothered him about this place.

He hadn't forgotten a single one of them.

The gang of kids had moved out of sight behind one of the shacks. A lone boy, eight or nine years old, stayed behind and stood watching him. Dark hair, a dirty face. Torn T-shirt and skinned knees. Could have been Caleb, twenty years ago.

The kid made his way across the road. "Hey," he said, "whatcha doing?"

"Just looking around."

"What's wrong with your leg?"

The boy must have noticed his awkward gait, the stiffness that always hit him after he sat in one position for a while. "I hurt my knee. Getting off a bull."

"Thought you were supposed to stay *on* 'em."

He shrugged. "That one had other ideas." Not too bad—in those three quick sentences, he'd managed to bypass two years' worth of rehab and pain.

The kid looked away and then quickly back again, shuffled his feet and jerked his chin up high. Caleb recognized the mix of pride and false bravado.

"Hey, mister...got a dollar?"

"Sure." How many times had he asked that question himself? How many times had he sworn he'd never ask it again? He reached into his pocket for his wallet, thumbed it open and plucked out a bill without looking at it. "Here you go."

"Wow. Gee, thanks. Thanks a lot."

Caleb grinned. The boy's grubby fingers clutched a hundred-dollar bill. He turned and raced across the road as if fearing Caleb would change his mind. He wouldn't. He had plenty of money now.

Folks in town would sure be surprised to see him again, especially when he started spending that cash. When he started showing them just how far he'd come. Maybe then they'd look at him differently than they had years ago.

His grin fading, he shoved the wallet into his pocket and nodded.

Yeah. He'd show them, all right.

Too early to tackle his first order of business.

Caleb looked down the length of Signal Street, taking in the storefronts along the way. Insurance agency. Harley's General Store. Pharmacy. Ice-cream parlor and clothing store. Everything the same as he remembered it from ten years ago. Except for the real estate office he planned to visit as soon as they opened.

How would Tess handle seeing him walk in the door?

The question stunned him, making him realize he wasn't sure how he'd react to their meeting, either. They hadn't parted on the best of terms.

He turned his back on the office and found himself staring at the Double S Café. Not much to look at, just a small square structure made of stucco. But Dori and Manny had brightened the place with pots filled with cactus plants all along the front and painted flowers and vines scrolling around the doorway. Above the door, a sign showed one letter *S* hooked on to another one. The Double S. That was new since his time.

Slowly, he made his way inside and along the jagged path between scattered tables to the rear of the café. He'd spent a lot of time in this cramped but cozy room, way back when, though not as one of the customers. How could he, when most days he went off to school without even any lunch money?

He settled on one of the stools that gave him a view through the open doorway into the kitchen. The owners, Dori and Manny, stood in conversation near the oversize oven. Dori spotted him first, her expression telling him she'd recognized him right away.

They hurried out to the counter.

Manny shook his hand and slapped him on the shoulder.

He stiffened when Dori leaned close to give him a long, sturdy hug. "It's so good to see you, Caleb."

Her voice hadn't lost the trace of Spanish accent that had always flavored her words or its gentle tone. Now he'd grown old enough to tell it masked concern for him. Or pity? He hoped not. She squeezed his hand, and he saw that same concern in her eyes.

"Good to see you, too." He had to clear his throat before he could continue. "Both of you."

"We read about you in the newspaper. We sent you cards."

Had they? If so, he'd left them behind unread when he'd transferred from the hospital to the rehab. He would have to give her the only response he could. "I didn't write to anyone—"

"No matter. You were busy with the rodeo. And after that…" She shook her head. "You weren't well enough, we know that. The judge called the hospital for more news. That was a terrible accident. Terrible." She squeezed his fingers. "But you're well again?"

How did he answer that?

As far as his body went, yes, he was back in one piece. As "well again" as the doctors said he might ever get. But in his mind and his gut…a different story there. All those months in rehab, he'd found himself with a lot of time to think about things. To run through the memories of his life up till then.

To develop a need that wouldn't let him rest.

He couldn't tell Dori about all that.

"I'm fine," he said simply.

"And you've come home?"

He shot a glance around the café, recalling the many nights he'd swept the floors and cleared off the tables after the last customers had gone. The small, brightly decorated restaurant had once represented so much to him. A place to work, get a good meal and feel less alone. That might explain what had driven him to come in here this morning.

He'd first talked to Tess here, too. The memory caused his stomach to clench. The fact she worked in the only real estate agency in town made their reunion inevitable. Suited his purpose, too. She'd get a firsthand look at how well he'd done for himself.

He looked back at Dori and Manny, once the only friends he'd had. Almost the only family. But…come home?

He couldn't tell Dori that, either.

"Just visiting," he said instead. "And while I'm here," he added, putting his plan into words, "I'm looking to buy some investment property."

"But that's wonderful," Dori said, obviously delighted. "You will find yourself a nice house and want to settle down here."

"I've got a house already—on a ranch in Montana." He smiled to soften the words. "But it'll be nice to visit for a while."

A short while.

Seeing Dori and Manny had revived some of the few good memories he had, but they couldn't outweigh the bad.

Once he did what he needed to do, proved he was

the equal of anyone else in this town, he'd leave Flagman's Folly behind him again.

For good.

Could anything beat showing up for work on a Monday morning and finding a long, tall cowboy waiting on the doorstep?

Yes, Tess LaSalle decided. Unfortunately, cowboys came by the dozen around here. What she needed was one with money.

It was a gorgeous first day of June, worthy of any advertising blurb she could write to attract new clients to Wright Place Realty. But in their tiny town, there was not a client to be found.

Unless…?

Half a block away, she eyed the man leaning against the dusty pickup truck parked at the curb. From his black Stetson to his Western shirt with the shiny pearl snaps, he might have dressed to play a role. Yet one glance at his formfitting, threadbare Wranglers and well-worn black boots plainly announced the truth: he was the real thing.

Whether or not he had cash on the barrelhead remained to be seen.

Still, she hurried along Signal Street toward the storefront office. As desperately as they needed clients, she wasn't about to let this one get away.

"Good morning," she called, digging in her canvas bag for her key ring. "Let me get the office open for you."

"Morning." When she neared him, he held out his hand.

Automatically, she responded. His hand engulfed

hers, the roughness of his fingers tingling all her nerve endings. She looked up to find his face hidden by the brim of his Stetson. She could see only a firm jaw and the dark stubble of five o'clock shadow. Another indication of a working cowboy and not a wealthy rancher?

As she watched, he lifted his head and tipped his hat, revealing thick, wavy dark hair and a pair of blazing green eyes.

Tess's fingers trembled in his. She'd have given anything to disappear at that moment. He couldn't have missed her reaction. Just as she couldn't miss recognizing those eyes.

Caleb Cantrell had planned that move to startle her. He'd succeeded, more than he could ever know. Shock warred with guilt inside her.

Belatedly, she realized his hand still covered hers. A treacherous longing to hang on to him stunned her. Appalled by her own emotions, she snatched her fingers away and dropped her arm as if she'd been burned.

She took a long, deep breath and set her jaw. Forcing her voice to remain steady, she asked, "What are you doing here, Caleb?"

He gestured toward the storefront. "That's a real estate office, isn't it?"

Before she could give the obvious answer to his question, a blue van pulled up to the curb behind his pickup truck. Tess's best friend and boss, Dana Wright, emerged from the van. She did a double take at seeing Tess's companion, then marched over to them. "I don't believe my own eyes. Caleb, is that really you?"

"In the flesh."

Good-looking flesh, too, with a nice even tan that

set off the whiteness of his smile as he grinned. Tess clutched the key ring she'd finally dug out of her bag.

"Well," Dana continued, "it's good to see you. You remember me? Dana Smith? Now Dana Wright?"

"Of course I remember you. Couldn't forget either of the prettiest girls in town, now could I?" He smiled at Tess.

She stiffened. He was wasting his time. No amount of sweet-talking would ever get her to believe in him again.

Sure, Dana could act natural and concerned. She didn't have Tess's history with the man.

Or Tess's secret.

"What brings you back to Flagman's Folly after all these years?" Dana asked him.

"Well, tell the truth, I'm looking to buy some land here."

"Is that so?" Dana stood taller and smiled wider.

Tess knew her friend's pulse must have quickened at the thought of a possible sale. Her own pulse was beating fast—for other reasons.

"As we like to say around here," Dana continued, "you've come to the 'Wright Place.' I'm sure we can help you out."

"So am I. I've got a list." He tilted his head. "I'd like to talk things over with Tess. Thought we'd go on along to the Double S. Over a cup of coffee, I can fill her in on what I need."

That wasn't what *she* needed. Not at all.

She sent her friend an agonized look.

Of course, Dana couldn't understand what it meant. Instead, she sent back an expression of wide-eyed innocence that said plainly, *We'll talk later.*

"Oh, I don't think I'll be able to do much for you," Tess protested. "I'm just the hired help. A glorified file clerk, really. Dana's the boss. You'll want to deal with her."

Caleb focused on her again. "I don't know about that," he drawled. "You and I've got some catching up to do."

She curled her fingers into fists. "No, we do not, and—"

"Ahh… Tess?" Dana broke in. She looked at Caleb. "If you'll excuse us for just a minute…?"

He patted the fender of the pickup truck. "I'll be waiting right here."

"Thanks."

Within seconds, Dana had unlocked the door and led the way into the office. She turned to Tess with a wide smile—most likely for the benefit of Caleb, who stood outside the storefront window—and said, "Girl, have you completely lost your mind?"

"I don't think so."

"Well, we're *both* going to lose our jobs if we don't make a sale soon."

Tess sighed. "I know."

As a single mom and the sole breadwinner for her small family, Tess clung to the paycheck she earned here. The money took care of their bills, if she budgeted carefully. When she had pennies left, she helped tide her mother over with her fledgling business, turning their home into a bed-and-breakfast inn and taking on guests.

Nonexistent guests, lately.

Things were bad all around. No one had much money on hand for vacationing in small-town inns. Or for buying property, for that matter. Losing this job would mean she'd have no income.

Roselynn and Nate depended on her. But as bad as things were for her, she knew Dana had it much worse. Widowed and left a single mom, her friend struggled to get by with three kids of her own.

Now Dana stood tugging on a lock of her honey-brown hair, her blue eyes narrowed in speculation.

"I have no idea what all this 'catching up' is that you and Caleb have to do—" Tess remained silent "—though I'm sure I'll hear about it sometime." She smiled as if to soften the words.

Since grade school, she and Dana had shared everything. But not that. She'd never told Dana anything about her connection to Caleb. Much as Tess loved her, she knew Dana couldn't have kept herself from broadcasting the news that Tess had found a boyfriend. Tess had had her own reasons for not wanting the news spread. And after what had happened, she'd given thanks that no one had known.

"I suppose," Dana was saying, "I could offer to show him around town, but I don't want to risk him taking offense. He obviously wants to work with you."

"Yes, I know." *Why?* That's what worried her. Caleb Cantrell didn't do anything without a reason. And he certainly didn't do anything he didn't want to. She had learned that years ago. After their last conversation way back then, she couldn't imagine why he'd want to speak to her again—or how he could have the nerve to believe *she* would ever have anything to do with him.

"Look," Dana said, "I can understand your reluctance to deal with Caleb. The man didn't have such a great reputation when he lived here."

"That has nothing to do with it," she protested truthfully.

"Fine. But if there's one thing we know about him, he's made money since he left town. Who are we to keep him from spending it in Flagman's Folly? And, let's face it, we need the commission."

"I know." She couldn't refuse to work with Caleb.

Besides, did she really want Dana working with him? Talking to him? Asking him questions about that so-called "catching up" he claimed they needed to do?

"All right," she said at last, choking on the words.

But it wasn't. No matter how much money she might bring in by making a sale for Wright Place Realty, dealing with Caleb Cantrell could cost her plenty. If he ever found out about the baby she'd kept from him, it might cost her the daughter she loved.

Chapter 2

"Now you know what I'm looking for," Caleb finished up. Across their booth in the Double S, Tess stared down at her notebook. "The best money can buy."

He had grabbed his coffee and her tea and headed to the empty booth at the far front corner of the room, close to the café's door. Not that he would need a getaway...

Tess didn't look too happy about sitting here with him. And she'd said next to nothing, leaving him to spend the last half hour doing enough talking to make his throat drier than New Mexico dust. Luckily, Dori kept the pot hot and full.

He glanced down at the woven place mat under his coffee mug, then around the room at the rough wooden tables and chairs, the bare planked floors, the colorful sombreros on the wall.

At anything that gave him the chance to think for a minute without staring at Tess.

Why he should find it hard to look her in the eye, he didn't know. Finding out she worked selling real estate had given him the best reason in the world for getting in touch with her once he'd come back to town. And her job made her just the person he needed to get his point across to everyone. He'd run down a list a mile long, throwing in every option he could think of for the kind of property he wanted to buy. The best, the biggest. The most expensive property.

He looked around the café. At this hour, too late for workers to stop in for coffees to go and too early for a lunch rush, the restaurant had only a few customers. Luckily, no one he knew. He'd returned to Flagman's Folly eager to get to work, but now that he had arrived, he'd realized he should've done more thinking beforehand about his great idea.

Much as he hated to admit it, seeing Tess again had shaken him more than he would have guessed.

But it was time to put his plan into action.

He looked back at her. "You got all that?"

"I believe so." Her head down, she flipped back through the pages of the notebook that lay on the table beside her.

He took the opportunity to check her out yet again.

Could have knocked him over with a frayed lasso when he'd seen her come walking along Signal Street. Luckily he'd gotten hold of himself by the time she'd reached him.

During the past ten years, Tess hadn't changed a bit. Well...naturally, she'd grown up and filled out.

Still, she had the same shoulder-length tumble of

dark curls, the pale skin that gave her away every time she blushed, the sparkling dark brown eyes. She looked up at him again now, those eyes wide, and said not a word.

He glanced down to see her hanging on to her tea-cup for dear life, it seemed. No wedding band. He wondered about that.

Not that it meant anything to him.

If only he could say the same about the way her fingers had trembled in his when he'd shaken her hand earlier...

Letting go of the death grip on her cup, she transferred her attention to the hem of her yellow shirt. The tug she gave on it pulled the fabric taut against her.

He forced himself to focus on taking a long swallow of his coffee.

"I think I've got everything we'll need." Her lips curved briefly. "Any last-minute items for your wish list?"

Yeah. A real smile. That one had looked so fake, he wouldn't have given her a nickel for it. "Nope. That about covers it for now."

"Then I'll get back to the office and start working on this. I'm sure we'll be able to find something to suit you." She flipped the notebook closed and dropped it into her bag.

When she started to slide out from the booth, he reached for her arm. Warm, soft skin met his palm. Holding her hand outside the office had given him a jolt. This about mule-kicked him across the room.

He pulled his hand away and cleared his throat. "What's your hurry? Been a long time since the two of us talked."

"Yes."

Obviously, if she had her way, it would be an even longer time before they had a proper conversation.

He settled against his seat cushions and stretched his legs out under the table, trying to find a comfortable position. "So, you wound up selling property for a living? Not a bad job. What does your husband do?"

And why the heck had he asked that?

Tess looked as if she wondered the same thing. "I don't have a husband," she said, clipping the words.

He frowned. "Last time I saw you, you were planning on getting married."

"I know," she said, her voice cold. "It didn't work out."

"Yeah. Neither did we." Again, he'd blurted the response without thinking. This time, though, he knew why. The bitter memory of their last meeting had driven him to speech.

He might as well have waved a red flag in front of her with his words. Her face went as belligerent as a bull getting ready to charge.

"There was no 'we,' Caleb. I seem to remember that maybe once there might have been. But *you* wanted to go off and start winding your way along the rodeo trail. So you did."

The acid in her tone seemed at odds with the hurt look in her eyes.

Well, he'd had his reasons. And she'd damned well given him another. One guaranteed to keep him away. Jaw clenched, he tried shrugging away the wave of guilt pounding at him. No such luck. He reached for the fresh pot of coffee Dori had brought a few minutes back.

The door to the Double S opened. Glad for the distraction, he looked up and watched a group of little girls roll like tumbleweeds into the place.

On the opposite side of the booth, Tess jerked to attention. He'd swear her face grew paler yet.

"Anything wrong?" he asked.

She shook her head.

She was lying. Something about that little crowd bothered her.

"Excuse me a minute," she said.

The girls had crossed the café and taken over the row of stools lining the counter in the back of the room. They looked innocent enough. Clean and respectable, too. A big contrast to the kid he'd given the cash to earlier.

The same thing people had thought about him when he'd lived here. He gripped the handle of his coffee mug, trying to get hold of his anger. At that age, neither he nor that kid had the power to control their worlds. Couldn't folks understand that?

He shook his head and looked again at the girls. Eight, nine years old, maybe. He'd seen plenty like them in his days on the circuit. Just a bunch of giggling kids who cared only about hanging out at the rodeo with their friends. Nothing to worry about with girls that age.

It was the older ones you had to watch out for.

Eyes half-closed, he sat back and admired the view of Tess's yellow shirt riding above well-fitting khakis as she marched toward the group of girls.

When she came up to them, they swung around on their stools. The sideways glances the four of them shot each other said plainly they hadn't expected to run into her here.

She leaned close to one of the kids, a pint-size version of Tess with dark curls and a stubborn chin he'd recognized easily. Had to be Tess's little girl.

All the coffee he'd swallowed that morning suddenly churned in his stomach.

The kid stuck that chin out now and shook her head. Then she crossed her arms over her chest and turned away from Tess. Trouble there, for sure.

The girl looked around the room at anyone and anything but her mama. Her gaze zeroed in on him, and her eyes widened to about the size of his competition champion belt buckles.

"Mom, look!" she said in a strangled whisper. She might've been trying to keep her voice down, but he could hear her clear across the room. She tugged on Tess's shirt. "Mom, do you *see* him?" Her voice rose with every word. She waved her arms frantically at her friends. "Guys—over there, in the corner. That's *Caleb Cantrell.*"

The trio surrounding her squealed like a sty full of pigs discovering a replenished trough. A familiar enough sound.

He smiled in satisfaction. Now, this was one group in Flagman's Folly he wouldn't need to work at impressing.

All four of them jumped off their stools.

To give her credit, Tess made an attempt to grab hold of her daughter and the girl next to her. They likely didn't even feel her hands on their shoulders as they slipped from her grasp. At that moment they were driven, with one goal in mind.

Getting to him.

From the look on Tess's face, she wanted to be anywhere but here.

Carefully, he set his half-full coffee mug aside,

moved his Stetson out of reach and braced himself, knowing what would happen next.

The girls headed toward him. No tumbleweeds rolling gently along now. Their eyes shining, their mouths tight with suppressed excitement, they stampeded across the room.

"All right." Tess looked from one girl to another, stopping at Nate. "You remember that list of chores you promised to do for Miss Roselynn in exchange for the sleepover tonight?"

They all nodded.

"Well, that's a start." She had spent more time than she could afford trying to drag their attention away from Caleb.

As rodeo-crazy as Nate and her friends were, she should have known Nate would recognize the champion bull rider immediately. If only the girls hadn't come into the Double S just when she happened to be there with Caleb. But that was a faint if only—and a useless one. In a town the size of Flagman's Folly, *everyone* would run into him sooner than later.

In the minute it took for those thoughts to flash through her mind, the girls had edged closer to Caleb again.

She tensed. "Get started now, girls," she said. "Miss Roselynn will be waiting for those groceries."

Even to her own ears, she'd sounded as firm as a blade of wet grass. Looking across the booth at Caleb, she felt just about as sturdy. After this run-in with him, she really needed peace and quiet. And time to practice the calm front she would have to present whenever he was around.

But there wasn't time enough in the world for that.

Besides, the way he sat smiling at her left no doubt he'd noticed her staring at him. He'd probably already seen right through her. As bad as the girls, she now had to drag her own attention away from the man, who obviously had plenty of experience in the spotlight.

"You've got the list for Harley's," she reminded Nate and her friends. "And you've got the money, too?" At their nods, she added, "Great. Then please get the shopping done—and don't forget to use the coupons."

Every penny saved meant a penny more she could use to help her mother put food on the tables at the bed-and-breakfast. The Whistlestop Inn might be empty of guests now, but with any luck, Roselynn would soon have every room occupied. And not by a houseful of chattering girls.

That was all she needed tonight.

After a burst of giggles and goodbyes to Caleb, the group ran toward the door.

One voice rose above the laughter. "'Bye, Mom. See ya later." The door slammed in her wake.

Tess sank back onto the booth's bench seat.

"Sleepover?" he asked.

"They're celebrating school letting out last week." She exhaled heavily. With the way Nate had behaved lately, she'd skated very close to *not* having this party. And if things didn't improve, it could turn into a very long summer.

The thought that Caleb might be there for a good part of it left her choking on her indrawn breath of dismay. She swore she'd do whatever it took to have him on his way as soon as possible. Focusing on him again, she realized she'd missed the beginning of his response.

"—can't be a bad bunch at all," he was saying, "if they're willing to do chores that cheerfully. And your daughter sure takes after you."

The blood seemed to rush from her head, making her dizzy. There were many subjects she never, ever wanted to discuss with Caleb Cantrell. On a scale of zero to ten, the topic of her daughter ranked at three hundred.

"Yes," she said shortly. She shoved one shaking hand through her hair. With the other, she picked up her canvas bag as she rose from the bench. "Well, I've got your information. Time for me to go and start working on it."

She turned away and waved a brief goodbye to Dori. The older woman stood with her elbows resting on the counter at the back of the room, taking a much-needed break.

"You'll come see us again soon?" Dori asked, directing the question to Tess but then quickly looking past her toward Caleb.

Was *no* female over the age of five immune to the man's charms?

"I'm sure *I* will," Tess said firmly.

"Be a real pleasure, Dori," he drawled. "For both of us."

Tess shivered and grabbed the door handle. She didn't want to share *any* kind of pleasure with him. Not now or in the future. And she refused even to think about their past.

Once outside, she stopped on the sidewalk near his pickup truck. He had driven them the couple of blocks to the Double S, and the close confines of the truck's cab had nearly left her hyperventilating. The two blocks had stretched to forty miles.

No way did she want to share that vehicle with him again, either.

"So," he said, resting against the fender, just as he'd been standing when she had first seen him that morning. "How old is she?"

"Dori?" She pretended to misunderstand, knowing full well what he meant. "I'm not sure. Around my mother's age, I would guess. Early sixties."

The deception hurt her. Badly. Because at her response, he grinned, making his green eyes blaze even in the shadow beneath his Stetson's brim. "I meant that girl of yours."

"Oh. She's nine."

"Nice-looking kid. What's her name?"

"N-Nate." Where was he going with this conversation? And why wasn't *she* going far, far away in another direction?

"Nate?" He sounded amused. "A real handful."

She frowned. He'd seen her daughter for all of five minutes, most of which Nate had spent amid the group of girls fawning over him. "What makes you say that?"

"The stubborn jaw." He reached up and touched her chin with his fingertip. "I'd have known her even if she didn't have your hair."

She swallowed hard and backed up a step, her legs threatening to give way beneath her. No, she would not get back in that pickup truck with him—even though it would give her a chance to sit down.

"I'll be in touch," she assured him. *When cows give orange milk.* "I'm sure it won't take long at all. And…" she held her breath a moment, then rushed on "I'm assuming you've reserved a place to stay closer to Santa Fe or Albuquerque."

His expression hardened. "I've got it covered," he said, his voice rough.

At another time, she might have thought twice about his reaction. Not anymore. "Good," she said firmly. "There's no need for you to hang around. I have your cell phone number. And you don't need to drive me to the office, thanks."

As she started along the sidewalk, he fell into step beside her. Though he matched his stride to hers, he walked with the stiff gait she had seen when he'd first gotten out of the truck in front of the Double S.

He'd been hurt during a rodeo. Very seriously hurt. The townsfolk had gone into an uproar when they'd learned about it. Nate and her friends had been despondent. Tess had managed to harden her heart against the news. Had tried not to think about Caleb's aborted career. About his injury. For the most part, she'd succeeded. Until now.

Reading about his accident was one thing. Seeing the results of it right there in front of her was something else. But she couldn't feel any pity for Caleb. Shouldn't feel any guilt, either.

Not after they way he had crushed her.

Keeping her gaze forward, she cleared her throat. "I—uh—know the way back on my own."

"That's good," he said. "A successful real estate person like yourself ought to know her way around. In fact, I imagine you're the perfect person to show me some of the sights in town."

Shaky legs or not, that brought her to a solid stop. "What are you playing at, Caleb? You were born and raised here, same as I was. You know all the sights there are to see."

"Maybe. And maybe some things have changed."

His gaze drifted from her eyes all the way to her toes. An answering shiver rippled its way along the same path, as if he'd run his finger down her body.

"You've got more curves than I remember." He grinned again.

Time to get away from him. "I have to run." *What an understatement.*

She needed to get to her office, research the list of his requirements, and find some property for him as quickly as she could—and as far away from Flagman's Folly as possible.

"Okay." To her relief, he nodded. "Tell you what. I've got some business to take care of, myself. Since yours won't take long, why don't I pick you up later? We'll ride around town a bit. Talk over your prospects at supper."

The most *un*likely prospect she'd ever heard.

The words rested on the tip of her tongue, ready for her to say them. But she couldn't.

Visions floated into her mind.

Nate. Roselynn. Dana with her three small children but no husband by her side. An Out Of Business notice plastered on the front window of Wright Place Realty. A For Sale sign decorating the lawn of the Whistle-stop Inn.

She thought of the commissions she and Dana would earn from the sale of a ranch to Caleb. The sale of a *substantial* ranch. He'd made it plain he intended to acquire the largest piece of property she could locate. He'd seemed obsessed by the idea of owning a big spread in New Mexico. Strange, when he'd told her he already ran a working ranch in Montana. She'd had to bite her tongue against the question she wanted to ask. Why did he feel such a need to branch out?

Fortunately, she'd kept quiet. What did it matter to her, as long as she managed to find him that ranch clear across the state? She ought to be grateful for his obsession. The income she could earn in satisfying his need would take care of every worry she'd envisioned, for a good long time. She couldn't afford—literally—to get on the man's bad side.

If he had one.

Everything she'd seen of him so far looked as good if not better than it had ten years ago.

"Sound all right to you?" he persisted. "You said you're still living at your mama's. Can she keep watch on the girls at the sleepover for a while?"

She swallowed hard. "Yes, she can. That sounds fine."

"Good. I'll be at your place early, then, around four."

She nodded and walked away before he could see the expression she knew she couldn't hide.

How many times as a love-struck teenager had she dreamed about Caleb pulling up to the house to pick her up for a date? Impossible, of course. Her grandfather had made sure of it. Even without Granddad's rules, she had known the pointlessness of her dream. She and Caleb had kept their relationship secret.

She sighed in frustration.

Back then, she had loved Caleb. Couldn't get enough of him. Yet he had left her. And now, when she didn't want the man anywhere near her, she was stuck with him.

The irony of the situation nearly overwhelmed her. But the damage was done. Her world had already caved in earlier that day, the minute he had forced his way into her life again.

Chapter 3

Caleb parked the pickup truck in his choice of spaces behind Tess's home. Only one other vehicle occupied the parking area, an ancient Toyota with more than its share of dents.

Funny to think he'd come calling here again. Twice in the past, he'd stopped by this place and hadn't made it beyond the front door. Her granddaddy had seen to that. Getting inside now would bring him a considerable measure of satisfaction.

Still, anger rose at the memory of her granddaddy. The same anger that had bubbled through his veins since he'd first set foot in town this morning. He'd have to watch that. Control that from here on. Anger wouldn't get him what he wanted from the townsfolk, or from Tess. No, he needed to give them all someone to look up to. Someone they'd respect.

A good storyteller. A bull-riding champ. A rodeo star.

Taking a deep breath, he stared at the clock on the dashboard. Three-fifty. Ten minutes early. Ten minutes to sit here. No sense letting Tess think he was too eager to see her again.

He couldn't have any illusions about her feelings, that was for sure.

She had looked less than thrilled to see him outside the real estate office that morning, and a good sight more unhappy once she learned why he'd been standing on the doorstep.

What he'd told her of his reasons, anyhow.

Pity she hadn't been more enthused.

As if she would forget about their past, just because he'd wanted her to. As if he could impress her, just by mentioning money. He'd known he would have to work harder with Tess than with anyone. Maybe he should have started with somebody who'd have accepted his return more readily.

Dori and Manny from the Double S, for instance.

Of everyone in Flagman's Folly, they were the people he should have harbored some guilt over. Maybe he did, somewhere deep inside. Someplace he couldn't get to right now. Not while he had grudges to tackle and axes to grind and scores to settle. He had all the bad parts of his past to resolve before he could look to the future.

Coming to the edge of dying had made him realize that. It had humbled him. It had scared the hell out of him. And it had finally made him understand just what all those early years and those bad parts of his past had done to him.

Returning to Flagman's Folly had to make up for some of that.

He glanced at the dashboard clock again. Time for the show to begin.

He climbed out of the truck and followed the path around the house to the front door. When he had driven by earlier that day, he'd seen the small sign near the sidewalk, proclaiming this the Whistlestop Inn. The sight had surprised him. Another thing that had changed since he'd left town.

Always, he had envied Tess this old house with its two stories, peaked roof and deep porch corralled by rails. A wooden-slatted swing dangled from chains in the porch ceiling. He'd always wanted to sit in that swing, too. It overlooked rows of plants with big pink and yellow and orange blooms and the yard that ran down to the street.

The porch alone took up more footage than that piece of crap trailer he'd lived in growing up.

He stabbed the doorbell and stepped back. Inside the house, he heard chimes, followed by some screeching and a lot of loud laughter. The girls, again.

Smiling, he shook his head. Kids were the same everywhere. Grown-up fans were, too. The autographs he'd signed all across the country proved that.

Abruptly the inner door swung open. Through the screened door, Tess's dark-brown eyes stared at him from a pint-size height. The kid could almost have passed as Tess's double. In a few years, grown up, she no doubt would. She'd look amazingly like the Tess he'd left behind.

Now those eyes rounded like the mouth beneath it.

"Better watch it, kid," he said. "Didn't your mama ever tell you your face might freeze that way?"

Her features went slack. "Yeah, all the time." She grinned. "My name's not kid, Mr. Cantrell. It's Nate."

"So I heard. And my name's Caleb."

She sucked in a breath. "You mean I can call you that?"

He nodded.

"Wow."

There went the eyes again. He chuckled. "What's the deal, if you don't mind my asking? Nate's a boy's name, isn't it?"

"Yeah." She looked down, suddenly shy, the dark curls falling to hide most of her face.

He couldn't help it. The urge came on him strong to tease her, just as he'd kidded her mama years ago, though Tess had been older then. "Can't be your real name," he said. "Come on, give."

She paused, considering him for a moment, then stared at her feet. "Anastasia," she hissed, her tone disgusted. She peeked out from under all that hair to see how he was taking the news.

"Hmm." He nodded thoughtfully. Now that he'd gotten himself into this, how should he handle it? "Well. Sounds like a right pretty name to me."

"It *does?*" She looked straight at him again. "Nobody has that name but me."

"That makes it pretty *and* special, then, doesn't it?"

"I don't know." Shrugging, she rubbed the toe of one shoe against the floor. "Ya coming in, or are ya just ringing doorbells for fun?"

He had to chomp down for a second on the corner of his lip before he could answer. "Is it fun?"

"Yeah. If nobody catches you."

"Hmm," he said again. "Well..." So far, he wouldn't take any prizes for his conversational skills. Hopefully, he'd have more luck with Tess later. But if he wasn't talking horses or rodeo, he sure felt at a loss when it came to kids. How could he answer this one? "Considering I did get caught ringing your bell," he said slowly, "and by you... I'll have to confess I was planning on coming in."

"*Really?* C'mon." She pushed open the screened door to let him in, then she turned and raced through the foyer. "Hey, guys," she yelled at a level that could quiet an arena without a bullhorn. "You won't believe who's here!"

He stepped into the foyer.

And found Tess staring at him.

She looked good in a tight-fitting Western shirt, almost a twin to his own, but more feminine in pink with a rose at each shoulder. He couldn't resist getting a full look at her snug jeans and brown cowboy boots.

Eventually, he worked his way up again to confront her unblinking gaze. He had frozen in the act of removing his Stetson. *Dang.* He was here to impress the woman, not stand gawking at her. Hurriedly, he swept his arm across his waist and bowed. "Well, hey. Didn't see you standing there, ma'am." He gestured between them. "The way we're dressed, we might almost be related."

Her mouth taut, she said nothing.

He frowned. "Aren't you going to welcome me in?"

She took a deep breath and let it out in an exasperated sigh. "I think someone already did."

* * *

Conscious of Caleb behind her, Tess hurried across the foyer and into the dining room. She had deliberately steered him away from the opposite side of the house, where Nate and her friends had claimed the living room. That was the last place she wanted him to go, and Nate was the last person she wanted him to see.

"Why don't we take a look at what I've pulled together," she said over her shoulder, "and then we can be on our way."

Or with luck, Caleb could leave on his own.

If she took care of all their business here and now, they might skip going out altogether. And if that didn't work, maybe she could at least avoid a tour of the town with him until absolutely necessary.

Still shaken by his greeting, she plopped down into a chair at the long central dining table and waved at the empty seats. Her briefcase rested on the chair beside hers, where she felt thankful to have it as a barricade. "I didn't expect you to stop in," she said. "I thought we would just hit the road."

Let him think she hadn't a worry in the world about going out alone with him.

"Seems like your daughter had different ideas. *She's* got the notion of Southern hospitality down pat."

She froze, a file folder half out of her case. "Meaning, I haven't?"

He considered. "Your welcome was on the cold side, wouldn't you say?"

"I'm not used to having people in my home, uninvited." That was rude. And so untrue. Sort of.

"Thought we settled the invitation part of it." He eyed the smaller tables scattered in various parts of the room.

"And looks to me like you're used to feeding a herd. I saw the sign outside. How's business?"

"Fine. But it's not my concern." He'd sounded surprised about the house's transformation and looked at her now with his eyebrows raised. "My mother owns the bed-and-breakfast. I just happen to live here."

"With Nate."

"Yes, of course, with Nate." She fought not to grind her teeth.

"And with your mother, of course. And your grand-daddy."

"No, my grandfather passed away a couple of years ago." She had no idea why he would care, but he seemed oddly surprised by the news.

"Well," he said, "surely you know if there are guests around the house or not."

She shrugged. "I'm too busy working to pay much attention."

"The real estate business keeps you hopping, huh? Never would have thought that, myself." He gave her a piercing glance. "Guess I was right—things have changed around town."

An even more touchy subject. "*Some* things," she said tightly. Years ago, she could never have let him into this house. Would never have been able to face the consequences. She only wished he wasn't here now. Part of her did, anyway.

Another part of her felt remorse. For Nate's sake, she wished she could be nicer to him, could forgive him for the past. At the thought, she hardened her heart. Would Caleb feel any remorse for the way he had treated her?

"How many years has it been?" he asked. "About nine? Ten?"

With his questions, all thoughts of forgiveness fled her mind.

"About," she muttered. She could tell him how long it had been since they'd last seen each other, down to the day. To the hour.

She folded her arms across her chest as if that could protect her. Too late. His questions had already triggered a whole list of thoughts she wanted—needed—to stay away from.

"This place never was an inn before," he said thoughtfully. "What made your mother go into business for herself?"

"As I told you, my grandfather died. He left the house to her, and she decided to start the bed-and-breakfast." Short and sweet and all he needed to know. She needed to get him out of here. "Now, if you don't mind, we'll concentrate on *your* business. I've got—"

Nate and her friends rushed into the room, their sneakers screeching on the polished floor as the girls skidded to a stop beside the table.

Tess's heart sank.

"Caleb—" Nate shot a glance at Tess. "He said I can call him that, Mom." She turned back. "Can you stay and have supper with us?"

"No, I don't think—" Tess began.

"C'mon, Caleb," Nate urged, her unblinking gaze on him showing she obviously hadn't even heard Tess's words. "We're having a sleepover. We're gonna grill hot dogs and burgers, and Gram's making potato salad."

"Yes, I am. The best red-potato salad you'll find this side of the Mississippi."

At the sound of her mother's voice, Tess swallowed a groan and looked across the room.

Just inside the doorway stood Roselynn and Aunt Ellamae, wearing smiles as alike as rows of kernels on a corncob. Tess eyed them warily. With those two, you could never know what to expect next. Just like Nate, as a matter of fact. "Caleb and I have some paperwork to take care of," she told them.

"Oh, sugar." Southern sweetness dripped from Roselynn's words. "You worked hard all day. Surely that can wait."

"Yeah," Ellamae added. "At least till after the fresh-made pecan pie."

Caleb grinned, and he glanced from one eager face to another—all six of them. With great effort, only Tess kept her expression carefully neutral.

"Ladies," he said, "I don't see how I can rightly refuse an invitation like that one."

Nate took him by the hand, and he rose to his feet.

Tess's eyes stung. Her heart sank even lower.

"C'mon," her daughter said. "Let's go out back by the grill." As she led him away, she added in a hoarse whisper, "Maybe you can do the burgers. Mom always burns 'em."

The rest of the girls followed in their wake like a row of baby ducklings behind their daddy and mama.

Her own mother and aunt looked at her, looked at each other, still beaming, and then disappeared from the doorway.

Tess put her elbows on the table and her head into her hands.

This couldn't be happening. It just couldn't. After almost a decade, Caleb couldn't be back here again.

But he was. Talking about the past and the changes

around here and how many years it had been. If it ever occurred to him to sit down and do the math...

That couldn't happen, either.

Tess shot to her feet. Determination propelled her across the dining room. She had to get that man out of her house. Had to make sure he never set foot in it again.

Most of all, she had to keep him from ever finding out that Nate—her horse-crazy, rodeo-loving, rebellious daughter Nate—was his daughter, too.

Chapter 4

The evening couldn't have gotten any worse, from Tess's perspective. She curled up on her lawn chair in the shadowy backyard and tried not to groan.

With the burgers and hot dogs and potato salad long gone, supper had given way to the night's entertainment.

Caleb.

He'd started in on tales of his life on the rodeo circuit, as if they had all come together to share stories over a cozy little campfire. Next thing she knew, they'd be toasting marshmallows over the grill and singing "Kumbaya."

Sighing, she wrapped her arms around her upraised knees.

Nate and the rest of the girls sat cross-legged at Caleb's feet. They stared up at him, their openmouthed looks of hero worship obvious for everyone to see. Even Roselynn and Ellamae had drawn their chairs over to the group, the better to hear his low drawl.

Traitors.

Yet, how could she blame them? Hadn't he roped her in, too, just with different kinds of stories? Not anymore, though. Never again.

"How did you ever get out of that field?" asked Lissa Wright, Dana's oldest child and Nate's best friend.

"Didn't that bull kill you?" another of the girls asked.

Nate rolled her eyes. "Of course not, silly. He's here, isn't he? Right, Caleb?"

"Right."

Even from across the yard, Tess could see him struggling to keep from laughing.

"As for how I got out of there, it's like this." With every word his voice grew more animated, holding the girls enthralled. "I whipped off my bandana and blindfolded that bull so fast, he didn't know what hit him. Got him so confused, he ran into a fence post harder than his own head. The darned fool knocked himself out."

Her Aunt Ellamae, always given to plain speaking, responded with a very unladylike snort. "Caleb Cantrell, that's a lot of bull, and you know it."

He grinned at her. "He sure was, ma'am."

Aunt El laughed.

Tess gave in to the groan she'd tried so hard to hold back and put her chin on her knees.

"Mom," Nate called, starry-eyed in the lamps' glow, "are you listening to all this?"

"I don't know if I'm hearing it just right," she said, forcing enthusiasm into her voice. "It sounds almost too good to be true."

The *real* truth was, except for the most exciting moments during his stories, when either Caleb raised his voice or the girls repeated in awestruck tones something he'd said, she hadn't heard anything at all. From her seat, Caleb's words came as a murmur. A low, sexy murmur. As much as the sound unsteadied her, she preferred not being able to hear him clearly.

Why would she want to know the details of the bait that had lured him away from her?

In the brief moment when everyone had turned to look at Tess, Caleb stared at her. His eyes shone as bright as Nate's. Not with the glint of excitement, though. Those eyes, his solemn expression, his stiff shoulders, all showed he had caught the false enthusiasm in her tone.

It seemed to bother him. She didn't understand why. But she didn't care.

"What's the biggest rodeo you were ever in?" Lissa asked.

"Well, let me think…"

Caleb broke eye contact with Tess, the audience focused on their star again, and Tess let her attention turn inward.

She knew nothing about Caleb's biggest rodeo, but she would never forget his *first* one.…

She'd known nothing about his dreams, either, when they'd first found each other in high school. Two lonely teenagers, they'd held on tight to a relationship made even more precious because it was theirs alone.

Their secret.

Yet a few months later, Caleb had left town—left *her*—to go off on the rodeo trail. When she didn't hear from him right away, she told herself not to worry. He had sworn he would call. He would write.

When the weeks went by without a word, it grew harder for her to believe in his empty promises.

And when two months had passed and she'd discovered she was pregnant, she'd had nowhere to turn. She couldn't tell her mom. She'd die before she would confess to Aunt El. And wouldn't survive if Granddad ever found out.

She couldn't even risk telling her best friend, Dana.

She *had* to find Caleb.

And she did.

After weeks of online searches, she had finally tracked him down at a rodeo outside Gallup. She'd had to use most of her babysitting money to buy a round-trip bus ticket that would take her there and back the same day.

She had arrived at the arena just in time to find Caleb flushed with success at his first major win—and with two girls wrapped around him. One giggled into his ear while the other one planted a lipstick-stained kiss on his cheek.

Her own cheeks flaming, Tess had approached the trio.

At first, Caleb looked as though he would deny knowing her. Then, he simply denied that he had any interest in her—by turning to walk away.

She stopped him, saying she had something important to discuss.

"Time to collect my prize," he told her. "Come and watch, Tess. *That's* what's important. That's what will save me from going back to some one-horse town with one-horse folks in it."

Obviously, his statement included her.

Raising her jaw, she stared him down. Sheer will-power kept her from telling him how he'd made her feel. She'd never in her life been so hurt. So humiliated.

Stubborn pride prevented her from telling him about the baby. Instead, she blurted out the news she was getting married.

That didn't interest him, either. He'd stood there, not saying a word, the silence hanging between them until, finally, he'd wished her well.

Best of luck, he'd said. Damn him.

Then they'd shouted his name over the loudspeakers, and even before he'd turned his lipstick-stained face from her, before he'd rushed off to claim his all-important prize, her heart had broken.

By the time she had walked away, she'd promised herself Caleb Cantrell would never know what he'd meant to her. And he would never know about their child....

In the glow of the hurricane lamp on the picnic table, someone moved toward her. She jumped. Gone so deeply into her thoughts, wrapped so completely in memories, she hadn't noticed anyone approaching. She looked up to see Caleb standing in front of her. It took her a long, startled moment to come to her senses.

When she did, she shot a glance past him, to find they were alone in the backyard.

She tried to rise from her lawn chair. Her legs, curled in one position for who knew how long, almost gave way. Staggering slightly, she managed to catch herself. Caleb didn't seem to notice. Still, to her dismay, she imagined him reaching out to steady her. Could almost feel the heat from his hands washing through her, as cozy and warm as if she *had* been sitting all that time in front of the campfire she'd thought about. She felt an overwhelming desire to move closer, to have him wrap his arms around her.

Was she crazy? Shaking her head at her own stupidity, she eased away from him.

She'd been burned by Caleb once. Hadn't that been enough?

Hoping her stiff legs would bear her weight, she moved aside and rested her hip against the nearest picnic table.

"Nice meal," he said.

She nodded.

"Still got that pecan pie to go."

"Yes."

"Good company, too. But you didn't seem to feel much like joining in the conversation."

What could she say in response? Nothing Caleb would want to hear. She shrugged, hoping he would leave it at that.

He didn't. Of course.

"Not into rodeo?" he asked.

Astonished, she stared at him. Could he really have asked that question? Could he have forgotten what happened the one and only time they'd been together at a rodeo? Or worse, did he not even care? She swallowed a bitter laugh. He didn't care at all. Of course.

Why should she? "I was at a rodeo with you, Caleb. Or I should say, I followed you to one. Once."

"Yeah, that's right." He tucked his thumbs into his belt loops. Not meeting her eyes, he said, "Sorry about that night."

She shook her head again, this time in stunned disbelief. He'd tossed out the offhanded apology with as much care as he'd tossed paper plates into the trash after their supper.

"It doesn't matter," she said. "That one time was enough for me. I never had much interest in going to rodeos after that."

"Look, I guess I got caught up in the win and wanted more."

"More what? Fame and fortune?" Not more time with her. "You got that, didn't you? And the stories to go with it." She couldn't resist adding, "But then, the rodeo didn't teach you that. You always talked a good line."

"Tess—"

She raised her hand to cut him off. "Sorry, I shouldn't have said that." Shouldn't have wasted her breath. At least *her* apology had held some sincerity.

Caleb hadn't changed, and she'd been foolish to think he might have. Even more foolish to hope she could ever feel close to him again. "Tell you what. Let's just leave the past in the past, where it belongs. It's history."

"Yeah, but you're part of my history. And I'm part of yours. No getting away from that."

No, she couldn't ever forget it. If he only knew how big a role their past played in her life every day...

A cold chill running through her now, she wrapped her arms around her waist, missing the warmth she'd so recently felt. "I don't know where you're planning to go with that, Caleb, but you can just stop right there. I won't have any more interest in your story than I did in your rodeo tales." She forced herself to stand straight again, abandoning the support of the picnic table. Then she steeled herself to look up at him. "Yes, I'm part of your history," she agreed. "The part you left behind."

* * *

Even though he now had his mind and hands occupied with two fistfuls' worth of playing cards, Caleb had plenty of focus left to dwell on the conversation he'd just had with Tess.

Or *tried* to have, more like it. She hadn't listened to what he'd already said and wouldn't let him get another word in edgewise. He had heard the hurt in her voice and knew part of him deserved the words she'd flung at him. Still, they'd stung.

He'd have protested, would have spoken up in his own defense, if her pint-size daughter hadn't returned to the backyard to lead him away and into the dining room, where the other girls had gathered around the long table.

Tess eventually joined them. Reluctantly, he could tell.

He had to fight not to crush the cards in his fist.

Yeah, dammit, he'd left her behind. But he'd meant to come back. He'd sworn it. Only things hadn't worked out that way. Life never did go the way you had it planned. Tess ought to know that. Hadn't she said as much herself when she'd told him about her marriage not working out?

Besides, she'd come to him first. To deliver her good news.

Slowly, he loosened his grip on the cards. He looked around the dining room again at the scattering of small tables he'd seen earlier, when he'd first arrived and she had brought him into this room. She'd cut him off quick when he'd asked her about business.

She'd lied, too, saying things were fine.

When Nate had taken him to the back of the yard to

get more charcoal for the grill, he'd seen the worn-out condition of the shed there and the broken-down fence sagging behind it. When he and the girls had put the card game on hold to rearrange the living room furniture for the sleepover, he'd seen the frayed edge of carpet behind the couch. Roselynn's business wasn't fine, and he knew it. He'd also bet real estate didn't keep Tess as busy as she'd let on.

He would eat this handful of cards if she could prove either of those things to him otherwise.

Well, if she wouldn't give him the truth, he would get it somewhere else.

She'd just headed into the kitchen to put the tea-kettle on.

He threw his leftover cards onto the pile on the table. While one of the girls shuffled the deck, he rose to straddle his chair backward, tilting it on its rear legs, moving closer to a small table for two placed against one dining room wall.

Roselynn and Ellamae sat there, polishing off a couple of pieces of Ellamae's pie. Roselynn turned her attention to him.

"Caleb, may I cut you another slice?"

He nodded. "Just a sliver."

When she handed it to him, he took a forkful, smiled his appreciation, then said, "The bed-and-breakfast here is new since my time. How long have you had it running?"

"Just a year now."

"Things going well?"

A slight wrinkle appeared between her brows and she fussed with the pie server. She didn't have Tess's flair for avoiding answers, though. "Fair to middlin', I guess," she said finally.

Ellamae made a choking sound. "Roselynn, your nose is gonna grow. Fact is," she said to Caleb, "the inn business is almost out the window."

"No guests?"

"No guests."

"We've had a few," Roselynn protested. Then she sighed. "But not for a long spell."

He couldn't state the obvious, that Flagman's Folly didn't have enough going for it to make it a tourist attraction. She'd have to do something to draw them in. "Are you advertising?" he asked.

"That's expensive."

"True. But as people say, sometimes you've got to spend money to make money."

"I suppose you're right." Roselynn lifted the empty pie plate. "Excuse me. I'll just run this into the kitchen."

When she'd gone, Ellamae chuckled. "*Run's* the word, all right. Looks like you've just scared her off. Not something you're used to with women, I'd reckon."

"They're usually headed in my direction," he acknowledged. "Used to be, anyhow."

"What happened?"

He blinked.

"Yeah, I know," she said. "I'm nosy. And I'm blunt. You ought to remember that from days past."

"I sure do." He laughed.

She was tough, too, and wiry, an older woman with graying hair and snapping dark eyes. Looked like any number of seasoned cowhands he could name. But Ellamae didn't herd cattle. She had an even more demanding job.

Keeping the peace in this town.

Ellamae worked as the court clerk. As a teen, Caleb had been up at the judge's bench a time or two, called in for jaywalking and riding with no lights on his bike—minor offenses not regularly requiring a court appearance. But in Flagman's Folly, things didn't always run the "regular" way. Another reason he'd left town at the first opportunity and never come back. Until today.

Judge Baylor kept a firm grip on his gavel inside the courtroom *and* out. And Caleb had always suspected Ellamae, with her direct way of dealing with folks, held as much power as the judge when it came to anything that went on around here.

Maybe that's why she'd unbent once in a while and let him off the hook when the judge cracked down on him. Maybe it's why she was conversing so freely with him tonight. And why he somehow felt he could trust her in return.

"We could use some straight talking right now," he said, thinking of his earlier conversation with Tess. You could tell she and Ellamae came from the same family tree. Tess's flat responses couldn't have gotten any more direct, though in a closemouthed way that left him more frustrated than before. He sensed it wouldn't be the same with Ellamae. But to get from her, you had to give. "As for what happened, I got bored with things. And then I got hurt."

"Yeah, we heard about it. That bull tossed you six ways to Sunday, didn't he?"

He nodded.

"I saw you limping some when you got here. Noticed it got worse after you stood at the grill a while. I thought that rehab place fixed you up."

He shrugged. "After a long day, I get to feeling some aches."

"Don't we all." She gave him a surprisingly sweet smile. "Well, you shoot pretty straight yourself, so I'll tell you this. Roselynn might come back here ready to chat with you, but she won't allow you much without a sugar coating on it. Tess won't allow you anything at all."

He nodded again.

"Found that out already, huh?"

"Yeah."

She smiled. "Then, it's lucky you got me. I'll flap my jaws in a good cause any day."

Together, they shot glances toward the doorway. All clear.

"Okay, then." Caleb tipped his chair forward another notch. "Start flapping."

Tess put the carafe of hot chocolate in the center of the tray and surrounded it with coffee mugs. The girls didn't need the extra sugar this late, but since they wouldn't sleep much tonight, anyway, that didn't matter.

What mattered was what *she* needed, and that was to get rid of Caleb. To safeguard her peace of mind. Her sanity. And maybe to protect her heart. Something inside still hurt after that unfeeling apology he'd given her.

Roselynn came into the kitchen and set the pie plate on the counter near the sink. "Need any help?"

"No, I've got it, thanks."

She looked over at the carafe. "You have enough for Caleb to have a cup of chocolate, too, don't you?"

"Yes, Mom. But I would imagine he'll be leaving any minute now."

Leaving...as he'd done so long ago.

She tightened her grip on the handle of the carafe. How could that one word, that one thought, fill her with both bitterness and longing at the same time?

"I don't know," her mother said.

Tess started, afraid she had spoken her question aloud.

But Roselynn stood looking through the doorway. "It appears he and El have settled in for a nice little chat."

"Oh, have they?" Tess grabbed the tray. If there was one thing Aunt El was known for, it was believing she knew what was best for everyone—and not hesitating to tell them.

Tess didn't want to think about the earful Caleb might be getting. But she certainly wanted to put a stop to it. "Can you bring the napkins, please?"

"Tess..." Roselynn frowned.

"What's wrong, Mom? Headache?"

"No...nothing. I'll go get some more napkins from the pantry."

In the dining room again, Tess saw her mother had been right. Caleb and Ellamae had their heads closer together than two sticky buns in a breadbasket.

She sailed across the room and plunked the tray on the table between them. Caleb backed off just quickly enough to keep from getting hit in the head.

A head that was as hard as that bull's he'd been talking about earlier. She ought to know.

"Hot chocolate!" Nate yelled.

The girls dropped their cards and clustered around the smaller table. Tess kept busy pouring drinks and passing out not-quite-filled mugs. No sense inviting spills. Upholstery and rug cleaning were expensive.

She looked through the doorway of the room to the grandfather clock in the hall. Almost nine. The girls would be up for hours yet, if they ever did get to bed.

She'd had to laugh. All those empty guest rooms upstairs, and they had chosen to sleep on the couches and floor in the living room.

"It's getting late," she told them. "Time to go off to the other room, now." At least that put them closer to their sleeping arrangements for the night.

"Come on in with us, Caleb," Nate said.

Tess could have won money on that being her daughter's next step. "No, Caleb's going to be leaving." Again, that word caught at her, made her want to sigh. Her voice shook just a bit as she added, "You girls go on."

Up went the stubborn jaw. Another step in her daughter's attempt to get her own way.

"But Mo-om," Nate wailed. So predictable. "He's drinking his hot chocolate, too."

"He can drink it here."

"Why can't he come with us?" Nate's bottom lip jutted out.

Tess gripped the edges of the tray. "Anastasia Lynn LaSalle," she said evenly.

Lissa poked Nate in the ribs. "C'mon, Nate. When it's all your names, you know you're in big trouble."

Before Nate could say another word that would get her in deeper, before Tess could add something she might regret, Caleb spoke up.

"You run off, now, like your mama says. I'll see you girls in the morning."

Tess turned to him. Bad enough her own daughter

was trying to make the rules around here. She didn't
need him attempting to call the shots, too. She didn't
need him at all.

"I don't think so, Caleb," she said, her chin as high as
Nate's had been. "From now on, if we need to discuss
any business at all, we'll meet at the office."

He smiled, took a sip of his chocolate, licked whipped
cream from his top lip.

Tess set her jaw and glared at him.

"Fine by me," he replied.

She narrowed her eyes. She'd never known him to
give in so easily.

"Business. Office. Got it." He smiled again and set
the mug on his table. "But I will see the girls tomorrow
morning, anyhow. At breakfast."

"What?"

He swept his arm out, gesturing at the space around
them. "This *is* a bed-and-breakfast. I assume your
mama serves breakfast to her guests. As I've just decided to take a room here for the rest of my stay in town,
I reckon that qualifies me for the meals."

The girls broke into cheers loud enough to make the
mugs on the tray rattle.

Or maybe that came from Tess's suddenly shaking
hands. She clutched the tray, wishing she could hold
it against her like a shield. She needed some kind of
armor against Caleb—because obviously no one else
in the room planned to help her.

The girls were too occupied in high-fiving Caleb
and each other. Aunt El was too busy smirking over
the turn of events she'd probably brought about herself.
And her mother...

Her mother was standing there smiling quietly, eyes aglow at the idea of a paying guest.

Tess swallowed a sigh verging on a sob of despair.

Much as she wanted to kick Caleb out of their home, she knew full well her mom couldn't afford to turn away any source of income. And as she gazed into his shining green eyes, she realized he knew it, too.

Caleb had himself a room at the bed-and-breakfast for as long as he wanted it.

And Tess had hold of a time bomb with an ever-shortening fuse.

Chapter 5

As Tess crossed the downstairs entryway, the grandfather clock in the corner chimed.

Two in the morning.

Fighting back a yawn, she climbed the stairs to the second floor again. She'd known not to expect the girls to settle down any time soon, but her patience had deserted her. She'd decided a little friendly caution to the group couldn't hurt.

The warning *had* reduced their giggles enough that she could barely hear them from the top of the stairway.

Roselynn's bedroom lay at the far end of the hall. The noise from the living room wouldn't bother her. Still, the warning to the girls had been good training for them, for the days when they had paying guests at the inn.

If they ever did again.

In the hallway, she came to an abrupt halt.

They *did* have a guest on the premises.

After the hour of troubled sleep she'd just tossed and turned through, how could she have forgotten that? Especially when that brief nap had been filled with images of their new boarder?

As if she'd slipped back into those fitful dreams, the door to her right opened slowly. Silently. Caleb stood framed in the opening, the glow from the hall fixture highlighting him. She gulped, staring at his tousled dark hair and eyes hazy with sleep, to a bare chest dusted with dark hair that arrowed down toward the pair of blue cotton pajama bottoms riding low on his hips.

He stood so close, she would need only to take a step to touch him.

She gulped again, feeling a stirring inside that sent her hands grasping to close her robe. Grasping—and finding nothing but her long sleep T-shirt. It covered her completely. She'd had no reservations about going downstairs to the girls without her robe.

But, oh, did she have her doubts about that decision now.

Caleb stood looking at her as if the T-shirt were made of see-through nylon with only a few velvet swatches in strategic spots for decoration.

"I'm sorry," she said coolly, though she'd grown hot all over in response to his hungry gaze. She forced herself to put her hands calmly by her sides. "Did the girls wake you?"

He shook his head emphatically, as if trying to clear it. "No, you did, pounding up and down the stairs. Thought we were having an earthquake."

"Very funny."

He grinned, a sleepy, crooked smile that only

cranked up the heat within her. "Didn't you feel the walls shake?"

She could feel herself shaking now, all right, to the point she had to fight her need to grab on to something solid.

Like Caleb.

"Sorry," she said again, abruptly this time. "I'll try to be quieter in future."

"Good." He slumped sideways, bracing one shoulder against the door frame. "I can't imagine you'd keep your guests very long if you go around disturbing their sleep."

"Then they shouldn't disturb mine." *Oh, great.* She'd snapped the words without thinking, more in irritation at herself for her weakness than anything else. Maybe he wouldn't realize what she'd said. Maybe he would think she meant the girls downstairs.

But, even half-asleep, he caught on quickly. "Did I bother your dreams tonight, Tess?"

"No."

He reached out to brush her hair back from her cheek. His fingertips whisked across her skin, sending a tickle along her jaw. He leaned close. Closer. She fought the urge to tilt her head the slightest bit, to let him cup her cheek with his palm. To lean even closer in anticipation.

"You never were very good at lying," he murmured.

The combination of his softened voice and less-than-gentle words made her breath catch in surprise. As she backed a step away, his fingertips raised a trail of goose bumps on her skin. "I try not to."

"Good. Then, you'll probably want to take back what you said. I *did* bother your sleep, didn't I?"

She attempted indignation, but the sound that came from her throat could have passed for a yearning sigh. Why couldn't things have ended differently years ago?

She stiffened her shoulders and raised her chin. "The fact you feel you can ask that bothers me," she said, sidestepping one truth but forcing herself to go full steam ahead toward another. "There's no sense in your worrying about whether or not you affect my dreams. The sleeping ones, anyhow. You gave up that right a long time ago."

He raised his hand again.

Smiling grimly, she backed another step, edging out of his reach. "I think you already know what you did to destroy my waking dreams. But that was a long time ago, too. We're beyond that and on to something new." Giving a firm nod, she added, "Breakfast will be served at eight. Then we'll take care of the business that brought you back to town. Meanwhile, have a good rest of the night."

She turned and walked away, blinking rapidly to hold back tears. Of frustration? Anger? Sadness? She couldn't tell.

She knew only that she'd been kidding herself when she'd thought about needing to hold on to something solid, like Caleb.

She'd felt the need, all right. To be close to him again. To relive the past with him. To revisit those days she had refused to talk about earlier when he'd brought them up to her.

Need had to give way to reality. Trying to make a relationship with Caleb into something solid, something lasting, would never work. The past had already shown her the truth. The real man didn't want her.

She'd just have to try harder to keep the dream-Caleb out of her bed.

No worries about that at the moment, unfortunately. This encounter with him guaranteed that in the hours until daybreak she'd find herself wide-awake and more restless than before. If a few minutes in the hallway had been that dangerous, what would happen if she spent all day tomorrow on the road with him?

She just wouldn't, that's all. She'd use her sleepless hours to revise tomorrow's schedule, making sure she and Caleb spent as little time alone together as possible until she could pull herself together....

On second thought, she'd better revamp her schedule for the week.

"Another sweet roll, Caleb?" Roselynn held the wicker basket toward him. Earlier she'd made a point of saying how nice it was to have a man at the table with them again.

He'd never had the pleasure of starting the morning off with a houseful of women. He found it a dubious pleasure, at best.

The little girls chattered constantly, sounding like a bunch of jaybirds perched on a humming telephone wire.

Roselynn seemed distracted now. The few times she attempted conversation, all she did was ask him if he wanted more of anything. Maybe the kids were giving her a headache.

He couldn't complain about the breakfast. He *could* complain about his second hostess, Tess, who didn't seem to care whether he ate or not. Obviously, she still felt riled.

So did he, as a matter of fact. Riled.

And intrigued.

Roselynn waved the sweet rolls at him again. "Yes, ma'am," he said hastily, "I'd like another of those."

Before he could pluck one from the basket, Nate snatched the top one out from under his hand.

"Nate," Tess snapped. "That was rude."

The girl shrugged. "Sorry," she muttered.

"Don't tell me, tell your guest."

Nate gave him a wide smile. "Sorry, Caleb. You want to share this one with me?"

"No, thanks, I'll get my own."

"Let me get some fresh from the oven," Roselynn said, reaching for the basket. She rushed off as though she couldn't wait to escape the tension between Tess and Nate.

He looked over at Tess, all prim and proper with a long-sleeved shirt buttoned up to her chin. A far cry from her outfit of the previous night. That loose, flowing T-shirt she'd worn hanging down to her knees hadn't given anything away. But his imagination didn't need a handout. He could envision what lay beneath the T-shirt just as easily as he could see how uncomfortable she still felt about getting caught in it.

All through breakfast, she'd refused to make eye contact with him. Her gaze kept moving to her briefcase on the chair in the corner. She wanted his business taken care of. She wanted him gone. He'd picked up on her feeling during supper the night before, and that—and sheer stubbornness—had only added to his list of reasons for taking the room at the inn.

Could he blame her for wanting to get rid of him? Maybe not. But he couldn't give her the satisfaction of leaving. He'd tried to explain to her what had happened years ago. She'd made it more than plain she didn't want to discuss it. Their past was in the past. She'd said it herself.

Looking down, he stabbed at the ham steak on his plate.

He still had his future to take care of.

She seemed equally certain of the need to make sure he didn't have a future around here.

After their standoff upstairs in the hall last night, he couldn't say she had things wrong. Staying this close to her might bring more trouble than he wanted to handle. He'd touched her face. Hadn't wanted to stop touching her. But she'd backed away as if he'd been a rattler with his tail rising. It had taken him a hell of an effort to let her walk off.

Another few minutes and he might've done something to get his face smacked. As if her verbal slap about her dreams hadn't made him feel bad enough.

You gave up that right a long time ago.

Maybe one of these days he'd find out what rights he did have with her. Now that could get interesting, at least for as long as he stayed in town. Money wasn't his only means of making an impression. He swallowed a grin along with another mouthful of coffee.

"Mom," Nate blurted, distracting him. "I forgot. When we went to the store yesterday, Mr. Harley said to say howdy."

"Oh, did he?"

He looked over at Tess. She'd sounded a little put out about the announcement. Asking her directly wouldn't get him anywhere. "I remember a Harley from school." Harley wouldn't remember him, though. The kid in his homeroom was too rich for the likes of him. "Doesn't his daddy own the general store?"

"He did," Tess said. "Joe has it now."

"Does he?" He smiled at Nate.

"Yep." She nodded. "And he makes money, hand over fist."

"Nate." Tess's voice had sharpened.

"Well, that's what Aunt El says. Right, Gram?"

Roselynn had just returned to the room and set the basketful of sweet rolls next to his plate.

Not waiting for an answer, Nate leaned closer to him. "Mr. Harley has the biggest store in Flagman's Folly. And he wants to marry Mom."

"Nate!" This time, Tess's voice could've cut the slice of ham steak sitting on his plate. "I think it's time for you and the girls to go and straighten up the living room."

Her friends promptly put their utensils down and began to rise.

Nate remained seated. "Why? There's nobody here but Caleb. He doesn't mind."

"Anastasia Lynn."

The girl rolled her eyes. "Oka-*ay*. Come on, Caleb, you can help me move the couch back."

Slowly, he released the death grip he'd held on his knife and fork.

"We'll take care of that later," Tess told her. "Caleb's still eating his breakfast. You go along, now."

The other girls pushed in their chairs.

Nate pushed out her bottom lip.

That had him biting back a comment. No doubt about it, Tess had her work cut out with this little one. But it wasn't his place to say anything.

Nate finally got up and shoved her chair up to the table. The kid had a lot of energy.

"See you later," she said to him.

He nodded. When she'd left the room, he turned back to Tess. Better to think about teasing her—and not about some guy who wanted her for his bride. "Paybacks," he murmured.

"What?"

"When you're a real handful as a kid, don't folks say to watch out, because 'you'll grow up to have kids of your own someday'?"

"No."

Roselynn laughed. "Oh, yes, they do, sugar. And he has a point." She turned to him. "Tess was an outright handful herself, you know."

"Mo-om," Tess protested, her tone sounding exactly like Nate's. "Let's not get into—" At the sound of footsteps in the kitchen, she stopped.

A real shame. He'd looked forward to hearing a few stories.

Ellamae ambled into the room as if she owned the place. She carried a coffee mug that matched those on the table. "Am I in time for breakfast?"

"Sweet rolls right out of the oven," he said, moving the basket to a space in front of an empty seat.

"That'll do for starters." Ellamae plopped into the chair and took a roll. "And just how is everyone this fine morning?"

"Lovely," Roselynn said. "We were just talking about Tess."

"Who is just getting ready to go to work," Tess said. "Speaking of which, aren't you on your way to Town Hall now, Aunt El? Is the Double S closed today?"

He almost smiled at her innocent tone.

"Oh, it's open." Ellamae turned to him. "Normally, I pick up an order to go and bring it over to the courtroom. But I felt a need to speak to my sister this morning."

"Perfect timing," Tess said. "Caleb and I are just leaving. Aren't we, Caleb?"

"Without brushing our teeth?" he asked, his tone as deliberately innocent as hers had been. "Does Nate get away with that?"

Her expression could have made a bull run for cover.

"*After* we brush, of course." She stood and pushed her chair beneath the table.

"Ah. Then we *are* just leaving," he said, following her lead.

"We'll see you at supper then, Caleb," Roselynn said.

"I'll be here," he confirmed.

He left the dining room at Tess's heels.

Much as he liked the thought of watching her squirm while her mama and aunt told tales on her, he'd come up with another idea he liked much better.

Getting her alone.

Her sister, Roselynn, made a sweet roll you could really sink your teeth into. Ellamae surveyed the breakfast table with satisfaction. But before she had eaten more than two rolls and a side of bacon, Nate and the girls came back into the dining room like a swarm of honeybees headed for the hive.

She held back a chuckle. If she'd guessed right by the look on Caleb's face, before too much time had passed, he intended to do a bit of swarming of his own—over Tess.

"Where's Caleb?" Nate demanded, looking wildly

around the room as if he'd hidden beneath one of the tables.

"He and your mama left just a few minutes ago," Roselynn said.

"Rats." Nate slumped in obvious disappointment.

"What's the trouble?" Ellamae asked. "He'll be back tonight."

"That's too late. We have to find him." Nate side-stepped closer to the two women. Her friends crowded in behind her. "We got a *great* idea," she announced.

Ellamae couldn't wait. "And what might that be?"

"We gotta get Caleb to stay in Flagman's Folly."

"But why, sugar?"

"Oh, Gram," Nate said, as if it were obvious. "This town is soooo boring. We need *something* to make it special. And Caleb's famous."

"He's a rodeo star," her friend Lissa added.

"Ex," Ellamae said flatly, but as she'd expected, no one paid any attention to that.

"So we got an idea to get him to stay." Nate put her hands on her hips and beamed at them. "We get him to marry Mom."

Roselynn choked on a mouthful of tea.

With one hand, Ellamae patted her back. With the other, she swiped another sweet roll. A conversation like this one called for extra sustenance. "And just how did y'all happen to come by that thought?"

"Easy," Nate said.

"She doesn't want her mom to marry Mr. Harley," Lissa put in.

"Caleb's richer," Nate said.

"And cuter," added Lissa.

"And *a star*," chorused the two remaining girls.

"Oh, sugar, I don't know—"

"Well," Ellamae broke in, "it's an idea, all right, Nate. But you and the girls better just forget about that for now. Let your mama and Caleb have some time together, see what happens. You never know. Everything might just come to pass the way you want it, without your helping things along."

"You like the idea, though, right, Aunt El? Right, Gram?" In her eagerness, Nate leaned so far forward she almost fell into the basket of sweet rolls. "You want Caleb to stay here, too, don't ya?"

"It has its possibilities, I'll admit," Ellamae told her. "But as I said, let's give it some time. You girls go on about your business. Unless you want to help clear the dishes."

"No, thanks." Nate backed up, almost trampling her friends. "We already have to fix the living room. Come on, guys."

All four girls turned and fled.

Ellamae laughed.

Roselynn smiled, shaking her head gently. "Those kids. What a wild idea."

Abruptly, Ellamae stopped laughing. "What's so wild about it?"

"For a rich man like Caleb? He has a ranch and a big house up in Montana. Why in the world would he want to move back to a little place like Flagman's Folly?"

"Two reasons." Ellamae held up a finger still sticky with icing. "One reason went out the door with him earlier." Another finger. "And the other just ran into the next room with her friends."

Roselynn stared at her. "Oh, no. That's not a reason. Not for Caleb. He doesn't know."

"He could find out."

Now Roselynn shook her head in earnest. "Not from us, he can't. Our lives wouldn't be worth the price of a three-day-old loaf of bread if Tess ever found out. Besides, *she* doesn't even realize that *we* know."

"Then I guess the girls are right."

"About what?"

"He's got to come around to the idea of marrying Tess."

Her sister gasped. "What makes you think she'd want to marry him now, after he already left her once and broke her heart? You remember how she moped around here."

"I do. But I also see how she's been acting since he's come back again. Like a firecracker ready to explode."

"She doesn't want to get hurt again."

"Of course not. And she's got her defenses up high against that, all right. Caleb's gonna have a time knocking them down. But you called it, too. He won't just up and decide on marriage all on his own. I imagine he'll need to be roped and hog-tied by his friends."

Roselynn set her teacup so firmly into its saucer, Ellamae felt sure it had cracked. "Those are children you're talking about, El. You are *not* going to get them involved in something like—"

"Settle down, settle down," she said, waving her hands to calm Rose. One of her hands just happened to pass over the basket, so she snagged another sweet roll. "I don't plan for those girls to do anything about it at all. This situation calls for a couple of mature, educated people to handle it."

"Like who?" Roselynn demanded.

"Like us, of course."

Her sister sighed. "Oh, Ellamae, it's so obvious our Nate's related to you. You both do come up with the wildest ideas." Grabbing a sweet roll, she smiled. "You always *were* good that way." She rested her elbows on the table and leaned forward. "So, what've you got in mind?"

Chapter 6

The sun had crawled well above the horizon by the time they finally left the bed-and-breakfast. A hot morning already, even for the start of June.

Caleb smiled to himself. Tess would soon regret that buttoned-up shirt she'd worn today.

She moved toward the parking area at a near-trot. He kept to a slower pace, but a steady one, eager for the chance to be alone with her. That spark he couldn't have missed between them last night had him curious. Had she felt it, too?

Then he recalled Nate's statement about the local store owner—the one who made money "hand over fist." She'd seemed impressed by that. What about Tess? What would she think when she found out how easily *he* could give the man a run for his money?

"So," he asked, "what Nate said at the table. You planning on marrying Harley?"

His question put a definite hitch in her stride. He smiled.

Without turning, she said coolly, "I haven't decided yet."

"Sounds like he could take care of you in style. According to Nate and your aunt Ellamae, that is."

"Yes."

Yes, *what?* He knew she and Roselynn were struggling. The man's financial status had to mean something to her. She stopped and faced him. His heart revved up with the crazy thought he'd just given her reason to decide in Harley's favor.

A frown line creased her forehead. "What was that my mother said about seeing you at supper?"

His heart settled back into its normal rhythm. Her mind hadn't been on Harley at all. "We renegotiated my reservation while you were in talking with the girls this morning. I'm paying a little extra and getting another meal. On top of the *other* perks," he said, grinning.

The glint in her eyes told him she'd understood his teasing. Her suddenly expressionless face let him know how little she liked the idea of sharing another meal with him at the inn every day.

"Well," she snapped, "since you've made arrangements of your own already, you won't mind that I've had a change to my plans, too. I've got some errands to run. I'm sure you'll be able to amuse yourself until supper tonight."

Now, *that* bothered him. He'd hired her to find him a ranch. "What do you mean, you've got errands? I thought you were all mine today." Despite his annoyance, it gave him satisfaction to see the soft pink blush filling her face. It also offered him a sliver of hope as sweet as Ellamae's pecan pie.

He thought back again to their meeting in the hallway last night. The look in her eyes then, the expression on her face when he'd touched her—they meant something. What, he didn't know, but he had a feeling it would be in his best interest to find out.

Besides, she'd said it herself, she hadn't yet promised herself to that Harley character.

"Actually," she said, "it may surprise you to hear this, but you're not the only item on my agenda. I've got business to take care of. First, I need to stop by the office to pick up some business cards and brochures."

He raised his brows. "You're planning on advertising to the critters out in the wild?"

"Very funny. No. Dana and I are doing an advertising blitz to try to...to increase our client list. I'm going to hit all the businesses on Signal Street today."

She turned and walked away, as if that ended their conversation. A few spaces short of his pickup truck, she stopped beside the old Toyota he'd seen yesterday.

If she thought she could shake him off with a trumped-up list of errands, she'd have to think again. Besides, her plans fit nicely into his own agenda. He would have had as much chance to flash his cash out in the desert as she'd have had passing out brochures. Now he could make like a rodeo star the length of Signal Street—with Tess right there to see him shine.

He moved to the passenger side of the Toyota and looked at her over the roof. "No problem. I'll go with you. Get a chance to say hello to folks I haven't seen in a while."

Her face fell, but she nodded shortly.

The cramped front seat wouldn't allow much room for him to stretch out his legs or ease his bad knee. Before he could suggest taking the truck, Tess had slipped inside and cranked the engine. He shrugged, then shoehorned himself into the car, sure he'd eventually wish he hadn't.

On the other hand, their close quarters kept her well within reaching distance. He recalled the warmth of her cheek against his fingertips the night before. This arrangement could work in his favor.

She looked away, carefully checking her mirrors before backing out of the parking space.

After they'd gone a block in silence, he decided playing along with her would work, too. "Good idea about the promo," he said easily. "You ought to work up some for the bed-and-breakfast. Your mama needs to get going if she wants any takers for those empty rooms upstairs."

She pulled over to the curb and jammed on the brakes so abruptly, his knee hit the dashboard. Pain radiated down to his ankle. He swore under his breath and made a big production of putting on his seat belt. She ignored that.

"Caleb, what exactly are you up to?" she demanded. "Why are you so interested in the inn?"

"I'm not int—"

She ran right over him. "And how is it you oh-so-conveniently had your suitcase in your truck last night? What happened to your plans to stay out of town? You had everything 'covered'—or so you'd said."

"This works out better." The idea of her seeing him throw money around town had started to appeal to him more than he'd thought.

"For *you,* maybe."

Yeah, his decision to take the room at the bed-and-breakfast had riled her. Not a good thing, maybe, in view of his plans. Even knowing it would make her more irritated, he couldn't help laughing at her response.

She exhaled forcefully. "Don't you have a reservation somewhere?"

"There's not a hotel, motel or town, for that matter, within fifty miles of Flagman's Folly, as you—being in the business of selling property and all—must surely know."

"All right, knock off the sarcasm." She pulled back onto the street and continued driving.

He shook his head. "Better watch yourself. I'm sure it wouldn't sit right with Dana to hear how her 'glorified file clerk', as you called yourself, is treating her biggest client."

She gave a snort equal to one of her aunt Ellamae's. "You mean 'the client with the biggest head,' don't you?" she asked sweetly.

"Maybe some people around here don't think so."

"You can't trust the judgment of *some people.* Especially when they're under the age of ten."

She'd noticed Nate and company's hero worship of him, too, then. She didn't need to sound so sour about it. "It's not like I'd asked for the attention."

"Of course not."

And she'd accused *him* of sarcasm.

She probably thought he'd encouraged the kids.

"Hey, it comes with the territory." When she didn't respond, he continued mildly, "We seem to have strayed from the subject of your mama. I was only asking about promo out of concern for her."

"Why would you even care?"

He looked at her without speaking, and this time her face flushed twice as fast. She grasped the steering wheel more tightly and swallowed hard before replying. "Never mind. But I'm sure she's working on some advertising for the inn."

"Not by the sound of it last night. Said it costs money."

"Which we don't have," she said flatly. "Is that what you're getting at?"

He raised his hands in mock surrender. "Whoa, now. I'm not getting at anything, only repeating what I'd heard from her. You know, I could give—"

"No." She stopped at a traffic light and stared straight ahead, her hands now in a white-knuckled grip on the wheel. "I know Mom's happy to have a paying guest, but that's as far as your money goes. I also know you're rich. Richer than anyone here in Flagman's Folly—probably everyone put together. But we don't need your charity."

"Where'd you get that idea?" he asked, trying to keep it low-key. "I was only going to say I could give my promo people a call and see if they could recommend some ideas for your mama."

"Oh."

"Yeah, *oh,*" he echoed, losing the effort to hold himself in check. "What do you know about charity, anyway?" he demanded. "I was at the receiving end of more handouts than you'll ever see in your life."

The light changed. The car jerked forward. Now he took a turn staring through the windshield. But he couldn't seem to shut up. "Your family *never* needed anything from me, did they? Never wanted it, either."

"You didn't meet my family."

"Not true."

"My mother never told me." It sounded like an accusation.

"She wouldn't know. It wasn't your mama I came across, anyhow, but your granddaddy."

She gasped. "You spoke with my grandfather? About what?"

He heard the edginess in her tone. Even after all these years, the idea that he'd talked to the man upset her that much? "I asked to do some work around your property. Yank weeds, cut grass. He just stood there in the doorway of that big old house and informed me he had 'no need to hire someone from the street.'"

She pulled the Toyota over to the curb in front of her office and threw the gearshift into Park. "You came to my house? Even after I'd asked you not to?"

Her voice shook, with rage or fear, he didn't know. But he could tell she hadn't gotten his meaning, maybe hadn't even taken in the words he'd said. She'd focused on what worried her most.

"No," he replied, as softly as he could. "That was before we were together."

"Oh," she said again. She ran her hands along the steering wheel. "Putting my foot in my mouth twice in one conversation, that's a record for me."

"It happens when people make assumptions."

"I'm sorry, Caleb." She looked away. "I… I'll be right back."

She'd opened the door and was out of the car before he'd taken his seat belt off.

All this, because he'd offered to help her mama. Would she have reacted as strongly if Harley had made the suggestion? Did she have a long history with the man, too? The questions left a bitter taste in his mouth.

He shouldn't care about her relationships with other men. About her anger. Or her apology. Or what she thought about him.

He shouldn't care about her at all.

Yet he did.

She hurried away from the Toyota, leaving him cooling his heels—but that's about as far as it went. His thoughts about her continued to keep the rest of him heated. The questions he'd obsessed over since the night before wouldn't leave him alone.

She crossed the sidewalk to her office, her dark curls gleaming in the sun. That pink shirt and her snug jeans sent his thoughts into a gallop. His memory, too. Once upon a time, he'd committed every inch of her to that memory. Did she ever think about that time, too? Maybe getting caught in her pajamas last night wasn't the only reason she'd covered up almost to her chin today.

He shoved open the door and climbed from the car. As he straightened his left knee, pain arced through it, making him grit his teeth. That knock into the dashboard had set any progress he'd made back a notch.

He leaned against the Toyota and recalled, once again, the scene outside his bedroom door last night. The thought sparked yet more memories. Was the rest of her still as soft as he recalled? Still the same shade of peach all over?

He wiped his brow, suddenly as sweaty as if he'd spent the morning sunbathing on a beach.

Yeah, she'd gotten him heated—in mind and body both.

That knowledge, and the fact he couldn't turn the feelings off, disgusted him. Just as he'd once disgusted her granddaddy.

The man had said a lot more to him that day, made comments he would never tell Tess. Or anyone. Comments about "streetwalkers" and "white trash" and "people who ought to stay where they belong."

That memory made him hot all over, this time with shame. A shame he'd sworn he'd never let himself feel again.

Years ago, those times he and Tess spent together, she had left her house to meet him. She had slept with him. But she'd never taken him to meet her family. Never wanted to bring him around her friends. He didn't have to ask why.

He wasn't good enough for them.

He wasn't good enough for anyone in Flagman's Folly.

Yeah, well, that had changed. As she had said, he'd gotten rich. He'd make sure she knew just how much he was worth now. And he'd make damn sure *everyone* in town knew it, too.

Chapter 7

A short while later, when the door of Wright Place Realty opened, Caleb forced his expression into neutral.

But it wasn't Tess leaving the office. Instead, a tall, dark-haired man stepped out and closed the door behind him. Too tall for Joe Harley.

What business did this guy have with Tess?

He shook his head at his own resentful thought. Real estate business, of course. What else? And what was it to him? Nothing. Same as Nate's claim that Harley wanted to marry her mama. He'd better remember that.

Hell, he'd do even better getting a handle on this sudden streak of jealousy he didn't know he had.

To his surprise, the man walked toward him, grinning, with his hand outstretched.

"Hey, Caleb. Long time, no see."

At the last second, Caleb recognized him. "Ben."

Ben Sawyer, one of his former classmates. It gave him satisfaction to see he could look the other man eye to eye now. All through school, he'd been a head shorter than Ben.

Though they were the same age, he'd wound up graduating high school a year behind the lot of them. Ben. Paul Wright, Dana's husband. Sam Robertson and a slew of others. He'd rather not think about the reasons for that.

"Yeah," he said, "it's been a long time. I'm a stranger to Flagman's Folly now."

"Are you kidding?" Ben laughed. "Around here, you're considered the most well-known person in the Southwest."

He smiled grimly. "Guess the media covered my downfall thoroughly enough." Not exactly the image he wanted to portray.

"I wasn't talking about your downfall, more like your local-boy-does-good career."

"The rodeo-crazy kids in this town." He knew it.

"Not just them. Everyone in the county followed your time on the circuit. But yeah, those kids really took an interest. You're their hero." The other man hesitated, then added, "You'll get back to riding again soon?"

He shook his head. "Not soon. Not ever."

Ben exhaled heavily. "That's tough."

Next, he would mumble something and make an uncomfortable exit, the way everyone else who'd known Caleb before the accident did. Not wanting to see that, he asked, "What are you doing in town, instead of working your ranch?" He looked over at Tess's office. "You thinking of buying some property?"

"No." Now Ben seemed uncomfortable. He turned,

gesturing to the storefront. "I own the building. I hear you're looking for some land in the area, though."

"Tess told you?" What else had she said about him? Then again, considering the fear she still seemed to have that folks would find out about their past, she probably hadn't said anything much other than that.

"Not Tess. I had to make a stop at Town Hall yesterday afternoon and heard the news there."

Caleb raised an eyebrow. He knew what that meant. "Let me guess. Ellamae filled you in."

"Ellamae did," Ben confirmed.

Odd. His return to town would've made the rounds instantly, of course. No getting away from that. But how had she known so early on about his plan to invest in property? Had Tess talked about him to her aunt, at least?

"Anyhow," Ben was saying, "you won't go wrong buying land here. And we all figured it was only a matter of time before you'd come back to your roots." He nodded as if to emphasize his words. "I'll see you around town."

Caleb watched the other man walk away, his stride steady and certain, strong evidence that Ben Sawyer felt he owned more than just the building in front of him. He owned a place in his hometown.

Not something Caleb could claim.

As for those roots Ben had mentioned…

He took a seat on a bench near the real estate office and stretched his good leg full length. The twinge in his bad leg told him not to risk it.

Back when he'd lived here, he wouldn't have called what he'd had "roots." More like a rolling mass of tumbleweed, with no ties and no reason for them. No atten-

tion from anyone. Positive attention, anyway. Except for
Dori and Manny from the Double S. Ellamae, at times.
And Tess. Or so he'd thought...

He shied away from going down that road. Better
to focus on Ben.

Ben, who had just spoken as if he felt Caleb was a
part of Flagman's Folly. And as if the townsfolk might
think the same. Did the man mean they believed that
now, based on Caleb's success in rodeo? Or could he
really have meant folks felt Caleb belonged even when
he'd lived here? Folks not like Tess's granddaddy?

He shook his head at the confusion the questions
had brought on.

The door of the office opened again, and this time
Tess did emerge from the building. She went over to the
Toyota and dropped a package onto the backseat. Then
she squared her shoulders and turned toward him, her
mouth set in a smile.

Maybe Dana had given her a talking-to in the office. And maybe Tess had accepted that she had to follow through on her duties—whether she liked the idea
or not.

"Let's go," she said.

He didn't much like her clipped tones. She'd sounded
almost like her granddaddy. Instead of rising, he patted
the wooden seat beside him. "Take a break."

Her gaze shot to his left knee and away again. She
probably thought he needed a rest. She opened her
mouth to say something pitying. He could see it in her
eyes. But then she closed her mouth without uttering
a word.

Two people in a row who hadn't voiced their sympathy. He ought to be grateful for that. He didn't need pity from them. From anyone.

He didn't need to bow down to them anymore, either. "Don't worry, that crack against the dashboard didn't do much damage. I'll be able to walk again." An ironic thing for him to say, considering the doctors had once held it in doubt. But she didn't need to know that.

Her cheeks red, Tess moved over to the bench and sat, cautiously, as if expecting the wooden slats to give way beneath her. She looked tense as a first-time bull rider.

Though the sarcasm had felt justified, he'd have to stop. Now. He needed to get her loosened up a little, more receptive to him again. A losing battle, maybe, considering their history. But he wouldn't know unless he tried. Besides, he needed to get more in touch with what had gone on in Flagman's Folly since he'd left.

"Saw Ben Sawyer when he came out of your office," he said easily.

Her shoulders lowered a notch. "Did you?"

"Yeah. It took me a second to recognize him."

"Really? He hasn't changed a lot since high school."

He shrugged. "I didn't see much of him back then. I wasn't in any of the clubs or on any of the committees."

"Neither was I, except when they desperately needed extra help and Dana dragged me along." She looked straight ahead. With one hand, she brushed at her jeans. Trying to sweep away memories?

Would she have any better luck at that than he had?

"Yeah, Dana and Paul and Ben, they had a hand in everything. You and I weren't joiners," he said, feeling his way.

He wouldn't have made it onto the debate team, as

Ben had. He'd never had a gift for quick answers. If he had, he might not have gotten knocked around so much by some of his mama's friends.

"Maybe," he ventured, "if we'd gotten tied up with more clubs at school or kept busier with friends, we might never have gotten together at all."

"Maybe not." Her voice sounded brittle, and she rushed on, "But Ben sure kept up with everything. They voted him onto the school council every year and made him president of both the junior and senior classes."

"I remember that. Always Mr. Personality, wasn't he?"

She nodded. "He still is. He's on the town council now."

"He told me he's your landlord."

She exhaled heavily, as if she'd been holding her breath, and curled her fingers into a loose fist on her knee. "Not mine. Dana's." Her tone had lost the brittleness, had become soft and low.

A car drove past on Signal Street, and he leaned closer, straining to hear her.

"Ben bought the building from the original owner. She rents the office from him."

"She? What about Paul? Doesn't he own half the business?"

Her shoulders stiffened again. "Paul—" Her voice broke. She cleared her throat and started again. "Paul isn't with us anymore."

Her reactions told him the man had done more than just leave town. He covered her hand with his. "What happened?"

"He was in the army and...he was killed overseas, a little over a year ago."

He shook his head in disbelief. When he could catch his breath, he asked quietly, "Dana's on her own now?"

Her eyes glittered suddenly. She looked away. "She has three children. Nate's friend Lissa is the oldest of them." She rose from the bench, her hand sliding free from his. "We ought to be going."

She said it as if she hadn't just dropped that news on him. Or as if she wanted an excuse to move away.

By the time he reached the car, she had slipped into the driver's seat and shut the door. He entered with less speed, trying to avoid hitting his knee. Attempting to recover from the shock of her words.

He felt no anger bubbling inside him now, just a churning mass of confusion. It left him uncertain of what to think. About anything.

In just a couple of conversations, his memories had been thrown offtrack, as unexpectedly as he'd been thrown off the last bull he'd ridden. And with just as many life-changing effects.

Paul...gone.

Ben...assuming Caleb would come home again.

The townsfolk...believing that he belonged.

It was a lot for him to take in at once.

Could he have gotten things wrong, at least as far as some folks were concerned? Did it matter? He still had more than enough reason to show the rest of them just what he'd become.

His cell phone vibrated. He pulled it from his pocket. Seeing the name and number on the screen gave him pause.

"I'll leave you alone," Tess murmured, getting out of the car and closing the door softly behind her.

He eyed the phone again and then greeted his foreman, who had a list of questions for him. Fortunately, he had answers. Yet by the time he'd ended the call, he wondered just how much longer he could leave the man on his own to manage the ranch.

He glanced at Tess. She was leaning against the front fender of the car.

She had as good as given him an ultimatum for today.

Ben Sawyer had given him things to think about that might affect his strategy.

He raised the phone in the air, indicating he'd finished his call. When she entered the car again, he turned to her. "I may have to leave town sooner than I intended." Her chest rose with her indrawn breath. Some might have mistaken it for disappointment. He knew better. "Looks like we're in for another change to our schedules. Now, how about showing me some real estate."

Three days later, he'd not gotten an inch closer to his goal. Caleb's jaw felt so tight he wondered how he could swallow his morning coffee.

"May I be excused?" Nate asked.

That was a first.

Even Tess looked astounded by the girl's politeness. She nodded as if afraid saying something to her might break the spell.

Nate got up and pushed her chair in to the table. "Can I go with you and Caleb today?"

Ah. That explained the sudden show of manners. Wouldn't last long. He knew without a doubt what Tess's answer would be.

"No, I'm afraid not," she said. "You'll be too busy,

anyway. Gram tells me you've slacked off on your chores around here."

"I don't want to do chores." Her intentions thwarted now, she'd turned ornery as an irritated bull.

"Neither do the rest of us. But we do them, anyway."

"Well, I'm not going to. I'm tired of chores. And it's summertime." Her chin came up and her dark eyes flashed.

Caleb bit down on the words he wanted to say. He didn't have any right to say them. But he wished for once he could take on some of Tess's burden. Take away some of the tension between her and Nate.

"That's enough," Tess snapped. "You have no other big plans for today. You're doing your chores. Besides," she added brightly, "there's no better time than a Friday morning to check everything off your list so you'll have a fresh start for the weekend."

Tess really took that "checking off" business to heart. She had driven him from one distant ranch to another this week, none of which came close to what he'd told her he wanted. It seemed any property at all would do for her, so long as she could check *him* off her list—and get a fresh start on her life.

Nate managed to hold her tongue but turned abruptly and ran from the room.

Despite his irritation at Tess, the despairing look on her face stunned him. He grabbed his empty mug and took a long swig of nonexistent coffee just to keep from reaching for her instead.

Chapter 8

"Give me a minute," Tess told Caleb. "I want to run up and see Nate before we leave."

"I'll be outside."

As if she needed the reminder. She hadn't made a move without him in days. At this point, she wasn't sure just how much more of his company she could take.

He'd seemed edgy and irritable during their long drives. She'd made a list of the most far-flung properties she could find, but he'd asked her about locating something nearer to Flagman's Folly—exactly what she *didn't* want to do.

She walked past his bedroom and tried not to think of how he'd looked that night she'd met him at his doorway. How he'd touched her and what she had felt. More stress piled onto what she already had to deal with.

Every day, no matter how she tried to avoid it, their

trips brought them closer to the town limits. Every day, her tension increased and her guilt grew. Thoughts ran continually through her head of Mom and Nate, Dana and her kids, and all they had to lose if she didn't earn this commission.

And none of that even came close to the most dangerous aspect of this whole disaster.

Caleb's story of meeting her grandfather had surprised her. But after jumping to conclusions with him that day, she didn't ask anything more. She didn't want to know. From then on, she'd stayed vigilant about watching what she said. Unfortunately, she didn't have that power over her thoughts.

Who was she kidding? She didn't have *any* control of her thoughts or emotions when she was with Caleb.

She pushed against Nate's door and lost her breath as she found herself looking straight at him.

At her daughter's insistence, the bedroom had been decorated in a cowboy theme, which she'd added to by covering the walls with rodeo souvenirs. From the poster beside the dresser, a larger-than-life-size Caleb Cantrell, Champion Bull Rider, stood staring back at Tess.

She had to force herself to drag her gaze away.

Nate lay sprawled on her bed surrounded by her collection of miniature horses.

"You okay?" Tess asked.

"Yeah." She didn't look up.

"Do you want to tell me what's bothering you? I know you don't like doing your chores, but you don't normally refuse like that."

"Nothing's bothering me."

"Oh. Well, then, I'll say goodbye. We're getting ready to go out to look at more property."

"Yeah, you said that. At breakfast. You're *always* leaving."

Tess looked at her in surprise. Was that what Nate's tantrum had been about? Missing her mother? "I know. But it's business."

"Yeah, and it's *always* business. Why can't you go by yourself for once? Why can't Caleb stay here with me and Gram and the guys?" She sat up on the bed and bounded to her feet, scattering toy horses over the floor. "Why do you *always* have to take him away?"

Before Tess could recover, Nate ran through the door.

Her knees shaking, Tess sank to the edge of the bed. Suddenly she felt thankful for the trip out of town. She would deal with her emotions around Caleb now, including the guilt that had begun to plague her almost daily. She'd have to. Anything would be better than letting him stay here and spend any more time with Nate.

Caleb had moved outside to lean up against the Toyota. He'd gotten tired of waiting in the kitchen.

He was impatient—for yet another day of self-imposed torture, of spending hours alone with Tess while keeping his hands off her. Evenings were better, since he'd taken it upon himself to fix up Roselynn's decrepit shed in the backyard of the inn.

But the days alone with Tess... If he didn't get a break from the days, the unfulfilled lust might just break *him*.

Still, those long rides with her along empty desert roads between available properties had left him plenty of time for thinking.

He had to keep his head around her. He couldn't start anything that might keep him tied down. That wasn't part of his plan. His life was in Montana now. He had a ranch to run, people dependent upon him, a foreman who might go rogue any minute. He had too much happening outside this town. And too many bad memories of it to stay here.

Permanently, anyhow. For the short term, that was a different story, one he'd told himself all those long months in rehab.

His life in Montana—or anywhere—would never mean a thing until he'd done what he'd set out to do right here. He damn sure wouldn't give that up for a roll in the hay.

Not even with Tess.

She came out of the house, and he caught another look at the bright, flower-printed shirt she'd picked to wear today. The shirt that made him think of hot nights in a garden and even hotter sex on the grass under the stars.

He slid into the Toyota and slammed the door behind him. He'd almost gotten himself pulled together by the time she buckled herself into the driver's seat.

"We're heading southeast today," she announced. "Going to look at a couple of places down near Carlsbad."

Grinding his teeth, he stared out through the windshield. Here he was, lusting after the woman no matter how much he tried to talk himself out of it, while she did her best to get rid of him. He'd asked her to find some property closer to town. Did she think he didn't know Carlsbad was about as far as they could go and still be in the same state?

"I think we'll skip the long trek today," he said.

She frowned.

Roselynn came out onto the back porch with a basket of laundry to hang on the line. Seeing them, she set the basket on the top step and crossed over to the car. "Since you're still here, I thought I'd ask if you'd like me to fix you up a picnic lunch or anything."

"No, thanks," he said. "I think the only trip we'll be taking today is down to Signal Street."

Her eyes lit up. "Nice to hear you'll be in town." She turned away and went right back past the laundry basket and into the house.

Shrugging, he turned to Tess. "We've got some unfinished business to take care of."

There she went with that white-knuckled choke hold on the steering wheel he'd seen the other day. It reminded him of himself as a kid, the first time he'd climbed onto the back of a mechanical bucking bronco and held on for dear life. It bothered him to think he gave her that same feeling of desperation.

It irritated the hell out of him that she didn't share his feelings of lust.

He forced a smile. "You never gave out that promo you have," he reminded her.

"Speaking of promo," she said tightly, "I see you've given Nate some of yours."

He nodded. "Yeah. I contacted my PR people, and they sent me some info to pass along to your mama. They threw in some of my stuff, too. Nate was there when we opened the package. So I gave her a poster. See?" He grinned. "I told you there was value in advertising. Now, handing your promo out today can do double duty. You never got around to showing me the sights in town, either."

Her fingers had loosened considerably on the steering wheel, but at his last words her expression turned downright suspicious. "Why is that important?"

What should he tell her?

Not the truth, that's for sure.

He planned to fling money around Flagman's Folly in a way that would make her and everyone else sit up and take notice—and then bow down and beg for more.

No, he couldn't tell her that. Instead, as always, he read his audience and came up with a good story.

"If I buy a sizable ranch, I'm going to need a good number of cowhands and someone to run it. I'd like to know what's available for them if they ever come this way. And for me, too, when I'm around."

Again, her mouth opened and shut again. No suspicion in her eyes now. Only a look of complete dismay.

Obviously, the thought that he would return to check on his property from time to time hadn't occurred to her. And now that he'd brought it up, she didn't like the idea one bit.

But she would keep quiet about that. He'd bet on it.

Sure enough, when he didn't say anything else, she nodded.

"Yes, I guess you're right," she said finally. Grudgingly. She started the car and proceeded to Signal Street without saying another word.

He'd called it right. She didn't want to risk the commission she'd get from a sale. She was only tolerating him for his money, only playing her game.

Just as he played his.

After all, it was money—and what he could do with

it—that had brought him back to town in the first place. And it was time he got down to business, instead of staying on the road penned up in a car with a woman who made him feel like a sex-starved teenager again.

Would everyone think the way Tess did? Instead of being impressed by his wealth, would they only want what they could get of it? Maybe that was why Ben Sawyer had played that coming-home-to-your-roots angle with him.

All week, the things Ben said to him had run around in his thoughts. Why would Ben—or anyone else in Flagman's Folly—have any other reason to care if he stayed around?

Ben had been one of the town's heroes, along with Paul Wright. Ben, the boy voted Most Likely to Succeed, and Paul, the football team's star quarterback.

He hadn't played any sport at all. Or done anything to show he might someday become a success in any area. He'd had no money, no charm. No claim to fame.

Unless you counted having a mama who made headlines like the one he'd once found scrawled in black marker with his own telephone number below it on the men's room wall at the Double S.

For a good time, call Mary Cantrell.

Caleb realized his great plan to stay in town to talk with folks—to keep from going off alone with Tess— had raised an issue he had never anticipated.

"Well," she said as they walked down the center aisle of the pharmacy, sacks in hand, "I think we've hit about every business in sight."

"Looks like it." Along with showing him around, she'd spread her business cards and brochures far and wide. "Not such a bad idea, after all. Maybe you'll get some new customers from the promo."

"If they even realize they have it," she said, sounding almost resentful.

"They all said they'd talk up your agency to anybody interested in a house."

"After that spending spree of yours, they'll probably forget where they put the brochures."

"I did buy the stores out, didn't I?"

"Close enough." She hefted one of the sacks she carried. "Did you really need fifteen razors?"

"Gifts for the ranch hands back home."

"How thoughtful."

"I'm a thoughtful man. Didn't I offer to buy you that box of chocolates?"

She groaned. "Don't start on that again, Caleb, please. I told you, the flowers and dishtowels for Mom and the pie tins for Aunt El were enough."

"Think your aunt will try them out soon?"

"How should I know? Let's get this latest haul of yours to the car, shall we? *If* we can find another spare inch to stow it."

He grinned. She hadn't wanted him to buy the gifts. He'd expected that.

As she turned away, his grin faded.

The walking and the many trips to Tess's car had shown him he wasn't ready yet for all this physical activity. As he'd told Ellamae, he felt his aches from time to time. Probably always would, the doctors had warned him, just as he'd always have the awkward limp when he got tired.

Today's pain didn't worry him too much, either.

The first time they'd exited a building and found his

new pint-size fan girls in the vicinity, he'd had a feeling they'd stick around.

Sure enough, as he looked through the plateglass window of the pharmacy, he could see the group standing on the other side of the street.

"Oh, Nate," Tess murmured under her breath. She shook her head and pulled the door open.

"Come on," he said, taking her by the elbow. "We forgot to make a stop over here." As he led her toward the next building, he felt her arm stiffen. Had she planned to skip this last store?

He slowed his step, knowing he couldn't insist on her going inside. But he needed to make this one last stop, to take one final shot at following his plan. Because, all morning, he'd felt thrown by the reactions of everyone they'd come across.

He'd wanted to show folks that money meant nothing to him, because he had plenty. But they'd appreciated his purchases. And they seemed more interested in talking with him about everything from the upcoming Fourth of July parade to their opinions of the politics of Flagman's Folly.

It hadn't made a bit of sense.

Tess stood staring at him. After a moment, she continued forward, and he fell into place beside her.

When they reached the automatic sliding doors of the building, she gave a little sigh.

As if in sympathy, a collective gasp rose from the opposite sidewalk. His fan girls exchanged looks of dismay and rushed into a huddle.

He smiled. What were they up to now?

Not waiting to find out, he walked with Tess into the air-conditioned coolness of Harley's General Store.

* * *

Tess froze. And not just because they'd turned the corner into the freezer aisle of the store, either.

She hadn't wanted to come in here, hadn't wanted to meet with Joe Harley while Caleb stood by her side. Until they'd talked to the clerk at the front register, she'd held out hope that Joe had business somewhere else this morning. But, no, there he was, kneeling in front of the frozen-food cooler, rearranging gallon-size tubs of ice cream. *Rocky Road.*

A perfect description of her life right now!

She could have argued about this meeting. And probably should have. But Caleb seemed determined to stop in at every business in town.

Including Harley's General.

Could his single-mindedness in coming here have something to do with Nate's little announcement at breakfast that first morning?

She shook off the idea. Sure, Caleb had asked her later if she planned to marry Joe. That didn't mean he cared about her. Or about any wedding plans she might—or might not—have. He had no reason to talk to Joe. But on second thought, better the two men should meet now, while she could be there to deflect the conversation away from subjects that shouldn't concern Caleb.

Joe had risen to his feet. Losing the battle to tug his blue smock closed, he gave up and held out his hand. "Well, now, Caleb. Heard you were back in town. It's right nice seeing you again, after all these years."

"Thanks. Same here." Caleb gestured. "I'm staying with Tess."

Joe frowned.

"You're *a guest* at the *bed-and-breakfast*," she said between clenched teeth, giving Caleb the coldest look she could manage.

"Right. That's what I said. Your house."

Joe looked at her, then back at Caleb. "You planning on staying long?"

Caleb's mouth curved slowly in a half smile.

The sudden shiver that ran through her didn't come from seeing that. No, it was from all the frosty air billowing out from the cooler. She reached over and smacked the door closed.

"Don't have a definite departure date yet," he drawled in answer to Joe's question. "But, I'll tell you something. Tess's sweet rolls are so good, they might convince me to hang around a bit."

She swallowed a groan. "*My mother* made the rolls," she corrected.

"Did she? I thought you did."

"No. I'm too busy selling real estate, remember? Or trying to." She turned away from him. "Which is why we're here today, Joe." She explained about the brochure for Wright Place Realty.

"Well, sure, I'll be happy to post one on the community bulletin board up front. In fact, give me a pile of them. And your cards, too."

His wide smile puffed up his face like a snowman's—appropriate enough considering their surroundings, but a poor contrast to Caleb's chiseled cheeks. She blinked, shoving the unkind thought from her mind even as she pushed a good number of brochures and business cards into Joe's outstretched hand. She might as well get something out of this humiliating situation.

"I'll pass these around at the next town council meeting."

"Thanks, I appreciate it."

He looked quickly at Caleb, then back at her again. "And we're still on for supper tonight, aren't we? It's Friday."

Caleb turned his head her way as if wanting to see as well as hear her response. She made sure to show him. She fastened her gaze on Joe, and said firmly, "Yes, we're still on. I'm looking forward to it."

A loud bang filled the air, followed by a child's high-pitched screech.

"Joe, breakage up front, aisle three," announced the clerk over the store's loudspeakers—and over the child's continuing wail. "That's Billie Jo's little one caterwauling. He's fine, but oh, my...we've got dill pickles bouncing *everywhere*."

"Excuse me," Joe said, backing away. "A store owner's work is never done. I'll pick you up at seven, Tess."

As Joe left, she turned to Caleb. "That was uncalled for."

He shook his head. "That's harsh, isn't it? I'm sure the man didn't mean to be rude. He had to go take care of his pickles."

She sighed. "Not funny. You know exactly what I meant—your remark about staying with me."

"Aw, you shouldn't let that upset you none. I'm sure Joe's a very understanding man. Although, come to think of it, he did look a bit taken aback by the idea, didn't he? Doesn't he know about your mama's bed-and-breakfast? Maybe you should tell him at supper."

So, he *did* care that she planned to go out with Joe.

Why? He had no right to interfere in what she did. He never would. She'd make sure of it. "Caleb Cantrell—"

"Tess LaSalle." He murmured her name, his voice low and husky, his exaggerated drawl long gone. He leaned forward until their bodies almost touched. "I am staying with you, aren't I? I'm even sharing your room—"

"You are not—"

"I am." He tilted his head down until their mouths almost touched, too. "I've got to be in your room, one way or another, if I'm in your dreams." He smiled. "Bet your good ol' pickle-picker-upper can't lay claim to *that* one."

"You're right," she said, keeping her voice low, as well. "Joe's no dream. He's a man that can be counted on." Shaking, she turned away, certain she'd had the last word. Knowing nothing could top the truth. And hoping Caleb had gotten the message.

He put his hand on her elbow. In the coolness of the frozen-food aisle, his fingers felt hot against her skin. She swallowed hard and tried even harder to keep from yanking her arm free. From letting him see how he affected her.

He opened his mouth, but before he could say a word, she blurted the most critical comment she could think of. "And at least Joe doesn't turn his down-home accent off and on."

He tilted his head again, putting his cheek close to hers. "Yeah," he breathed into her ear, "but I'll bet he doesn't turn you on, either."

A few minutes later, after saying their goodbyes to Joe, Caleb trailed after Tess, who stomped toward the front door of the store. She hadn't looked his way once since they'd left the ice cream section behind. Could he blame her?

He shook his head in amazement at what had happened back there.

His plan called for impressing Tess just the way he would drive home his message to the rest of the folks in town. It didn't involve teasing her. Or getting so close he could have kissed her. But his brain had had other ideas, and his body had followed along, same as that first night at the inn, when he'd stood in the upstairs hallway with her. Now, at last, he knew why—though it galled him to admit he'd have to credit the news of her date with old Joe for smartening him up.

He intended to rub everyone's noses in his wealth, to prove he was just as good as they were. But that wouldn't work with Tess. With Tess, he needed something more.

He wanted her to see what she had missed. To know just what she'd walked away from when she took off to marry some other guy.

And yeah, dammit, to realize he was the best thing she could ever have had.

A few steps ahead of him, she came to a dead halt just inside the automatic doors. His revelations had put so much kick in his stride, he barely reined himself to a stop in time to keep from trampling her.

As the doors slid open, he followed her gaze to the sidewalk outside, where his local fan club stood waiting.

"Not again," she muttered.

"Yep, again. Or still. And it seems like their numbers have swelled." They had additional reinforcements with them. Reinforcements that weren't so pint-size. "Your mama and aunt have joined them."

"They'd better not have." Her words sounded threatening. She barreled through the front doorway like a bull down the chute.

"Hello, *again*," she said to the crowd on the sidewalk.

Her forced cheerfulness couldn't have rung true to any of them, yet they all smiled back as if she'd meant it.

"And my," she went on, looking at the women, "isn't it nice to see you two here. But Aunt El, don't you have to go to work this morning?"

"We're on our way over to the Double S." Her aunt made a production of looking at her watch, then stretching her wrist out at arm's length. "Noon, see? I normally get a lunch right about now."

"The judge lets you off for good behavior?" Caleb asked.

The two older women laughed and glanced at each other.

Finally Tess made eye contact with him again—only to shoot him a look that told him she didn't appreciate his humor. Or, more likely, his interference.

"How did your morning go?" Roselynn asked.

"Fine." Tess clipped the word.

"Not bad," he said more easily. "Just a few visits to touch base with folks again."

Roselynn smiled. "That's good. Did they get you all caught up on things?"

"I don't know about that. They talked politics, mostly."

"Heck, that wasn't worth the trip," Ellamae assured him. "We've had the same mayor for years, and he was a shoo-in this time around, too. What else did you talk about?"

"Not a lot. We didn't have enough time for any real conversation."

Tess made a strangled sound. Probably thinking again about his spending spree.

"Is that so?" Ellamae looked at Roselynn, who smiled.

Without their saying a word, he had the feeling they'd spoken volumes between them.

"Our visiting's done now, though." He turned to Tess. "We'll be heading out of town to look at property again, won't we?"

"Tomorrow," she confirmed.

"Then can we go to lunch with you and Gram, Aunt El?" Nate asked. "Caleb can come with us."

"No, I don't believe that will work," Tess said.

He registered the strain in her voice and guessed her thoughts had flown to how much a meal for this gang would cost.

No problem there. He'd willingly pick up the check. It would pay Dori and Manny back some for all they'd given him. But as he opened his mouth, Tess cut him off, just as she had at the store.

"Gram has your lunch ready at home," she told Nate.

"I'll eat it for supper," she shot back.

She looked on the verge of having a tantrum right there on the sidewalk. Tess looked about to explode. A gut feeling told him his arrival in town might have added to her parenting troubles. The thought made him feel low.

"Well," he said quickly, "we're here now, all together. Why don't we walk on over to the restaurant? My treat."

The girls cheered. The two women smiled.

Tess looked up at him. "How nice of you, Caleb."

She'd muttered the words for him alone, and again her tone fell far short of matching her words.

"Just trying to be hospitable," he said. Besides, along with adding to the profits of the Double S, he'd have been a fool not to grab this opportunity to show a few more folks the big spender he'd become.

The sour look she sent him—eyes squinted, lips pursed—made him think she'd seen right through to that last goal.

And that she didn't much like what she saw.

Chapter 9

Tess had hoped for an empty table at the Double S—a nice, long table that would put distance between her and Caleb. She should have known Roselynn and Aunt El would immediately claim their favorite booth up front next to the window. From there, they could see both everything that went on in the café and anything that happened within sight on Signal Street.

With luck, nothing of interest would happen at their *own* lunch table. She had noticed the look they'd exchanged outside Harley's General Store. They were up to something, no doubt about it.

Uneasily, she followed her aunt across the room.

"I'm sitting next to Caleb," Nate announced.

"There's not enough room for all of us," Tess said before her daughter could put the statement into action. "You girls can take the next booth."

To head off any argument, she promptly dropped onto one of the bench seats and scooted over to the space near the window. She expected her aunt, who had hovered near her elbow, to follow. Instead, Aunt El gestured to Caleb.

Squaring her shoulders, Tess locked gazes with him. As strongly as she could without words, she attempted to send the idea that he'd do much better to choose a seat somewhere else.

He nodded, as if confirming receipt of her message. Then, just as she began to relax, he smiled, sat on the end of her bench, and slid across it nearly to the center.

"Well, thank you," Ellamae said, plopping down beside him. "Just give a gal a little more elbow room, would you?"

"Sure thing."

Caleb moved closer to Tess, close enough that she could feel the warmth radiating from him, the slight press of his thigh against hers.

His mouth had tightened into a straight line, but the skin around his eyes crinkled. The man was laughing at her. Was probably trying to unnerve her.

Gritting her teeth, she fought the idea of edging closer to the window. That would only give him proof of how well he'd succeeded.

Ridiculous. Here she sat at high noon, in a crowded café, in front of her entire family, and she was allowing this man to get to her.

To her dismay, her aunt waved again. "Come on over, girls. Plenty of room now. Nate, you settle there by your gram. Lissa, hop up beside her. The rest of you, pull up a couple of chairs and we'll be all set."

Tess swallowed a groan. Trust Aunt El to take over.

But what could she say about it? Besides, her aunt's grin showed how pleased she felt at coming up with a solution she thought suited everyone.

Not quite.

Even more apprehensive now, Tess watched as Nate scrambled across the bench, eager to take the next-best place of honor—the seat opposite her hero.

As the rest of the group grabbed at menus, Tess rubbed her temple, feeling a monstrous headache coming on, all thanks to the man beside her. When she caught Caleb looking at her, she froze.

"Sun in your eyes?" he murmured sympathetically. "Want to switch places?"

The others were too busy to hear this side conversation. She looked pointedly from the booth's tabletop to the small space between them. "What do you plan to do," she muttered, "climb over me?"

The wicked gleam in his eyes made her flush. She hadn't meant anything by her sarcastic question except to vent her frustration. But that gleam and his soft laugh told her he'd found an underlying message in it.

Another great choice of words. Good thing she hadn't said *that* aloud, too.

"Whatever it takes, Tess." He dipped his head toward her, and his eyes looked suddenly serious. "That's a promise."

She laughed bitterly. "No, thanks. You can keep your promises to yourself." She didn't want anything to do with them.

"What *do* you want, Mom?"

Startled, she looked up to see Nate waving a menu at her.

"Everybody's ready but you and Caleb."

Oh, she was ready all right. To get him on the road again tomorrow and on the way to a sale that would take him out of her life. Their lives.

What he was ready for...

She recalled that gleam in his eyes and had a very good idea of what he had in mind. She didn't want that from him, either.

No matter what her dreams said.

She looked over toward the end of the booth, where Dori stood waiting to take her order. "I know what I'm having," she said, forcing a smile. "A bowl of Manny's good, hot chili."

"Act like it, too," Caleb muttered. "*Real* chilly."

"What?" she asked, struggling to keep her voice down in front of their witnesses.

"I said I'd like that, too." He smiled and turned away to place his order. "A bowl of real, homemade chili."

After Dori had gone back to the kitchen, the others returned to their conversation.

She slumped back against her seat and raised her hand to her temple again. "Caleb," she muttered, "why don't you just give me a break."

Lunch had gone downhill from there, in Tess's opinion.

Just as they had done ever since they'd met him, the girls hung on Caleb's every word. Worse, Roselynn and Aunt El did the same, while occasionally sending each other meaning-filled glances. Once in a while, they let their gazes slide her way.

They'd cooked something up between them. Who knew what—but one thing was certain. Aunt El had instigated the plan.

She would have an easier time dealing with Nate's belligerence than she would trying to get anything out of her aunt. Instead, she'd have to corner her mother.

Meanwhile, stuck beside Caleb in their booth, she was literally held captive for more of his rodeo tales. Did the man's stories never end?

Though she had to suffer through watching the adulation on Nate's face, at least she had the satisfaction of knowing the conversation didn't stray into any dangerous topics.

When their group left the Double S, Tess trailed behind, trying not to grumble under her breath.

Caleb held the door for her, and as she stepped outside, she saw everyone had gathered beside a car that had pulled to the curb. Kayla Robertson sat behind the wheel. Tess smiled. Kayla had lived in Chicago, but since marrying Sam last year, she had become a part of Flagman's Folly and Tess's good friend.

Their daughter's puppy hung his head through the rear passenger window. The dog, a Labrador-Shepherd mix, had a tan face, with one eye completely surrounded by dark fur.

"This is Becky's puppy," Nate told Caleb. "His name's Pirate. Becky can't hear, so she talks in sign language. This is how you say 'Pirate.'" She put her hand over her right eye.

"Like an eye patch," Caleb said.

"Right." Nate beamed at him.

Tess stepped forward and made introductions.

Kayla reached through the window to shake Caleb's hand. "I've heard a lot about you from Sam," she told him.

"Have you?" He seemed taken aback.

"Oh, yes. And he's heard you're in town again. He plans to be in touch."

"Where's Becky?" Nate asked.

"Home." Kayla laughed. "She's getting to be a real rancher. My sister's coming for a visit soon, and Becky's already excited about showing her aunt how she feeds the chickens. Her daddy and the ranch hands are going to build her a chicken coop one of these days. Now that the subject's come up," she said to Caleb, "I'll warn you Sam mentioned having you stop by the house." Her gaze shot toward the two older women and back again. "And once I tell him what Roselynn said about knowing your way around with a hammer and a paintbrush, you're doomed."

He grinned at her. "Any time. Just say the word."

Tess swallowed her frustration. Or tried to.

"I'd better get going," Kayla said. "I'm taking Pirate to the V-E-T."

"Is he sick?" Nate asked in alarm.

"No, just going for a checkup. Tess, call me." Kayla waved to them all, then pulled the car away from the curb.

Before anyone could move, Aunt El announced, "Well, we've got a busy day on the books for tomorrow."

Tess looked at her. "You mean at Town Hall?" she asked warily. Hopefully.

"You know I told the judge I don't work on Saturdays. That's family time."

She shook her head. "Sorry, Aunt El, I'm afraid I'm busy, too. Whatever you have planned, you'll have to count me out."

"Oh, sugar, that's a real shame," Roselynn murmured.

Her aunt stared steadily at her for a long moment. Then she drawled, "Why, that's not a problem, Tess. We can work around you. We just need this man standing by your side." She put both hands on her hips and grinned up at him. "It's high time we reintroduce Caleb Cantrell to the gentry of Flagman's Folly."

So *that's* what those two were up to. "Really, that's not necessary."

"It surely is."

"No, Mom," she said, trying not to sound as desperate as she felt. That would be all she needed, to have Caleb distracted from their business. Maybe to have him extend his stay. Just the thought made her shudder. "Caleb's here to look at property."

"Can't spend all our time doing that," he said.

"We don't have time to waste, either," she shot back, refusing to look at him.

"What's gentry?" Nate asked.

"Besides," Tess rushed on, feeling her control of the situation beginning to slip, "we've already lost today."

"Well, I don't see—"

"And I don't see why you have all this interest in visiting with folks."

"Why wouldn't I?"

He'd asked calmly enough, but from the corner of her eye, she saw him tense. She couldn't antagonize him now. She couldn't upset him at all.

Facing him, she said, "I thought you'd want to get your business taken care of so you can go back to Montana."

"What's gentry?" Nate asked again.

Tess sighed. "It means people. Gram and Aunt El want to introduce Caleb to folks."

"That's a great idea, Mom! We can help."

"Yeah." Lissa nodded. "We know lots of people."

"Good. You just hold on to those thoughts," Aunt El said cheerfully. "They're sure to come in handy. But for now, we've got plenty of things lined up."

"Yes," Roselynn agreed. "Starting with a potluck tomorrow afternoon at Ben Sawyer's place."

"Ben?" Tess asked. "He's invol—?" She caught herself, took a deep breath, and tried again. "I mean, he's invited us out to the ranch tomorrow?"

Smiling, Roselynn shook her head. "Not just us. The potluck's open to the entire town."

"Oh, that's great," Tess said brightly. As the others began walking up Signal Street, she added under her breath, "Just great."

Only Caleb hung back, looking down at her, his expression unreadable.

She frowned. "What?"

"You got something against potlucks?"

"No, not at all."

"You don't care for Ben Sawyer?"

"Of course I like Ben."

"Hey, Caleb," Nate yelled from several yards ahead. "You comin'?"

"Be right there," he called. He turned his attention back to her. "What it is, then? Something's bothering you about this *invitation*."

His emphasis showed he had picked up on the way she'd stumbled over her words. "Nothing's bothering me."

"Good. Then you ought to be happy about getting me out of your hair tomorrow. After all, you said you wanted a break." He turned and left her standing open-mouthed on the sidewalk.

She clamped her jaw shut on the words that threatened to spill out this time. Then she shook her head.

If he thought he'd be going off to Ben's ranch without her tomorrow, he was in for a surprise. She didn't trust him alone long enough to have lunch with her family. She couldn't risk leaving him on his own with them all afternoon.

Darn it, why couldn't Ben Sawyer stay out of this? Why should he feel the need to get involved in anything to do with Caleb? And why hadn't he mentioned something to her about the potluck earlier this week—when she would have had time to set up any number of appointments to keep Caleb out of town?

She stole a glance up the street.

The group had stopped and stood waiting for Caleb.

The first thing she saw was the satisfied smile on Aunt El's face. And the first thing she realized was that Ben hadn't thought of the potluck all on his own. He'd had help.

She had no doubt whatsoever about just who had come up with the terrible idea.

Come to think of it, Kayla Robertson had looked to Roselynn and Aunt El in the middle of her conversation. Sure, Sam might have intended to get in touch with Caleb. But that request from Kayla—for him to help build a chicken coop for their daughter, of all things—had come at a very opportune moment. Accompanied by her comment about Caleb's handyman skills, how could that request have been a coincidence?

It couldn't. Grinding her teeth in irritation, she looked at the crowd up ahead again.

Caleb stood head and shoulders above her mom and Aunt El and all the girls around him. He smiled and joked with them as if he didn't have a care in the world but to keep them entertained.

Well, of course.

He'd been stuck in a car with her almost the entire week while she'd taken him all over the state. He'd probably sat counting the minutes until he would have his audience around him again.

He laughed at something Aunt El said, then turned to listen to Nate.

The smile and the adoring look she gave him made Tess's stomach tighten. As she watched, he reached out and ruffled Nate's hair. Even from this distance, she could see the color rush to fill her daughter's face.

It was nothing compared to the flash of fear that shot through Tess.

Chapter 10

*W*hat a week.

Tess slumped into her swivel chair and rested her head on her hands.

After lunch, Caleb had announced he needed a haircut. She had made sure to see Roselynn and Nate off to the inn in the company of all Nate's friends. Then she had escaped to her office, desperately seeking a few minutes away from everyone.

It had been bad enough to know she would have to sit down to every breakfast and supper with Caleb.

She hadn't anticipated how tough the times alone with him would be.

She had envisioned them firmly belted into their separate seats of her car. Or maybe outside, tramping over some of the property she wanted to show, with plenty of wide, open space between them. She hadn't thought about the long hours beside him in her small car, where the simmering attraction she felt for him only added to the heat inside the vehicle. Between the mileage and her need to turn up the air conditioner, she was spending a fortune on gas.

Yet being nearly glued to his side in front of everyone they'd met this morning had been worse.

And then lunch. After Caleb had offered to treat everyone, she had wanted to run away. But she couldn't risk leaving him alone with Nate. Or with Roselynn and Aunt El. So she had given in and gone along. And what a meal *that* had been!

The sound of footsteps on the hardwood floor of the office made her jump. She raised her head and found Dana eyeing her in concern.

"Are you all right?" Dana asked.

"I'm fine. I didn't hear you come in."

"I didn't. I was in the back office."

Despite her worries, the phrase made them laugh, as usual.

She looked around. Their two oversize desks took up most of the floor space in this storefront room that no self-respecting real estate agent could call anything but tiny.

Beyond the wall behind them lay a minuscule strip of footage their new building owner had dared to label a second office. They'd managed to fit in a drop-leaf table—with both leaves dropped. A two-drawer filing cabinet did double duty as a resting place for a minirefrigerator, a coffeemaker and a hot plate for their teakettle.

"The 'back office.'" She shook her head. "Ben ought

to try selling houses for a living. He's got such a way with words, you should hire him."

"No, I should not." As if to underscore her emphatic response, Dana dropped into the chair beside Tess's desk. "You look done in. What's going on with you and Caleb?"

She jumped again. "Wh-what?"

"Caleb. You know, our client? The one you're showing properties to? How's it going?"

"Oh." She began rearranging the office supplies on the desktop. "Fine—except for today. He wanted to stay in town. We walked the length of the business area and back again, stopping in at every store and office along the way."

Dana frowned. "What for?"

She shrugged, recalling all he had told her but not feeling a bit certain he'd shared his real reason with her. "He said he wanted to see the sights. While we were at it, I took care of handing out our promo."

"That's good. We need to drum up some business."

"I know." Guilt ran through her yet again. At the feelings she shouldn't have for Caleb. At the secret she'd kept from him for so long. At the worry her refusal to show him property close to town would ultimately hurt her best friend.

The wasted day today had only increased her distress.

As if she had picked up on Tess's thoughts, Dana said, "You didn't go out of town with him, then?"

"We didn't even get off Signal Street."

"You've been doing your best. Just keep at it." Her eyes sparkling, Dana leaned forward. "Seems to me he's dragging his heels with you about looking at property. What's he up to?"

That's what *she* had asked him.

And now she had stirred Dana's interest—exactly what she needed to avoid. "Nothing much. He just wanted to relive old times, I guess."

"And catch up with you?" Dana asked. "That's what he said when he came in here that first day."

She hurried to change the subject. "Everywhere we turned, we found Nate and Lissa and crew waiting for us—no matter how often I tried distracting them with the idea of going somewhere else."

"He's certainly caught their eye."

"Uh-huh." She sure hadn't. He'd asked her about leaving Flagman's Folly the next day. Because he wanted to find his big, expensive ranch property.

Not because he wanted to be alone with her.

Why did that thought hurt so much? Especially when she didn't want to be alone with him, either. Not after that episode at the store. But she had to do something to get him out of town. Nate's reaction to him had proven that.

Roselynn and Aunt El had made her goal impossible, at least for tomorrow. Once Caleb had heard their grand plan to reintroduce him to folks at Ben's potluck, he seemed to have lost all interest in leaving town.

Glancing down, she swept a handful of paper clips from the desktop into her palm and clenched her fingers around them. "Having Caleb around Nate is the *last* thing I need right now," she muttered.

"Why?"

For a long moment, she sat frozen. Then she opened her fist and let the clips trickle into her pencil drawer.

She had almost forgotten Dana, who now looked even more interested. Worse, she had almost slipped. Had come close to blurting out a truth her best friend had never known. One no one knew.

Easing the drawer closed, she searched frantically for a response that would take them off this dangerous topic. "Well… I'm having enough trouble with Nate as it is. We've always gotten along fine, always acted like two of a kind. But lately, she seems to go out of her way to disagree with every word I say."

"Lissa's the same. It comes with being a preteen. They have to go through that confrontational stage. We did, too."

"I suppose." She'd told herself that many times. But even armed with the knowledge, she'd been helpless to stop the tension between them. That shouldn't have come as a surprise. Much as she hated to admit it, her daughter's rebellious streak matched her own at that age—as her mom had seemed all too eager to tell their guest at breakfast that first morning.

As if she didn't have enough on her mind, now she had Caleb to contend with. Despair made her cheeks flush as she faced what she'd been trying to deny. His presence made her more short-tempered. Stretched her nerves nearly to breaking point. And added a whole new layer of tension to her life.

A shiver rippled through her at the memory of their conversation alone at the store, ending with his cheek close to hers and his words whispered into her ear.

I'll bet he doesn't turn you on…

"—Caleb?" Dana asked.

"*No!* Not Ca—" She broke off in confusion. "What?"

Dana frowned. "What's gotten into you, girl? You'd

said having Caleb around Nate was the last thing you needed. I repeat, what's Nate got to do with Caleb?"

"Everything."

"Really?" Dana looked more interested than ever.

She clutched the arms of her chair. "One major thing, anyhow. He might be off the rodeo circuit now, but as far as Nate and all the girls are concerned, he's still a walking, talking reminder of it. They're more eager than ever to get to a rodeo. And you know what *that* means."

"I sure do. Money we don't have." She sighed. "Who knew we'd come to this, Tess?"

The office phone rang. Dana went to her desk to answer it. Tess held her breath, hoping this would be a call from a new client. A moment into the conversation, she could tell it wasn't.

She thought again of Dana's question. *Who knew we'd come to this?* She'd meant more than just their current financial dilemma, bad as it was. She was thinking about how different she'd expected her life to be. So had everyone else.

All the while they'd been growing up, even in high school, quiet, bookish Tess had been the one without a steady. Without boyfriends. Without any dates at all. Until…

Another topic she'd better stay away from.

Chatty, ready-to-be-liked Dana had been the one with a longtime steady. A boy who had always loved her. Who had become her husband and the father of her children.

And now Paul was gone.

Everyone in town had been touched by his death. Caleb had seemed affected by the news, too. She couldn't forget his stunned expression or the bleak look in his eyes when she'd told him. He'd probably never considered the idea of someone they knew—someone their age—dying.

Dana hung up the phone and stared out the front window for a moment. After a sigh, she looked at Tess and returned immediately to their previous conversation. "It bothers me, Tess, always having to deny our kids everything."

"We don't," she said earnestly. "It's only the extras we can't give them, and only for now. That will change. Soon."

"Yes, it will." Giving a decisive nod, Dana pushed herself away from her desk. "Just as soon as you make a sale to Caleb."

Tess slumped in her chair and tried to swallow her groan.

Later that evening, after getting whupped by Nate more than once over a checkerboard, Caleb gave in and suggested they move outside for some fresh air. While she ran up to her room with the game, he went outside to the wooden porch swing.

Roselynn followed a moment later, carrying a tray with a couple of glasses and a pitcher of lemonade. "Thought you might like something to wet your whistle." She poured a glassful and handed it to him.

"Thanks." He took a sip of the drink. On the sour side, the way she'd discovered he liked it. The way he'd had to fight to keep from feeling tonight. Sour and cranky and...

Jealous.

While the rest of them had eaten their supper, Tess had gone off for her date with old Joe.

As Roselynn entered the house, Nate came out and took her usual seat on the porch. She leaned back against the railing, one leg stretched out across the front step.

The sun threw the lengthening shadow of a pine over them, cooling the air a little.

It had been a good while since their noon meal at the Double S. But not nearly long enough for him to forget Tess's attitude. Or her words.

He took another swig of his lemonade, trying to quench his thirst. And to drown his irritation.

When her aunt had announced the plan of having him get together with folks, Tess had shown all too plainly how little she liked the idea. And at lunch, she had outright told him to keep his promises to himself. She couldn't have made it any clearer that she didn't want anything from him. She didn't even want him around.

Hell, was she *still* ashamed to be in his company?

The thought riled him.

"Caleb, you're rich, aren't you?"

He started at Nate's question, unexpected in the quiet moment and unnerving in its bluntness. She had more than a little of her aunt Ellamae's personality in her.

When he looked across the porch, he found her with her head bent over her glass as if she were analyzing the contents. "Well…" He paused, wondering how to respond. Honesty ought to work. "I've got more money than some people have. And not as much as others."

"Do you have as much money as Mr. Harley?"

He rubbed the back of his neck. "I don't rightly know how to answer that. I wouldn't know how much money he has."

"Lots."

"Yeah, so I gathered." *Hand over fist,* Nate had said at breakfast the other day, quoting Ellamae. Then she'd added the man wanted to marry her mama. He thought she intended to pick up on that again now, but she threw another question at him.

"Are you dirty?" she asked.

He looked down at his jeans, then whacked his good knee with his free hand, brushing the fabric. "Nope, no dirt on me."

"Not *dirt.* Like, dirty rich."

He had trouble keeping his eyebrows from climbing. "I'm not sure I follow you."

"Aunt El says people who are dirty rich don't have a lick of sense."

"Oh." He smiled. "'Filthy rich,' you mean?"

"Yeah. Like I said."

"Uh-huh." Unable to help himself, he asked, "She was talking about me?"

"No." She shook her head so firmly, her curls bounced. "Aunt El says you've got plenty of sense."

He raised his cup to his mouth to hide another smile. The compliment pleased him more than it should have. Too bad Tess didn't have as good an opinion of him.

"She says you just need some direction."

Caught between a laugh and swallowing his lemonade, he wound up coughing. When he could finally catch his breath again, he asked, "Your aunt Ellamae said that to you?"

She shook her head again, her eyes hidden by her curls. "I listened in the hallway when she talked to Gram."

"I see." He sat there weighing his options.

First off, he could—and probably should—say something against her eavesdropping. He couldn't hold back a small smile, just imagining how Tess would take it if she learned he'd disciplined her daughter. And judging by Nate's chattiness, it wouldn't take long for Tess to find out.

At the same time, he hated the idea of stopping the flow of conversation—even if it made him feel like a heel for merely thinking about getting information from a nine-year-old.

He'd deal with the talking-to later. For now, curiosity won out.

"So…this filthy-rich person with no sense. Was your aunt talking about Mr. Harley?"

"No, somebody on TV."

"I see."

"But she said rich people look down on other people." She lifted her chin, finally making eye contact with him again. "You don't do that, do you?"

Now it was his turn to shake his head. If she'd only known the irony of that question… "No, I try not to look down on folks." Too bad everyone didn't do likewise.

"I figured."

"What's this all about, Nate? I mean, what's got you asking the questions? You feeling a need for money?"

"No. Mom and Gram are always talking about it." She shrugged. "But I was just wondering."

They sat there in silence.

A minute later, a dark green Chrysler came into view on Signal Street. He could see Joe and Tess inside. As Joe drove up to the bed-and-breakfast and turned into the drive leading around to the back, Tess waved. Nate returned the greeting with a definite lack of enthusiasm.

He frowned. "Nice to have your mama home," he offered.

"Uh-huh." She slumped back against the railing.

"Or not so nice?" he asked.

"She's always grumpy."

"And you're always in a good mood."

She glanced at him, then away again. "Most times," she mumbled.

They heard the slamming of the car's door. Seconds later, Joe turned the Chrysler back onto Signal Street and drove away. After a moment, Tess's footsteps crunched on the walkway.

Nate took a quick drink, wiped her mouth with the back of her hand, and said in a rush, "Are you gonna move here? 'Cause it's a really good place."

Another irony now.

He'd come back to Flagman's Folly only to do what he needed to leave it behind him forever.

He felt a sudden chill, cold as the ice-filled glass in his hands. Nate was already a self-confessed eavesdropper. Was she basing her questions on something she'd heard the adults say about him? He tried a smile. "You sound like your mama now. Next thing I know, you'll be wanting to sell me some property."

"But are you, Caleb?" She stared at him, her dark brown eyes unblinking and as serious as if everything in the world depended on his answer. "Are you gonna live here?"

The sound of Tess's footsteps grew louder. The steady rhythm of her shoes on the gravel walkway sounded like a clock ticking a countdown.

Leaning forward slowly, he set his glass on the tray Roselynn had left on a wicker side table. Then he rested his elbows on his knees and linked his fingers together in front of them. Finally, he looked again at Nate.

The eager look on her face told him the answer she wanted.

Honesty would have to work here, too.

"No, Nate. I just came back for a short while to visit. I don't belong in Flagman's Folly."

Tess turned the corner of the house. Their gazes met over the porch railing. Her dark brown eyes were as serious as Nate's.

But while her daughter's expression had looked full of hope, Tess's face couldn't hide her relief.

Chapter 11

Early the next afternoon, Caleb followed Tess and Roselynn across Ben Sawyer's yard.

After hearing Ellamae's news yesterday about the potluck at Ben's place, he'd looked forward to the chance for a relaxed, enjoyable meal.

Not that he had any complaints about the food at the Whistlestop. Roselynn's breakfasts and suppers more than satisfied his hunger. But the conversation sure had lacked something lately.

Last evening, it had been just the three of them. Nate had sat picking at her plate, wearing the most mournful look he'd ever seen on a child. Roselynn had caught on quick and spent most of her time going back and forth between the dining room and the kitchen.

At least whupping him at checkers had cheered the kid up.

Since coming back to the inn after her date, Tess had ignored him.

They took their places at the end of the line wending its way toward one of the trestle tables. The makeshift tables were loaded down with food, which pleased him no end.

"Looks like enough here to feed a couple of armies."

"It will go fast," Tess said.

"It surely will," Roselynn added. "Better take enough first time around, Caleb, so you don't get done out of it."

"No worries about that." They'd been here awhile now, and after more than a few conversations with folks already, he'd worked up an appetite.

He'd come today prepared as he always was when meeting with a crowd—same as he had with Nate and her friends—ready to regale them with tales of his rodeo days. To his surprise, he'd received responses similar to those he'd gotten in the shops on Signal Street. The folks of Flagman's Folly seemed less concerned about hearing his stories and more interested in welcoming him home.

He couldn't understand it.

The line shuffled forward and he followed, conscious of how close he stood to Tess. So close he could see a few tiny freckles on the back of her neck.

As he loaded potato salad and pickled beets onto his plate, he contemplated the situation with her.

Ever since their arrival, he'd expected her to put as much distance between them as possible. Yet except for helping Roselynn bring their contributions into the kitchen and later setting out the food, she'd stayed by his side nearly every minute. He couldn't understand that, either.

As he and Tess turned away from the trestle table now, he said, "Guess we're going to have a time finding somewhere to sit."

Before she could answer, Nate came running up. She and her friends seemed less inclined to hang around him today, probably due to all the games they'd had going on.

"Mom, do you know where Becky is? I can't see her anywhere."

"And you won't. The Robertsons aren't coming today. They already had plans to go up to Santa Fe."

"Oh, rats." Frowning, Nate stomped off.

Her mention of the Robertsons had jogged his memory. "It surprised me," he told Tess, "when you introduced me to Sam's wife outside the Double S yesterday. I didn't know he had a kid, either."

"Neither did he."

Raising his brows, he waited for her to say more, but she turned her back on him without another word. He could get that she put up defenses when they were alone out in the desert, when the heat of the day couldn't hold a candle to the heat between them inside the car—no matter how high she cranked up the air.

But even this afternoon, in front of other people, she had seemed to want nothing to do with him, had acted about as friendly as she had during their meals at the Whistlestop. So why was she sticking to him like a burr under a horse's saddle?

Again, he scanned the area. Ben definitely had invited a crowd.

A good thing, too. With so many people around, he hoped eventually to get his distance from Tess. Something he sorely needed. Any time he got near her, he couldn't help trying to get a rise out of her. And he always succeeded. But he had a feeling one of these times his teasing would come back to bite him.

If it hadn't already.

He hefted the plate of food in his hands and looked around again.

"Caleb. Over here!" Ellamae waved at them from a group of lawn chairs near one corner of the house.

As he headed across the yard, Tess fell into step beside him. It wasn't until he'd gotten closer to Ellamae that he saw who had taken one of the chairs—an older man with a tanned and wrinkled face and snowy white hair arranged in a style that would've looked good on a country singer back in the Fifties.

Judge Baylor.

Too late to back out now. Caleb gripped his paper cup of punch and tried to smile. Tess took one of the vacant lawn chairs. He set his food on the other one and reached down to shake hands with the judge.

"Didn't think y'all would miss the festivities," the man drawled, focusing on the pile of chicken wings on his overflowing plate. "I'll say one thing for Ben Sawyer. He does know how to entertain in style." He chomped down on a wing and grunted in approval.

Then, true to Caleb's memory of the judge, he proceeded to talk at length while the rest of them ate.

Caleb dug in to his potato salad.

Beside him, Tess pushed the food around on her plate, much as Nate had done last night and again this morning.

After a while, Judge Baylor wound down, took a long swig of sweet tea and sat back in satisfaction. Caleb found himself being inspected from head to foot, as if the judge had just seen him for the first time. "Well, now, aren't you a sight to behold."

He tensed. "That supposed to be a compliment, Your Honor?"

The judge's eyes narrowed. "Yes, son, I do believe it is. In any case, you're looking considerably better than the last time I saw you."

"You remember that far back?"

"Why, it wasn't that long ago. You were trussed up like a side of beef in that hospital bed you spent so much time in."

Startled, Caleb grabbed the plate that had begun to slide from his lap. "You're saying you saw me in the hospital? In Dallas?"

"You spent time in any other one since I've known you?"

He shook his head.

"That would be the place, then. You were an awful sight. Though I must say—" the judge's bushy brows— the same snowy white as his hair—lowered in a frown "—you keep on with that high-and-mighty tone of yours, I might find your inability to converse back then a marked improvement over today."

"Sorry," he muttered. "I've had a lot on my mind."

"I'll bet," Ellamae murmured. She put the last bite of her hamburger into her mouth and eyed him as she chewed.

Tess kept her attention glued to her plate.

Obviously neither of them planned to rush to his defense.

He focused on the older man again. "I never knew you'd come to Dallas."

"Yep. Me and Sam Robertson both. We'd heard the

news on the television, of course, but folks in town wanted to know firsthand how you were doing."

He had to struggle to find his voice. "No one told me you'd visited."

"That's understandable. We didn't leave our calling cards." The judge picked up another chicken wing. "The nurse said they had you knocked out and you'd stay that way for a while and likely not get up to much when you came to."

"It might have been days before they would ease back on the medication, the nurse told them," Ellamae said, taking over the story. "So Sam and the judge turned tail and came back home again. They'd seen enough to tell everyone how you were doing."

"Poorly," the judge stated.

Hell of an understatement, there. "Yeah, that's a stretch of time I'd just as soon forget."

From the corner of his eye, he saw Tess shift, stabbing her fork into a pile of potato salad she hadn't yet touched.

"Ellamae, you're needed!" called one of the women from over near the house.

She waved in answer and began to struggle out of her lawn chair. "Well, you two just go on reminiscing about old times. Tess, you come along with me. I'm sure whatever's up over there, they can use an extra pair of hands."

Tess hesitated as if doubting she ought to leave. He frowned once again. Did she think he needed a guard? When she found him staring at her, her cheeks flushed pink and she staggered to her feet. The plate of salad nearly went flying.

As the two women hurried away, the judge turned

back to Caleb. "Quite a few folks have said you've stopped in to visit with them in town."

"Yeah," he said, grinning. "We hit Signal Street. Tess said I'd gone on a real spending spree."

The judge shrugged. "Didn't hear anything about that."

Caleb stopped grinning and looked at him suspiciously. "No one mentioned it at all?"

"No. Just said it was good to see you again."

"Huh." Lost in thought, Caleb gathered up his own plate and his empty punch cup. Judge Baylor knew everything that happened in this town. Why hadn't he heard the news?

"Sit back, boy, take it easy." The judge waved his hand lazily. "No sense rushing off just yet. I don't see anybody starting up with the horseshoes, like at Sam Robertson's place." He sounded disappointed.

"I wouldn't know about that." But he could sure envision the older man flinging horseshoes with the same energy he used to throw out sentences in his courtroom.

"No, you never were at any of the Robertsons' barbecues, were you?"

"We weren't that friendly," he said, intending to leave it at that. But his tongue overrode his good sense. "I can't think why Sam would have come to see me in Dallas. Or you, for that matter, Your Honor."

He nodded. "Yeah, that was a good part of your problem all along. You couldn't think."

"I didn't need to." The paper plate crumpled as he tightened his grip. "Everybody in town made it obvious what *they* thought."

The judge grasped the arms of his lawn chair to pull himself upright. He leaned forward, his expression grave. Instead of the heated glare Caleb remembered from the past—and expected now—he found the man staring at him with something like compassion in his eyes.

"We watched you with some concern, true," the judge said. "Couldn't have been easy, growing up with a mama who gave her favors away like yours did."

Caleb narrowed his eyes. "You don't hold anything back, do you, Your Honor?"

"I did then. You're man enough to hear it now. And I'll say it again. You didn't think much in those days." He rose from his chair. "Folks saw you as a boy with a bad home life and—no surprise—a bad attitude to match." He shook his head. "What worries me now, son, is it seems like getting thrown from a bull and cracked to pieces still hasn't knocked that chip off your shoulder."

Once the furor in Ben Sawyer's kitchen had calmed down, Tess could finally make out why her aunt had received such an urgent summons. The women had required her services to settle an argument over the proper way to prepare nuts for a pie. She had to smile. In her own way, Aunt El held just as much power in this town as Judge Baylor did in his courtroom.

"Looks like my help's not needed, after all," she said to no one in particular. "I'll just slip back outside…"

On the porch, she stood and shook her head at herself. Maybe she had misjudged Aunt El. She and Roselynn had a long history of butting into things that didn't concern them. It hadn't taken much of a stretch to wonder whether, for some reason of her own, Aunt El had used the trip to the kitchen as an excuse to get her away from Caleb and Judge Baylor. Had she let the knowledge of her aunt's reputation color her judgment?

What about her suspicions of Caleb? Why *had* he come back to town? With his off-again, on-again interest in property, she was beginning to doubt his claim about wanting to buy a ranch. The thought of *not* making a sale to him made her hands suddenly clammy.

The fear of what he might really be up to made her entire body break out in a sweat.

She recalled what she'd overheard him saying to Nate last night. What he'd deliberately wanted her to overhear, she was sure. *I don't belong in Flagman's Folly.*

The memory of those words made her heart ache.

He had probably always felt that way, and she'd never realized it. He'd left town—and left her—because of it. Hadn't he said so, that night outside Gallup when she'd gone to find him? More words to make her heart ache.

All he'd worried about was his prize. His fame.

That's what's important. That's what will save me from going back to some one-horse town with one-horse folks in it.

Even back then, ten long years ago, he'd felt too good to stick around. Too good to be with her.

Shaken by those thoughts, she descended the porch steps and forced her gaze to the corner of the house. Then she froze. The lawn chairs now had new occupants. She ground her teeth in frustration. Regardless of Aunt El's intent, she'd managed to separate her from Caleb. Where was he?

"Tess?"

She started at the sound of her name and found Ben Sawyer standing beside her. "Sorry, I didn't see you."

"Obviously. Looks like you have something on your mind. You had a heck of a scowl on your face, too."

"I was just squinting. The sun's so strong today."

"Uh-huh. Everything okay in the kitchen?"

"Yes, fine. And there's still plenty of food, too. The women of Flagman's Folly won't let you down."

"They do things right, don't they? Why do you think I had this potluck?"

So much for getting away from her suspicions. And he'd just asked a loaded question. "Why did you, any-how? What made you decide to have the potluck today?"

He shoved his hands in his back pockets and shrugged. "It's been a while since I hosted a get-to-gether for folks."

"Uh-huh. And who suddenly reminded you of this long passage of time? Were you by any chance chatting with Aunt El?"

"Yeah, I saw her here earlier on—"

"No, I meant before today. Did she put you up to this?"

"Huh?" He blinked.

She laughed. "Come on, Ben. You handled much tougher questions on the sixth-grade debate team. Aunt El talked you into having this potluck, didn't she?"

No answer.

She had opened her mouth to repeat the question when she noticed him staring across the yard. She'd lost him completely. Something else had caught his attention. Or someone. She turned to look, too.

Out by the roadside past the other parked vehicles, she spotted a new arrival. Dana's blue van.

She smiled with relief. When she'd mentioned the potluck to Dana yesterday afternoon, her friend had shown an odd reluctance about committing. Tess had done her best to convince Dana to come. She'd kept to herself too much since Paul's death. It wasn't good for her or for her kids.

Nate's friend Lissa now hurried away from the van with her four-year-old brother tugging to get out of her grip. But she held him tightly by the hand as she towed him toward the rowdy group of kids playing in a shady corner of the yard.

Dana appeared around the end of the van. In one hand, she balanced a casserole. With the other, she struggled to push her baby's stroller over the uneven ground.

Before Tess could move a step, Ben muttered, "'Scuse me."

He took off across the yard, his ground-eating stride indicating *he* was the one with something on his mind now. But even from here, Tess could see the less-than-welcoming expression on Dana's face.

She groaned. Now what? No matter how she tried to ignore the friction between her best friend and their landlord, it seemed evident that trouble was on the horizon.

And speaking of trouble…where was Caleb?

If it wasn't one thing, it was another.

Ellamae shook her head as she herded her sister across Ben's yard to a quiet spot for a quick private chat. She'd finally gotten the argument in the kitchen straightened out when Roselynn had pounced.

"Ellamae," she started in again now, "I don't know that we're doing the right thing. I just saw Caleb, all alone and looking like a thundercloud, stalking off."

"He left?" She hadn't expected that.

"No, he went out past the barn."

"Oh, well. That's no worry. He probably wanted to look over Ben's horses." She grinned at her sister. "Loosen up a little, Rose. Don't want folks thinking something's up." After watching Roselynn force her lips into a stiff smile, she continued, "Tess and I left him with the judge, and I imagine the man said something to him he didn't take to. You know how blunt the judge can be."

That earned a small but genuine smile from Roselynn. "And you're not?"

"Never mind that. Where did Tess get off to?"

"I don't know. I thought she was with you. That's why I came looking." She sighed. "I saw her earlier, as well, and she didn't seem any too happy, either."

"She didn't eat a bite when we were chowing down with the judge."

"Again? She hasn't been eating a thing at home, either. El, she's breaking her heart over Caleb a second time."

"You should've seen her when they were talking about Caleb being in the hospital."

Roselynn shook her head. "She never would look at the news whenever they talked about him. Or read the articles in the paper. What are we going to do?"

"Just what we said we'd do. What we *are* doing. Getting him out and about with folks."

"But that's not helping Tess."

"It will. Give it some time. You're about as impatient as Nate."

Her sister's face softened in a smile. "She does have a case over him, doesn't she?"

"She sure does. Uh-oh," Ellamae muttered, "here comes Dana. She's not acting too happy, either. What is it with these young'uns? They're all looking sorrier than wet hens and behaving about as cheerful. Brace yourself. And mind what you say to her. Well, hello there, Dana," Ellamae said, pitching her voice to be heard clear out past the barn. "And how are you on this beautiful day?"

"I could be better," she said, her tone grim. "But it's not me I'm worrying about right now, thank you."

"The children?" Roselynn asked in alarm.

"Oh, no, they're fine. It's Tess and Caleb I meant. There seems to be some tension between them."

"Do you think so?" Roselynn asked.

"Can't say as we've noticed." Ellamae met her sister's gaze and held it. "Well, Rose, we've got to get back to the kitchen." She moved forward, only to have Dana sidestep in front of her, blocking their escape route.

"Just spare me a minute, ladies," Dana said, and it didn't sound like a request. "I've got a feeling there's something we need to discuss."

Chapter 12

Out by Ben's barn, Caleb stood with one foot braced on the bottom rung of the fence.

No one had come racing after him, surrounding him, clamoring for his autograph, wanting to take his photo. He wasn't the star of the show today, wasn't even in the running. That didn't quite fit his plan. But he couldn't seem to do anything to change it.

Folks treated him as though he'd always been around.

Maybe he should never have left town.

The idea—and what went with it—froze him in his seat.

Would he really go back to that time and place if he could? Back before the rodeo and the buckle bunnies and the fall that had brought him down from a bull one last time? The fall that had ended his career permanently?

Back to when he was nothing but the son of the good-time girl of Flagman's Folly, New Mexico?

He breathed in the good scent of the horses that stood in the corral, twitching their tails at annoying flies and occasionally neighing as if they were talking with him.

A much nicer conversation than the previous one he'd had, when the judge had gotten the last word by throwing out that accusation about his attitude when he was a teen.

He would have called the man on it—if he hadn't been so taken aback over the rest of what the judge had told him.

He gripped the top fence rail as he recalled his first day back in town, when he'd stopped in at the Double S before going to find Tess. Then, Dori said the judge had contacted the hospital for news about his condition. Judge Baylor himself had confirmed that and more.

If he could believe everything the man had told him—

"Caleb?" Tess's voice, sounding uncertain, interrupted his thoughts.

When he turned his head, he found her standing by the corner of the barn, looking as tentative as she'd sounded and as young and nervous as…as that time outside Gallup.

Almost subconsciously, his hands tightened on the rough wood. But a second later, she strode over to stand beside him and rested her hand on the rail with an assurance that somehow irritated him.

He couldn't resist the chance to unsettle her. Maybe because he felt so ill at ease himself. "Miss me?" he asked, forcing a smile.

She frowned. "Let's say I wondered where you'd

gone off to. You seemed a little shell-shocked over what the judge told you."

He laughed shortly. "And you didn't hear the half of it."

"What else did he have to say?"

Without thinking about it, he shrugged, then froze in position for a second. Exactly which shoulder did the judge think he had a chip on, anyway? "Nothing important. He likes to hear himself talk."

"You really didn't know he and Sam went to the hospital to see you?" The skin around her eyes crinkled as if she felt pain.

He had to look away. Inside the corral, a filly shook her head and snorted at a persistent fly.

"Never heard a thing about it. No big deal. I wasn't in shape for visitors, anyhow."

"I'm sorry for all your suffering," she murmured.

It was the first time she'd come straight out with her sympathy. He wasn't sure how to take it. Didn't want to take it at all.

Could he accept the opportunity she seemed to be offering, the chance to tell her everything he'd gone through in those long months in the hospital and the even longer months in rehab?

No, he didn't want sympathy. But the prospect of telling her what no one else knew, well, that was tempting.

He could tell her the things that bothered him most.

How close he'd come to dying.

And how sometimes, in the middle of the night when the pain ate at him and he fought taking his pills, how little the thought of that scared him.

He let go of the fence and shoved his hands in his

back pockets. Took a deep breath and let it out an inch at a time.

"No big deal," he said again. "I got through it."

The setting sun cast a deep red tinge over the barren landscape around them. Running the back of her hand across her forehead in frustration, Tess scowled at the horizon and tried to ignore the man by her side.

They'd been together all day, something she certainly hadn't been able to claim in the week following Ben Sawyer's potluck. She'd spent most of her time asking herself the same question she had faced that day: where was Caleb? As hard as she tried to keep an eye on him, he somehow kept slipping from her grasp.

Between Aunt El's social calendar and Roselynn's list of odd jobs around the bed-and-breakfast, he stayed busier than she did. They'd barely had any time alone together. On the one hand, she counted herself lucky. On the other hand, his full schedule didn't do anything to help her speed his departure.

She had finally put her foot down. Working around his *additional* social engagements, they'd managed to carve out some time during this second week to do what he'd supposedly come here for.

Part of her wondered whether her mom and Aunt El were solely to blame for everything. The other part of her suspected Caleb had purposely avoided being alone in her company.

At one point on the day of Ben's potluck, when she had finally tracked Caleb down near the barn, she'd thought for a moment he was going to open up to her. Was going to give them the chance to get close again.

And damn her, despite all the reasons she shouldn't even think about getting close to him, she wanted it.

She plucked at the neckline of her peasant blouse, pulling the soft fabric away from her in an effort to cool herself. The air had become much too warm for comfort. Or maybe she felt overheated because Caleb stood much too close.

"That's enough sightseeing for today," she said abruptly. "It's getting late."

"Sounds good to me." He started toward his rented pickup truck.

She followed, stopping just short of muttering under her breath. What she'd really meant was, she didn't have the energy—or the patience—to keep playing the role of tour guide.

She desperately needed a day off from everything and everyone. A day away from the long list of grievances about her life.

Her situation with Nate had gotten worse than ever. She had done nothing to earn Dana's faith in her ability to make a sale to Caleb. She hadn't even come within a mile of getting him to make a preliminary offer.

Every chance she could, she had taken him around the state, showing him the available ranches and acreages on her listing. Every one of which he had found reasons to turn down.

Every one of which brought them in closer and closer to the outskirts of Flagman's Folly.

When she reached the truck, he opened the passenger door for her. She stood beside him, hesitating. She needed to make a sale. To get him out of town, away from Nate. Pushing a stray lock of hair from her forehead, she fought to keep the frustration from her voice. "You haven't seen anything yet that interests you?"

"I wouldn't exactly say that." He grinned down at her.

"Very funny. Too bad I couldn't *hold* your interest." The minute she'd spoken, she wished she hadn't.

But wishing wouldn't bring the words back, any more than longing for Caleb had brought him home to her. Ten years too late didn't count.

Besides, he hadn't returned to town for *her,* anyway.

His grin faded, but he continued to look down at her, his green eyes sparkling like sunshine on glass. "Tess—"

"Never mind."

Her cheeks burning, she stepped up into his truck and let him close the door behind her. As he walked around to the driver's side, she waved her hands furiously, hoping to cool her face. Maybe he'd think her flush had come from the setting sun.

He'd insisted on bringing the truck these past few days. Knowing the price of gas and the amount of territory she planned to cover, she hadn't said a word. Why couldn't she have held her tongue a minute ago, too?

And she'd thought Dana was the chatty one!

When he opened the driver's door, she clenched her hands into fists and dropped them to her sides. Breath held, she waited for him to start the truck. He didn't. Instead, he turned to her.

Her throat tightened, trapping the air in her chest.

He exhaled heavily, as if he'd held his breath, too. "You don't know how much I wish things had been different."

"Wishing doesn't get you anywhere." Hadn't she just

acknowledged that? "And I don't want to talk about the past."

"You haven't made that hard for me to figure out."

"You didn't make things easy for me by leaving." Mentally chastising herself, she turned her head away. Why couldn't she stop blurting out the wrong things?

He reached up to touch her cheek, so gently she could barely feel his knuckle against her skin. Still, she flinched. But he'd managed to get her to face him again. Just as he'd succeeded in setting off her anger once more, stirring up the resentment that had bubbled inside her for days now. For years.

"I tried to see you before I left town," he said.

As if she could believe that. "Did you?"

"Yeah, I did. Went by your house to tell you good-bye. That made the second and last time I ever saw your granddaddy, when I rang the bell and he came to the door and said you were out."

She wouldn't have gotten any word he'd left for her. But she had to know. "Did you...leave a message?"

"Not likely, when he shut the door in my face." His voice had hardened. "Besides, what was I going to say? He didn't know about us."

"He did, once I got back from Gallup," she said grimly. "He told me I was wasting my time chasing after you." She wouldn't tell Caleb a single detail about how her life had gone after that. Not for a million-dollar sale.

"He was right."

She stared, unable to speak. Unable to believe how much his words had hurt.

"Where were you going to get with me, Tess? No-where. You knew that well enough not to tell folks about us. You knew the way everyone looked down on me. I was the poorest kid in town."

Understanding washed through her. Compassion, too. He'd directed those hurtful words at himself, not at her. "No," she protested. "That wasn't why I didn't tell anyone. It didn't matter to me how much money you had."

"Whatever the reason, I don't blame you. Folks didn't want to bother with someone like me, with a mama no one could be proud of. Without a daddy even willing to give me his name."

At his last words, she clutched the armrest by her side. He was hitting much too close to home, if only he knew it. And she was coming much too near to doing something she should never do—telling him what was in her heart. In their history.

She could see the pain in his face, could hear it in his voice. She had to will herself to remain still and not reach out to him.

"At least leaving got me away from everyone's pity. And worse." He spoke so quietly, she could barely hear him.

"People knew your mother...slept around. And yes, some of them pitied you, Caleb," she said, her throat so tight she had to whisper the words. "Some of them thought less of you, too. But not everyone."

"Did you?"

She shook her head.

He looked at her, his eyes gleaming even in the now-dusky light. "If that's so, then maybe we ought to go back to where we were."

Her throat tightened another notch. What was he saying? That he'd had wishes about their relationship, too?

Regrets about how it had ended? No. She couldn't let herself believe in that. Things could go just as wrong again as they had years ago, and now she had so much more to lose.

Still, she couldn't stop herself from blurting, "Back—" she had to clear her throat and fight to keep her tone neutral when she was racing out of control inside "—to the last time I saw you, you mean?"

"No, to where we left off before I went away. We had good times together. We had fun."

We had a baby.

No, she couldn't say that. He'd tossed out an apology not long ago, one she couldn't accept. Just as now she couldn't let him so high-handedly toss aside what they did have when they were together. "We had more than fun."

"Yeah, we did. I was getting to that." He paused, looked away for a moment, then brought his gaze back to hers. "I'd have come back home again, too. But you told me you were getting married—"

"And I'm sure you didn't stay lonely too long."

He gave her a half smile. "You *are* thinking about the last time you saw me, aren't you?"

"No, I'm not." She swallowed her rising panic. "I'm just...just wondering how things went for you after that. I know you found fame and fortune, but did you learn a lot from the rodeo life? Did you enjoy moving from place to place, living on the road?" She was babbling, but anything was better than letting the conversation head in the direction he'd been taking it. "Did you like all those girls hanging on you?"

She swallowed a groan. That wasn't where she'd meant to head, at all.

And darn him, this time he laughed outright.

"Buckle bunnies are part of rodeo. No living without them."

Just what did that *mean?*

Better not to ask. Probably better not to open her mouth again. Ever.

Still, she couldn't stop her surge of anger. He had seen right through her. Her thoughts *had* focused on the day she had tracked him down.

And the girls hanging on to his arms.

Irritation spilled out of her. "You certainly didn't feel hounded by your groupies back then!"

His eyes glinted. From the last rays of the sun as it made its way to the horizon? Or from more amusement he couldn't hide?

"No need to get in an uproar over it," he said. "Those girls were just wanting to hitch their wagons to the nearest star."

She exhaled forcefully. "Well, let me tell you something. I have never thought of you as 'Caleb Cantrell, rodeo star.' And I don't plan to start thinking that way now."

"You don't?"

She'd responded honestly and openly, not stopping to analyze a thing. If she'd thought twice, she might have held back, knowing her words would have to upset him. Yet the expression on his face now looked anything but upset.

The look in his eyes made her head swim. She had to tear her gaze away.

And at that moment, with that brief loss of contact, in that tiny little window of time when she let down her guard and allowed her true feelings to show, she realized she'd contributed to her own undoing.

Before she could react, Caleb slipped his hand behind her head and gently urged her to turn toward him again. When she did, she found his face close to hers, their mouths only inches apart.

She tensed her hands, planning...wanting...*needing* to push him away. But after the past weeks of nerves stretched to the breaking point and the past ten years of unfulfilled wishes and destroyed dreams, she needed this just as much.

The chance to kiss Caleb.

No.

The chance to have Caleb kiss her, to let him realize what he had done and how he had hurt her and everything he had missed—and then the best chance of all, for her to tell him to *kiss off*.

That's what she needed.

But instead of moving forward as she expected, he leaned back. And brushed his finger teasingly along her skin just above the elastic neckline of her peasant blouse. Her heart began to pound.

Again, he did the unexpected. Instead of touching her mouth with his, he dipped his head. He brushed his warm lips against the fluttering pulse point below her ear, slid his finger beneath the elastic and eased the neckline aside to travel a path along her collarbone. She traveled, too, back to the time he'd discovered that very sensitive place on her body. The first time *she'd* known about it herself.

The reminder made her freeze in place.

And now, finally, his eyes dark and glittering, he

leaned close and kissed her. The weight and heat of his mouth against hers made her heart race even faster.

She raised her hands to his chest, longing only to pull him against her, to relive the closeness they'd once shared. But the knowledge of what had happened between them then—what she had to prevent him from discovering now—told her she couldn't cuddle against him. Couldn't risk letting him take her into his arms. She had to push herself away from him.

But could she?

Chapter 13

Caleb let Tess's words replay in his head.

I have never thought of you as 'Caleb Cantrell, rodeo star.' And I don't plan to start thinking that way now.

For once, he didn't have a lick of trouble with her outspokenness.

He'd never tell her that, or let her know how relieved she had made him feel. Or admit that her words had made everything right for him.

She flattened her palms against him, and the deep breath he took made his chest swell. With pride or contentment that she still wanted him, he didn't know. *Could* she still want him?

The question managed to slap some sense into his head.

What he was doing here was crazy.

When he and Tess had been together before, they

were kids. They were adults now. Consenting adults. That knowledge *should* have provided the go-ahead to do what he wanted. And what was he doing? Behaving like a randy teen with his first crush, about to go too far in the front seat of a pickup truck.

A truck he didn't even own. Somehow, that made it worse.

Tess didn't deserve this.

Out of respect for her, he needed to stop.

In the same instant Tess pressed her palms against his chest, he leaned back and slid his arms from around her. Ignoring the twinge in his knee, he slid across the bench seat and behind the wheel again.

Damn. He'd come here to make things right for himself. Not to do everything wrong.

It was dark enough now inside the cab of the truck that he couldn't see Tess's face. Good. That meant she couldn't see his. He made a fist and tapped the side of it lightly on the dashboard. Then he started the pickup. "Time to head back," he muttered.

Silence.

"Got a little carried away there."

More silence.

He kicked the shift into gear. "It won't happen again."

From the other side of the cab came only a long, drawn-out sigh.

Of frustration? Irritation? Regret?

Yeah, he felt the same.

If he'd been thinking straight, he'd never have taken things this far. Or gotten this close to actions he might never escape. Accidents happened, and he wanted nothing to do with the consequences that could result from them.

He jammed his foot on the gas pedal. With a roar of the engine and a tug on the steering wheel, he swung the truck around in the direction of town.

He'd fought hard during this damned long week to keep his mind on his goals. As if he didn't already have enough to deal with, his conscience would bother him now, for sure.

Should've listened to those instincts.

Should've kept those hands off her.

Should've realized you can't trust yourself around her.

Tess hurried to finish loading the dishwasher.

Simple exhaustion from all the stress had made her sleep like a rock that night. No dreams of Caleb. No nightmares.

But no escaping him at the breakfast table the next morning, either. She had struggled to survive the meal without staring at him as if she were some lovestruck teenager.

Like mother, like daughter.

She would have laughed at the irony of it—if her heart hadn't broken for her daughter's sake.

It was going to be a long day. The work party at Sam Robertson's ranch had expanded to include a barbecue afterward. And if that wasn't bad enough, just as they'd finished breakfast, Kayla called, asking her to bring Nate over early to keep Becky company.

Of course Tess had said yes, although agreeing had almost broken her. Now, more than ever, she needed to keep an eye on Caleb whenever he was with Nate. That would mean nearly all day and probably half the night at Sam's.

After breakfast, Caleb had disappeared without a word. Roselynn had left to drop Nate at Lissa's until they needed to leave for Sam's. Then she planned to pick up a few things at the store.

Finished loading the dishwasher, Tess hurried out to the yard to take down the laundry. She welcomed the chore to keep her mind occupied. She welcomed even more the chance to be alone.

In the hot sun, the bed linens had already dried. She folded as she went, dropping the items into her basket. As she took down the remaining sheet, she got a clear view of the opposite side of the yard. And what a view it was.

Caleb had just come around the corner of the shed. He'd taken off his T-shirt, and she couldn't drag her gaze away. Her mouth went as bone-dry as the sheet in her hands.

That first night he'd stayed at the inn, she'd seen how good he looked standing half-undressed in the dim light of the hall outside his bedroom. Yesterday, in their encounter in the front seat of his truck—the encounter she'd since tried so hard to forget—she had touched all that goodness. Even through the fabric of his shirt, she'd felt hard muscle and heat.

Now he crossed the yard toward her. She shivered and clutched the sheet in her suddenly trembling hands—as if that would do any good. She'd be better off sitting on those hands to keep them out of temptation's way. And off temptation's six-pack abs.

Caleb closed in.

Walking—or running—away now would only make her look like a coward. Standing there shaking wouldn't give any better impression. She gathered up the sheet, crossed to one of the picnic benches and collapsed onto it.

Temptation came to a stop in front of her, looking hot—in more ways than one. Sexy, no doubt about that. And slightly sweaty, with his hair curled at the edges and a light film of moisture riding his tanned cheekbones. The urge to kiss that moisture away left her clutching the sheet so tightly, her fingers hurt.

To her dismay, he took the seat beside her. He sat backward on the bench and stretched his legs out in front of him. She saw him wince and had to swallow her murmur of sympathy.

As she glanced down, she saw what the hallway light *hadn't* shown her that night—a long, thin scar, sliced white against tanned skin, traveling up his rib cage and ending to one side of his chest in a sunburst of scar tissue.

This time she couldn't swallow her response. She gasped and looked up to meet his eyes. "Caleb…" She couldn't finish. Didn't know how.

His shrug puckered the scarred skin even more. "That's nothing compared to the knee."

She licked her dry lips and fought to match his matter-of-fact tone. "They happened in the same accident?"

He narrowed his eyes, and she could read his question in them. She looked away, afraid to answer. No, she hadn't followed the news about him, or she would have known already. She wouldn't have asked him now.

After a moment, he said, "Yeah, the same time. That bull wasn't satisfied with throwing me off and stomping on my leg. He tried to run through me in a few places, too."

The statement made her lose any pretense of calm.

Reaching out with her shaking hand, she traced the long, thin scar. "Does it hurt still?"

"Not right now, it doesn't." He half smiled, but she didn't need to see that to know what he meant.

"I'm sor—"

He lifted his hand and touched one finger to her lips. "Don't say it. I don't want that."

She moved her hand upward, sliding it to the patch of scar tissue. His heartbeat thrummed steadily beneath her palm. After a moment, she dropped her hand to her lap. But not before she'd felt his heartbeat pick up speed.

She sighed. "I wish I knew what you *did* want," she murmured, looking away. "You say you're here to buy property, but you don't seem interested in anything I've shown you so far. And then yesterday... Caleb," she said, unable to stop herself from blurting the thing that had bothered her most since then. The apology she'd never made. "When we were out in the desert and you'd talked about us, you said I knew I wasn't going to get anywhere with you."

She waited. He didn't respond, didn't look toward her, but she could tell by the way he sat, without moving a muscle, that he was listening to her.

"You said I knew it so well, that's why I didn't tell my family about you. And you thought it was because I pitied you. But I never have." She hung on to the sheet in her lap, needing to do something with her trembling hands. "I didn't keep our relationship from my family because of *you*. I did it because of me."

"You?" He still wouldn't look at her. "Why?"

She sighed. "Because my grandfather would have skinned me alive if he'd found out I was dating anyone."

At that, he turned his head, his eyes squinted in a frown. "You were seventeen."

"I know that. But he didn't think I should date anyone until I graduated. He was strict about it, almost obsessed over the idea of my focusing on my education. My mother dropped out of high school, and I think he thought I'd do the same." She shrugged. "It didn't matter. There wasn't anyone I wanted to go out with, anyhow. Until that day at the Double S."

Now she was the one who wouldn't make eye contact.

She and Dana had stopped in at the café after school for sweet teas. Football practice ended early, and Paul had shown up unexpectedly. The three of them shared a booth, but Paul made it so obvious he wanted to be alone with Dana that Tess couldn't help but catch on. Before she could speak up, could think of an excuse to leave, he had made the first move, and he and Dana had left her alone in the café.

"I was in pretty bad shape that day," she said, able to smile about it now. "It felt like Dana and I never had time alone together anymore. She was always somewhere with Paul. That was the first time in weeks we'd been able to hang out, just the two of us. Then they went off without me." She laughed. "It wasn't till they were gone that I discovered I didn't have enough money to pay for the sweet teas."

"I remember," he murmured.

"You saved me that day, giving me the change from your tips to make up the difference. If Granddad ever found out I'd tarnished his reputation by not paying what I owed, he would have grounded me till graduation."

"Dori and Manny would've let you slide."

"I didn't know that. But you were there for me. I never thanked you for that."

"I didn't hold it against you."

"No." But he'd held her against him not long ago, about as tightly as she now clutched the sheet. She dropped it to her lap and said, "Another thing about yesterday...when you said you'd gotten carried away..."

"And you won't hold that against me, will you?"

"You said it wouldn't happen again."

He leaned closer.

She stiffened, still not able to look at him. And now not daring to breathe.

"It won't happen," he said, his voice low. "Unless you want it to."

He stroked her jaw lightly with one finger.

Warmth spread up her neck into her cheeks. "I—"

"Oops. Well, excuse me!"

She jumped, startled by the unexpected interruption, though not at all surprised by whose voice she had heard. She turned away from Caleb to face her aunt.

"I didn't mean to interrupt."

"You're not," Tess said, rising from the bench.

Just as Caleb had saved her from an embarrassing situation that day in the Double S, Aunt El had saved her now—from giving in to temptation. From making yet another mistake. "I was just collecting the laundry, but I need to go over to my office for a while. Lots of paperwork to do before we go off for the rest of the day."

As she'd spoken, she had gathered up the sheet, crossed the yard again and grabbed the laundry basket.

Then she smiled at them both and fled.

* * *

Tess had forgotten about Roselynn borrowing the car.

She took her bag with the office keys in it and walked the few blocks to Wright Place Realty, hoping to burn up her nervous energy. She couldn't. And once at her desk, she had nothing to occupy her. So she simply paced the floor of the sunlit room and wondered how she'd managed to get herself into this predicament. And how she was going to get out of it in one piece and with her emotions intact.

Why couldn't she just have been satisfied with Joe Harley? Why couldn't she have accepted his proposal one of the many times he'd offered it? Then she wouldn't have had to face this dilemma at all.

But good old Joe didn't... Joe couldn't...

She sighed, forced to admit what she knew.

Joe wasn't who she wanted.

She'd been so foolish with Caleb just now, reminding them both of what had happened the night before.

The rush of excitement she'd felt when he'd held her proved how much she still cared about him. His kiss had only increased her desire to get closer. Whether she would have found the strength to push him away, she would never know.

He'd moved first, backing off in a rush. Admitting he'd gotten carried away. Assuring her that kiss would never happen again.

At the same time, she'd become obsessed by a wish that it would never end.

Again, she berated herself for mentioning anything to him.

So foolish. So naive. So completely idiotic.

How could she have left herself that vulnerable to him? And in front of Aunt El, too?

A sudden flash through the office window caught her attention. Outside, sunlight glinted off the windshield of Dana's van as she eased it to a stop at the curb.

Groaning, she dropped her head into her hands. They had spoken on the phone and exchanged emails but hadn't seen each other since the day at Ben's ranch.

She didn't want to see Dana now. How could she, when her best friend would take one look and know something was wrong? She would have to bluff her way through this. After a long, deep breath, she pasted a smile on her face.

The front door swung open.

Dana stood on the threshold and shook her head. "You'll give me a bad name with folks for making you come in on a Sunday."

"We can always claim work overflow."

"Ha." Dana closed the door and went to take a seat behind her desk.

Tess raised her brows in surprise. "What are you doing here?"

"I saw the lights on and thought maybe our landlord was up to something sneaky."

Tess laughed, sure that's what Dana had intended. "That's ridiculous. Squeaky-clean, boy-next-door Ben?"

"Just kidding. Actually, I didn't come in to discuss Ben. I saw you sitting here."

"Oh." Suddenly wary, she looked down at her desk and brushed an imaginary speck of lint from its surface.

"I'm as sure as I can get," Dana said, "you've got something you want to tell me."

Tess put her palms flat on the desk and breathed

deeply again. After all these years, how could she confess to her closest friend? But how could she keep on the way she was now, holding back the truth from her?

And from Caleb?

A chilling wave of guilt rushed over her. Shivering, she pushed the thought aside. She couldn't tell him. Not now. Not ever.

But the time had come for her to confide in Dana.

"You're right," she admitted. "I do need to talk to you. About Caleb. He... I..." She could find no easy way to say this. "We went together senior year in high school. Just for a while, right before he left town."

"Yes, I know."

She almost choked on her indrawn breath. "You *what?* How? For how long?"

"Since high school." When Tess's mouth dropped open, Dana laughed. "And how? Come on—I was your best friend. I knew when you suddenly had no time to hang around after classes. And when you started leaving my house early on the weekends." She smiled and added gently, "And I saw the way you looked at him when we got to school every morning."

"You didn't. *I* didn't."

"Yes, you did."

"Oh, great." She slumped and ran her fingers through her hair. "Did everyone figure it out?"

"No, just me."

"Well, that's some consolation." She looked up. "I'm sorry I never told you, Dana. I couldn't let anyone know. If Granddad had ever found out..."

"You don't need to explain that. Why do you think I kept it to myself? So, now Caleb's here. And you are...?"

"In a mess. A real mess. I don't know why he had to come back again." She couldn't keep the bitterness from her tone. "He's not planning to stay, whether he buys property or not. Nate worships him, and he told her point-blank he doesn't belong in Flagman's Folly."

"And you haven't told him about Nate?"

"No, and I sure don't—" The blood drained from her face. She gripped the edge of the desk. "You know that, too?"

"I guessed. And just to make sure, I cornered Rose-lynn and Ellamae when I saw them at Ben's. Your mother confirmed it."

"She didn't!"

"Of course she did. Your aunt wouldn't budge when I asked. But you know your mother's nothing like El-lamae."

"*Nobody's* like Aunt El," she muttered, thinking of the campaign her aunt was running to reintroduce Caleb all over town. A sudden chill shot through her. How much had her aunt overheard earlier? How much had her own unwise decision hurt her?

She shook her head, forcing herself to stay on track. "Mom couldn't keep a secret if she— Oh…" She laughed weakly. "Of course she could, if she's known about Caleb all these years. Aunt El has to know, too. But how?"

"Not from me."

"Dana…" She hesitated. "I'm sorry I never told you about Nate, either."

Dana shrugged and looked away, making her feel worse than ever. "Everyone has secrets."

"I don't anymore. Not from you. But I haven't told

Caleb anything." She still couldn't. How could she have let herself forget that long enough to get so close to him?

In as few words as she could, she shared the story of her long-ago trip to Gallup to find him, of how he had treated her, of how she had flung out the news about her marriage.

Of the way he'd wished her luck.

"What would I know about luck?" she asked scornfully. "If I'd understood it at all, I'd have known getting involved with him was the unluckiest thing that could have happened."

"But then Nate happened," Dana said softly.

Tears sprang to Tess's eyes. That was one thing—the only thing—she could never regret. "Yes, I have Nate. Thanks to Caleb. And," she added, her voice shaking, "I have to get him out of here before either of them finds out."

Caleb looked around the kitchen in amazement.

Roselynn had already cooked a mess of stuff to bring to Sam Robertson's that afternoon. And now she and Ellamae had started in cooking again. Far as he could tell, between them, they'd cleaned out the store. And still they'd forgotten a couple of things.

When Ellamae had left to go to Harley's, Roselynn came up with a long list of items she needed him to get down from the highest shelves in the pantry.

"I can't tell you how much I appreciate all you've done around here," she told him.

"My pleasure." He meant it. Especially this minute, when work could take his mind off the talk he'd had with Tess such a short while ago. And keep him from dwelling on how close he'd come to doing something he shouldn't have.

He'd worked up a sweat fixing the shed in the yard. Tess's hands on him had made him hotter. They'd been alone, the house deserted. He'd wanted to pick her up, sheet and all, and carry her inside. When he'd stroked her face, the look in her eyes told him he might just have gotten his wish. If Ellamae hadn't come along.

If Ellamae hadn't saved him from himself.

"Tess tries to help out," Roselynn said with a shrug. "But neither of us has money to burn."

He did. He'd just somehow gotten offtrack about his idea of setting it to flame. Gotten too hot over Tess to keep his thoughts and his hands where they belonged. And damn him for forgetting his plan to make Tess see what she'd walked away from. Instead, he'd started obsessing about everything *he* had missed.

He had to struggle to focus on her mama.

"And she's got so much on her mind with Nate."

"I noticed. A lot of friction between them." But anyone could tell they and Roselynn and Ellamae all loved each other. The way a family should.

Sighing, she reached for the baking dish he'd handed down from the stepladder. "You're right, those two are always at sixes and sevens. It's awful to see. You must think they don't care for one another at all."

He shook his head. "I'm certain it's the opposite. They just don't let it show often enough."

"That's so true." She set the next baking dish beside the first one. "I try to take on some of the responsibility with Nate, but you know Tess. She's always too hard on herself."

"Yes, she is." Too quiet, as well. "Must be a challenge having to raise the child on her own. With your help, of course."

She smiled. "I've tried to do what I could. It's not easy. Nate's a bit rebellious at times."

"I noticed that, too."

They both laughed, but he sobered quickly. Their talk reminded him of that first day he'd come back, when Tess had told him her marriage hadn't worked out. Maybe it had fallen through before it even got started. He went with his hunch. "Tess never married at all, did she?"

"No, she never did." She hesitated, then said, "She didn't tell you about that herself?"

"Yes." He added grimly, "Though not in so many words."

"She's had plenty of chances." Roselynn sounded proud, the way a mama should sound when she talked about her kids. "Joe Harley's asked her more than once. But she's always said no. She's always put Nate first, you see. After you left, I think she felt—" She cut herself off and swallowed hard.

As if trying to take back her words? Too late. In these past few weeks, he'd already taken note of some things that didn't add up. She'd just given him another item for his list. "Why would you think my leaving had anything to do with Tess?"

"I didn't. I mean, I don't."

"And what's Nate got to do with this?"

"Nothing. Nothing at all. That was just me running my mouth again, as usual. If Ellamae hadn't left for the store already, she'd tell you so." She started fussing with the dishes on the counter.

He frowned. That first night he'd spent here and

many times since, he'd seen how quickly she had left the dining room when the conversation made her uncomfortable.

The same way Tess had fled just a little while ago.

What was it Ellamae had said about Roselynn that night? That her sister "won't allow you much without a sugar coating on it." How much was she sweetening the truth now? He needed to know.

Stepping down from the ladder, he moved to stand in front of her. "Roselynn," he said in the voice he'd use to calm a spooked mare, "what is it you're trying not to say?"

"I don't know what you mean." She kept her gaze on the baking dishes.

Between her innocent slip and her unwillingness to explain, he now had enough to figure things out—and he sure as hell didn't care for the total he'd come to.

"Roselynn," he said again, "is there something Tess won't tell me that I ought to know?"

"Please, Caleb," she said urgently, "don't ask me that." She scooped up both dishes, clanking them together. Finally, she met his eyes. "That's between the two of you."

Chapter 14

"Don't worry, I'm turning off the lights," Tess reassured Dana as they prepared to leave the office. That done, she followed her friend outside and pulled the door closed behind them. "I don't want you to—"

Abruptly, she stopped.

At the curb behind Dana's van sat the rented pickup truck with Caleb at the wheel. And she thought she'd managed to escape him for a while.

"Here comes Nate." Dana pointed along Signal Street.

The three of them converged on the truck at the same time.

"All aboard for the Whistlestop," Caleb said.

Nate opened the passenger door and climbed in, moving to the seat in the rear of the cab. "C'mon, Mom."

Tess hesitated, not wanting to sit that close to Caleb

again. And especially not wanting to get in that truck after what had happened between them in it.

Nate sat staring at her impatiently. Though Caleb's dark sunglasses hid his eyes, she could tell he watched her, too. Even Dana stepped back so that Tess could climb into the cab.

"Talk to you soon," Dana said.

As she nodded and climbed in, she gave thanks that this would be a quick and painless trip. Nate's chatter made the short ride go even more quickly. Still, she gave a sigh of relief when they reached the parking area of the inn.

Caleb opened the driver's door, and Nate jumped to the ground and ran toward the house.

When Tess reached for the passenger door handle, she was startled to feel his hand clasp her wrist. She looked at him in surprise. He released her arm, closed the driver's door and rested back against his seat.

"Let's compare notes," he said.

He could have chosen a better time than this. But she couldn't say that. She couldn't risk reminding him again of why they hadn't discussed the property last night. She grabbed her canvas bag from the seat beside her and began rummaging in it for her pen. "All right. Where do you want to start?"

"With Nate."

Her fingers closed convulsively on the notebook she'd just slid from the bag.

"You know," he continued, "the first day I met her, she told me she wasn't too happy with what you'd called her. 'Anastasia.' That's different. How'd you come up with it, anyhow?"

Her nails dug half-moon dents into the notebook's

cover. She had to swallow hard before she could answer.
She had to sound natural. Unconcerned. "I...looked
it up in a baby-naming book. I thought it was pretty."

"And so it is. Goes nice with the rest of her name,
too. 'Anastasia Lynn LaSalle.' You've called her that
a couple of times when she's mouthed off to you. Of
course, you didn't have to find that last one in a baby
book, did you?"

"No, I didn't." She loosened her grip on the notebook but took a firmer hold on her emotions. Nothing
to worry about here. He was only making conversation,
more than likely prompted by Nate's chatter. "Now,
what about that property we looked at just after lunch
yesterday? The acreage is suited to what you need, and
I'm sure we can get the asking price down. I've calcu-
lated—"

"Before we get into prices, let's calculate a few other
things."

"Such as..."

"Years."

She frowned, puzzled. "For a mortgage?"

"For a marriage. Yours."

Her fingers convulsed again. If she gripped any
tighter, she would risk a handful of ink when the pen
broke in two. But there was no getting away from it.
These weren't idle questions Caleb was asking. The
confrontation she'd dreaded since the first day she'd
seen him again had now begun. That didn't mean she'd
go down without a fight. "What does my marriage have
to do with anything?"

"A lot. Maybe more than I'd thought. You told me a
while back it 'didn't work out.' How many years would
it be if you were still married now?"

"That's none of your business."

"I'm calling you on that one, Tess. I think it *is* my business. You were never married at all."

"What makes you think that? Just because Nate has my maiden name? That doesn't mean a thing. Besides, whether I was married or not—or will marry Joe Harley or not—has nothing to do with you."

"Maybe not. But it's got something to do with Nate. And I should've seen that sooner. She's nine years old. I've been gone for ten. That's a simple enough calculation for me."

"Don't be so crude. Or so conceited." She forced a laugh. "I had plenty of time to—to find another boyfriend after you left."

"I'll give you crude, Tess. You teased me long enough before you let me into your jeans. What are the chances you'd give away your favors to someone else only a couple months later?"

She gasped. Yes, his words had shocked her, as he'd planned. But worse, they'd hit the truth, too. She *wouldn't* have gone with someone else so soon after she'd given herself to him.

Nate came out of the back door and jumped down the steps, then headed in their direction. The huge grin on her face made Tess's heart hurt.

"Nate's mine, isn't she?" he demanded.

With shaking hands, she shoved her notebook and pen back into her bag. She had to get out of here.

He clasped her wrist again. "I'm not leaving this truck till you answer."

He would feel her tremors. Would see them. She couldn't help that. But as tears sprang to her eyes, she turned her head away. At least, she could keep him from seeing those.

Nate ran across the yard toward them.

Tess blinked furiously again. She couldn't let Nate see her this upset, either.

"Tess." He spoke her name gently. But relentlessly.

She slumped against her seat. Why did this conversation have to happen here? Why did it have to happen at all?

Nate was just a few yards away and coming closer, and still he pushed. "Tell me."

"Nate is not *yours,*" she burst out, her voice low but harsh with threatening tears. "She's ours." She reached blindly for the handle and yanked it, slid from the truck and slammed the door closed behind her.

"You coming in the house?" Nate asked.

"Yes." She'd go anywhere, do anything to avoid having to be alone with Caleb again. From behind her, she heard the driver's door slam shut.

Surprising herself and Nate, she wrapped her arms around her daughter and squeezed tightly, wishing she would never have to let go.

To her shock, Nate returned the hug with equal enthusiasm.

Caleb still felt thrown by the news he'd learned.

Not discovering he was Nate's daddy. No, that was the best of it all.

After he'd left Roselynn, he'd walked around with his legs as shaky as the day he'd gotten out of his hospital bed to see if he could stand again. Maybe that's the way real daddies felt when they first saw their babies. He'd missed that step—and a few thousand others.

Thanks to Tess's deceit.

Her refusal to tell him about Nate only underscored the feelings he'd grown up with, the beliefs that had been reinforced in his time on the circuit. *Don't get too close to people.* He'd almost done that, almost trusted Tess. Almost shared his fears about having come so near to dying. Only to find she'd kept this secret from him all along.

Deep inside, he had to admit he understood that. At least, part of him did. He could see why she hadn't told him about the baby at first. That night in Gallup, he'd obsessed over winning his event, claiming his prize. Gaining the proof that showed how right he'd been to leave Flagman's Folly. And then wanting to show that proof to Tess. He'd sure messed that up.

Yet, another part of him didn't understand Tess's betrayal at all. That had been one night, one conversation. Since then, she'd had years to make another attempt to contact him, and still she'd kept the truth hidden. Even when he'd come back to town, she hadn't told him.

A while after he'd left Roselynn, he'd driven to Tess's office. Finding Nate and Dana there had put an end to any chance of talking to Tess alone. And when they'd gotten back to the inn, she had nearly run from the truck into the house.

Now he heard her footsteps in the hallway coming from the direction of her room. Easing his door ajar, he stood in the opening, waiting. No way would she get by him again, as she'd done downstairs, sticking close to Nate from the minute they'd come into the house so he wouldn't have a chance to talk with her alone. She'd come up here the same time as Nate, too, managing to cut him off again.

But she had run out of options for evading him.

Roselynn and Ellamae had never left the kitchen. Nate had gone into her room but had barreled down the stairs a few minutes ago. No one left up here but the two of them.

Her footsteps neared. He stood his ground, and when she saw him in the doorway, she froze.

He caught her gaze and held it long enough to send his message. Then he backed a couple of paces and swung the door open wider.

She sighed and waited.

So did he.

It could almost have been a replay of that first night he'd spent at the inn. Only now, a lot more had passed between them. A lot of empty words. *No one pitied you, Caleb. Not everyone thought less of you.* When he'd asked her if she'd felt that way, she had shaken her head.

Yet she'd kept his daughter from him.

She stepped into the room, closed the door and turned to face him. She had freshened up, pulling her hair back with some sparkly combs, putting color into her cheeks. Adding something shiny to her lips that made them look softer than ever and ready for a kiss.

And damn him, he wanted to kiss her again.

She leaned back against the door, as if wanting as much distance between them as she could get. "Can we just let this go?"

Anger fired through him, making his hands shake. "I don't know," he said, proud of keeping his voice low. Not so proud of his struggle to drag his attention from her mouth. "You could try distracting me."

The flare of anticipation in her eyes almost crushed him.

She didn't want *him,* she just hoped to put off having this conversation. To avoid making the truth known to everyone.

Disgusted with himself, he moved over to the bureau and pawed through a drawer for a couple of bandannas. It would be hot working outside in the sun.

Not as hot as he felt inside this room.

In the mirror, he could see her staring at him. Could almost see her thoughts turning in her head. She might not want him, but he sure as hell felt the need for her—to make love or to settle a score, he couldn't tell right now. Just as well he'd never find out.

"No sense getting off course, is there?" he asked. "That's what brought us here today." He faced her again, opened his mouth, then shut it. Wincing inwardly, he thought of what she'd said to him in the truck earlier.

Don't be so crude.

He had the right to what he was going to say now. But he didn't have to be offensive about it. Despite everything, she had done a good job raising their daughter, with no help from him. He had to give her that.

That's all he'd allow.

"I'm going to talk with Nate."

"No." She surged forward, stumbled to a stop halfway across the room to him. "I won't let you do that."

"Let?"

She lifted her hands palm-up, then dropped them to her sides, but not soon enough for him to miss seeing she was the one shaking now. "All right. Then I'm asking you, Caleb. Don't do this."

Unable to stop himself, he laughed shortly. "Did you think I'd just walk away and forget what you told me?"

"No, I didn't expect you to forget. But walk away? Yes. Why wouldn't I think that? You've done it before."

"And you'll never let me off the hook for it."

She shoved her hand through the air, pushing his

words away. "That's not what I meant. Not what we're talking about. It's Nate I'm thinking of. We can't just tell her this now and then go out for the day as if nothing had happened."

Being called crude, he'd accepted, but he'd be damned if he'd let her think him cruel and not defend himself. "What the hell makes you think I'd do that? Give me some credit, Tess. I won't tell her today. And I won't hit her point-blank with the news. You can pave the way for the conversation. But I'll be the one to tell her."

"What good will it do for you to talk to her? You're leaving again soon. She's never known about you. She doesn't need to know now."

"Who said that's for you to decide?"

"I'm her mother."

"And I'm her daddy."

"Yes," she shot back, "and it will be better for her if she never knows that."

The heat of her words slammed into him. She couldn't have made her feelings more plain, her rejection more final. He'd wanted the real reason behind her refusal to tell him about Nate even after all the years. Now he had it.

Even after she had said she'd never looked down on him.

He had to take a breath before he could respond. Before he could think at all. Still, her belief didn't make him any less determined.

He crossed the room, walking past her without looking, and threw open the door. "I'm telling Nate the news, Tess. When I do, you can be there for the conversation or not. Your choice."

* * *

Caleb drove the final nail into the wood and eyed Sam Robertson's new chicken coop with satisfaction. Amazing what a little hard labor could do for a man's aggressions.

All afternoon, he'd managed to act as though he hadn't a worry in the world.

The way Tess had kept up her lies for all these years. How hard had that been for her? And after the truth she'd kept from him, why should he care? Because she was the mother of his child?

The thought made him hot and cold at the same time. He swung the hammer again.

"Not bad for amateurs, huh?" Sam asked.

A few of his ranch hands had helped with the work, but they'd all taken off to shower, leaving the two of them to finish up.

Caleb dropped the hammer into the box with the other tools. "Looks like a pro job to me. Besides, I wouldn't call you an amateur. I saw that workshop of yours in the bunkhouse. And Dori told me you made the sign over the door at the Double S."

Sam shrugged. "Thanks." He finished rolling up the last of the tarps they'd used.

"I could do with a couple of those for next week," Caleb said. "I'm getting ready to do some painting over at the Whistlestop."

He'd already told Roselynn he'd do the work. Besides, he planned to stick around, no matter how Tess felt about him. No matter how much he wanted to walk away from her now. He wouldn't leave until he'd told Nate the truth.

"Help yourself," Sam said. "Let me know if you need a hand. I can send some of the boys over your way."

"That's not necessary. It's only one small room. It won't take much time."

Sam grinned. "Tess has you working, huh?"

"Roselynn does."

"Good thing. It'll keep you out of trouble."

"Maybe." More than likely, it would keep him in Roselynn's good graces, that was all. If she would still speak to him after she found out he'd confronted Tess.

Roselynn and Ellamae had been working hard in the kitchen when he'd left to drive over here with Nate. And with Tess, who hadn't said anything at all to him directly since she'd walked out of his room.

"Let me get us a refill." Sam went over to the insulated water cooler his wife, Kayla, and Tess had kept refilled.

Caleb stripped off his T-shirt and felt the pull of the scar tissue on his chest. Remembered the feel of Tess's hand as she'd touched him there.

He used the T-shirt to scrub the sweat from his face. Along with working off aggressions, the hot sun and hard labor made for good physical therapy. His knee hadn't given him much trouble at all. Too bad he couldn't say the same about his thoughts.

Despite everything, thinking of Tess while he'd worked had made him hot, bothered *and* troubled.

Catching sight of her across Sam's yard throughout the day hadn't helped, either. She wore a pair of jeans that fit her well enough to destroy his concentration—a dangerous thing for a man with a hammer in his hand. If that wasn't bad enough, she wore another blouse with an elastic neck that had him fixating on what had happened the day before.

He'd obsessed over that damned blouse all day yesterday, waiting for the chance to slide it off her shoulders and do just what he had done. He shook his head at the memory.

They had experienced some intense times as teenagers, but he'd never felt the way he had in that truck. Their talk had broken new ground, too, carrying them to the verge of a closeness they'd never arrived at years ago.

A closeness that could lead him into making promises he couldn't keep.

That morning, as he'd sat staring at her during breakfast, his mind had kept running through the whole list of reasons he didn't want to get involved with her.

Now he had to get involved. At least at some level.

Sam returned and handed him an oversize tumbler filled with cold water. He downed a gulp of it and settled back against the fence beside the coop. Across the yard, Tess and Kayla and Sam's mother worked at setting up for the barbecue. Folks would start showing up before too long.

On the back porch, Nate sat with Sam's five-year-old, Becky. Their hands waved in the air as they talked to each other in sign language.

"Looks like the girls get along," he offered.

Sam smiled. "They do. Nate's a good kid to spend so much time with a little one like Becky."

Nate *was* a good kid, despite her frequent shortness with her mama. He'd begun to care too much about both of them. At the same time, he couldn't stop thinking about how much he'd missed of Nate's life—thanks to Tess's lies.

Why was he wasting time over thoughts that would only tear him apart? In the long run, obsessing wouldn't change anything. He knew what he would do. His childhood here in town, his ten years in rodeo, his talk with Tess just the day before—they had all paved the way to his decision.

He tightened his grip on the T-shirt he'd stripped off, trying to stop thoughts of yesterday. They came to him, anyway.

Tess had wanted to know what knowledge he'd gained from being on the rodeo circuit. Chances were, his answer wouldn't have pleased her. He'd learned a lot. And of all the lessons the circuit had taught him, he thought again of the one he'd learned especially well: *No sense in forming personal ties. They don't last.*

For some people, anyhow. They seemed to have worked out fine for Sam Robertson. Caleb could hear the pride in the man's voice every time he talked about Becky.

He swallowed another gulp of water that seemed to clog in his throat. Clearing it, he said, "Tess told me Becky came to live with you not that long ago. That must have made some big changes in your life."

"It sure did." Sam looked across the yard at his wife and daughter.

The smile on his face made Caleb feel suddenly envious. On the one hand.

On the other hand, it made him want to bolt.

What did he know about being a daddy?

"I guess you've gone through a few changes lately, too," Sam said.

Caleb frowned. Then he realized Sam must have meant his rodeo career. "Been a crazy time," he agreed. He paused, then went on, "Judge Baylor told me about you two coming to the hospital."

"Yeah. The news stories had started to slow down. Folks wanted an update on how you were doing."

"I wouldn't think they'd send a posse as far as Dallas to find out."

"We figured firsthand was the only way we'd get information. We'd have gone clear to the East Coast, if we'd needed to. Trust me on that." Sam picked up the water cooler. "I'd better go check the barbecue before I hit the shower."

Caleb nodded and watched the other man walk away.

Somehow, he did trust Sam Robertson. They hadn't run into each other much when he lived in town, but when they did, the man had always been decent.

Sam said folks had cared when he'd had the accident. A big concept to wrap his head around. Growing up, hardly anyone had bothered about him. Yet, since his return, all the townsfolk had shown him interest and concern.

Sam said pretty much the same things the judge had said.

Did that mean he had to trust the judge's words, too? About everything?

He unclamped his fingers from his T-shirt and tossed it onto one shoulder. Slowly, he smiled. That chip Judge Baylor claimed he carried around had just started to slide out of place.

Then he glanced across the yard again and felt his smile slide out of place, too.

Since his return, all he'd gotten from Tess was the feeling she wanted him gone. Or was it?

In the truck yesterday, he'd taken it upon himself to back off, out of respect for her. Before he'd done that, though, she had started warming up in a way he sure liked.

She'd seemed willing enough to get close to him that morning, too. At least till Ellamae had shown up.

He looked over toward the trestle tables in the yard.

Tess's face lit as she listened to something Kayla told Sam. Her cheeks flushed pink from sunshine or laughter or her movements as she leaned down to smooth a cloth over the tabletop. Even from here, he could see a sparkle in her eyes.

What would've happened if he hadn't backed off yesterday?

And why the hell was he thinking about it?

After that confrontation in his bedroom, nothing could happen between them now.

Chapter 15

Tess looked over toward the porch, where Nate and Becky carried on their play, half in sign language and half in the way they moved Becky's toys through a dollhouse Sam had made for her.

Her puppy, Pirate, lay flat on his belly beside them.

Every time they saw Becky, she and Nate picked up a few more signs. And Nate always enjoyed the little girl's company. Still, knowing her tomboy daughter would much prefer to muck out the stalls in Sam's barn than play with dolls, Tess couldn't help but smile. Nate looked up, caught her gaze and smiled back.

Tess blinked rapidly, fighting off a wave of tears.

Prickly, exasperating and *belligerent*. No one with any sense could deny those words applied to Nate. *Precious, loving* and *beloved* did, too. How was she going to react when Caleb told her the news?

Tess braced her hands on the picnic table. Hurt and humiliation washed over her. She had sworn Caleb would never know about their child. Too late for that now.

Resignation flooded through her, too. Much as she didn't want to admit it, she'd made the choice years ago to hold back from Caleb something he had the right to know. Now he'd found out. Now she had no choice. She had to accept his need to tell Nate the truth.

He strode across the yard toward Tess, as if he'd heard her thought and planned to act on it that very moment. Even as a cold sweat broke over her, she told herself it couldn't be true. He wouldn't talk to Nate here.

As he approached, she stared. He was shirtless again now, and the memory of touching him made her fingers tremble just as they had that morning.

She wanted to touch him again.

Her cheeks burning, she grabbed the pile of napkins Kayla had left on the table. Napkins now, sheets and pillowcases earlier today. None of them could occupy her hands well enough.

She looked over her shoulder, but Sam, who might have provided some interference, had just entered the bunkhouse. Kayla had followed his mother into the house. Even Nate and Becky had left the porch swing and were rushing toward the barn, Pirate bounding at their heels. Everyone had deserted her.

She tried to swallow, but her throat wouldn't cooperate. Tried to rise, but her legs wouldn't obey her.

Then she got a grip on her napkin—and on her emotions. If she couldn't be strong for herself, she'd damned well better practice being strong for her daughter.

Just as Caleb neared her, she heard the sound of a car

on Sam's gravel drive. The familiar chugging noise of its engine made her sag in relief. She'd fight Caleb for what she had to. But not here. Not now.

Tess rose, and they both started toward the Toyota, where Roselynn and Aunt El had begun unloading the backseat. They seemed to have brought enough to feed the crowd on their own.

"Let me take some of that off your hands," Caleb offered.

Aunt El looked at her, then eyed him up and down, her gaze lingering on the T-shirt that only partially hid his bare chest. "Seems like you might have enough on *your* hands already."

Tess felt her cheeks burn. What did she think the two of them had been up to? Then again, how much had she seen this morning? Sighing, Tess said, "Never mind, Caleb. You need to go shower. I'll take care of these two."

He shrugged, then nodded and headed in the direction of the bunkhouse.

"Hey, Caleb," Ellamae said, "need someone to scrub your back?"

He pivoted, his face split in a grin. "Why, thanks, ma'am, but I wouldn't want to put you out."

She laughed. "Don't be silly. I wasn't offering to do it myself." She looked at Tess.

Shaking his head, he turned away.

Shaking with fury, Tess turned on her aunt, but pent-up emotion made the words catch in her throat. The tension with Nate. The angry confrontation with Caleb. The years she'd spent keeping a secret that wasn't a se-cret from those closest to her at all. Finally, she found her voice. "Aunt El. Mom. What is it you two are trying to do?"

"Help you, sugar," Roselynn said.

"Like always," Aunt El added gruffly.

"Oh-h." The word threatened to become a wail. Tess swallowed hard, her eyes misting. "I know you've always meant well," she began. "I just didn't realize how much, until today. Dana told me you both know...everything about me and Caleb."

"I heard tell you were out walking with him a few times," Ellamae said.

"'Heard tell'?" Tess shook her head. She could laugh about it now. Sort of. "What you mean is, you sicced your spies on me."

Her aunt shrugged. "Whatever it takes."

"We were worried about you."

"I know you were, Mom. You, too, Aunt El." Tess reached out and gave them each a quick hug. "Thank you. I appreciate it more than I'll ever be able to say. But I'm a big girl. You've got to let me act like one. Let me take care of this myself, all right?"

"Hey, Gram!" Nate shouted from the barn doorway. She and Becky ran up to them, followed by Pirate.

"Gram, did you bring the chocolate pie?"

"We sure did," Roselynn said. "And we've got to get it into the house."

"Along with the rest of this food. Here, Tess."

Aunt El shoved the foil-covered casserole into her hands and proceeded to lead the way to Sam's back porch.

It wasn't till much later that Tess realized neither her aunt nor her mother had made any promises about letting her take care of her problems on her own.

* * *

Hours later, Caleb would eagerly have swapped the back scrub he didn't get for the back massage he now needed. Though on second thought, he could have fared worse if Tess had taken up Ellamae's suggestion. He still couldn't hold back an unwilling smile every time he recalled the look on Tess's face when she'd heard what her aunt had said.

He put both hands to his lower back and stood straighter, trying not to look like he hurt as much as he did. So much for his hard labor being good therapy. He hadn't finished his shower yet before the aches had set in.

"Grab yourself a chair before they're all gone," Ben Sawyer advised him.

"Don't mind if I do," he said.

He took one of the lawn chairs Ben offered him and sat in it. With a sigh, he stretched his feet out toward the fire they'd just started in a cleared ring well away from Sam's house and barn. And the brand-new chicken coop that didn't look half bad at all.

"Did that big supper do you in?" Ben asked.

"That and the games," he confessed. He wasn't about to mention the coop, which had started it all.

After the barbecue and a few rounds of horseshoes— in which Judge Baylor whupped most everyone's butt— he felt more than ready to take a break. The need for the rest bothered him, but there it was. He would never be the same man he'd been a couple of years ago.

Did it matter much, when that man might not have been the person he'd always thought, anyhow? Folks like the judge and Sam and even Tess, he admitted reluctantly, were making him change his perceptions about himself. And about the past.

On the opposite side of the ring, Tess had just taken a vacant chair. She sat staring at the fire, her eyes glowing from the reflected flames.

They hadn't had another chance that day to be alone. Much better that way.

"Hey, Caleb, can we sit with you?" Nate asked.

"Sure," he said.

Today, same as at Ben's potluck, Nate had gotten too involved playing games with her friends to pay much attention to him. Come to think of it, their tendency to hang around had slacked off lately, too. As if the girls had started to get used to seeing him. As if they, in agreement with Ben's statement about the townsfolk, took for granted he belonged.

The thoughts left him with a funny feeling beneath the scarred skin of his chest.

Nate and Lissa and Becky squeezed their way between his chair and Ben's. Becky's pup hovered behind them, his tail wagging. Ben shifted his chair to give them more room, and Caleb did the same.

"Thanks." Nate plopped onto the ground next to him.

Her friends took places beside her. Pirate dropped to his haunches and rested one paw on Becky's knee.

The girls unfolded a game board and started to divvy up cards.

A burst of laughter broke out from one point in the circle of chairs around the fire ring. Voices rose left and right as more people pulled up chairs.

Caleb sat back and recalled the questions that had taken over his thoughts more often than they should have today.

What if he and Tess hadn't split up permanently? Would they have lasted till now?

He looked down at Nate's dark head. If he and Tess had gotten back together, they could have raised Nate with both a mama and a daddy. Might have had a few other kids along the way.

But they hadn't, thanks to Tess.

Like a flame in the fire ring, a flare shot up inside him. He had to get beyond that thinking. What had happened—or not happened—couldn't matter anymore. He had to look forward, keep his eye on the future.

Do right by his child.

He couldn't follow what his own mother had done. Ignored him. Virtually abandoned him. Left him wondering about his daddy.

He clutched the metal armrest of his chair and swallowed the bitterness that rose to his throat. Yes, in another way, he had deserted Tess by turning from her years ago. But he'd never known about their baby. He did now.

He wouldn't let his daughter think he'd abandoned her.

At that moment, Nate looked away from her game and up at him. Her eyebrows wrinkled in a frown. Grasping the arm of his chair, she leaned toward him. "What's the matter, Caleb?"

"Not a thing," he said. "I'm just sitting back and enjoying myself."

She leaned closer and whispered, "Then why do you look so sad?"

All through breakfast, Tess's stomach churned. She couldn't touch her eggs, could only pretend to sip her tea.

Last night, Caleb had insisted he would talk to Nate this morning.

Tess had spent a long time after that closeted in the kitchen with her mom and then an even longer night awake in her room.

The three adults had eaten little. They said even less.

Nate picked up on the tension.

By the time Roselynn had gone into the kitchen, closing the door firmly behind her, Nate looked apprehensive. When Tess asked her to come into the living room, her expression froze. She looked over at Caleb.

"You comin', too?"

"Wouldn't miss it."

In the living room, feeling suddenly chilled, Tess grabbed the crocheted afghan from the couch and crossed to the rocker in one corner. She took her seat and clutched the afghan in her lap. Somehow, she had to start this conversation that would change all their lives forever. At least Caleb had given her the chance to make the news easier for Nate to hear.

He sat on the couch and leaned forward, resting his elbows on his knees and linking his fingers together in front of him.

Nate plopped onto the leather ottoman. "I'm in big trouble, right?"

"Of course—"

"No, you're—"

Tess and Caleb each cut themselves off.

Not looking at him, she said, "You're not in any trouble, Nate. Why do you think that?"

"I just do." She scuffed her sneaker on the braided rug beside the ottoman and added in a rush, "Aunt El said I'd get in hot water soon for mouthing off."

Tess couldn't help wondering if Aunt El ever thought about just where Nate got her sass. She smiled gently. "It's true, we could have less of that all around."

"I'm trying not to," Nate mumbled. "It's not easy."

"I know." She paused. Caleb sat watching them intently. If ever she had an opening to show him how well she could handle Nate—and how little she needed his interference in their lives—this was it. "I didn't mean just you, honey. I imagine I could snap a little less often, too."

"Yeah. That would be good."

Caleb met her eyes briefly, and her sudden contentment at the sense of a moment shared gave way just as quickly to a feeling of dismay. Sharing a moment with him had gotten her into more hot water than she could believe. With shaking hands, she clutched the afghan again.

"Nate, Caleb and I wanted to talk to you together."

Her daughter's eyes immediately sought his. He gave her a smile that made Tess's eyes mist.

Oblivious to her, Nate grinned back at him. "You feel better now? You're not sad anymore?"

Tess frowned. What was that about?

He shook his head. "No, as a matter of fact, I'd say I'm feeling pretty darned happy."

"Then, you mean," Nate said slowly, "you're going back to the rodeo?"

Tess almost sighed aloud at the irony of those words. No, Caleb would never go back to the rodeo circuit. But he *would* leave again. That's why she had fought with him about not telling Nate the truth. He'd left *her* once and she'd gotten over it. Eventually. But what would happen when he repeated history with their daughter? Would he break Nate's heart, too, when he left town?

"No, I'm not going back to rodeo, Nate."

"Oh, wow." She bounced on the ottoman. "Then you're staying here, right? I knew you would! Boy, wait'll I tell the guys."

"It'd be nice to stay, Nate." He looked down at his linked fingers. "But I can't do that permanently."

"Oh."

Tess took a deep breath. "Nate," she began, "you know that Caleb grew up here in Flagman's Folly."

"Yeah. That's why he came back."

"That's part of it, yes. But there's more. He also has something to share with you about when he lived here." She stopped and looked over at him.

He cleared his throat and took up the story. "When your mama and I were teenagers, we went together."

"Went where?" Nate asked.

"Uh, we went to high school together. And then we dated each other for a bit. You know what I mean?"

"Yeah." She nodded emphatically. "Like, boyfriends and girlfriends."

"Right. And then…" He faltered.

"And then you missed Mom and then you came back, and now you're gonna get married! I knew it."

"Nate—"

Before Tess could finish, she interrupted. "Wait a minute. You said you're not staying here." She frowned. "Then how are you gonna marry Mom?"

Tess watched as Caleb's fingers tightened, clamping his hands together.

"I'm not going to do that, either."

"You're not?" Nate spoke in a dull tone now, her eyes downcast. "Then you're just…leaving?"

Tess inhaled sharply and blinked back the moisture suddenly blurring her vision. This was ten years ago, all over again. Ten years ago, but much worse.

"No, I'm not leaving yet." He shifted to the edge of the couch and took a deep breath, as well. "Nate, I know this'll come as a surprise to you. A good one, I hope. What…your mama and I want to tell you is that… I'm your daddy."

Nate's head snapped up. Her eyes opened wide. Her jaw dropped. A bright red flush filled her face. "You are not! You're Caleb Cantrell."

"Nate," Tess said softly.

"Listen—" Caleb said.

"No, I won't listen!" Nate jumped up from the ottoman, her eyes glistening. "Don't let him say that, Mom." Her voice broke. She backed away. "You're a rodeo star. You can't be my daddy. You *can't*."

Before Caleb or Tess could say anything more, she turned and ran from the room.

They heard the sound of her sneakers slapping on the bare entryway floor, the front door opening, the metal screened door banging against its frame.

And then silence.

An uncomfortable, agonizing silence that lasted forever.

Caleb broke it, finally, by clearing his throat. He said nothing, only moved his hands in a groping, almost helpless gesture. She could envision him on the back of a horse or astride a bull, holding on to reins or grasping a saddle horn, fully in control.

Caleb was never helpless. Until his accident.

And until now.

She dug her fingers into the afghan in her lap, knowing she had to keep quiet for her own sake and for Nate's.

The look on his face and the hurt in his eyes wouldn't let her. But how did she find the words?

"It… This was a shock to her. You had to know it would be. You'll need to give her some time." She took a deep breath, bracing herself, knowing the only thing she could think of to help him was guaranteed to hurt her. "Nate's a preteen with a crush on you, Caleb. A girl who thinks she's in love. At some level, though, she realizes that's just a dream." She swallowed hard. "Believing you would…we might marry gave her a way to hold on to you. And now, she doesn't have that, either. All she's left with is the feeling she's humiliated herself."

He stared at her.

She stared back, unable to look away. Her pulse pounded at her temples. Her eyes felt tight from her effort to hold back tears.

Finally, he nodded slowly. "Yeah, I reckon you're right."

Chapter 16

Tess stood outside Nate's bedroom door.

When she hadn't returned after a short while, Tess had tried not to panic. When an hour had passed with still no sign, she'd given up and called Dana. It seemed Nate had run directly to Lissa's house.

After Nate had arrived home, only to run right upstairs, Tess gave her a few minutes alone. And allowed herself a few minutes to compose herself before following.

Nate sat on her bed, leaning against the headboard, with her arms crossed over her chest. Her gaze rested on the poster of Caleb that now lay in a torn, tangled heap on the floor.

When she saw Tess looking at the poster, she muttered, "He's not my daddy."

Tess sat carefully on the side of the bed and put her

hand on Nate's knee. "Honey, I'm sorry I never told you, but what Caleb said is true."

"How?"

With her free hand, she gripped the edge of the mattress. This was not the talk she'd planned to have right now. But she owed Nate an answer. "Well…we read that book together, remember?" she said. "The one about babies—"

"Not the babies," Nate said, anger blending with scorn. She refused to look up. "I know all about that and how the boy's whatchamcallit—"

Good thing she wasn't watching Tess, who couldn't help staring in surprise. She didn't recall the book going into that much detail. "'Whatchamacallit?'"

"I can't remember the word. You know—the boy's swimming thing hits the girl's egg—and wham! There's a baby."

Tess opened her mouth and closed it again.

Nate continued, "The eighth-grade girls are always going on about that stuff in the cafeteria. But I'm not talking about that." Nate tilted her head down farther, her dark hair hiding her face. She hesitated, then went on in a softer tone. "I never saw Caleb. Except at the rodeo, I mean. And on posters. If he's my daddy, why wasn't he here before?"

Tess shook her head. Trust Nate to ask the tough questions. Before she could decide how to respond, Nate looked up.

Her expression made Tess's breath catch. Her tomboy daughter's eyes filled with tears.

"Didn't he even want me?" Nate's voice shook. Tears spilled over and ran down her cheeks. She scrubbed them away with the backs of her hands.

"Oh, honey." Tess reached for her.

As Nate sobbed against her, Tess held her close and kissed her hair.

Caleb looked around the breakfast table, where they all sat quietly, thinking their own thoughts.

In the couple of days since he'd learned he had a daughter, his life had changed. And not for the good, it seemed.

The morning he and Tess had talked to Nate, she'd disappeared afterward in a halfhearted attempt to run away from home that had ended by suppertime. Since then, she'd made sure their paths only crossed during meals, when she would sit scrutinizing him every time she felt sure he wasn't noticing.

Roselynn tried hard to keep things normal, yet the expression of pity he saw every time he caught her off guard didn't help much.

And Tess…

As clearly as if she'd put it on paper, Tess had drawn a parallel between the way she and Nate felt about him.

She'd drawn battle lines now, too. Their interactions remained all business, all the time, but even with that, she had trouble looking him in the eye.

He should have known better, about Nate. About Tess.

As luck would have it, she had found some nearby available acreage, a ranch that sat closer to the outskirts of Flagman's Folly than anything she'd shown him yet.

Another change he couldn't put on the good side of his life.

His grand plan for returning to Flagman's Folly had fallen as flat as the paper-thin crepes Roselynn had

just served him. Sure, he'd come back to town knowing he was down and out of rodeo for good. But he'd
gone out on top, dammit—and he'd wanted to show
them all. Wanted to rub their noses in the proof of his
success. Hard to do, though, when no one cared about
those things but him.

With the way things stood, he couldn't deny Tess her
commission. Well, he'd put all those rodeo winnings
he'd saved up to good use and just buy the danged ranch.

"The property has about everything on your wish
list," she said, her attention focused on her plate. "And
it's ready for immediate purchase."

Nate's head shot up. She looked from Tess to him
and back again.

"A stroke of good fortune," he said, "finding that
property available right now."

"Yes," Tess said.

Nate's fork hit her plate so hard, the clank echoed in
the suddenly quiet room. "Does that mean he's leaving
soon?" she demanded, looking at Tess.

He tried not to wince at her eagerness to have him
gone. How could he expect anything otherwise?

"Yes, that's what it means," Tess said.

She sounded relieved about it. He should have known
that prying the truth from her and sharing it with Nate
wouldn't make a difference to either of them.

"He's leaving 'cause of you, Mom!" Nate burst out.

Now he heard anguish in her tone. The realization
forced him back in his seat in astonishment. Maybe
he'd read her wrong.

She raised that strong jaw the way she had the first
time he'd seen her, talking to her mama at the Double
S, in the way that made her look so much like Tess.

"You told him he was making comp—complications for everybody."

"Nate," Roselynn said hurriedly, "I'm sure that's not true."

"Yes, it is, Gram. I was in the hallway and I listened to them talking."

Tess sighed. "You know you shouldn't—"

"I *have* to listen! If I don't, nobody tells me anything. Like, about my daddy." She held such a grip on her fork, her knuckles turned pure white.

Tess's face paled to nearly the same shade. "Nate—"

"Everything's your fault!"

"Hold it," Caleb said. He couldn't let Tess take the brunt of Nate's anger. Now it *was* his place to speak up. "That's no way to talk to your mama. Let's try an apology."

The look Tess gave him would have made a better man turn tail and run.

Roselynn, about to reach for a platter, sat back empty-handed.

Nate looked from him to Tess. Carefully, she set her fork on her plate. "I'm sorry. May I be excused?"

"Yes, you may," Tess said.

"From the table," he added. "If you ask me, Nate, your bad manners are another story."

For a second, he'd have sworn her dark eyes shone with tears. Then she blinked and the image disappeared. "You sound just like Mom."

No one said a word as she shoved her chair backward, the legs screeching against the wood floor. She stood and pushed the chair up to the table, then looked at him again.

He waited for her to raise her jaw. She didn't. His

hopes took a sudden leap. Maybe sounding like her mama had earned him a mark on the good side of his tally.

"I'm sorry for my bad manners, too," she said.

He nodded and tried a half smile. "Glad to hear it."

She smiled slightly in return. After taking one last, quick look at her mama, she turned away from the table.

"Don't go off too far, sugar," Roselynn said. "We promised Becky we'd bring over those books of yours, remember? Just give me a bit to get the dishes cleared up."

Tess rose and took the platter from Roselynn's hand. "You two go ahead. Caleb and I will take care of things."

He raised his brows. Helping with repairs around here didn't bother him. But when had he gotten nominated to do housework?

"Are you sure?" Roselynn asked.

Tess nodded, her mouth set in a grim line. "Oh, I'm sure. We've got a lot to clear up. Besides dishes." She grabbed a serving bowl, too, and stalked out of the room.

Roselynn sat wearing her pitying expression again.

"Oh, boy," Nate mumbled, her eyes wide. "Maybe you shoulda asked to be excused, too."

The image of Caleb sitting at the table smiling at Nate, of Nate smiling back at him, had filled Tess with dismay. But now, as she rinsed dishes in the kitchen sink, her hands shook from a very different reason.

After Roselynn and Nate had left the house a short while ago, she'd gone into the dining room to continue clearing the table, only to discover Caleb had conveniently disappeared, too. If he thought his absence from the kitchen would save him, he'd have to think again.

She couldn't understand what had led her to behave the way she had these past couple of days. She had given in to his determination to tell Nate the truth. She had felt compassion when she'd seen how much Nate's rejection had hurt him. And she had kept up appearances as well as she could since then, even though she'd wanted to do nothing but take Nate and run with her as far away as she could.

But now this!

The way he'd stepped between her and Nate enraged her. All through these weeks, he'd seen how rebellious Nate was, how hard to handle at times. Didn't he know what his involvement would do to Nate? It would only confuse her. Only make it more difficult for her to understand after he'd left her.

After he'd left them both.

Behind her, she heard heavy bootsteps on the kitchen floor. She whirled from the sink, heedless of the water she'd sprayed across the counter, and faced him.

"How could you do that?" she demanded.

"What?"

Gritting her teeth, she grabbed a dish towel to dry her hands. "Don't give me that. You know what. How could you discipline my daughter in front of me? What makes you think you have that right?"

"I'm her daddy."

"No, you are not. Not in the ways that count." To her horror, her voice broke. She clenched her fists and pushed on. "You haven't been her daddy from day one."

"And whose fault is that?" He crossed the kitchen and snatched the dish towel from her hands, slammed it down on the counter. "Quit worrying that damn towel, Tess, or you'll have it in shreds. And start making some sense. You never gave me a chance to be Nate's daddy. You never even told me you were pregnant."

"I tried to tell you. When I found you outside Gallup. That day I had to track you down." Suddenly, she realized her anger was less about his interference with their daughter and more about his indifference to her. About the way he'd tossed her aside. But she couldn't seem to stop her words, to keep the bitterness from her voice. Or the images from her mind.

"You don't remember anything about that day, do you?" she demanded. "How you were so eager to leave your one-horse town and the one-horse people in it. So eager to run into that arena to claim your trophy. Or your new belt buckle." Tears blurred her vision, threatening to spill. "Whatever it was, you got it. I just hope it was worth what you gave up."

She attempted to rush past him, but he reached out, catching her around the waist and turning her to face him. Her chest heaved with her ragged breaths as she fought for control. She could see him breathing unsteadily, too. Could see his eyes light with an emotion she couldn't name.

"Yeah, I remember," he said, his voice low. "I acted like a jackass. But that's not what all this is about, is it?" he demanded. "I said it to you the first night I came back here. You'll never let me off the hook for leaving."

"Well, all right," she cried, reaching down, intending to push his arm away, "give the man a prize."

"I'll take it," he said.

She froze, confused. "What are you talking about?"

"You just offered me a prize. And I know what I want."

Her hand clamped involuntarily on his forearm. Her heart beat faster.

"You said it yourself, I'm leaving soon." He tucked his finger under her chin and with gentle pressure tipped her face up to his. He leaned down, leaving her no choice but to make eye contact with him.

In truth, she couldn't have looked away.

He waited the space of several heartbeats, then to her shock, he dropped his hand and stepped back.

Her hand fell to her side. Her heart raced. The pulse in her neck thudded against her skin. She'd barely regained control of her breath and he'd stolen it away again.

"Before I leave here, I want what you had for ten years and never gave me," he said, everything—his eyes, his face, his tone—hard and uncompromising. "I want time with Nate."

He turned and walked out of the kitchen without a backward glance, as if aware of how thoroughly he'd unsettled her. As if certain she wouldn't say a word.

As if knowing she couldn't refuse him.

She reached unseeingly toward a chair at the table and dropped into it.

He had forced the issue with Nate, and the damage had been done. If her daughter were an infant, a toddler, too young to understand, the situation would be different. She could get away with telling Caleb to leave and never come back.

But Nate was a rebellious preteen with a mind and a will of her own. And she now knew Caleb was her daddy.

Tess gulped a mouthful of air, exhaled it on a long, shaky breath. No, she couldn't refuse Caleb. She wouldn't be able to live with herself if she forced him to walk away and break her daughter's heart.

The question was, would she be able to protect her own heart when he finally went off on his own again?

These past weeks had taught her another truth she wanted to ignore. That kiss they'd shared in his truck had opened her eyes to the possibility. Her compassion for him in the face of Nate's rejection reinforced the feeling. And the way she'd responded just moments ago, when she thought he was going to kiss her, turned that feeling into fact.

If the time had come for telling truths, she had to be honest about it. Finally. Not with him. She could never share it with Caleb. But she couldn't keep lying to herself.

She'd never gotten over him.

Worse, that kiss, that compassion, that moment of breathless anticipation, the yearning she couldn't deny—they all made her hope that, despite everything, Caleb's determination to get to know their daughter would bring them together again, too.

Chapter 17

Caleb stretched his bad leg sideways on the porch swing and looked over at Nate, who'd already settled into roughly the same position on the top porch step.

Another week had passed. Phone calls from Montana made him feel pressured to get back home. Still, he stayed. He had important business here, too.

He'd tried to prepare Nate for his leaving, but she hadn't taken it well. He couldn't walk out on her right away.

Just yesterday, he and Tess had taken care of the paperwork for the property he'd agreed to buy. Knowing how much she and Dana needed the income, he couldn't resent the purchase. And he would find some way of making the investment pay off.

A good part of his time, he'd helped out with repairs around the inn and painting that room Roselynn needed done.

As the week had gone by, he'd continued to stop in often at the Double S to visit with Dori and Manny. He'd kept in touch with Sam and Ben and with others in town, too. It felt good to know he could talk to them all without that chip on his shoulder.

Resentment weighed him down only when he talked to Tess.

Along with their business discussions, they'd managed to have a few amicable conversations. Somehow, he'd handled the constant temptation to touch her without giving in. But he'd started getting cramps in his fingers from clenching them into fists when she came anywhere close to him.

Better to keep from spending time alone with her, to have Roselynn and Nate around—and Ellamae, when she dropped in. Safety in numbers.

He wouldn't have to worry about that tonight. Tess had just gone upstairs to get ready for another date with good old Joe. The best thing, all around.

He looked over at Nate again. They'd made peace on Signal Street during the Fourth of July parade. For the price of a double-dip ice-cream cone.

Well, a sort of peace, and probably as close as they could have come then. But he continued to work at it and had felt gratified to see he'd made real progress.

Every day, he managed some time alone with her. Nothing special, just having her help while he made his repairs. Playing cards and checkers after supper. Relaxing with her outside, where he took his usual seat here on the swing and she settled onto her favorite spot on the step.

"You want grape or lime?" she asked, holding up a couple of wrapped candies.

"Lime." He pretended not to notice her relief. He'd already figured out she liked the grape-flavored best.

She got up to give him his candy, then returned to her seat. "Gram sure has lots of stuff for you to do around here."

He nodded. "She sure does. Good thing I have a great assistant."

She gave him a smile. She hadn't warmed up to him enough to reach her previous level yet. Maybe she never would. Fine by him—he didn't want the hero worship, the adoration, the crush. What he did want…he had no right to expect.

Plenty of times, he'd found her eyeing him as if she'd been trying to figure out what made him tick. She sat watching him that way now. He waited, knowing that sooner or later she'd come out with whatever she had on her mind.

This porch was the place they did most of their talking.

And the place he did a lot of his thinking whenever he found time hanging heavy. He tried not to let that happen often. Didn't want to risk getting too deep into his troubled thoughts.

"Before," Nate said suddenly, "did you ever wish you had kids?"

He froze in the act of rubbing his knee. She hadn't called him by name since the day he'd told her he was her daddy. But she'd asked a slew of intense questions about his relationship with her mama, his life on the circuit, and what he'd done since he couldn't ride.

With all those questions this week, she'd never brought up anything like this. He knew where she had to be headed.

"You know," he said, "I never did wish for kids, Nate. Never thought I'd have a family." Never wanted one. But he couldn't be that blunt.

That night around the fire ring at Sam's place, when she had asked him why he looked so sad, he hadn't known what to say. So he'd come up with something else. In all the time he'd thought about it since, he still didn't know how he'd find the right words.

He couldn't tell a nine-year-old anything he'd thought about while sitting in front of that fire. How his own mama had told him straight out he was nothing but a burden to her. Nothing but deadweight dragging her down.

That's the kind of family he knew about.

He couldn't give her an honest answer about that. He didn't want to talk about his past at all with Nate. With anyone. Yet with the truth he'd revealed to her just a week or so ago, how could he not tell her something about his life, too?

"Growing up," he began slowly, "I didn't have much of a family."

"You didn't?"

"No. No brothers or sisters. No cousins."

"Like me."

He nodded. He'd had no father, either. Like her, too.

Tess had shown him a photo album filled with pictures. Of herself and Roselynn and Ellamae. Of Sam and Paul and Dana and of other folks from town.

And of Nate. Lots of pictures of Nate, showing how she'd grown and changed through the years.

He clenched his jaw so hard, the candy split in two. He should've been here for her. He should've been her daddy all along.

A movement through the screened door caught his eye. Tess stood in the entrance hall, looking down at Nate's bent head.

Unaware of her mama's presence, she tugged at the lace on her sneaker. "I guess I'll never have brothers and sisters." Before he could think of what to say, she took a deep breath and added, "Why can't you stay here?"

His turn for a deep breath, one he let out by degrees. "I told you the other day, Nate," he said softly. "I have a ranch to run—in Montana. I'll have to go back there sometime soon. But you'll get to visit. I promised you that, remember?"

"Uh-huh."

She kept fiddling with her sneaker, refusing to meet his eyes. He could feel Tess's gaze on him now. He kept his focus on Nate.

"So," she continued, "when you go there, are you ever coming here again?"

"Of course I am." But no matter how many times he returned, he would never get back all he'd missed.

He couldn't escape the irony of the situation. Or the parallel between this conversation and those he'd had in past weeks with Tess.

"It's just a quick plane ride," he told Nate. "Montana's not that far away."

"It's far. I looked it up on the computer." She shot to her feet.

He glanced toward the door. Tess no longer stood in the entry.

Nate bolted into the house and yanked the door so roughly, it bounced before slamming shut. The quick slap of her sneakers told him she was running.

"Nate, stop," Tess said from inside the house.

The sound of running steps continued.

As he reached the door, she spoke again. "Anastasia Lynn La—"

"Don't call me that!" Nate shrieked. "My name shoulda been *Cantrell!*"

Her cheeks flushed beet-red, she stood near the stairs and stared back in their direction. Tess had frozen just beside the doorway, her face drained of any color at all.

He stepped into the house, closed the door gently and looked from one to the other of them.

"Nate," he said, "don't be in such a hurry to take on my name. Your own's got a lot more going for it."

She looked down at the toes of her sneakers.

"And," he added, "don't be so quick to sass your mama. She doesn't deserve that kind of talk from you."

There was a lot more Tess didn't deserve.

Roselynn entered the hall from the doorway into the dining room. Her eyes widened when she saw the three of them standing motionless. "What's all this? Tess, did you let Caleb and Nate know supper's waiting? Isn't anyone planning to come eat?"

"I told them," Tess said. "I'm leaving now. Joe just pulled up." She slipped past him and through the doorway without a backward glance. In a hurry to go meet the man. Well, she'd be better off with Harley.

Roselynn turned and went into the dining room again.

Caleb hesitated, then looked toward the stairs.

Nate had disappeared from sight.

He swallowed a taste of guilt more bitter than that lime candy he'd crunched to shards.

Nothing but a burden to me. Nothing but deadweight dragging me down.

His own mama had said that about him, and he hadn't wanted to hear the words. Hadn't wanted to believe them. But he couldn't deny how well they now applied to his relationship with Tess.

Showing up here had done nothing but cause more trouble for her with Nate.

They'd both be better off with him gone.

"Joe," Tess said quietly. She sat in the passenger seat of his car as he drove her home from their date. Early. "I hope you can understand."

"Of course I can, Tess. Come on, now. It's not like I'm just some stranger walking in on this."

"I know. You've always been there for me."

"And your heart's always been with Caleb." He shrugged, his eyes on the road. "Even before you told me tonight, I knew I'd lost my chance."

"I'm sorry."

And she was. Yet her thoughts had already made the leap across town to the Whistlestop.

It had been a crazy week.

Caleb had received what he'd asked for, the chance to get to know Nate better. With her explosion tonight, he might have gotten more than he'd expected.

She would have to talk to Nate in the morning. Not to scold her. How could she scold her daughter, when she felt the same way?

Her name should have been Cantrell, too.

She'd gotten what she'd hoped for, also, the chance to get closer to Caleb. The purchase of the property had given them a lot to discuss, but they'd found other things to talk about, as well.

In silence, Joe turned the corner onto Signal Street.

She couldn't drag her thoughts from Caleb.

Seeing his concern over Nate, watching how much time they'd spent together, she had to believe her hopes would come true. That the temporary agreement she and Caleb had come to for their daughter's sake would lead to a permanent reunion for them.

She and Joe rode the final blocks in silence. When he pulled over to the curb, she could see Caleb in the swing on the front porch. He sat staring out at Signal Street, his expression brooding.

She fumbled for the door handle. "I'll see you at the store, Joe."

"Tess." When she turned to look at him, he reached over and took her hand. "Just so you know, those times I asked you to marry me, that was me talking, nobody else. I asked because I wanted to."

Emotion clogged her throat. She simply nodded and squeezed his fingers. On the sidewalk, she waited until he'd driven away before turning to walk up the path.

After taking a deep breath and letting it out slowly, she climbed the steps and took the empty half of the swing. Caleb said nothing. After a while, she asked, "How was Nate at suppertime?"

"She didn't show."

She sighed. "I'll speak to her. She needs to apologize. And I owe you an explanation."

"You don't owe me anything."

"Yes, I do. For why I never contacted you later, to tell you about Nate."

He didn't respond.

She licked her suddenly dry lips, then went on, "I told you about my grandfather, how he felt about my going to school. He was strict and hard and unyielding about everything, and I knew if he found out about us, he'd take that away. I made you keep our relationship a secret because I was afraid of that. Afraid of him."

He continued to stare out at the street.

She sagged back against the swing, knowing she faced the most difficult part of her story now. "After Nate came, I didn't try to contact you, either. Granddad wasn't happy about my having a baby, but he knew I was dependent on him." He didn't like that, either, but that wasn't something Caleb ever needed to know. "To give him credit, he took care of me and Nate when she came along. And I was afraid of doing anything to upset that. Anything that would get me into trouble."

He rose from his seat and moved to lean up against the post near the stairs where Nate always sat. "You'd already wound up 'in trouble.'"

The words hung between them for a long moment.

Finally, she nodded, knowing what he meant by the emphasis. "When I first found out I was pregnant, I didn't dare tell anyone. My mother's never been good about keeping things from me…most of the time. She tells Aunt El everything, too. And," she said grimly, "Aunt El's so blunt, she would have told Granddad he drove me to it—and then expect him to accept the news calmly because she was the one who delivered it."

"So you came looking for me."

She nodded again, knowing there was nothing else she could add. He knew the rest.

"I didn't do right by you, Tess. I *am* sorry about that. There's not much I can do about what happened back then. No way we can go back in time."

She held her breath. This was nothing like that throwaway apology he had made the first night they'd seen each other again. The crack in his voice, the shadows in his eyes told her he meant what he'd said. He regretted what happened between them. Maybe even wished, as she did, that they'd always been together.

"I'll do something now," he said.

His determination brought tears to her eyes. Her heart raced, making her pulse flutter. She rose from the swing, began to reach out, but he looked away.

She stood frozen. Then she let her hands fall to her sides.

"Tomorrow," he said, "I'll head back home."

She managed to choke off the cry that rose to her throat. In that one flat statement, he'd shattered all her hopes. Again.

The screened door creaked open, breaking the silence.

Nate stepped out onto the porch. Her eyes were huge and shining and her lips trembled, and Tess longed to reach out to hug her the way she'd wanted to do with Caleb.

But he had already moved across the porch and put his hand on Nate's shoulder.

Nate blinked rapidly and bent her head.

"I'm sorry I was never a part of your life," he said softly, then glanced at Tess. "And I'm sorry I wasn't there for you."

"Me, too," Nate said, staring at her sneakers. "And I'm sorry I listened again. It was just for a minute. I *had* to."

Shaking his head, he looked down at her. He smiled with such tenderness, Tess now could not hold back a small sob.

Nate lifted her jaw to that rebellious angle Tess knew

so well. "I heard what you told Mom," she said, her words tumbling together, "and I know you're gonna leave. I want to go, too. I want to live in Montana with you."

Chapter 18

"Go to sleep, now," Tess said.

After she had coaxed Nate upstairs again, it had taken a long while to settle her down enough to get ready for bed.

"But—"

"I told you, honey," she said gently, "we'll all have a lot of talking to do in the morning. And, Nate," she added, forcing more firmness into her tone, "remember what else I told you. Nothing good will come of it if I find you out of your room and anywhere you shouldn't be tonight."

"I know," Nate mumbled, dragging the sheet up almost over her head. "And I said I'm sorry I listened again."

Torn between tears and a smile, Tess leaned down to kiss her forehead. "I'll see you in the morning."

She closed the bedroom door quietly behind her.

As she went down the stairs, she cringed, knowing she hadn't been entirely truthful with Nate. Yes, they would talk in the morning. But by then, the important things would have been said.

She could understand Nate's feelings at the thought that Caleb planned to go off and leave her. How could she not understand, when she'd once suffered through the experience herself? When she'd dreaded it happening once more?

But she'd learned something tonight, with Caleb's announcement. While the thought of losing him again had broken her heart, too, this time she was strong enough to handle it.

The idea of losing her daughter was a whole other subject.

For the second time in her life, Tess was going to take a stand against a man who wanted to force her into a situation she wouldn't accept. And now, it wasn't just her own future at stake, but her daughter's.

Caleb was about to find out just how rebellious *she* could be.

She marched into the living room, where he sat on the couch staring down at a magazine.

She tossed the afghan from the rocker onto the ottoman and took a seat. She didn't need anything to hold on to now—but her temper.

"Caleb, I haven't said this to Nate, but I'm saying it to you. You told her you were sorry you weren't part of her life, and you seemed sincere about it. I'm glad to know that. I'm sorry for the way things worked out for all three of us—though you had a lot to do with that." She paused, pressed her lips together for a long moment, then went on. "I had a lot to do with it, too." Clamping her hands on the rocker's arms, she struggled to keep her voice calm. And failed miserably. "I don't care how much you regret not being around for Nate. You'll never be able to make up for lost time with her. It's gone. Just as you'll be gone, as of tomorrow. But you are *not* taking her with you."

She stared him down, daring him to argue.

He looked back at her for a long time, his green eyes glowing in the light from the table lamp. Finally, he said simply, "Of course not."

She blinked. "Just like that?"

"Yeah, just like that. I don't want Nate with me."

His arrogant tone, so like her grandfather's, stunned her. His careless attitude made her heart hurt. And as irrational as it might be, as a mother she felt overwhelmed by the need to rage at him for the cruelty of his words. How dare he dismiss Nate so coldly?

"You must have one hell of an opinion of me, Tess, if you think I'd take a nine-year-old away from her mama." He laughed just as arrogantly as he'd spoken, and she realized his attitude had been directed at her, not Nate. He rose from the couch. "Good night."

He turned to leave the room. She did nothing to stop him. There was nothing she could do to make the situation any better. Saying anything at all might make things worse.

Nate would stay here with her. That had to be enough.

She had gotten what she'd wanted.

And lost the dream she'd unknowingly been holding on to since the day Caleb had left Flagman's Folly years ago.

* * *

Caleb had put a good number of miles behind him before the sun sent even a glimmer into his rearview mirror. He'd wanted to be away from the inn and out of town long before anyone else was up.

After he'd left Tess in the living room last night, he'd knocked first on Roselynn's door and then on Nate's to say his farewells. Better to do it right away than wait till morning.

Easier than running into Tess again.

Roselynn took the news hard, but he told her she hadn't seen the last of him. He'd be back. He just didn't say when.

Nate stared at him, blinking away tears she wouldn't let fall, and near broke his heart. He tucked her in and kissed her forehead and said goodbye. He told her the same things he'd told Roselynn, but unlike her gram, Nate didn't accept his word. She wouldn't let him leave her room until he'd made promises. So he'd made them, wondering how many he could keep.

Tess...

He didn't want to think about Tess. To think she could even suggest he'd take Nate away from her. It proved how little respect she had for him.

About as much as he had for himself.

He gripped the steering wheel and squinted through the windshield. Now, away from the inn and Flagman's Folly, he could finally get some perspective. And he didn't like what he saw.

The road ahead of him was bare. Empty. At the end of it he would find the airport and the flight home to his ranch in Montana.

Behind him lay the only things that really mattered.

Flagman's Folly itself, the place where he'd found acceptance from folks. Where he'd had it all along, no matter what he'd told himself over the years.

Roselynn and Ellamae, two women who looked out for his interests, something his own mama had never done.

Nate, the daughter who cared about him even though he'd never been a daddy to her.

And Tess.

Again, he didn't want to think about Tess, but he had to face the truth. To admit she had good reason for feeling the way she did about him.

Yet she'd never given him a chance to make peace with her.

With that thought, he acknowledged what he hadn't been able to admit before. What he couldn't put into words even now.

And with that thought, he also knew he couldn't go.

For better or for worse, he had to tell Tess how he felt. He had to hope she could find it in her heart to let him make up for his past mistakes.

Leaving the bare road ahead, he gunned the engine and swung the truck in a tight, hard U-turn. A loud thump sounded from the back of the truck, and he muttered under his breath. He'd forgotten about his suitcase.

But suitcases didn't yell "Ow!"

He pulled to the side of the road and parked with his flashers going. After he'd walked around to the back of the truck, he rested his crossed arm on the edge of the tailgate and waited.

When he had put the suitcase into the truck bed that morning, he'd seen the tarps he had tossed in there after he'd finished painting and then had forgotten to bring them back to Sam. He'd shrugged, figuring he would have the car rental place get rid of them. Sam wouldn't lose sleep over a couple of drop cloths.

Now a pair of hands crept out from the edge of a tarp and pushed it aside. Nate sat up and stared at him.

"Good morning," he said. "How's everything?"

"Coulda been fine, except that big bag rolled over and squished me."

"Are you hurt?"

"No, I'm okay." She paused, then said tentatively, "Are you mad 'cause I'm here?"

"No. But what brings you here?"

"You did." She sounded surprised. She crawled across the truck bed over to where he still stood with his arms on the tailgate. Slowly, she rose to her knees in front of him and looked him in the eye. "I got in the truck because I didn't know what time you were leaving. Then I fell asleep."

"I told you last night," he reminded her quietly, "I can't take you with me."

"But I thought if I hid till we got to the airport, you'd have to."

"Nate…"

"Never mind." She gave a long, drawn-out sigh. "I can't go, anyway. I can't leave Becky and Gram and Aunt El. And Mom." She squinted and looked away, but not before he saw the tears filling her eyes. "I know I fight with her a lot. I'll try to get better about that. 'Cause I really need my mom." She blinked, swallowed hard and looked back at him. "But I… I need a daddy, too."

His chest tightened until he could barely breathe. He had to blink several times, himself.

He could see in Nate's eyes and face how she felt. She couldn't say the words yet, and he wouldn't, either. It was too soon for both of them.

But she loved him. As much as he loved her.

His daughter loved him. The knowledge gave him confidence even as it raised another question in his mind.

Could her mother ever love him, too?

"You look kinda funny," she said. "You sure you didn't stop the truck 'cause you're mad at me?"

"No, I'm not mad at all. I didn't know you were here."

"Then why?"

"I was headed home."

"That's why you almost killed me with that bag?"

Swallowing a laugh, he nodded.

She looked past him and then over her shoulder, east and west along the highway. Her eyes widened in astonishment. "This truck's going back to Flagman's Folly!"

"So are we, Anastasia Lynn."

"Really? Wow!" She grinned. "Okay… Daddy." She flung her arms around his neck and hugged him tight. "Let's go home."

She'd looked everywhere, and still, she couldn't find Nate.

Tess tried to stay calm, to keep from letting her mom know how upset she was. She must have succeeded, because when she went to the kitchen to share the news of Nate's disappearance, Roselynn simply gave a rueful shake of her head.

"Oh, sugar, don't fret. She's probably just run off again to Lissa's like she did the other day."

"I'm not sure about that. I imagine when Caleb told

you last night he was leaving, he stopped by Nate's room, too. I think she's run away over that, because when I went up there a couple of hours ago, she was already gone."

That got her mother's attention. *"Before 5:00 a.m.?"*

Nate never woke up that early. Tess didn't often, either, but then, she'd never gone to sleep last night. "Yes," she said, "before five."

"Have you called Dana?"

She nodded. "Nate wasn't there."

"How about the other girls?"

"I didn't want to try them too early. Besides, you know Nate would go to Lissa."

"But it's been two hours. Or more."

"I know. I'm going to call the girls after I check the house one more time, just to make sure she's not hiding somewhere." She had gotten as far as the dining room when she heard the front door open.

She hurried to the doorway and gave a sigh of relief when her daughter entered the house.

"Nate! Where in the world have you—?"

Caleb stepped into the entryway behind Nate and closed the door. He put a hand on Nate's shoulder. "She was with me."

He'd taken Nate with him, after all? Immediately, she shook her head. No, of course, he wouldn't have done that.

As if he'd read her thoughts, he said, "She stowed away in the truck."

Nate nodded emphatically. "Yeah, I hid in the back. He didn't know I was there."

As calmly as she could, Tess nodded. She and Nate would discuss her new habit of running away some other time. Right now, she felt so relieved to see her daughter, she could have cried.

But she hated herself for the briefest second of hope she'd felt when Caleb had stepped into the house. He had come back only to return Nate.

She looked at him and said stiffly, "Thank you for bringing her home."

"He was coming back, too, Mom. He turned the truck around *before* he found me."

Tess nodded again. But she couldn't read anything into that. She knew better than to believe in her dream.

"Nate," Caleb said, "your mama and I have an errand to run. Why don't you go find your gram and tell her we'll be back in an hour or so?"

"Sure."

She smiled up at him, and he ruffled her hair.

Tess had to blink away tears.

Nate crossed the entryway and almost threw her off balance with an unexpected hug. Then she slipped past her into the dining room and shouted, "Hey, Gram, what's for breakfast?"

Her voice faded, her footsteps did, too, and still Caleb stood in the doorway. "Can we talk?" he asked. "Away from here?"

Shrugging, she nodded. Talk couldn't hurt her. Not any more than she hurt already.

Chapter 19

Caleb drove down Signal Street and a good way farther, needing to pull his thoughts together.

Nate had chattered all the back to the Whistlestop, leaving him no time to figure out how to tell Tess what he needed to say. He'd never been much good at talking about things. And he'd never faced any conversation as important as this one.

In the passenger seat, Tess sat with her eyes forward and her fingers twined together in her lap.

When they reached the edge of town, he pulled to the side of the road and cut the ignition. The engine noise died, leaving nothing but silence.

He hoped this conversation wouldn't end the way their talk had finished the night before, with him vowing to leave town. He didn't know what to say to prevent that. He didn't even know where to start, except with some hard truths.

He pushed open the driver's door. "Come on, I've got something I want to show you."

When they had both exited the truck, he led her across the road, past the collection of ramshackle houses and tar-paper shacks to the place he'd once had to call home.

He'd come here again a week ago. Hard as he'd found it to believe, he'd discovered the trailer he had once lived in still sat way in the back, its rusted hulk twenty years more decrepit, its curtains hanging in shreds.

Now he stopped a few feet away from the trailer.

Tess's expression told him she wouldn't need an explanation of why he'd brought her here. Still, he needed to give one.

"This is where I come from," he said, scuffing his boot against the weed-choked ground. He looked from a broken wooden fence to the rusted trailer and then beyond them to a blue sky that went as far as his eye could see. "I couldn't wait for the day I'd leave this behind me. And the day I'd leave this town. I guess we pretty much covered that already."

"Yes," she said, so softly he could barely hear her.

"I hated Flagman's Folly and almost everyone in it. I thought folks looked down on me because I was dirt-poor and had no daddy. But mostly because of the kind of mama I had. All I could think of was getting the hell out. And then I started seeing you." He took a deep breath and let it out slowly. "This next part probably won't make a lot of sense. Back then, I'd never have brought you here, but after we'd gone together a while, I got resentful that you wouldn't take me to your house or introduce me to your family. You wouldn't even let anyone know we were going together."

"Caleb—"

"It's all right," he interrupted, knowing if he didn't get this out he might never have another chance. Or the nerve. "We covered that, too. I understand why now, but back then I didn't know. I thought you looked down on me, too. The only thing I could figure to do was prove myself to you. To everyone."

Tess moved away, and his heart seemed to lurch.

She stopped a few feet from the trailer, where some kids had piled cinder blocks together to make a small house or a fort. She sat down on one of the walls and looked at him, her expression neutral.

Seeing her settle made his heart settle down again, too.

"Once I got away from here," he continued, "my life changed. For the good. That night you came to Gallup, that night I had my first win, felt like a sign that I'd done the right thing. I'd made a start. But I knew one win wouldn't get me far. When you showed up, I was fixated on getting that trophy so I could show you what I'd done. Only I went about it like a jackass. We covered that, too."

He shoved his hands into his back pockets. The next words didn't want to come, but he had to say them. "Then you told me you were getting married. And I swear to you, Tess, nothing in my life had ever hurt that bad."

He heard her let out a half sigh but couldn't look at her. Not yet.

"I felt like I had nothing left. Nothing but the rodeo. I went on to win all those trophies and buckles you talked about. Won a lot of money, too. I had sponsors lining up to sign me, buckle bunnies hanging on my arms. They proved I was someone. Someone important. Not just Mary Cantrell's bastard son." He clenched his jaw so hard, he thought he might crack a molar or two.

"I told you—" she began.

"I know you did. Wait, please. Or I may never get to finish." He continued more slowly. "After that, I didn't think about Flagman's Folly very often. But when I got thrown from that bull and wound up in the hospital, and then all during the physical therapy at the rehab, I had a lot of thinking time on my hands. And I thought about what they'd told me—I almost didn't make it."

The memory alone made his bad knee twinge. He moved over to the steadiest-looking section of the broken wooden fence and leaned back against it. Then he slid his foot up to plant his boot flat against the post, removing some of the pressure. From his knee, not his confession.

"The doctor's news brought me up short, I tell you. Made me take a look at what I wanted to do with my life. Or what was left of it. I needed to start over again. But I knew I couldn't move forward, until I could finally shake off my past. Until I'd come back here and done what I'd sworn I'd do, show everybody I was just as good as they were." He laughed shortly. "Only, nobody appeared to think I *wasn't* just as good. They all seemed to like me fine. Dori and Manny at the Double S. Judge Baylor and your aunt, Ellamae. Sam and Ben.

"That day at Ben's, when you and Ellamae left, Judge Baylor told me I'd always had a chip on my shoulder. The more I talked to folks and saw how they acted with me, the more I realized the judge was right. But getting to know folks knocked that chip right off."

Now he could look at her again. Even from here,

he could see her eyes shining with tears. The sight almost broke him, but he couldn't go to her until he had earned the right.

"I learned something else, too. It didn't matter if I was poor or not then. It doesn't matter that I'm rich now. Folks aren't measuring my worth by my bank account but by the respect I show them. And the respect I have for myself."

He hadn't had the courage to open his heart completely to Tess until now. Watching her, he saw the dark curls he'd never been able to keep from threading his fingers through, the dark eyes he'd always loved to gaze into. Those eyes held so much more now, and so did Tess herself. An inner fire and an inner strength—both equal to the ones he'd have to draw upon now.

He braced himself, knowing he'd have to lay himself bare, tell her things he hadn't understood himself. Until today.

"Respect for myself was something I *didn't* have, till I turned that truck around this morning to come back to town today. Because I knew I wouldn't leave again without telling you the truth. About everything." He shook his head. "I'd made my peace with everyone but you. And I figured out why. I need more than just peace from you, Tess, because you mean the most to me."

Now he had to look her straight in those dark eyes when he said what came next. She sat staring at him, her lips pressed together, her hands flat against the cinder block wall.

"I ran off ten years ago, after convincing myself everyone looked down on me. I ran out on you, and you were the best thing I had in my life." His hands trembled. He rested them on the fence rail to steady himself.

"I ran out on you again today. This time, I didn't want to leave, I swear. But I thought I had to give up what I wanted—to do the right thing for you and Nate. Now I know that's not true. I should've listened to my instincts. And now I want to come back. If you'll have me."

Accepting he still couldn't go to her, knowing he wasn't done, he held on to the railing for all he was worth. Which wasn't much. And never would be, if she wouldn't take him on again.

Trying to keep herself from going to Caleb, Tess grasped the cinder blocks so tightly the rough concrete dug into her palms.

She'd seen the struggle reflected in his face, in his stance, and the depth of emotion in his eyes. She'd heard all he had said till now. Words she had always longed to hear. But did she really understand them? "You mean... you want your room back again?"

"That'll do for starters, if it's the way it has to be." He gave a half smile that made her heart beat faster. "But to be honest, I'm hoping that option won't last long at all. Because I want a permanent reservation. A place here with you. Being a husband and daddy. Everything all rolled up into one."

She opened her mouth, but before she could speak, he shook his head and moved to take a seat on the wall beside her. He studied her, his eyes clear but his expression troubled.

"Please hear me out," he continued. "I know I can't expect you to take me up on just my say-so that I'm ready now, when I wasn't before. Or that I've changed." He shook his head ruefully. "To tell you the truth, just a few weeks ago, I'd never have expected to be saying all this. And there's more."

He lifted her hand from the wall between them, rubbed his thumb across her knuckles, the way he'd always done years ago. His hand was callused now. His touch was familiar, yet changed. So were they.

"Once I got back here, at some point, I finally realized I'd come for your forgiveness. But the longer I stayed, the more I realized I hadn't earned it yet. And then I realized even more. Hard to admit," he said slowly, "but I don't think I knew the reason that mattered most until this morning when I found myself leaving you again. I love you."

His eyes brightened with the light of sincerity and hope…and something else. Her throat closed so tightly, she could barely breathe.

"I can't change what happened, Tess, and I know we've lost so much since then. But I want to make up for it. If I can."

He squinted, and the skin around his eyes crinkled. Though she couldn't see the tears in his eyes, she heard that emotion in his voice. "You're the only woman I've ever loved. The only person who gave me love unconditionally. What's more, you're real with me."

He squeezed her fingers gently, as if to prove his point, and she felt her chest tighten, too.

"Those buckle bunnies you keep talking about—all those women hanging on me for all those years. They didn't want me. They worshipped my fame and fortune, that's it. I don't want that. I want your reality. I want *you*. Now. And forever."

He released her hand and sat back, waiting.

Still, she couldn't catch her breath. Rising, she moved to lean against the fence where he'd stood previously, needing the distance from him. The perspective. Needing the railing to keep her from falling.

Not falling for Caleb's words. She didn't have any doubt of the truth of them.

Not falling down in a heap on the dusty ground. She felt stronger than she ever had in her life.

But to keep from falling into his arms.

Bowing her head, she held on to the railing, one hand on either side of her as Caleb had done.

She knew he'd said what he had to and was waiting for her to begin. So she did.

"When you left us this morning, I knew I'd be strong enough to survive it. I've grown that much since you left the first time." She gave a half laugh that sounded more like a sob. "Back then, I wasn't so sure I'd make it. When you left me, I hated you. I never wanted to see you again."

He shifted, yet made no move to come to her. She felt grateful for that.

"Then I discovered I was pregnant. When Granddad found out, eventually, he tried to force me into a marriage. I told the boy I couldn't marry him. And I've told him that every time he's asked me since."

"Harley." He spoke softly and shook his head in wonder.

She nodded.

"Good old Joe," he said with a crooked smile. "I owe that man."

She would have smiled back, if she hadn't had to brace herself for what came next. "Once Granddad put his foot down, I had nowhere else to go. Except to you." Her voice shook so badly, she needed to wait a moment before she could continue. "When you were there in that arena, with your buckle bunnies and your trophy and the announcer calling your name, something inside me snapped."

"Tess—"

Though she heard the pain in his voice, she shook her head. "No, Caleb. Not till you've heard me out. I let my pride get the best of *me* then. You didn't give me a chance to tell you about the baby. But I didn't take a stand and tell you, anyway. Instead, I came home and stood up to my grandfather, who only wanted me to get married to give the baby a name." She swallowed hard and looked at him, knowing he would see the tears in her eyes. Hoping he could see her sincerity now, too.

"That's why I told you—and how I can feel so sure it's true—that not knowing your own daddy's name doesn't matter. Nate never knew hers. That doesn't make her any less a person. Or make me love her less. I wasn't going to get married just to keep Granddad happy. Or to give our baby a name that wasn't yours."

A tear spilled down her cheek, but she couldn't reach up to brush it away. Her hands were still clamped on the fence rail. Now it *had* become the only thing holding her up.

This time, when Caleb shifted, it was to rise and cross the space between them. She felt grateful for that, too.

He thumbed away the tear that had trickled down to the corner of her mouth. His hand lingered there, brushing her jaw, tilting her chin up.

"I'm sorry," she said. "I was wrong not to tell you about the baby."

"I was wrong in a lot of ways, too. I love you, Tess. I just hope you can love me again."

"That's something else I've learned since you've come home." She smiled tentatively, trying to hold back her tears. "Even when I thought I hated you, I never stopped loving you."

He wrapped his arms around her and pulled her close, nestled her head beneath his chin. She could feel the pulse in his neck pounding and his heart thundering against hers.

They stood that way for a long time, and their heartbeats gradually returned to a steady pace. She knew she'd never been happier.

But then Caleb kissed her and said the one thing that could make her happier still. The one thing she'd hoped all these years to hear.

"Let's get married, Tess."

Once Caleb had turned away to leave the rusted shell of the trailer behind, he knew he would never go back there again. He'd never want the reminder of a life no kid should live. Never need to see the place that had made him believe he deserved less than anyone else.

When he and Tess reached the Whistlestop Inn and crossed the yard to the back porch, he had to pause for a moment to hold her close again. To take in all that he *did* deserve.

Self-respect. A home and family. Tess.

He heard the back door open.

They both turned to look.

Nate stood on the porch with her hand still on the door latch, as if unsure whether or not she should stay. "I wasn't listening," she assured them.

"We weren't saying anything," he returned.

"Yeah, I noticed. You look funny, Mom."

"I feel funny. The happy kind." Smiling, Tess squeezed his hand. "Your daddy just asked me to marry him."

Nate's eyes widened. "Really? Wow! I gotta tell Gram and Aunt El!" She bounded through the door, then stopped and turned back. "I'm coming to the wedding," she added, "but don't expect me to wear a dress."

The door slammed against the frame. They could hear her shrieking as she ran through the kitchen.

Tess laughed. "I don't know," she said, drawing the words out and shaking her head. "Are you sure you understand what you're asking? If you want reality, you'll get it here. A meddling mother-in-law and an aunt who's worse. A belligerent preteen daughter. And a wife who gets rebellious at times, too."

"Yes, I'm sure."

A flash of movement against a windowpane caught his eye. Nate and Roselynn and Ellamae had all gathered at the dining room window and stood smiling down at him.

He smiled back, then looked at Tess again. "Don't worry about me," he said. "After riding my share of angry bulls, I can handle a few ornery women."

* * * * *

After writing more than eighty books for Harlequin, **Stella Bagwell** still finds it exciting to create new stories and bring her characters to life. She loves all things Western and has been married to her own real cowboy for forty-four years. Living on the south Texas coast, she also enjoys being outdoors and helping her husband care for the horses, cats and dog that call their small ranch home. The couple has one son, who teaches high school mathematics and is also an athletic director. Stella loves hearing from readers. They can contact her at stellabagwell@gmail.com.

Books by Stella Bagwell

Harlequin Special Edition

Men of the West

The Arizona Lawman
Her Kind of Doctor
The Cowboy's Christmas Lullaby
His Badge, Her Baby... Their Family?
Her Rugged Rancher
Christmas on the Silver Horn Ranch
Daddy Wore Spurs
The Lawman's Noelle
Wearing the Rancher's Ring
One Tall, Dusty Cowboy
A Daddy for Dillon
The Baby Truth
The Doctor's Calling
His Texas Baby

Montana Mavericks: The Great Family Roundup

The Maverick's Bride-to-Order

The Fortunes of Texas: The Secret Fortunes

Her Sweetest Fortune

The Fortunes of Texas: All Fortune's Children

Fortune's Perfect Valentine

Visit the Author Profile page at Harlequin.com for more titles.

HIS TEXAS WILDFLOWER

STELLA BAGWELL

To my husband, Harrell, for all those times
he's taken me to the mall when he'd rather
have been on his horse. I love you.

Chapter 1

Rebecca Hardaway swayed slightly on her fragile high heels and for one horrifying moment she feared she was going to topple forward and straight across the silver-and-white casket suspended over the open grave.

Dear God, give me strength, she prayed as she struggled to brace her trembling legs and stop the whirling in her head. She had to be strong. If not for herself, then out of an odd respect for the person who was about to be lowered into the earth.

Up until five days ago, Rebecca hadn't even suspected she had an aunt much less known Gertrude O'Dell existed. If Gertrude herself hadn't left strict instructions with a lawyer to notify Rebecca of her demise, she doubted she'd ever have known.

When the law offices of Barnes, Bentley and Barnes had called Bordeaux's, the department store in Houston where Rebecca worked as a fashion buyer, she'd thought a coworker had been pulling a joke on her. Her mother didn't have a twin sister in New Mexico! Surely there'd been some sort of mix-up.

But shockingly, there had been no mix-up and now questions continued to tear at Rebecca. How could such a secret have been kept for so long? Why had her mother, Gwyn, done such a thing? Her father had died eighteen years ago. Had he known about Gertrude? Or had Gwyn kept her twin sister a secret from everyone?

You don't understand, Rebecca. Gertrude and I were never close. Even though we were sisters, we were very different people. She had her own life and I had mine. We chose to go our separate ways.

Her mother's lame response to Rebecca's grilling hadn't answered anything. In fact, Gwyn was still evading her daughter's questions. And each day that passed without answers filled Rebecca with more and more resentment and puzzlement. She'd thought herself alone in the world except for her mother and now she realized she'd been cheated out of the chance of knowing her aunt!

And now it was too late. Too late.

At the head of the casket, a minister finished reading the 23rd Psalm, then added a short, comforting prayer. As Rebecca whispered "Amen," she felt a strong hand cup her right elbow.

Lifting her head, she looked straight into a pair of gold-brown eyes framed by thick black lashes. The face was partially shaded by the brim of a gray cowboy hat, but she recognized the man as one of the eight people who'd seen fit to attend her aunt's simple graveside services.

"I thought you might need a little support," he said softly. "The day is hot and grief has a way of draining a person."

Grief. Oh, yes, she was feeling all kinds of grief. She'd lost more than an aunt. She'd lost the whole foundation of her family. And her mother was still evading the truth. But this man had no way of knowing that.

"Thank you," she murmured.

A few steps away, the minister concluded the services, then offered Rebecca a few consoling words before he walked away. Beside her, the young cowboy continued to hold her elbow. He was dressed in a starched white shirt and blue jeans, the creases razorsharp, the fabric carrying the faint scent of grass, sunshine and masculine muskiness. His hand was warm, the fingers wrapped against her skin, incredibly tough.

Who was this man, she wondered, and what connection did he have to Gertrude O'Dell?

"They'll be lowering the casket in a few moments," he said in a low husky voice. "Would you like one of the roses for a keepsake?"

Grateful for his thoughtfulness, she glanced at the lone spray of flowers lying upon the casket, then at him. "Yes. I would like that."

He dropped his hold on her arm and moved forward to pluck one of the long-stemmed roses from the ribbon binding. As he handed the flower to Rebecca, her throat thickened and tears rushed to her eyes.

Up until this moment, she'd not shed a tear or given way to the emotions washing over her like stormy waves. But something about this man's kindness had pricked the fragile barrier she'd tried to erect between her and the awful finality of her aunt's funeral.

"Thank you," she told him, then lifted her watery gaze from the rosebud to his face. His dark features were masculine and very striking, making the soft light in his eyes even more of a contrast. "I'm Rebecca Hardaway, Gertrude's niece. Did you know my aunt well, Mr.—" She paused as a slight blush heated her cheeks. "Uh, I'm sorry. I have to confess that I don't know any of her friends."

Once again his hand came around her elbow and with gentle urging, he moved her away from the casket and over to the limp shade of a lone mesquite tree. "My name is Jake Rollins," he told her. "And I'm sorry to say I didn't know your aunt personally. I only saw her from time to time as I drove by her place. I came to the funeral today—well, because I thought she might like having someone say goodbye to her."

"Oh."

The tears in her eyes spilled onto her cheeks and she wiped helplessly at them with the pads of her fingertips. He pulled a white handkerchief from his back pocket and offered it to her.

She thanked him, then used the soft cotton to dab at the tracks of moisture on her cheeks. While she tried to gather herself together, she was keenly aware of his broad frame, the way his brown eyes were studying her. There had to be a lot of compassion in this man, she thought, for him to attend the funeral of a person he'd not really known.

He began to speak. "My friends, the Cantrells—the people I'm here with—own a ranch just west of your aunt's place. It's called Apache Wells. Maybe Gertie mentioned it to you?"

She shook her head. She didn't know how to explain to this man that she'd never spoken to Gertrude O'Dell. Never met her. It was all so unbelievable, yet terribly true. "I'm afraid not. But I do thank you and your friends for coming today. I—well, if it weren't for you and your friends, there would have been only a handful of people here to see her laid to rest."

Faint cynicism quirked his lips. "People nowadays tell themselves they don't have time to go to funerals. If I were you, I wouldn't worry myself over the lack of mourners."

Interest suddenly sparked in her misty blue eyes. "You called my aunt Gertie," she asked. "Is that how people around here knew her?"

Jake tried not to appear stunned as he studied the beautiful woman standing before him. This couldn't be Crazy Gertie's niece, he thought. The old woman had been a recluse who'd always been dressed in old clothing and was known for firing a shotgun at anyone she didn't deem welcome on her land. Rebecca Hardaway was the complete opposite. She looked exactly like one of those women whose photographs filled a fashion magazine.

She was wearing a black dress that hugged her slender hips and draped demurely across her breasts. Her high heels were just that—high. With little straps that fastened around her shapely ankles. A black straw hat with a wide brim and a band swathed with white chiffon covered her pale blond hair and framed a set of pale, delicate features. Her lips were red and so were her short fingernails. And even with her blue eyes filled with tears, all Jake could think was that she was one classy chick.

"Well, I'm not exactly sure about that," he said.

"We—Abe, old Mr. Cantrell that is—always called her Gertie. I imagine that's what her friends called her, too."

Everyone around here had assumed Gertie had no family. Down through the years no one had witnessed any outsiders visiting. In fact, Jake figured he'd fudged when he'd pluralized the word *friend*. The only person who'd had much contact with the woman at all was Bess, an older lady who worked in a small grocery store in Alto. A moment ago Jake had seen her climb into her car and drive away from the cemetery. If Rebecca wanted information about Gertie, then Bess would be her best source.

"I see," she murmured.

At that moment, she glanced over her shoulder just in time to see the coffin being lowered into the ground. Sensing the sight was cutting into her, Jake moved the two of them a few more steps away from the grave site and did his best to distract her. "Did you make the trip here by yourself?" he asked.

"Yes. I live in Houston and—there was no one available to make the trip with me."

No family, husband, boyfriend? Even though Jake had already glanced at her left hand in search of a wedding ring, he found himself looking again at the empty finger. It was hard to believe a beautiful woman like her wasn't attached. And if she was, what kind of man would have allowed her to travel all this way to attend such an emotional ceremony by herself?

"That's too bad," he said. "You shouldn't be alone at a time like this."

She drew back her shoulders as though to prove more to herself than him that she wasn't about to break down. "Sometimes a person has no other choice but to be alone, Mr. Rollins."

His lips twisted to a wry slant. Women had called him plenty of things down through the years, but never Mr. Rollins. "I'm just Jake to you, ma'am." He tilted his head in the direction of the Cantrell family, then suggested, "Let me introduce you to my friends."

"I'd like that," she murmured.

For May in Lincoln County, New Mexico, the sun was hot in the cloudless sky. Every now and then a faint breeze rustled the grass in the meadow next to the lonely little cemetery and carried the scent of Rebecca Hardaway straight to Jake's nostrils. She smelled like crushed wildflowers after a rainstorm. Sweet and fresh and tempting.

Forget it, Jake. She's not your kind of woman. So just rein in that roaming eye of yours.

By now Abe, Quint and Maura had gathered near the wrought-iron gate that framed the exit to the cemetery. As Jake and Rebecca Hardaway approached the group, Maura, a pretty young woman with dark red hair, was the first to greet them. Quint, a tall handsome guy who was the same age as Jake, followed close behind his wife. Next to him, Abe moved to join the group. The elderly man was somewhat shorter than his grandson and rail-thin. His thick hair was white as snow and matched the drooping walrus mustache that covered his top lip. Abe was a legendary cattle rancher of the area and Quint was quickly following in his footsteps. Both men were like family to Jake.

Quickly, he made introductions all around and had barely gotten the last one out of his mouth before Maura reached for Rebecca's hand.

"You must be awfully weary, Ms. Hardaway," she said gently. "We'd love for you to join us at Apache Wells for refreshments. That is, if you don't have other plans."

Gertie's niece glanced at Jake as though she wanted his opinion about the invitation. The idea took him by surprise. A fancy woman like her had never asked him for the time of day. But then he had to remember that Rebecca Hardaway was obviously under a heavy weight of grief and probably not herself.

"Well, I don't know," she said hesitantly. "I wouldn't want to be a bother."

"Nonsense, young lady," Abe spoke up. "We always have the coffeepot on. And everybody's welcome. We'd enjoy having you."

Rebecca smiled at the old man, which was hardly a surprise to Jake. Even though Abe was in his mid-eighties, Quint's grandfather hadn't lost his charm with the ladies. What did surprise him was how the tilt of the woman's lips warmed her, made her appear all too soft and touchable.

"Thank you, sir," she said to Abe. "It would be nice to have a little rest before I drive back to Ruidoso."

"Great," Maura chimed in. "Just leave your car here and ride with us. The roads might be too rough for your rental car. Someone will bring you back to pick it up."

"That's kind of you," Rebecca told her. "Especially since I—well, I'm not sure I'm up to driving at the moment."

Quint suggested it was time to get out of the hot sun and be on their way. Jake didn't waste time helping Rebecca over to the truck and into the front passenger seat.

She gave him demure thanks, but no smile and as

Jake climbed into the back bench seat next to Abe, he wondered what the old man had that he didn't.

Hell, Jake. If you want a woman to smile at you all you have to do is drive down to Ruidoso and saunter into the Blue Mesa for a cup of coffee or the Starting Gate for a cold beer. There were plenty of women around those hangouts who would be more than happy to smile at you.

Yeah, Jake mentally retorted to the cynical voice in his head. He knew plenty of women who were willing to give him whatever he wanted, whenever he wanted. But none of them were like Rebecca Hardaway. And if any of them were like her, he'd steer clear. He was a simple man with simple taste, he told himself. If a man understood his limitations, he was more likely to avoid trouble.

And yet as Quint guided the club cab truck over the dusty road, Jake's gaze continued to drift to the back of Rebecca Hardaway's head. Once she'd gotten settled in the leather seat, she'd removed her hat and now as she turned her head slightly to the left to acknowledge something that Quint was saying, he could see a drape of fine blond hair near her eyebrow and wispy curls tousled upon her shoulder. The strands were subtly shaded and obviously natural.

There was nothing fake about Rebecca Hardaway, he thought. At least, not on the outside. As for the inside, he'd have to guess at that. Because there was no way in hell she'd ever give a working man like him a glimpse.

Abe's cattle ranch, Apache Wells, consisted of more than a hundred thousand acres and had been in existence long before either Jake or Quint had been born. The property was only one of many the old man owned and though he was rich, Abe lived in a modest log house nestled at the edge of a piney foothill.

Once inside the cool interior, Maura and Quint quickly excused themselves to the kitchen to prepare refreshments. While Rebecca took a seat on a long couch, Abe settled himself in a worn leather recliner and Jake stood to one side trying to decide if he should escape to the kitchen with his friends or take advantage of these few minutes with the Texas wildflower.

"Don't just stand there, Jake. Sit down," Abe practically barked at him. "You're makin' me tired just lookin' at you."

Stifling a sigh, Jake pulled off his hat and carried it over to the opposite end of the couch from where Rebecca was sitting.

As he sank onto the cushion, and placed his hat on the floor near his boots, he said, "Sorry, Abe. I was thinking I should go help Maura and Quint. But I guess they can manage without me."

"Sure they can," Abe replied. "Besides, I need you to help me entertain Ms. Hardaway."

Since when did Abe need help entertaining a woman? Jake thought wryly, but he kept the comment to himself.

"Oh, please. You don't have to make conversation for my sake," Rebecca spoke up. "Just sitting here in the cool is nice and restful."

She'd leaned her head against the back of the couch and crossed her legs. From the corner of his eye, Jake let his gaze wander down the length of shapely calf and on to the delicate ankle. Like the black leather strap of her high heel, he could easily imagine his thumb and forefinger wrapped around her smooth ankle and tugging her toward him.

Jake's thoughts were turning downright indecent when Abe spoke up and interrupted them.

"I'm right sorry about Gertie, Ms. Hardaway. She wasn't an easy person to know, you understand. She liked her privacy and I respected that. As neighbors we got along. 'Cause we didn't bother each other—just exchanged a few words from time to time." He wiped a thumb and forefinger down his long white mustache. "She was way too young to leave this world."

"Yes. She was only fifty-six. But she…suffered from some sort of heart condition." At least, that was what Gertrude's lawyer had explained to Rebecca about the cause of her death.

"That's too bad," Abe replied. "Could be that's why she didn't socialize. Guess she didn't feel like it."

Rebecca's gaze dropped to her lap. Was the old man trying to say in a nice way that Gertrude O'Dell had been a recluse? If so, he was probably also wondering why Rebecca or other relatives hadn't been around to visit or check on the woman. Oh, God, the whole situation was so awful. She didn't want to explain to these people that for some reason her family had been split down the middle. She didn't want them to know that her own mother had refused to attend her sister's funeral. It was embarrassing and demeaning.

"Well, I wouldn't exactly say that, Abe," Jake countered. "Gertie visited some with Bess."

Rebecca looked at the cowboy named Jake. Without his hat, she could see his hair was thick and lay in unruly waves about his head and against the back of his neck. It was the color of dark chocolate and even though the lighting in the room was dim, the strands gleamed like a polished gem. As her gaze encompassed his broad shoulders and long, sinewy legs, she decided he was a man of strength. No doubt he worked out of doors. With his hands and all those muscles.

She swallowed uncomfortably, then asked, "Who is Bess?"

"Gertie's friend," he answered. "She was the older woman at the funeral. She left the cemetery before we had a chance to introduce you. I guess she must have been in a hurry for some reason."

"Oh. Yes." Rebecca vaguely remembered an older, heavyset woman dressed in a simple print dress standing on the opposite side of Gertrude's coffin. "I would have liked to have met her. And thank her for coming to the services."

"I'm sure Jake can make that happen for you," Abe said. "He knows where everybody works and lives. He gets around."

Rebecca didn't find that hard to believe. Even though she didn't know him, Jake Rollins looked like a man who would never have a problem socializing. At least, with the female population.

He had that rangy, rascally look. The sort that tugged at a woman's dreams, that made her want to learn how it felt to be just a little naughty, a bit wild and reckless.

Had Gertrude ever had those womanly feelings? Rebecca wondered. Had her aunt ever looked at a man like Jake and wondered what it would be like to make love to him? To have him make love to her?

From all appearances, Gertrude had died a spinster. And at the rate Rebecca was going, the same was going to happen to her. Men were drawn to her, but they didn't stick around for long. Once a guy learned she enjoyed her demanding career, he chose to move on and find a woman who could devote her time solely to him.

Rebecca was doing her best to push those thoughts away when Quint and Maura entered the room with a tray of refreshments. And thankfully for the next half hour, the conversation moved away from Gertrude O'Dell's untimely departure, and on to the daily happenings of these people who had chosen to show her a bit of hospitality and kindness.

While Rebecca sipped iced tea and nibbled on a sugar cookie, she learned that Maura and Quint had been married for nearly two and a half years and had two young sons, the latter of which had been born only a few months ago. Abe was a widower and had been for nearly twenty years. As for Jake, she could only assume he was a single man. During the conversation he didn't mention family of any sort and there definitely wasn't a ring on his finger. At the cemetery when he'd handed her his handkerchief, she'd noticed that much about him. But it wasn't the lack of a wedding band, or the mention of family, that told Rebecca he was a bachelor. He had that independent look. Like a mustang who knew how to avoid the snares and traps made by human hands. Even though she was a city girl, she could see that about him.

But in spite of the prickly awareness she had of Jake Rollins, Rebecca decided she could've sat in Abe's house for hours, letting the easy conversation take her mind away from all the hurt and betrayal she'd been feeling since she'd learned of Gertrude's existence. But the day was getting late and she needed to do so many things before she returned to Houston.

After placing her empty glass on a tray situated on

the coffee table, she rose to her feet. "Thank you so much for the refreshments and for inviting me to your home," she told Abe, then included the others in a hasty glance. "You've all been so kind, but I really need to stop by my aunt's place before dark. If someone could drive me to the cemetery to pick up my car, I'd be ever so grateful."

Quint looked questioningly at Maura and then Maura smiled suggestively at Jake. "Jake, I know you'd be more than happy to drive our guest to pick up her car. Wouldn't you?"

"That's a fool question," Abe shot at Maura. "Jake would give up his eyeteeth to drive Ms. Hardaway to wherever she wants to go. And if I were twenty years younger I wouldn't give him the chance." Winking at Rebecca, he pushed himself out of the chair and fished out a wad of keys from the front pocket of his jeans. Tossing them to Jake, he said, "Here, son. Take my truck. That way you won't have to hurry back with Quint's."

With a bit of dismay, Rebecca watched Jake rise to his feet. She'd expected Quint or Maura to be the one to drive her. Not the brown-eyed cowboy with the charming dimple in his cheek.

"Thanks," Jake told him. "And don't worry. I'll take care of your truck."

"Dammit, I'm not worried about you taking care of my truck. Just make sure you take good care of Ms. Hardaway."

Abe walked over and with a gnarled hand patted Rebecca's shoulder. For a moment the old man's gesture of affection stung her eyes with emotional tears. It had been years since she'd had her father in her life and with both sets of grandparents passing on before she'd been born, she'd never had a grandfather. Abe made her realize what she'd been missing and how much she needed a wise, steadying hand right now.

Jake cast Abe a wry grin. "Don't worry about that, either. I know how to be a gentleman."

Behind them, Quint chuckled and Rebecca didn't miss the dark look that Jake shot back at him. Obviously the two men were such good friends they communicated without words, she thought. And from what she could read from the conversation, Quint viewed her as a lamb about to be thrown to a wolf.

That was a silly thought, Rebecca told herself. She was twenty-eight years old and had been around all sorts of men. She hardly needed to worry about one New Mexican cowboy.

But moments later, as he wrapped a hand at the side of her waist and helped her into Abe's truck, her heart hammered as though she'd never been touched by a man.

"I noticed that Mr. Cantrell called you 'son.' And you and his grandson appear to be very close," she remarked as he climbed beneath the wheel and started the engine. "Is Mr. Cantrell your father? I mean, I know you have different surnames, but—well, sometimes that doesn't mean anything."

He thrust the truck into first gear and steered it onto the graveled drive. "No. Quint is just a good friend. Has been since the third grade. And Abe isn't my father. I don't have a father."

"Oh." His last words weren't exactly spoken in a testy nature, but there had been a faint hardness in his voice. She wondered what that could mean, but realized she was in no position to ask. Besides that, Jake Rollins shouldn't be interesting her. Not now anyway. She was here to say goodbye to her aunt and deal with the woman's estate. Certainly not to get involved with a local. "Neither do I," she told him. "Have a father, that is."

He shot her a questioning glance and she explained, "He died when I was ten. He worked for a major oil firm and was involved in an accident while he was in the Middle East. Something happened to cause an explosion on the job site."

"I'm sorry. That must have been tough."

She shrugged. "It's been nearly eighteen years and I still miss him."

He remained silent after that and it was clear to Rebecca that her revelation about her personal life hadn't given him the urge to expound on his. Biting back a sigh, she forced her attention to the passing landscape.

Once they'd moved away from Abe Cantrell's house, the forest of tall pines had opened up to desert hills dotted with smaller piñons and huge clumps of sage. To her extreme right, the sun was quickly setting, bathing the whole area in shades of pink and gold.

During Rebecca's many travels, she'd never been to New Mexico. And before her small commuter plane had landed in Ruidoso, she'd not expected the area to be so open and wild or for it to touch something deep within her.

Was that why Gertrude had come to live in this state? Because she'd thought it beautiful? Or had she simply wanted to put a great distance between herself and her sister. Oh, God, there were so many questions Rebecca wanted, *needed* answered.

"What is that cactus-looking stuff with the pretty

blooms on it?" she asked Jake as she forced her thoughts back to the moment. "See? Over there to your left with the pink blossoms."

He nodded. "That's cholla cactus. It blooms in the early spring and summer. You don't have that in Texas?"

"Not in the city of Houston."

His gaze slanted her way. "Guess you don't get out in the country much."

He'd not spoken it as a question but more like a statement of fact. As though he already knew the sort of person she was. The idea that she appeared so one-dimensional to this man bothered her a great deal. Though why it should, she didn't understand at all.

"Not in a while," she replied. "But I've been in the desert before. In Nevada. It didn't look like this."

"No. That state is pretty stark in some areas. But Lincoln County, New Mexico, is just plain pretty," he said with obvious bias.

Even though the cab of the truck was roomy, Rebecca felt as though there were only scant inches between them. His presence seemed to take up a major part of the space and try as she might, she couldn't seem to make her eyes stay away from him for more than a few seconds at a time.

While she went about her daily life in Houston, she was accustomed to seeing businessmen dressed in boots and Stetsons. Yet she had to admit that none of those men looked like Jake Rollins. He was the real deal and she was embarrassed to admit to herself that his raw sexuality mesmerized her.

"Well, here we are at the cemetery already," he announced as he geared down the truck and pulled to a stop in front of her rented sedan.

She avoided looking across the wrought-iron fence to the mound of fresh dirt covering Gertrude's grave. Instead, she smiled at Jake. "Thanks for taxiing me back to my car. It was very kind of you."

His grin was crooked and caused her breath to hang for a moment in her throat.

"And I didn't have to give up my eyeteeth to do it," he teased.

In spite of everything, she chuckled. "Mr. Cantrell is quite a character. I think I could fall in love with him."

He let out a humorous snort. "Most women who meet him do. How he's stayed a widower all these years is a mystery to me."

He climbed out of the truck and Rebecca waited for him to skirt the vehicle and assist her from the cab. Once she was down on the ground and standing next to him, she quickly started to step away, but his hand continued to rest on the side of her waist, causing her to pause and glance up at his dark face. His brown eyes flickered with a light that was so soft and inviting, she couldn't tear her gaze away.

"I guess this is goodbye," he said.

The husky tone of his voice sent shivers over her skin and she could only think how his touch soothed her, thrilled her in a way she would have never expected.

Her heart was suddenly hammering, yearning for some elusive thing she couldn't understand. Unconsciously, she moistened her lips with the tip of her tongue. "I—uh—don't suppose you would like to stop by Gertrude's house with me? I mean, if you're not in any hurry. I need to shut things up before I head back to Ruidoso."

His brows arched faintly, telling Rebecca he was

clearly surprised by her invitation. So was she. It wasn't like her to be so impulsive. Especially when it came to men. But during her aunt's graveside services, Jake Rollins had been so kind and caring. And though she couldn't explain it, his presence made her feel not so alone and heartbroken.

"I'd be pleased," he said.

"Fine." She drew in a long breath, then stepped away from him and quickly headed to her car.

Gertrude's house was only two short miles from Pine Valley cemetery. As she drove carefully over the country dirt road, Jake followed at a respectable distance behind her. When she finally parked in front of her aunt's small house, she climbed out of the car and waited for him to pull his vehicle to a stop next to hers.

When he joined her, she said, "I only arrived in Ruidoso last night, so I didn't get a chance to drive out here until this morning. I've still not looked over the whole property. Only the house and its surroundings." She glanced at the house and tried not to sigh with desperation. "I have to admit it wasn't what I expected."

As she walked toward a small gate that would lead them to the front entrance of the house, Jake followed a step behind.

He said, "I take it you've never been out here to your aunt's home before."

There was no censure or disbelief in his voice and that in itself drew out her next words before she had time to think about them.

"You're right, I haven't. And I'm very sorry about that."

"Well, you're here now. That has to stand for something," he said, then with an easy smile, he touched a hand to her back and ushered her up the small steps and onto a concrete porch.

By the time Rebecca reached to open the door, his comment had tugged on her raw emotions. Pausing, she bent her head and swallowed hard at the tears burning her throat. What was the matter with her? She hadn't known Gertrude O'Dell and until an hour or so ago, Jake Rollins had been a stranger. Neither of them should be affecting her like this.

"Rebecca? Is something wrong?"

Lifting her head, she looked at him and her eyes instantly flooded with tears.

"Oh—Jake."

The words came out on a broken sob and before she could stop herself her head fell against his chest, her hands snatched holds on his shoulders.

She felt his strong arms come around her and then his graveled voice was whispering next to her ear.

"Don't cry, Becca. Your aunt wouldn't want that. And neither do I."

Chapter 2

The comfort of his arms felt so good. Too good, she thought, as she sniffed back her tears and pushed herself away from him. She didn't know how long she'd allowed her cheek to rest against his broad chest, or his hand to stroke the back of her head. For a while she'd seemed to lose all sense of control over herself.

"I'm so sorry, Jake," she mumbled in an embarrassed rush. "I didn't mean to fall apart on you like that. I— The day has been long and everything just seemed to hit me all at once. And now I've gotten mascara on your nice, white shirt."

She darted a glance at his face and saw that his brown eyes were studying her with concern. Amusement, disgust, surprise. Anything would have been easier to deal with than his compassion. She struggled to keep her tears from returning.

"Forget that," he murmured. "Are you okay?"

While she'd been in his arms, while her cheek had rested against him, he'd called her Becca, she thought. No one had ever called her that and she wondered why it had sounded so endearing and natural coming from him.

Drawing in a deep breath, she nodded and turned to open the door. "Yes. I'm fine now. Please come in and I'll show you around," she invited.

They stepped into a small living room crammed full of old furniture, stacks of magazines and newspapers, and shelves of dusty trinkets. The windows were open, but outside awnings shaded the sunlight and left the cluttered interior dark and gloomy.

As Rebecca switched on a table lamp, Jake said, "I suppose I was eight years old the first time I ever visited Apache Wells with Quint. As best as I can remember your aunt was living here then. It's going to feel strange to drive by and know that she's not here anymore."

With one hand Rebecca gestured around the room. "It's clear that my aunt lived modestly. I suppose she wanted it that way."

"Maybe she couldn't afford anything else," he suggested.

"My aunt wasn't exactly a pauper," Rebecca revealed. "She had a nice nest egg in her savings account."

"Guess she was saving it for something more important."

More important? The money, the property, everything had been left to Rebecca. Nothing about her aunt's life or final wishes made sense. Had the woman lived miserly just to leave Rebecca a small fortune? She'd not even known her niece! Oh, God, Rebecca wished she could understand what it all meant.

"Come along this way to the kitchen," she told him. "I'd offer you something, but I'm afraid there's nothing in the house to eat or drink."

"I'm fine," he assured her. "It hasn't been that long since we had refreshments at Abe's."

The kitchen was a tiny room with one row of cabinets and a single sink with a window above it. Through a pair of faded yellow curtains, a ridge of desert mountains loomed in the far distance. Between them and the house was an open range filled with green grass, clumps of purple sage and blooming yucca plants.

"Would you look at that refrigerator," Jake remarked. "I'll bet it's at least fifty years old."

Rebecca glanced at the appliance with its rounded corners and chromed handle. In spite of the paint being worn and rusted in places, the thing was still working. Although someone, she didn't know who, had removed nearly all of the food from the shelves. In order to keep it from spoiling, she supposed. Perhaps Gertrude's friend, Bess, had done the chore.

"Yes. I guess Aunt Gertrude didn't believe in getting rid of anything that was still working." Which was the complete opposite of her twin sister, Rebecca thought wryly. In Houston, Gwyn was constantly refurnishing her house with the newest and best. The contrast of how the two sisters lived was completely shocking and made Rebecca wonder even more how the split had happened.

Rebecca pointed to a short hallway that led off the kitchen. "The bedrooms and bathroom are down there. I'd show you, but they're all a mess. Would you like to see out back?"

"Sure."

He followed her out of the kitchen and onto a porch. This portico was made of planked wood and shaded with a roof. At one end, the thin branches of a desert willow moved in the breeze and scattered lavender blossoms on the dusty boards. The grass in the yard was long, scraggly and full of weeds and Rebecca couldn't help thinking about her mother's well-manicured lawn in Houston. There, thick St. Augustine grass was fed and groomed on a regular basis by a hired gardener. Expensive lawn furniture was arranged in an eye-pleasing manner beneath the deep shade of a live oak. From the looks of it, Gertrude O'Dell hadn't even owned an old porch swing, she thought dismally.

"Looks like things need a little cleaning and fixing up here, too," Jake remarked. "I didn't realize there was a barn behind the house. The trees hide it from the road. Are there animals or equipment in it?"

"No tractors or anything that could be deemed as equipment," she told him. "But there are three barn cats. And a horse was here this morning. I think it must come and go in the pasture. At least, it wasn't locked inside a pen when I saw it. There's a dog somewhere around here, too."

"Let's go have a look," he suggested, then glanced down at her high heels. "Or maybe you'd rather not."

"The ground is hard and dry. I'm not worried about my shoes, Jake."

He smiled and for a moment she was reliving those few moments she'd stood in the circle of his arms. His body had been warm. Incredibly warm. And his muscles thick and hard. His male scent had engulfed her and she'd wanted to bury her face in the V of his shirt, to cling to him until nothing else in the world mattered.

Her strong reaction to the cowboy was startling and continued to confuse her. Although Rebecca had always enjoyed male company, she'd never relied on a man to keep her happy. How could she, when all the ones she'd known had been as fickle and unpredictable as the wind? Down through the years, she'd learned, somewhat the hard way, that men perpetually put themselves first. To them, sacrificing meant giving up football tickets to take her to the opera. She could do without that. And do without them. At least, she believed she could.

Still there were times, like earlier at Apache Wells, when she'd watched the loving exchange between Maura and Quint Cantrell, when she'd listened to them speak of their young sons, that she wondered if she would ever find that sort of love, ever have children of her own.

"Good," he suggested, breaking into her thoughts. "Lead the way."

As they stepped off the porch, a reddish-brown dog with long hair scurried beneath the yard fence and came loping toward them. From the wag of his tail, he was happy to see Rebecca again and she paused to bend and stroke his head.

"I was surprised to find that my aunt had left pets behind," she told Jake. "I suppose before I leave I'll have to take them to a place where they can be adopted out to new homes. And I need to find a trustworthy Realtor to deal with the property."

After giving the animal a few strokes on the head, she straightened to her full height to see Jake was studying her closely.

"Gertie didn't have a will?" he asked thoughtfully.

Color rushed to Rebecca's cheeks, although she didn't understand why his question should unsettle her. It wasn't a crime to be an heiress, even to a run-down property like this.

"Uh—yes. Actually, Gertrude made me the sole beneficiary."

She began walking on toward the barn and he strolled beside her. A stand of aspen trees grew at the back of the yard and as they passed beneath the shade, the air was dry and pleasant. She suspected that by nightfall the temperature would be downright cool.

"So why don't you stay on and make use of the property?" he asked. "Or do you already own something in Houston?"

As they walked along, she stared at him. "No. I rent. In the city. I don't have any use for property."

Was the man crazy? Why would he even think she'd want or need Gertrude's old homestead? Even though she'd told him and his friends that she worked as a fashion buyer, he obviously didn't realize the importance of her job. At least, its importance to her. He didn't understand that her mother and friends would be shocked to see her spend one night on this ramshackle property, much less want to hold on to it for herself.

But she kept all those thoughts to herself. She didn't want to give him the impression that she was a snob. Because she wasn't. She was just accustomed to a different life than this. That was all.

"That's a shame," he said. "With a bit of loving care this place could be a nice little home. But I guess a fancy lady like you would never settle for anything this simple."

There was no sarcasm or accusation in his voice.

He'd simply stated a fact the way he saw it. And she wasn't at all sure she liked the image he'd formed of her.

Pushing a hand through her tousled hair, she wondered if she looked as bad as she felt. But that hardly mattered. When Jake Rollins had called her a fancy lady, he'd not been referring to her looks, but her substance as a person. She couldn't remember the last time anyone had noticed anything more about her than her outward appearance, the latest fashion she happened to be wearing. It was a jarring realization.

"Actually, I won't be leaving tomorrow," she told him, while trying to decide why she felt it important to give him that bit of information. "It will take me a few days to deal with everything and get the property ready to sell."

"Well, I hope everything turns out the way you want," he said quietly.

"I do, too," she murmured, then quickened her pace on to the barn.

The structure was built of lapped boards with a low roof made of corrugated iron. The outside had once been painted white but had long since faded to a tired gray. At one end, two wide doors stood open, allowing a shaft of waning sunlight to slant across a floor of hard-packed dirt.

Inside, two female cats, one gray striped and the other a solid white, were lounging on a low stack of old hay bales. Nearby, a yellow tom was stretched out in the shade of a metal water trough full of rusty holes. Everywhere she looked, everything about the place seemed to have been long forgotten, as though her aunt had quit living years ago, instead of days ago. The idea saddened her even more.

While Rebecca tried to get near the wary felines, Jake walked around the structure, testing the supporting beams for structural soundness. Perhaps he knew someone who was looking to buy a place like this, she thought.

"This morning the horse was standing out in that wooden corral. But the gate to it is open and I suppose he or she wandered away," Rebecca suggested.

"Grass is probably the only feed it's been getting. Do you know how much acreage goes with the house?" he asked.

"Two hundred and ten acres."

"Well, I wouldn't worry about the horse. With that much grazing area, he has plenty to eat."

Rebecca moved away from the cats and walked to where he stood gazing out the wide-open door. "Do you cowboy for a living, Jake?" she asked.

His expression faintly amused, he looked at her. "That depends on what you mean by cowboying."

She shrugged, while wondering why he made her feel just a bit foolish. She was an educated woman with a college degree in business, along with being well-read on a variety of subjects. She kept up with current events, politics and the stock market. She was independent and had lived on her own for some years now. Yet when Jake looked at her with those brown eyes of his, she felt like a piece of mush, a woman who didn't know the first thing about dealing with a real man like him.

"Well, I'll put the question this way, do you do your job on horseback?"

He chuckled softly. "Most of the time. I own a ranch over by Fort Stanton, near Capitan. I raise cattle and horses."

She looked at him with interest. "Oh. Somehow I got the impression that you worked for the Cantrells."

"I used to work for Quint. On his ranch, the Golden Spur. But once he got the place built up to the way he wanted it, I decided he didn't need me anymore. And by then—" he paused, his lips twisting to a wry slant "—I had fish of my own to fry. From time to time I still help Quint. Whenever he has roundup going. And Abe occasionally asks me to do things for him, too. For instance, a few of his special horses he won't let anyone shoe, except me."

Her brows arched. "You do farrier work?"

He nodded. "I did a lot of farrier work when I was younger. And then for a long time I managed the training barns at Ruidoso Downs."

"So you know a lot about horses."

He chuckled again and the sexy sound drew her gaze straight to his. There was a gleam in his amber eyes that could only be described as provocative and she found herself drawing in a deep, cleansing breath and releasing it slowly.

"I like to think so," he drawled.

Finding it more comfortable to look at her feet rather than him, she noticed her high heels were now covered with dust and one of the pointed toes scuffed. But she didn't care. Bordeaux's supplied her with clothing, shoes, bags, jewelry and anything she wanted as a way to advertise their merchandise. There were plenty more high heels where these came from.

"I don't know much about the outdoors," she admitted, then glanced over her shoulder at the lazy cats. "Or animals. I've always loved being around them, but never had the opportunity to have any of my own."

As a young girl, she'd begged her mother for a dog or cat, but Gwyn had refused. Yet that hadn't deterred Rebecca's interest in animals. She'd visited the Humane Society every chance she'd gotten and fussed over her girlfriends' furry pets. By the time she entered high school, she'd had her heart set on becoming a veterinarian and had tried to gear her studies in that direction. In her mind, it would be the perfect job. Not only would she get to spend her days with a variety of animals, she'd be caring for them, making them well and happy.

But once her mother had learned of her daughter's plans, Gwyn had been outraged. She'd absolutely forbidden Rebecca to even consider such a career, insisting that her daughter was too fragile, too beautiful to be dealing with animals in a dirty barnyard.

Rebecca had argued the point. But by that time her father, Vance, who'd been a gentle, easygoing man, had already died, leaving Rebecca with no one to help support her wishes or desires. Gwyn had always been a forceful, strong-minded woman and Rebecca had never wanted to be a rebellious child. So she'd tried to consider the fact that her mother could possibly be right and that years down the road, after Rebecca had grown to womanhood, she'd eventually see that her wish to be a veterinarian was ridiculous.

In the end, she'd caved in to Gwyn's wishes and put aside her own dreams. But now, after all these years, Rebecca often wondered if her childhood pursuit would have suited her, would have given her more fulfillment than the materialistic job she had now.

"Well, looks like now is your chance to change that," Jake remarked. "There are plenty of animals here for the taking."

Lifting her head, she smiled wanly. He made everything sound so easy and uncomplicated. How would it feel to live that way? To not be hurrying and scurrying, constantly flying from one city to the next, continually worrying about maintaining her looks and asking herself if any of it really mattered, did *she* really matter in the scheme of things?

"Perhaps," she murmured, then said, "If you're ready, I need to be shutting the house and driving to Ruidoso. I'd like to get back to my hotel room before dark and from here the trip is at least thirty minutes."

"Sure. I'll help you."

It didn't take the two of them long to shut the windows and lock the doors. Once they made their way back out to their vehicles, Rebecca paused at the driver's door of the sedan and extended her hand to him. When his warm fingers wrapped around hers, she was once again flung back to those moments she'd been wrapped in his arms. Somehow she knew she would never forget how it had made her feel to be that close to him, to have his voice in her ear, his hand in her hair.

"Thank you, Jake, for taking time out of your day to attend my aunt's services. It means very much to me. More than you can imagine."

"I was glad to do it."

Instead of dropping her hand, he continued to hold it tightly, his thumb moving ever so slightly against its back. Rebecca suddenly had to remind herself to breathe.

"Well, perhaps we'll see each other again—before I leave to go back to Texas," she said, trying her best to keep her voice light and natural, even while she was feeling the quiver of her words as they left her tongue.

"I'd like that, Rebecca. Very much."

She waited for him to drop his hold on her hand. When he didn't, she forced herself to extricate her fingers from his and turn toward the car.

Before she could reach to open the door, he did it for her and without looking his way she quickly slid beneath the wheel and started the engine.

When he shut the door between them, she dared to glance at him through the open window.

"Goodbye, Jake."

He lifted a hand in farewell, then stepped back and out of the way. As she turned the car around and headed down the short drive, she looked in the rearview mirror to see him walking over to his truck. As he went, he lifted his hat from his head and raked a hand through his hair as though he was either puzzled or weary, or simply gathering himself after the stress of dealing with an emotional woman.

Dear God, what had made her fall into his arms like that and weep against his chest? She wasn't that sort of woman. What could he be thinking of her?

It doesn't matter, Rebecca. You'll probably never see the man again.

The idea left her very, very empty.

Rafter R Ranch, the place Jake called home, was located only a few miles from Fort Stanton, a military facility that had once played an important part in New Mexico's early growth as a state, but was now only a preserved part of its history, where tourists could view the past. If Jake needed to drive to town for any sort of supplies, he had to head northwest to Capitan. The trip took more than twenty minutes and the town was actually only a village of about fifteen hundred people or so, but Jake didn't mind the isolation. In fact, he felt lucky to have snagged the precious river land.

Several years ago, when the property had gone on the real estate market, Jake hadn't seriously considered trying to purchase it for himself. At the time he'd been doing farrier work around the county, making a decent enough living for himself, but nothing that could secure enough money to buy choice river acreage. Besides, why would a guy like him want a house and several hundred acres? His mother already had a place of her own, and as for himself, he didn't need much to make him happy. A place to eat, sleep and hang his hat was enough to satisfy him.

But Quint, who'd always been more like a brother than a friend, had insisted that someday Jake would want to settle down and raise a family, that one day he'd want a ranch, a place to build a dream.

At first Jake had laughed at him. Jake didn't have dreams, he dealt in reality. And the reality had been that he couldn't raise enough money to buy an outhouse, much less a house with hundreds of acres surrounding it. But Quint had stepped up and offered to help Jake get a loan and as a result, he'd somehow managed to purchase the first and only place he could truly call his own.

At that time it hadn't mattered that the property needed lots of work. The house had seen plenty of neglect and outside the fences and barns were crumbling. But he'd looked past the drawbacks and on to the possibilities. He might have been short on cash, but he was an able-bodied man who could do plenty of things with two hands and a strong back.

Acquiring the ranch had put a dream into motion for Jake. And along the way, he'd gone from farrier work to running the stables at Ruidoso Downs, to helping Quint build the Golden Spur into a cattle empire. His financial security had slowly and surely changed. Especially three years ago when gold had been discovered on the Golden Spur and Jake had purchased shares in the richly producing mine. Now, the Rafter R was taking shape. He was gradually building the place the way he saw fit and answering to no one but himself. And that meant the ranch's success or failure rested squarely upon his shoulders.

For Jake, it was a heavy weight of responsibility and one he'd never grown accustomed to carrying. But he was trying. And for the most part, Jake couldn't complain. He had a large herd of cattle and horses, a home, and a ranch yard full of sturdy barns and plenty of equipment. He even employed two hands to take care of the animals. He had most everything a cowboy could want. Except a family.

That lonesome thought entered his mind as he pulled his horse to a stop outside the barn, then swung himself down to the ground. But he tried not to dwell on it as he loosened the sweaty girth and pulled the saddle from the animal's back. He wasn't the family sort. Being a husband and father and doing it right meant loving one woman for the rest of his life. He couldn't imagine putting himself in such a confinement, much less succeeding at it.

Jake had just finished putting away his horse and tack, when he heard his mother's voice calling to him from the edge of the barn door. More than surprised that she'd ventured away from Ruidoso so late in the evening, he strode down the wide alleyway to greet her.

Clara Rollins was a thin woman with wispy brown hair and a face that could only be described as tired. Jake could remember a time, back before his father, Lee, had left the family, that his mother had been a beautiful, vibrant woman. But that had been nearly twenty years ago, before his parents' marriage had begun to crumble and before she'd been diagnosed with cancer.

She'd beaten the disease, but the fierce treatments had weakened her heart and for the past five years Jake had watched her movements grow slower, the light in her eyes fade away. Not because her heart condition had worsened, but because she'd lost all will and hope. He loved his mother and wanted to make her life better, but her mind-set was always on the negative. She refused to get better, because she believed she had no reason to get better.

"This is a nice surprise," he said, as he leaned down and planted a kiss on her forehead. "You've not driven over here to the ranch in ages."

"I haven't seen you in days," she said in a faintly accusing tone.

Jake bit back a sigh. In spite of his affection for his mother, she often tried his patience. Probably even more than Abe tried Quint's. But at least Abe was full of life. The old man would go to the end kicking, joking and enjoying his time on earth. Clara was content to simply wait for her life to slip by. He hated her attitude, but as yet hadn't found a way to change it.

"I've been very busy, Mom. I've been riding fence line this week." He gathered his arm around her shoulders and urged her away from the barn. "Let's go to the house. I'll see if I can scrounge us up something for supper."

"No need for that. I've brought you some pot roast. It's already in the kitchen, waiting to be heated."

He rewarded her with a look of approval. "You've been cooking? You must be feeling better."

"I just like to know my son is eating right," she said wanly.

Jake's house was located about fifty yards from the block of barns and sheds that made up the ranch yard. Even though he kept his pace slow to match his mother's, she was breathing hard by the time they reached the back door and stepped into the kitchen. A part of him wanted to shake her for not following the doctor's orders and keeping herself in shape by taking routine walks.

"Sit down, Mom. And I'll get everything together and on the table," he told her as he washed his hands at the sink.

She did as he suggested and he went to work putting plates, utensils and iced glasses on the table.

"I talked to Quint's mother yesterday," Clara said as Jake heated the meat and vegetables in the microwave. "She said she was home watching the babies for Maura, while you went to a funeral for Abe's neighbor."

"That's right. Gertie O'Dell passed away and graveside services were held for her yesterday. I doubt you knew her. She—well, I don't think the woman hardly ever got off her place. She was a recluse. Abe said she'd been his neighbor for nearly thirty years and he could count the times he'd talked to her on two hands."

"No. I don't recall that name," Clara said thoughtfully. "How old was the woman?"

"Fifty-six, I believe."

A worrisome frown collected between Clara's brows. "That's only a few years older than me."

"That's right. It's unfortunate, but people of all ages die."

He carried a dish of potatoes and carrots over to the table, then went back for the roast.

"What was wrong with her?"

Jake wasn't about to tell his mother that Gertie O'Dell had died from some sort of heart failure. Clara already considered herself an invalid. He didn't want to add the notion that, like Gertie, she was headed toward her deathbed.

"I'm not sure," he said evasively. "Some sort of illness she'd had for a long time."

With everything on the table, he took a seat kitty-cornered to his mother's chair and poured sweetened tea into their glasses.

Clara spread a napkin across her lap. "I'm surprised you attended the funeral. Guess you made the effort for Abe's sake."

He paused to look at her. "No. I made the effort for Gertie's sake, Mom. I don't do everything in my life just to make an impression or score points."

Clearly flustered by his retort, she clamped her lips together. "Well, you didn't know the woman personally," she pointed out.

"Maybe not. But she was a fellow human being, a fixture in Abe's neighborhood. Whenever she saw me pass, she would always give me a wave. And coming from Gertie that meant a hell of a lot. She hated most folks."

"Her family—"

"She had none," Jake interrupted. "Not any immediate family. Only one relative showed up for the funeral."

Clara's expression was suddenly regretful as she looked at her son. "How awful," she murmured.

Jake sighed. "Yeah. That's my thinking, too."

He didn't go on to tell his mother about Rebecca Hardaway. She'd press him with questions that he couldn't answer. Like why Gertie had left her estate to a niece who'd clearly never been a part of her life. At least, not while Gertie had been living in New Mexico. And from judging Rebecca's age, he'd guess that had been as long or longer than the pretty blonde had been living.

"Wonder what will happen to her estate?" Clara asked as she ladled food onto her plate. "I suppose with no husband or kids, some distant relative will put it up for sale."

The image of Rebecca drifted to the front of Jake's mind, the way her blue eyes had glazed with tears, the sobs he'd felt racking her slender shoulders. He'd been a bit shocked when she'd fallen into his arms. Not that a crying woman was anything new to him. Down through the years, he'd seen plenty of waterworks sprout for all different reasons. And most of the time he had to admit that tears on a smooth pink cheek left him unaffected. There wasn't a woman on the face of the earth who couldn't be a good actress when she wanted to be and turning on the tears was just a part of her act.

But Rebecca hadn't been acting, he realized, and her emotional state continued to puzzle Jake. She'd said she'd never been to her aunt's house before, but seeing it had disturbed her. She didn't appear to have even known Gertrude or how she'd lived, so why had the woman's death hit her so hard? None of it made sense to him. But then, Gertie had lived what most people would call a bizarre life. Maybe learning all of that about her family member had been too much for the Texas wildflower, he considered.

Jake had to admit he'd been disappointed that Rebecca had so quickly decided that she didn't want Gertie's property. As though it was all meaningless to her. For some reason he'd wanted to think she was a deeper sort of person than that. But then maybe he wasn't being fair. Maybe she wasn't in a position to care for the place, the way it deserved to be cared for. She obviously had a life back in Houston. She might even have a special man waiting for her return, he thought grimly. The lack of a ring didn't necessarily mean anything nowadays. She might even have a husband.

The idea bothered him far more than it should have.

Trying his best to shake it away, he glanced up at his mother. "You're probably right," he replied to his mother's comment. "And selling it won't be much of an effort. The land joins up with Apache Wells. Abe would be glad to fork over a very fair price to make sure it becomes a part of his ranch, instead of watching it go to some developer."

"Maybe someone should give this information to Gertie's relatives?" Clara suggested. "They'd probably be grateful to have someone drop a buyer into their lap."

When Rebecca Hardaway had spoken of finding a Realtor to deal with selling the place, he probably should have spoken up and told her that a Realtor wouldn't be necessary. Abe would buy the property without batting an eye.

But something had kept the words inside him. Selfishness? The hope that Rebecca Hardaway would be forced to stay in New Mexico longer than necessary? The hope that while she was here he'd get the chance to know her, spend time with her, maybe even get physically close to her?

Dream on, Jake. Rebecca might have leaned that sexy little body against you once, but there won't be a next time. If you do see her again, there won't be any tears in her eyes and she'll see you for just what you are—a cowboy who can offer her little more than a lusty roll in the hay.

Picking up a steak knife, he sliced ruthlessly into the meat on his plate.

"Maybe I'll do just that, Mom."

Chapter 3

At the same time, some twenty miles south in Ruidoso, Rebecca sat in a luxurious hotel suite. From her seat on the long moss-green couch, she could look out the plate-glass wall at the picturesque view of Sierra Blanca. Next to her right arm, a telephone sat on a polished end table and all she had to do was lift the receiver from the cradle and press a button to have a full course meal delivered to her room.

But at the moment she wasn't seeing the beauty of the tallest peak in the southern part of the state, or concerning herself over ordering dinner. She was thinking about Jake Rollins. Something she'd been doing ever since she'd driven away and left the man standing in front of her aunt's house.

So why don't you stay on and make use of the property? With a bit of loving care this place could be a nice

*little home. But I guess a fancy lady like you would
never settle for anything this simple.*

Today Rebecca had planned to get a list of things
done. First of all, to ask around town and find a Realtor she could trust. Secondly, to contact the nearest
animal shelter to find homes for the pets Gertrude had
left behind. But Rebecca hadn't attempted to do either
of those things. She'd walked a short distance around
town, ate lunch, returned to the hotel and for the past
two hours sat wondering why Jake Rollins's words continued to haunt her.

It wasn't like the man had anything to do with her
life, she mentally argued. Up until yesterday, she'd
never met him. Yet the things he'd said to her, the way
he'd looked at her, had done something to her thinking.

With a heavy sigh, she rose to her feet and walked
across the room to where a gilt-edged mirror hung over
a small accent table. The image showed a young woman
dressed casually but fashionably in a pair of summer
white jeans and a sleeveless cashmere top. Her blond
hair was twisted into a sexy pleat and her face touched
with just enough color to look pretty but not overdone.

Her friends would tell her that she looked perfect,
but that had come to mean very little to Rebecca. On
the inside she felt far from perfect. And she didn't understand why.

Even before she'd learned about Gertrude and traveled here to New Mexico, she'd been feeling empty, as
though spinning wheels were quickly carrying her to
nowhere. Then yesterday, when she'd stood beside her
aunt's grave with hardly a soul there to tell the woman
goodbye, a heavy sense of reality had stung her. She
wasn't sure why thoughts of missed opportunities and

connections were upsetting her, but she couldn't get rid of them.

Across the room, her cell phone rang. The sound cut into her dark thoughts and with a heavy sigh, she walked over to collect the small instrument from where she'd left it on a low end table.

Her mother's name and number were illuminated on the front and she braced herself with a deep breath before she flipped the phone open and lifted it to her ear. Gwyn had been ringing the phone all day, but Rebecca had ignored her calls. She wasn't ready to talk to the woman, but years of being a devoted daughter couldn't be wiped away in a matter of days. And Gwyn deserved to know that she'd arrived in New Mexico safely.

"Hello, Mother."

Gwyn let out a sigh of relief. "Oh, thank God you finally answered! Is everything all right?"

Rebecca's jaw tightened. "Is that question supposed to be some sort of joke? How could everything be all right? I just watched my aunt—an aunt I didn't even know I had—be lowered into the ground!"

"Now, Rebecca, honey, please let's don't start in about all of that now. Gertrude is gone. There's no use talking about her anymore."

If it hadn't been for disturbing the other hotel guests, Rebecca would have actually screamed into the phone. Instead, she tried to calm the rage boiling inside her. "Sure. Just forget her," she said, in a voice heavy with sarcasm, "and get on with our neat little lives. The way you've seemed to do for the past thirty years."

There was a long stretch of silence and then Gwyn asked, "When are you coming home?"

Clearly Gwyn was still refusing to open up about

Gertrude and her indifferent attitude about her own flesh and blood caused something to suddenly click inside Rebecca. Feeling strangely calm, she said, "I'm not. At least, not for a good while. I have things to do here. And I want to make sure they're done right."

Gwyn gasped. "What sort of things? What are you talking about?"

"Listen, Mother, my aunt left everything she had in this world to me. And even though she's gone now, she still deserves my attention. I owe her that much—" Emotions suddenly filled Rebecca's throat, choking her. "That and so much more."

"But, Rebecca—she—your job—you'll have to be getting back here to Houston soon!"

"You worry about my job, Mother. You seem to love it much more than I do, anyway."

"Rebecca! You—"

"I'm sorry, Mother. I'm very busy. I've got to get off."

Rebecca hung up the phone, then purposely walked over to the closet and pulled out the luggage she'd brought with her. An hour later, she'd packed all her things, checked out of the hotel, and after purchasing a few items at the grocery store, headed north to Gertie's place.

As she drove northwest, out of the mountains and onto the desert floor of the Tularosa Basin, she picked up her cell phone and pushed a button that would connect her with her boss in Houston.

"You're going to do what?" the woman exclaimed loudly in her ear.

Rebecca felt the ridiculous urge to smile, but forced herself not to. Even before her father had died, she'd been a responsible child, who'd grown into an even more responsible adult. She'd never done an impulsive thing in her life and she was shocked at how good it felt to be doing it now.

"I need to take a leave, Arlene."

"Yes, but you said indefinitely! Surely this break you're taking won't require that much time! What will I do without you? The Dallas show is coming up and then New York City. I have to have a buyer there! Otherwise—"

Outside her car window, the sun was casting a purple and gold hue across the desert floor. She'd never seen anything so wild and beautiful. "Send Elsa. She knows what she's doing and she'll be more than happy to step into my shoes."

Arlene snorted and mouthed a curse beneath her breath. The woman's reaction didn't surprise Rebecca. Arlene was in her late fifties and had spent more than thirty years working for Bordeaux's. Still single, she'd made the famous department store her life and believed that Rebecca and its other employees should, too.

"Elsa doesn't have your taste or finesse with people. I want you back here in two weeks. That's all I can afford to give you, Rebecca."

The demanding ultimatum brought an angry flare to Rebecca's nostrils. She'd given so much of herself, her life, to Bordeaux's and all she could expect in return for her commitment was two weeks?

"That's not enough, Arlene. Not by a long shot."

Her retort must have shocked the woman because the line went silent. It stayed that way for so long that Rebecca actually pulled the phone away from her ear to see if the instrument was still receiving a tower signal.

"What's come over you, Rebecca?" the woman finally retorted. "I realize you must be grieving, but from what I understand this death was a distant relative. Surely you can put it behind you and get yourself focused on business again."

She was nearing the turnoff to Gertrude's house and the road that eventually led to Apache Wells. Jake and the Cantrells had shown her more compassion in one afternoon than this woman had shown her in the six years she'd been working for Bordeaux's. What did that say for the people she'd surrounded herself with?

"Taking this time off is important to me, Arlene. If you feel you need to replace me permanently, I'll understand. Just mail my final paycheck to my apartment."

Another long silence followed Rebecca's statement and then Arlene said in a mollified tone, "Now wait a minute, Rebecca. Let's not get so hasty about things. You're a great asset to Bordeaux's and I don't want to lose you." She paused and released a long sigh of surrender. "All right. Take as long as you need. Your job will be waiting when you do get back to Houston."

Arlene's concession should have inspired Rebecca, filled her with joy to know that she was that good, that appreciated at her job. Yet she felt nothing but relief that her conversation with the woman was over.

"Thank you, Arlene. I'll be in touch soon."

Ten minutes later, she parked her vehicle behind a Ford pickup truck that sat beneath an expanse of sagging roof connected to the left side of the house.

Rebecca recalled a truck being listed in Gertrude's will and she assumed the old red F-150 had belonged to her aunt. In this isolated place a person had to have transportation of some sort. She wondered if the vehicle was still in running condition and made a mental note to check the thing out after she'd put away the perishable groceries. Keeping a rental car for an extended length of time would run into a huge expense. The truck would solve that problem.

At the back of the car, she opened the trunk and started to lift a sack of groceries when she suddenly heard a low whine and felt a nudge against the back of her leg.

Turning, she saw the dog had spotted her arrival and come to greet her. His mouth was open and he appeared to be grinning as though he couldn't be happier to see her.

For a moment, Rebecca forgot the grocery bag and squatted on her heels to wrap her arms around her furry brown friend.

"Well, here you are again, big guy," she said to him, then stroked a hand down his back. Beneath his long, thick hair she could feel his backbone and realized the animal had obviously not been getting enough to eat since Gertrude had died. "I'll bet you're hungry, aren't you? I'll bet you'd like a big bowl of juicy dog food."

As if on cue, the dog let out a long, loud whine. Rebecca smiled and patted his head. "All right. Come along and I'll see what I can do," she told him.

With plastic bags dangling from both hands, she urged the canine to follow her onto the porch. Once she opened the door, she pushed it wide and invited him in.

"Just for a while," she warned him as he shot past her, his tail wagging furiously.

During her visit yesterday morning before the funeral, she'd discovered several dozen cans of dog and cat food stacked in a small pantry. She emptied two of the cans into a plastic bowl and set it on the floor.

While the dog gobbled it hungrily, she stored what perishable food she'd purchased in the refrigerator and found places for the rest of the things in the cabinet.

By the time she was finished with the chore, the dog had cleaned the bowl and was looking up at her, his head tilted curiously to one side. No doubt he couldn't understand why his mistress was gone.

The notion was a sad one. Especially when Rebecca tried to imagine her aunt and the dog together. It was difficult to form such a picture in her mind when she didn't have the tiniest idea of what Gertrude had looked like. There were no photos of the woman sitting around the house and even in death, she'd clearly been a private person by leaving orders with her lawyer to keep her casket closed.

If Gertrude and Gwyn had been identical twins, then the woman would have been petite and dark-haired with hazel-green eyes and a square face. But her mother hadn't seen fit to tell her even that much about her sister, so Rebecca could only guess and imagine Gertrude's appearance.

Trying not to dwell on the loss and become maudlin all over again, Rebecca spoke to the dog, "I have no idea what your name is, boy. Is it Furry? Smiley? Buddy? No. None of those fit. What about Beau? Back in elementary school I knew a boy named Beau. The tips of his ears sort of flopped over like yours. But he was nice. And I liked him."

The dog responded with another whine and pushed his head beneath Rebecca's hand. Smiling, she gave him a loving scratch between the ears. "Okay. Beau it will be. Now let's see if we can start cleaning up this place."

* * *

A week later Jake was at Marino's Feed and Ranch Supply, purchasing several sets of horseshoes, when he heard a woman's soft voice call his name.

Turning, he was completely shocked to see Rebecca Hardaway standing a few feet away from him. What was she doing in a place that was mostly frequented by farmers and ranchers? More important, what was she doing still here in New Mexico? He figured she'd probably already wrapped up her business and gone back to Texas.

His heart was suddenly beating fast as pleasure ricocheted through his body. "Hello, Rebecca."

He started toward her and she met him in the middle of the dusty aisle filled with pesticides and grass fertilizer.

Smiling, she extended her hand to him. "Hello, Jake."

He took her hand, while his gaze quickly encompassed every inch of her. She was dressed casually in blue jeans and a pink hooded T-shirt. Her blond hair was pulled into a ponytail and her face was completely bare of makeup. She looked fresh and beautiful and rested. And just looking at her made something inside of him go as soft as gooey candy.

"This is a surprise to see you," he admitted. "I figured you'd already left the area."

She shook her head. "No. I've decided to stay on for a while. I'm living out at my aunt's place now."

It was all Jake could do to keep his mouth from falling open. That day he'd visited Gertie's place with her, she'd seemed almost indifferent to the place. What had changed her mind so much that she'd actually been motivated to move out there?

"Oh. How's that been going?"

She laughed softly and Jake warmed to the sound, warmed even more to this different, more approachable Rebecca.

"Well, let's say I've never done so much cleaning in my life, but the house is coming around. I've decided I'll have to hire a man to help with the outside. There's so much heavy junk that needs to be hauled away. But I did get the truck going and turned in my rental car."

He peered toward the front of the building where plate-glass windows looked out over the graveled parking lot. Was she driving Gertie's old truck? He couldn't imagine such a thing. But perhaps there had always been another side of this woman and he'd not yet had a chance to see it.

His mind racing, he said, "Uh—that's good. Is it running okay?"

She nodded proudly. "Great. I took it by a mechanic's shop and had it checked out. The only thing it needed was new tires so I had those put on."

"Sounds like you've been busy."

She smiled again and as he looked at her, he realized the expression on her face was genuine. The fact made him happy. Very happy.

"I've made a start."

He glanced at the red plastic shopping basket dangling from her hand. "You needed something from the feed store?"

"A few things for the cats and dog. Flea collars, wormers, things like that. They're probably not going to be too happy about it all, but I want them to be cared for properly."

"So you didn't give them up to a pet adoption agency?"

Her cheeks turned pink and her gaze drifted away from him as though she was embarrassed she'd ever mentioned doing such a thing. Jake was truly baffled by this turn of events.

"No. I changed my mind about all that." She directed her gaze back to his. "That day of the funeral was—well, I was very upset and said some things before I had a chance to think them through."

And done some things before she'd thought them through, Jake decided. Like bury her face against his chest and grip his shoulders like she never wanted to let him go. Now she was probably embarrassed about that, too.

But she didn't appear to be uncomfortable with him holding her hand. In fact, she wasn't making any sort of effort to draw it away from him. The idea encouraged him.

"We all do that from time to time," he told her.

She let out a faint sigh and then a tentative smile curved the corners of her lips. Jake couldn't tear his eyes away from her face or even consider dropping her soft little fingers.

"I'm glad I ran into you like this," she said. "I've been wondering if you might do me a favor. That is—if you have the time and happen to be going by my place."

My place. So she was calling it *her* place now. He couldn't believe how such a little thing like that could make him feel so good. And he wondered if he was coming down with some sort of sickness that was throwing his thinking off-kilter. He'd always been drawn to women. Down through the years he'd probably had more girlfriends than Quint had cattle, but he'd never had one that made him feel like happy sunshine was pouring through him and painting a goofy grin on his face.

"I'd be glad to help if I can," he told her.

She said, "The horse has been coming up and hanging around the barn. I found some feed for it stacked away in a storage room, but I wasn't sure how much to give it. The cats and dog I can deal with, but I know nothing about horses. And I remembered that you do. If you would be kind enough to look it over and make sure everything is okay. Maybe show me the correct amount to feed it? I'd be very grateful."

God was definitely smiling down on him today, Jake thought. For the past week, he'd struggled to get this woman off his mind. He'd tried to think of any reasonable excuse to drive over to Gertie's place and see if she was there. But he'd figured if she was still in New Mexico, she'd be staying in a hotel in Ruidoso and hardly likely to be around the old homestead. And then, too, he'd tried to convince himself that she was off-limits, a woman who could never fit into his simple life, even for a short while.

Now here she was inviting him to her place as though it was as natural as eating apple pie. He couldn't believe his good fortune and it was all he could do to keep from shouting with glee.

"Sure," he said as casually as he could manage. "I was thinking about driving out to Apache Wells this evening, anyway. Would that be soon enough?"

She smiled. "That would be great," she said, then glanced around his shoulder. "You were looking at horseshoes when I first spotted you. I don't want to keep you from your business."

She extricated her hand from his and Jake felt ridiculously bereft. "It's nothing that pressing." He glanced at his watch. "I have to be over at the track—Ruidoso Downs—in an hour or so to shoe some racehorses for a trainer that I'm friends with."

"Oh. Is that something you do often?" she asked curiously.

"Occasionally. There are some folks I just can't say no to."

Like you, he thought.

"Well, I should let you go, then."

Before she could turn to leave, he reached out and caught her by the hand. She looked at him, her brows arched in question.

Jake was amazed to feel warm color creep up his throat and onto his face. Hell's bells, women didn't make him blush. Nothing did. So why was he doing it now?

"I was wondering if you'd like to go have a cup of coffee?" he invited. "That is, if you have the time."

"Do you?"

He grinned. "It doesn't take me ten minutes to get to the track. I have plenty of time."

"In that case, I'd love to," she replied. "Just let me pay for my purchases and I'll be ready."

They both took care of their business in the feed store, then walked out to the parking lot together. Jake was about to suggest that she ride with him to the Blue Mesa, but before he could get the words out of his mouth, he noticed Gertie's dog was sitting in the cab of the old Ford.

Surprised, he asked the obvious. "You brought the dog to town with you?"

"Yes. I discovered that Beau loves to ride in the truck. And I enjoy his company. He'll be fine while we have coffee," she added. "I'll leave the windows rolled down and there's a nice breeze. He'll probably curl up on the seat and go to sleep."

Wonder of wonders, Jake thought. Was this the same fashionista who'd walked across the barnyard in a pair of high heels? No matter. She was here with him now and he was going to enjoy every second of her company.

"Okay," he told her. "Then follow me. The café is only a few blocks down the street."

Since it was midmorning, the crowd had mostly dispersed from the little café and they both found parking slots directly in front of the entrance.

Jake suggested they sit at an outside table. That way she could keep an eye on Beau. As they climbed onto the wooden deck filled with small round tables, she looked around with obvious pleasure.

"How nice of you to bring me here, Jake. This is so quaint and lovely," she exclaimed. "Can we take any table we like?"

"Sure. As long as it isn't already occupied."

Since there was only one other couple making use of the outside seating, Rebecca chose a table at the far corner, where a few feet below them a small brook trickled through tall pines and blue spruce trees.

A waitress appeared almost instantly after they were seated and Jake didn't waste time ordering coffee and a piece of chocolate pie.

"You're having pie, too?" Rebecca asked with a

shocked tone that implied eating such a thing in the middle of the morning was absolutely sinful.

Jake chuckled. "I have a lot of work ahead of me today. Besides, the Blue Mesa makes the best pie in town. Try some. It won't put any pounds on you," he added with a wink, then glanced up at the redheaded waitress. "Will it, Loretta?"

The waitress laughed and Rebecca could tell by the light in the young woman's eyes that she knew Jake well and found him more than attractive. Probably one of many, she thought, then wondered why the idea annoyed her.

"Not at all," the waitress answered. "I eat it all the time and I don't get any complaints."

Rebecca deliberately avoided giving the waitress's curvy figure an inspective glance. "Okay," she said to Jake, "you've talked me into it. I'll have a piece of peach." Glancing up at Loretta, she added, "If you have peach."

The woman's smile was faintly suggestive. "We have every flavor a person would want. Just ask Jake. He's tried them all."

Rebecca assured the waitress that she'd be satisfied with the peach and the redhead quickly swished away to fill their orders.

"Don't mind Loretta," Jake said. "She's a big flirt, but she doesn't mean any harm."

He probably didn't mean any harm either, Rebecca thought. But she figured he'd broken plenty of hearts with that dimpled grin and amber-brown eyes. Was she trying to be the next woman on his roster?

No. She simply liked him. Liked being around him. That didn't mean she wanted anything serious to develop between them. In fact, where women were concerned, she doubted the word *serious* had ever been in Jake Rollins's vocabulary.

"So how has it been staying out at Gertie's—uh, your place?" he asked after a moment.

She leaned back in her chair and wished she didn't feel so self-conscious about her bare face and messy hair. But for the past few days she'd felt like a child again, free to be herself. When she'd driven into town this morning, the last person she'd expected to see was Jake.

"It's been different to say the least. I'm still not used to the lack of an air conditioner. Or the idea that I can't drive a couple of blocks to a convenience store whenever I need something. But I like the quietness. Last night while I was sitting on the porch I heard a pack of coyotes howling in the distance. It was an eerie sound."

"Guess a city girl like you never heard anything like that."

"No. Actually—" The sound of approaching footsteps interrupted the rest of Rebecca's words and she turned her head to see Loretta arriving with their orders.

Once the waitress had served them and ambled away, Jake prompted Rebecca to finish what she'd been about to say.

"It was nothing important," she told him as she spread a napkin across her lap. "I was only going to say that since I've come out here to New Mexico I've been learning about a lot of things. Mainly about myself."

His expression was gentle on her face as he stirred a spoonful of sugar into his coffee. "Are you liking what you're learning?"

She grimaced. "No. But I'm trying to change what I don't like."

He didn't ask what she meant by that remark and Rebecca was relieved. She didn't want to admit to this man that it had taken the death of her aunt to open her eyes about her own life.

As she cut into the peach pastry, he leaned back in his chair and studied her with open curiosity. "This probably isn't any of my business, Rebecca, but are you planning on staying here in Lincoln County for an extended length of time?"

A faint frown creased her forehead. For the past week, his question was the same one that had gone round and round in her head. Was she going to stay for long? At the moment everything about being in this new place felt right and wonderful. But was that only because she was away from her demanding job? Away from the rift between her and her mother? Or was the contentment she'd been feeling these past few days trying to tell her that she'd finally discovered where she was truly meant to be?

"Maybe," she answered slowly. "It depends. On a lot of things."

He sipped his coffee, then thoughtfully reached for his fork. "Well, I suppose there's a man back in Houston who won't take kindly to you staying out here for very long."

She looked at him with faint surprise. "Not hardly. I don't have a boyfriend. And even if I did, I wouldn't allow him to tell me what to do. Unless I was madly in love with him."

He arched a brow at her. "That would make the difference?"

"Of course. Love always makes the difference. Doesn't it?"

One corner of his mouth curved upward as he reached across the table and closed his hand around hers. "You're asking that question to the wrong man, Rebecca."

He was telling her that love was not an important commodity on his list of needs. The reality should have put her off, should have made the warmth of his hand insignificant, the race of her heart slow to a disappointed crawl. But it didn't.

Like the rich pastry in front of her, she understood Jake Rollins wasn't necessarily good for her. But he was too tempting to resist.

Chapter 4

"You're going where?"

Amusement slanted Jake's lips. Even over the cell phone, he could hear the dismay in Quint's voice.

"To Gertie's place. Or I guess I should be calling it Rebecca's place. Since it belongs to her now."

As Jake motored his truck down the narrow, two-lane highway he could have counted at least twenty-five fence posts before Quint eventually replied and even then Jake figured the other man was rolling his eyes.

"I always did think you'd make a good detective, Jake. Maura's brother, Brady, could probably find you a good job in the sheriff's department if you wanted it. You're better at pulling information from people than a dentist pulls teeth."

Jake chuckled. "I can't help it. It just falls in my lap."

Quint's groan could be heard over the telephone connection. "Oh, sure. You've probably been harassing the lady all week. How many times have you called her? No. Better than that, how did you get her phone number?"

"Quint, I've not called her once. I don't even have her number."

"Really? How did you miss that piece of information? You seemed to know other, more personal things about the woman."

"Look, I just happened to run into her at the feed store. She asked for my help and I couldn't refuse her. Could I?"

"You? Refusing a woman? That might have actually killed you."

Jake frowned. Normally Quint's sarcasm would have made him laugh, but for some reason this evening he wasn't finding it amusing. More like downright annoying.

"You're being a real jerk about this, Quint. Especially when I was planning on driving on to Apache Wells to check on Abe—after I finish meeting with Rebecca."

Quint sighed. "I'm trying not to be. But you took me by surprise, that's all."

"Why? What's so surprising about me seeing Rebecca Hardaway? She's gorgeous and nice and I happened to like a woman's company."

"No bull," Quint said with a wry snort, then added, "If you want the truth, I figured Gertie's niece would have already left here by now. Along with that, she's not your type."

Jake's jaw unconsciously tightened. "You mean she's not a barfly?"

"I didn't say that," Quint countered. "You did."

"You meant it," Jake shot back at him.

"All right," Quint conceded with a dose of frustration. "You'd be the first to admit that you don't go around seducing schoolmarms."

"Rebecca is hardly a schoolmarm."

"No. But she seems like a nice, decent woman. And after five minutes of conversation, I'm not sure you'll know how to treat her."

Even though Quint was his childhood friend and the two of them always spoke frankly to each other, Jake was struck by his comment. It was true that Jake had always directed his likes toward "experienced" women. But he knew when and how to be a gentleman. He resented Quint implying otherwise.

"I'm not a heathen, Quint. Besides, she wants me to look over her horse. Not her."

"Poor thing. Someone should have told her you're an expert at both," Quint said.

"You're really on a roll this evening, Quint."

Quint paused, then said, "I don't mean to get on your case, Jake. I'm just thinking about you. From what I saw of Rebecca Hardaway, she's the type of woman who—well, who could hurt a man without even trying."

Jake let out a wry snort. "What are you talking about? She's a fragile little flower who couldn't hurt anything or anyone."

Quint didn't say anything to that. Instead he abruptly changed the subject. Jake figured his friend had decided he was wasting his time giving him advice about the opposite sex.

"So what did you decide about buying the alfalfa from the producer in Clovis?" Quint asked. "I thought it was a fair price. And they always have good, clean hay."

"I haven't decided yet," Jake told him.

"What are you waiting on? Cold weather? The price to go up?"

"I was hoping the price would fall a bit," Jake admitted. "If it doesn't, I might be better off sticking to creep feed. I want to do more figuring before I decide what feed program to plan for this coming winter."

"I can understand that. I just wouldn't wait too long, though. Otherwise, you might get caught with your pants down."

Jake realized that Quint's advice was well-meaning. He even appreciated his friend's guidance, but it did little to bolster Jake's self-confidence. 'Course, Quint didn't have any idea that his longtime friend lacked in that department. At one time, before Jake had purchased the Rafter R, Quint might have believed he needed a big dose of ambition, but never self-confidence. That was something that Jake had kept carefully hidden from his friend, his mother, anyone who was close to him. He didn't want them to know that he often lay awake at night wondering if he was on the right path, if the business decisions he made would be the right ones and hopefully keep the ranch out of the red.

"I'll make my mind up about the alfalfa in the next few days," he told Quint, then spotting the turnoff to Rebecca's place in the far distance, he added, "I'm almost here. I'll talk to you tomorrow."

He started to snap the phone shut when Quint's voice stopped him.

"Jake—all that stuff I said earlier about you and Ms. Hardaway, I didn't mean to sound insulting."

"I never thought you did."

Quint sighed. "I just worry about you getting involved with a woman here on a temporary basis. I don't want to think of my best buddy moving to Texas and away from me. And I sure don't want to think about you getting that hard heart of yours cracked open."

A surprised frown crinkled Jake's features. "Oh, hell, Quint, there's not a woman on this earth that would make me leave New Mexico. And there sure isn't a woman who can break my heart."

"I'm glad to hear it."

Jake grinned as he wheeled his truck into Rebecca's graveled drive and told his friend goodbye. But as he slipped the phone into his jeans pocket and climbed down from the truck, he wondered why Quint had made such a fuss about him seeing Rebecca in the first place. The other man had never voiced an opinion one way or the other over Jake's female conquests, he didn't see why he should start now.

Shoving that thought away, he started toward the house.

Rebecca had been down at the barn, locking the horse up in the dry lot, when she'd caught sight of Jake's white truck pulling into the drive. Now, as she hurried through the backyard, she called his name.

"Jake! I'm back here."

He spotted her immediately and quickly changed directions.

She stood where she was, taking in his tall, muscular stride until he reached her side. This evening he'd changed his denim shirt to a teal plaid accented with flapped pockets and a long row of pearl snaps down each cuff. He looked very Western and extremely sexy and as he smiled at her, she could feel her heart reacting like a runaway drum.

"I was going to the house," he told her. "I thought I'd find you there."

It was impossible for her to keep her lips from spreading into a wide smile. Though she didn't understand completely why, just seeing him made her happy.

"I've been down at the barn, shutting the horse in the corral so it wouldn't leave before you got here," she explained. "Would you like to go have a look at her now?"

"Sure. We're already halfway there anyway," he reasoned.

With Beau on one side and Jake on the other, she led the way to the barn. As they moved forward, she noticed he was taking in the heaps of neatly piled junk she'd gathered from all corners of the yard.

"I've been trying to clean up the clutter," she explained. "Gertrude must not have believed in getting rid of anything. Even after it was broken. I've never seen so many old tires and rusted buckets."

"I'm surprised at how much better the place is beginning to look. And while we're on the subject, I could haul this stuff away for you," he offered. "That is, if you don't already have someone to do it."

She gave him an appreciative smile. "It's nice of you to offer, Jake, but Abe has already offered to send some of his hands to come pick it up for me."

"You've talked to Abe?" he asked with surprise.

She nodded. "This afternoon after I got back from Ruidoso I drove down for a little visit. I wanted to let him know in person how much I appreciated his kindness the day of Gertrude's funeral. He's such an easy man to talk to. If I tried, I couldn't have picked a better neighbor."

He chuckled. "If Abe wasn't eighty-five I'd be jealous."

Jealous of her with another man? Even though the idea was ridiculous, it thrilled her to imagine this man getting possessive ideas about her. But no one had to tell her he was teasing. This morning while they'd drunk coffee at the Blue Mesa, he'd confessed to her that he'd never been in love or intended to be. And she'd spent the rest of the day wondering why.

Trying to keep a blush from stinging her cheeks with pink color, she purposely turned the conversation in a different direction. "Did you get your work done at the racetrack?"

"Finished up about an hour ago. I'm still trying to get the kinks out of my back."

"Oh, I'm sorry. I shouldn't have bothered you with Starr. You should have told me to call a vet."

"Starr? Is that what Gertrude called the horse? Or did you find registered papers?"

"If Starr has papers, I've not found them. But then I haven't begun to sift through all the drawers and cabinets filled with Gertrude's papers and things." She glanced away from him as she realized there was nothing for her to do but answer honestly. "You see, up until the morning of her funeral, I had no idea my aunt had any sort of pets." Trying to smile, she directed her gaze back to him. "So I've given them all names of my own. They might not like what I've christened them, but it's better than calling them dog, cat or horse."

"Well, looking over Starr is hardly a problem for me," he assured her, then added with a wink. "And moving around helps the kinks in my back."

At the barn, they walked to the small fenced lot connected to the left side of the building. Inside the enclosure, the gray dappled mare that Rebecca had named Starr ambled over to them. Beau flopped down in a nearby shade, content to simply watch.

While Jake sized up the animal's overall appearance, Rebecca decided it best to keep her questions to herself until he had a chance to voice his opinion.

Finally, he said, "From this side of the fence, she looks like she's in reasonably good shape."

"Do you have any idea how old she is? Or what sort of horse she is?"

"With a closer look I might be able to give you a good guess about her age. Do you have a halter or bridle that I could put on her?" he asked.

"Yes. Just a moment and I'll get it," she told him.

When she returned with a rope halter, she found Jake already inside the corral and his hands on the horse. Rebecca scrambled over the fence to join him and he took the simple piece of tack from her and slipped it on the mare's head.

Dismayed at how easy he'd done the task, she groaned with frustration. "I tried putting that thing on her several different times yesterday. But each time she kept lifting her head higher and higher."

Chuckling, Jake glanced at her. "Don't let her beat you at that game. Before you try to slip it on her nose, put your arm behind the back of her head. That tells the mare to keep her head down to your level."

"Oh. Well, I did warn you that I know very little about horses."

He cast her an appreciative glance. "You knew enough to see that this one was a mare."

The color on her cheeks deepened. "Thank you for giving me that much credit."

His hand stroked down the mare's neck and then his fingers began to comb through Starr's long, black mane. For a man with big hands, Rebecca couldn't help but notice how gently he touched the mare.

"You're welcome," he said. "But I can't figure why you named her Starr. She doesn't have a star in her forehead."

She shot him a hopeless look. "Does everything have to be so literal with a cowboy? I wanted to name her Starr because she is one—to me. Isn't that a good enough reason?"

"Best reason of all," he answered, then with a soft laugh, motioned for her to come closer.

Since she was already standing only a couple of steps away, she could hardly get much closer without touching him, she thought. Confused by his gesture, she took a cautious step toward him and Starr, then paused.

"Come on over here," he coaxed, while pointing to the spot directly in front of him. "Neither one of us is going to bite you. I want to give you a lesson."

Rebecca wasn't sure she was ready for the kind of lesson he could give her, but she stepped forward anyway.

Immediately, he slipped the rope halter off the mare's head and pushed the dangling straps into her hands.

Gasping, she stared at him. "Jake, I can't do this! I've already told you—"

Before she could finish, he positioned her next to the horse, then situated himself close behind her. Rebecca drew in a sharp breath as the front of his hard body pressed against the back of hers. Heat flooded her senses, raced over her skin to leave every pore puckered with awareness.

She was trying to catch her breath and assure herself that she wasn't going to melt, when he suddenly aligned his arms with hers and slipped her hands into his.

"I'm going to guide you," he explained in a low voice. "Let's open the halter like this." With his hands moving hers, the strands of rope fell into the right position. "Now we're going to put this arm around Starr's neck and this one is going to loop the rope over her nose."

The subtle movement of his body against hers was sending currents of excitement shivering through her, making it difficult to breathe, much less think. Thank goodness he couldn't see her face or guess how overwhelmed she was by his nearness.

"She—she'll try to run away." Rebecca finally managed to speak.

"No. She won't," he murmured. "She likes human contact. Don't you?"

Rebecca shouldn't have to answer that question, she thought wildly. The mare wasn't trying to move away from them any more than Rebecca was trying to pull away from Jake.

Swallowing again, she admitted, "When the time and the place is right."

He didn't say anything to that. But then he didn't need to. The slow, sensual shift of his body was already telling her how much it liked being next to hers. How much he wanted to prolong the experience.

She tried to swallow and ended up gulping as his low voice vibrated close to her ear.

"This piece goes behind Starr's ears. And this one beneath her throat. Now latch the two together and pull it snug. But not tight." He easily thrust two fingers between the halter and the mare's jaw. "See. You should be able to get your fingers comfortably beneath the rope."

"Yes—I see."

Her voice sounded more like a strained squeak than anything and he glanced over his shoulder to look at her. "Are you okay?"

She tried to smile, but ended up merely nodding at him. "Sure."

"Want to try again?"

Again? She'd barely survived this one lesson. "Um… no. I think I can manage now. Thanks."

Before he could insist on another haltering session, Rebecca quickly stepped back until there was a safe distance of space between them.

Glancing over at her, he said, "You must be a fast learner."

Superfast, she thought, as she took in the faint grin on his face. In a matter of moments, she'd learned that standing next to Jake was like snuggling up to a piece of red-hot dynamite. "I am. I pick up on things—quickly."

"That's good. Especially around animals. You always need to be on guard around them." With his gaze still on Rebecca, he stroked a hand over Starr's rounded hip. "Just because Starr is standing still and behaving nicely now doesn't mean that something couldn't frighten her and make her rear or bolt. She wouldn't be trying to hurt you—she'd just be trying to save herself. But you could get hurt in spite of that. You understand what I'm trying to tell you?"

Yes, she understood far more than he could possibly know. That he and Starr could both be unpredictable. And that she needed to stay on guard when she was around either of them. Yet that wasn't the way to enjoy the horse, him or even life in general. Strange how she could think in those terms now that she'd traveled out here to New Mexico. Before, back in Houston, she'd carefully thought out every step she'd taken.

"Don't worry, Jake. I'll be very cautious when I'm around her."

"Good."

He gave her a lazy smile, then turned his attention back to the mare. For the next few minutes, he made a slow, thorough inspection of Starr's teeth, ears, feet and coat. Once he was finished, he led the horse over to the fence and loosely tied the lead rope to one of the cedar post.

"Well, I'd say Starr looks to be somewhere around ten years old. And she's a quarter horse most likely mixed with a bit of Thoroughbred. The kind we use on the ranch to work cattle."

"Is ten old? For a horse, that is?"

He ambled over to where Rebecca stood and lazily leaned a shoulder against the fence. "Not at all. She hasn't even reached her prime yet."

She smiled with relief. "Oh. I'm glad. I mean, well— I guess I've already gotten attached to her and I hated to think that she might be in her waning years. And—I might not have her for much longer."

He casually folded his arms against his chest. "Hmm. Does that mean you'll be taking her back to Houston with you?"

His question brought her up short. What had she been thinking? That she was automatically going to stay here from now on with her little family of animals? Had she been speaking her dreams out loud without bothering to think how ridiculous they must sound to this man?

She groaned inwardly. "I don't know about that, Jake. I've not thought that far ahead. I just like to think that she'll be with me for a while. You know what I mean?"

An easy smile came upon his face and she suddenly realized that he did understand what she was trying to say, that maybe he didn't find her dreams ridiculous after all. The way her mother had so many years ago.

"Sure I do."

A breath of relief escaped her. "So, is there anything else I should know about her? Any problems?"

"Nothing serious that I can see. She needs to be treated for parasites and her feet need attention. A set of shoes would help. Especially if you plan on riding her."

Rebecca's lips parted with eager surprise. "Oh! Could I ride her?"

The smile on his face deepened and her gaze zeroed in on the dimple at the side of his mouth. Oh, my, he was a charmer, she thought. And he didn't even have to utter a word. Just one long look from the man was enough to melt a woman's bones.

"I don't see why not. She appears to be gentle. If you'd like, I'll bring a saddle over and see how she handles first. Do you know how to ride?"

Rebecca shrugged. "I know how to get in the saddle and make them go and stop. That's the extent of it. My friend and I went to Padre Island one summer on vacation and we hired horses from a stable to ride on the beach. I'm sure they were what you'd call nags. But it was such fun."

He chuckled. "I don't know what Gertie was doing

with Starr, but she's definitely not in the nag department."

Rebecca walked over to Starr and pressed her cheek against the mare's neck. Jake followed and as he came to a stop just behind her shoulder, she looked thoughtfully up at him.

"I wonder what my aunt *was* doing with Starr?"

His expression solemn, he shook his head. "I'm not sure if Abe or Quint ever spotted her on horseback. I certainly didn't. Maybe she wanted the mare for company," he suggested.

A tiny pain squeezed somewhere in the middle of Rebecca's chest. "Yes. She probably was lonely," she murmured, then embarrassed by a sudden sting of tears, she turned her gaze on Starr's gray coat.

Behind her, Jake cleared his throat, then closed his hand over her shoulder and gently squeezed.

Touched by his sensitivity, she turned toward him and tried her best to smile. He was so close that she could see the golden flecks in his brown eyes, smell the subtle scent of cologne clinging to his shirt. His lips were not exactly full, neither were they thin. The word *perfect* kept coming to her mind as her gaze inspected the way the lower one squared off at the corners, the way his strong jaws blended upward into a pair of lean, hollow cheeks.

Doing her best to curb the urge to moisten her own lips, she said, "There is something else about Starr that you can advise me on. A couple of days ago, I purchased feed for her. From Marino's—where I ran into you this morning. The man behind the counter suggested I give her a certain kind. But I'd like your opinion. I have it in the barn, if you'd care to look."

"I'd be happy to," he replied.

Drawing in a bracing breath, she stepped around him and started to the barn. When he didn't follow immediately, she glanced behind her to see him removing the halter from Starr and opening the gate so that she could come and go whenever she liked.

Rebecca paused to give him time to catch up with her, then led the way to the back of the barn where a small room with a door was located. When she opened it and Jake spotted the four sacks of feed, each weighing fifty pounds, stacked against one wall, he looked at her with surprise.

"How did you get that stuff in here?"

She shrugged as though it was no special feat. "I drove the truck as far as the fence would allow and then I used the wheelbarrow to get the sacks back here."

"But you had to lift them to get them inside this feed room."

"I'm not as fragile as I look. I work out at the gym and I have some muscles."

Whenever Jake looked at this woman, he didn't see muscle. He saw gently rounded curves and soft, soft skin. He saw things he wanted to taste and touch. This evening she was wearing a purple top with a scooped neck and tiny little straps over her shoulders. The garment exposed her creamy skin and for the past few minutes that he'd been here, he'd had to fight with himself, remind himself that he had no right to reach out and touch, to let the pads of his fingers savor all that smooth, heated skin.

"Then I guess I can quit worrying about you taking care of yourself."

Her brows arched faintly above her blue eyes, the corners of her lips curved upward. "Worried? Why? I've been taking care of myself for a long time now."

"Maybe so. But not out here in the country. Like this. With no one around."

"Abe isn't that far away. And if I needed help, he has dozens of cowboys."

Jake didn't want to think about dozens of cowboys coming to Rebecca's aid. He didn't want to imagine just one. Unless that one was himself. Dear Lord, could Quint be right? he wondered. Was this woman the type who could hurt him? Really hurt him? He didn't want to think about it.

"Yeah. I suppose he does," Jake murmured, then stepped inside the little feed room.

She stood outside the open door and waited while he bent to inspect the feed and read the nutrition list. When he finally rose to his full height she said, "I've been giving her two of those scoops full twice a day. Is that enough? Or too much?"

Jake looked at the plastic scoop lying inside a black rubber feed bucket.

"That's good for now. After a couple of weeks, you might increase it to three scoops in the morning and evening. By then she'll be getting used to digesting more food on a regular basis. From the looks of her she could stand to gain about fifty to seventy-five pounds."

He stepped out of the room and shut the door behind him. It looked as though his job was now finished and for the life of him Jake couldn't think of one excuse to stay longer.

"That's great to know. I'll mark it on the calendar to remind me when to give her more," Rebecca told him, then smiled brightly. "Thanks for giving me all the horse lessons and for being so patient with such a—greenhorn."

He laughed softly. "I'd be as lost as a goose if I had to tell anyone about the fashion business. All I know is that I want my jeans to bend, my shirts to snap and my boots to have enough heel to stay in the stirrup."

She laughed along with him. "Yes, I guess we all have our own fortes."

Fighting the urge to clasp his hands around her arms and draw her to him, Jake jammed his hands in the front pockets of his jeans. Saying the next words was going to be worse than downing a dose of bitter medicine, but Jake didn't want to overstay his welcome and have her thinking he was a man who'd take advantage of her privacy.

"Well, I guess if that's all you needed from me this evening, I'll be going."

The disappointment on her face was like a burst of sunshine to Jake.

"Oh, you don't have to go yet, do you?" she asked quickly. "I was hoping you could stay and have supper. I've made enchiladas and I can't begin to eat them all."

Jake was more than a little stunned. True, she'd asked him out here for his help, but he'd never expected it to go any further than a few minutes of pleasant conversation over the mare.

"Are you sure?" he asked. "I wouldn't want to intrude."

To his amazement, she reached over and looped her arm around his. "Intrude? I'm the one who's been asking for all the favors," she said. "And I hate eating alone. Don't you?"

If Jake truly wanted to be honest with this woman, he'd tell her that he hated doing everything alone. But he couldn't admit such a thing to her. He wanted her, wanted everybody to believe he was a man who was happy with his life and himself.

"I'm not particularly fond of it," he replied.

"Great. We'll be doing each other a favor. Then let's go on to the house. It won't take but a few minutes to get things together."

As they left the barn and headed toward the little stucco, she kept her arm firmly clasped to his and Jake was amazed at how much the simple touch was affecting him.

It didn't make sense, he thought. Over the years, a heck of a lot of women had touched more than his arm. But none of those women or their touches had made him feel as though he was stepping two feet off the ground, as though he was someone important and wanted.

She's the type of woman who could hurt you without even trying.

Quint's words suddenly echoed through his mind and a nagging unease followed right behind them. He still had his ranch to improve, his mother to care for, and no experience of settling down with a woman—particularly one who wasn't used to hard work and the realities of "cowboying," as she'd said. His friend had been right, he thought. Rebecca could easily hurt him.

If he let her. And Jake wasn't about to do that. She might have a firm grip on his arm right now, but he'd never give her soft little fingers the chance to touch his heart.

Chapter 5

Moments later, at the house, Beau followed them onto the porch and before Rebecca could open it, the dog stuck his nose in the crack of the screen door.

With a wry smile, she looked up at Jake. "Do you mind if Beau joins us? He'll be a good boy and lie on the floor, out of the way."

"I don't mind at all."

Jake followed her into the kitchen and was instantly struck by the delicious smell of just-cooked food. Glancing around the small room, he could see she'd made major headway in cleaning the piled cabinets and dusty linoleum.

The evidence of her hard work surprised him somewhat. That first day he'd laid eyes on her at Gertie's funeral, she'd seemed like the last sort to pick up a mop or broom or manhandle heavy feed sacks. But then, he'd not known her any more that day than he really knew her now.

"Is cooking something you do regularly?" he asked. She laughed softly. "Not in Houston. I don't have time for it. And I'm not really that good at it. I can do a few certain dishes. But now that I've moved out here, I'm trying to get the hang of making regular meals. It's not like I can walk down the road to a deli or restaurant."

"No," he agreed, while thinking what a drastic change in lifestyle this must be for her. About as drastic as him trying to survive in Houston.

Gesturing toward an open doorway on the opposite side of the room, she said, "I'm sure you'd like to wash Starr's hair from your hands. The bathroom is right down that hallway on the left. There should be soap and towels and whatever else you might need."

He nodded. "Thanks. I'll be right back."

Since the house was very small, it was no problem finding the bathroom. Along the way, Jake caught glimpses of the two bedrooms branching off the short hallway. In one, cardboard boxes and clothing were piled and strewn every which way. The other was neat and clean with a double bed made up with a white bedspread.

As he washed his hands, he tried not to think about her lying upon that white bed, the night breeze blowing gently across her body. No. Those were thoughts he shouldn't be dwelling on. Those were the kind of thoughts that could only get him into trouble. Yet he couldn't quite shove them aside or quit wondering what it would be like to kiss her, make love to her.

You can forget that, Jake. Rebecca might want you to share her supper table. But that's a far leap away from

her bed. Remember, you told Quint she's not a barfly.
So don't expect her to behave like one. She's a lady. A
lady not likely to make love to rough-edged cowboys.

Downright annoyed by the mocking voice in his
head, Jake switched off the bathroom light and hurried
to the kitchen. He'd told Quint that he knew how to be
a gentleman. So now was the time for him to prove it.

He found Rebecca setting the table with big red
plates that were chipped around the rims and tea glasses
foggy from years of handling. Even though Rebecca
came from an easier life, he thought, her aunt certainly
hadn't lived one.

"What can I do?" he offered.

"Nothing. It's all ready."

She plucked a bowl of tossed salad from the cabinet
counter and placed it in the middle of the small table
alongside the casserole dish containing the enchiladas.

As she made a move to take one of the chairs, Jake
quickly pulled it out for her, then helped her onto the
seat. He couldn't remember the last time he'd done such
a thing for a woman, but somehow it felt right with Rebecca.

She looked up at him and smiled. "Thank you, Jake."

"My pleasure," he murmured, forcing himself to
drop the loose hold he had on her forearm and take a
seat in the chair kitty-cornered to hers.

"I have all the windows open," she said, "but the
oven has made it very hot in here. I hope the heat doesn't
make you uncomfortable."

The heat he was feeling had everything to do with
her. Not the oven. "Don't worry about it. I'm fine."

She picked up a spatula, then motioning for him to
hold out his plate, she ladled a hefty portion of the meat

and tortillas concoction onto the surface, then did the same for herself.

A few feet behind them, Beau had curled up on the floor and now had one eye cocked curiously on their movements.

"For a girl who never was around animals, you sure seemed to take to them," Jake commented as he glanced at the contented dog.

Smiling faintly, she said, "I guess you could say I feel like a child let loose in a toy store. I'm so enjoying Beau and the cats and Starr."

"You never had pets when you were a kid?" he asked curiously.

Her gaze avoided his as she shook her head. "Not one. Mother wouldn't allow it. She said they were messy and costly and would require too much care."

"Sounds like she's not an animal lover."

Looking over at him, Rebecca grimaced. "Not hardly. She—uh—is not the outdoor sort."

"And you are?" he asked with an impish grin.

She shrugged. "I've always thought I could be." Her blue eyes caught hold of his. "You'll probably laugh when I tell you this, Jake, but when I was young, I desperately wanted to become a veterinarian."

His fork paused in midair as he looked at her. A sheen of sweat dampened her forehead and her cheeks were flushed from the heat. She looked beautiful and sad and sexy all at the same time, he realized.

"What happened? Why did you change your mind?"

Her lips pursed together. "I didn't change it. Mother changed it for me."

"Oh."

She helped herself to the salad bowl. "You see," she

began, "when my father, Vance, was still alive my life was fairly rounded. He understood that I needed and wanted to do things other than what my mother had planned out for me. But after he died, I didn't have him to back me up on anything. And when it came to me wanting to become a vet, she thought doctoring sick animals was too primitive for her daughter. That it was just a childish whim on my part."

"Was it?"

She sighed and Jake sensed there was something lost in her, some missing piece that she was yet to find. But then he supposed most people were that way to some degree. For years now his father's leaving had left an empty spot in him and he'd often wondered how he would feel if he ever found the man and stood face-to-face with him. Yeah, he figured everyone was a little lost at some time in their life.

"I don't know," she said. "Being here with Beau and the rest of the animals makes me wonder if I should have stuck to my guns and gone after my own wishes."

"You're still very young," he pointed out. "You have plenty of time left to go after your wishes."

She looked at him with faint dismay. "You make it sound so simple. But it's not. I have a job that pays extremely well. I've worked hard to build my career to this point. In fact, it's taken years. Throwing all that away and going back to college would be a huge change in my life, not to mention a whole lot more work."

"Work isn't work if you like what you're doing."

She remained silent for a long moment and then she grinned at him. Jake felt his heart begin to kick like a trapped pony.

"And do you like what you're doing?" she countered.

He chuckled. "We were talking about you."

"Yes, but that's all we seem to do is talk about me. I want to hear about you."

"I'm not that interesting, Rebecca. I live a boring, everyday life."

"I don't believe that. Tell me about your ranch. What do you call it?"

"The Rafter R. That's my brand, too. A gable of rafters with an R beneath it."

"Abe says the property is a very pretty piece of land."

"Abe did, did he?"

"Yes. He says it's near an old fort that the cavalry used years ago."

"That's right. The Rafter R is out in the middle of nowhere. But the majority of the ranches around here. have to be in the middle of nowhere. You need lots of acreage to run cattle in New Mexico. Forage is a scarce commodity. It's not like the area you live in where the Bermuda grows knee-deep."

"I see. So do you like being a rancher?"

Did he? There were many aspects of the job that he loved. Working outdoors, tending to the livestock, seeing the results of his handiwork. But working for Quint or managing the training stables at the Downs had been much easier. At those jobs, the responsibility of making major decisions had lain on someone else's shoulders, not his.

"For the most part. It's the sort of work I've done all my life. I went to college for a couple of years thinking I might eventually do something different in the agriculture field. I even got an associate degree, 'cause I believe everybody ought to learn. But doing a thing is sometimes better learning than what books can tell you. And it just isn't in me to be anything else besides a cowboy. Horses, cattle. They're what I know."

He didn't go on to tell her that he'd been born into ranching, that his father had taught him all he knew about raising cattle and horses. Even his ability to become one of the best farriers in Lincoln County had come from Lee Rollins.

You're like your daddy in every way, Jake. The good and the bad.

His mother had spoken those words to him more times than Jake could count. And he supposed Clara was right. He did take after Lee in plenty of ways. But Jake didn't want to believe he was exactly the same man as his father. He didn't want to think he was the sort of guy who could callously walk away from his own child, from the woman he'd sworn to love and cherish.

"And I'm sure you're very good at what you do."

Her reply broke into his roaming thoughts and he looked over just in time to see her cast him a furtive glance.

"I'd love to see the Rafter R sometime," she quietly suggested. "Whenever you're not too tied up with work."

Did she really want to see his ranch or was she simply trying to be sociable because he'd gone out of his way to help her with Starr?

Jake quickly decided to keep the questions to himself. He didn't want to take the chance of offending her. Especially if she really meant what she was saying.

"I'd be happy to drive you over to see it some evening," he said. "Just don't expect too much, though. I've only been working on the place for the past couple of years. It's coming along. But it's not quite where I want it to be yet."

"So it wasn't in tip-top condition when you purchased it?"

He grunted with amusement. "If it had been I could have never afforded it."

Her smile was gentle. "Well, I'm sure I'll be rightly impressed."

Impressed? With him? What was wrong with this woman? Couldn't she see he was just a regular Joe?

After that their conversation turned to less personal things. She asked him about the winters in Lincoln County and other local interests. As they talked and enjoyed the food, Jake tried to think of another time he'd had such an evening. But he couldn't recall even one.

He'd never really had many meaningful conversations with women he dated. Not that Rebecca could be considered a date. But she was definitely a woman and they were alone together. If this evening wasn't a date, it was pretty close to being one. Yet nothing about it felt like anything he'd experienced in the past. Most of those encounters had been spent throwing out sexual innuendos and nonsensical jokes, while subtly maneuvering his date to the bedroom. Getting to know his companion had never been important to Jake

So why did it seem important now?

"I'm so full I don't think I can eat another bite," Rebecca announced as she pushed back her plate. "Would you like something else? Dessert? I have chocolate cake that I purchased from a bakery in Ruidoso. I'll make coffee to go with it."

Jake wasn't sure he could eat another bite either, but

the cake and coffee would prolong the evening. And he wasn't ready to leave. Not by a long shot.

"That sounds good," he told her. "While you make the coffee, I'll clear off the table."

Rising to her feet, she looked at him with surprise. "That's not necessary. I'll deal with the mess later."

Ignoring her, he got to his feet and reached for the dirty plates. "I insist," he said. "It's the least I can do."

As they moved around the kitchen, the close quarters caused their shoulders to inadvertently brush each other more than once. Each time it happened Jake warred with the idea of grabbing her and whirling her into his arms. If Rebecca had been any other woman, he would have already made his move and showed her just what her presence was doing to his libido.

But Rebecca wasn't any woman and even though his body was yelling at him to shift to a faster gear, his mind was telling him he had to take things slowly. If he didn't, he might scare her off and ruin the easy companionship that had developed between them.

When the coffee finally finished brewing, Rebecca filled two cups and placed a hefty serving of chocolate cake on a small plate.

"If you'd like, we could take our coffee and sit out on the back steps," she suggested. "It's much cooler than this kitchen."

And much safer, she thought, as she poured a dollop of cream into her cup. From the moment they'd entered the house and sat down to supper, she'd felt as though all the oxygen had been sucked from the room. She'd hardly been able to keep her eyes off him. And the more she'd looked at him, the more her mind had wandered to things she had no business thinking. Like how it would be to kiss him, to have him hold her the way a man holds a woman whenever he wants her.

"I'm good with that," he agreed.

Releasing an inaudible sigh, she called to Beau and the three of them passed through the door and onto the back porch.

"I apologize for not having a porch swing or lawn furniture," she told him. "I couldn't find any around the place and I've not taken the time to shop for much more than groceries and pet supplies."

"The steps are fine," he assured her. "I'm not used to doing a lot of chair sitting anyway. Most of my sitting is done in the saddle."

He waited until she'd eased down on the top step before he joined her and as he stretched his long lean legs out in front of him, Rebecca immediately wondered if she'd made a mistake by leaving the kitchen. At least in there their chairs had been a respectable distance apart. Now that they were sitting side by side on the wooden step, there wasn't a hand's width of space between them.

What are you whining about, Rebecca? You've been itching to get close to the man. Now that you are, you want to run like a scared cat.

She wasn't feeling scared, she mentally argued with the mocking voice in her head. She was only trying to be cautious. Jake was obviously a love 'em and leave 'em sort of guy. He'd never taken a wife, or as far as she knew a fiancée, but she'd be ready to bet he'd taken plenty of prisoners of the heart. Would she be willing to become one more?

Sipping her coffee, she tried not to sigh, to let him see that just sitting here close to him was shaking her like the winds of a hurricane. "I'm ashamed to admit that a lot of my work is done sitting behind a desk. I have so much reading to do, so many photos and catalogs to view, I don't get to exercise as much as I'd like."

"You look like you get plenty of exercise."

She'd not been fishing for a compliment and the fact that he'd noticed such a personal thing about her sent a flash of pink color to her face.

"At the gym," she explained. "I meant natural exercise."

Between bites of cake, he glanced at her, his mouth curved in a suggestive grin. "What sort of exercise do you consider *natural?*"

She cleared her throat and wondered again why he made her feel so naive and inexperienced. She'd had plenty of boyfriends, even a few lovers. This one shouldn't be causing a flash fire of heat to rush from the soles of her feet to the top of her head. This one shouldn't be making her heart pitter-patter like those first few drops of rain right before a storm.

Dating had never been simple or easy for Rebecca. Losing her father had taught her that loving someone with all her heart also carried risks. And for a long time after she'd first started dating, she'd kept everything simple and platonic as a way to keep her emotions protected. But then, as she'd grown older, she'd realized if she never allowed a relationship to grow between herself and a man, she'd always be living alone. Unfortunately, each time she'd let a man into her life, he'd found a reason to leave. Now Jake was knocking on the door of her heart and, crazy or not, she was desperately wanting to open it up and let him in.

"I meant like…riding a horse."

"Oh. So tell me, Rebecca, back in Houston what did you do for play?"

The question brought her up short and for long moments her mind was stuttering, searching wildly back through her regular routine. To her dismay, the days and nights of the past few years were mostly an uneventful blur of work and travel, exhaustion and sleep.

"Well—I go to the movies," she finally said. She didn't add that the outing was mostly a form of work, a chance to see what types of fashions were being worn on the big screen and how the more popular movies would influence the next round of designs to be introduced to the buying public.

"Is that it?"

She thought for another long moment. "I like going to the beach down at Galveston—whenever I get the chance. But that's not often."

His gaze slipped over her face and she could feel her lips tingling, burning beneath his lazy inspection.

"No dining, dancing?"

She looked away from him to focus her gaze on the open field sweeping away to the left of the property. Twilight had fallen and in the gloaming she could see a pair of nighthawks circling over the desert brush. As she watched the birds dip and dive for insects, she wondered how Jake's simple questions could make her see herself more plainly than looking at her image in the mirror.

"On occasions. I stay very busy with my work, you see."

"Yes. I am beginning to see," he replied.

He placed his plate and cup aside, then reached for her hand. Rebecca tried not to outwardly shiver as the pads of his fingers slid gently back and forth over the top.

"And I'm thinking it's a good thing that you decided to stay on here for a while. For me, 'cause I like your company. And for you, 'cause I get the feeling that you needed some time away."

Her throat was suddenly thick and she tried to swallow the sensation away. "I hadn't planned on staying. Not at first. But I—well, I decided that my aunt deserved a little of my time. God knows she didn't have any of it while she was alive. And now—well, everything she had in her life, she left to me. It's—"

She was suddenly too choked to speak and she looked down at her feet as she tried to regain her composure. Finally, she spoke in a broken voice. "It's hard for me to bear, Jake. I don't deserve anything from her. None of it."

"Rebecca, why would you say such a thing?"

"Because I never visited her. Never spoke to her." She looked at him, her expression full of despair. "Jake, this is going to sound crazy, but I never even knew I had an aunt! I didn't find out about Gertrude until a few days before her funeral."

Clearly stunned by her admission, he stared at her. Then finally, he said, "I understood that you'd never been out here to visit. But I thought—well, sometimes people have good intentions that never come through and I figured you were busy with your own life."

Her head swung shamefully back and forth. "I wish it were that simple. But it's not. My family—everything feels like a lie—a sham!"

"Whoa now, Rebecca. That's a pretty harsh way of putting things. Maybe you ought to back up and explain from the beginning," he gently suggested.

Realizing half of what she'd just said probably hadn't

made sense to him, she nodded. "You're right. I should start at the beginning. So I'll begin by saying that I've always been from a small family. I never knew my maternal grandparents. My mother had been born to them in their latter years. By the time she'd grown to adulthood they were both suffering from age-related health problems. They passed away before I was born."

"What about your paternal grandparents?" he asked. "During the time I was a very young child they lived in Florida and came for short visits. But a few years before my father lost his life, they were killed in an automobile accident."

"That's hard," he said softly.

Her lips took on a wry slant. "That's life. At least, that's the way it is in mine." She drew in a deep breath and let it out in a heavy rush. "So neither of my parents had siblings. Or that's what I was led to believe. So I had no aunts or uncles or cousins. For most of my life it's just been my mother and me."

His forehead puckered in a frown, he squared around to face her. "How did you find out about Gertrude?"

"A lawyer from Ruidoso called me at the department store where I work. He explained that Gertrude had left strict instructions to notify me of her death, but not before. And that all of her belongings, including the land and mineral rights, go to me."

As she talked he rested their entwined hands upon his knee and Rebecca was amazed at how one minute his touch could be so exciting and the next comfort her like nothing had before.

"Dear God, that must have been a wham in the gut."

She sighed. "At first I thought someone was playing a tasteless joke. I even argued with the lawyer and told him that I ought to know my own family." The faint noise she made in her throat was something between a self-mocking groan and a sob. "Can you imagine how I felt when I learned that I didn't know my own family? Initially I was in denial. Then when I realized he was serious, I was stunned and embarrassed."

He stared thoughtfully out to the stand of aspens and the barn partially hidden by their branches. "I can't imagine what any of it must have felt like. You learn you have an aunt at the same time you learn that she's already died." He focused his gaze back on her face. "How did all this happen, Rebecca?"

Shaking her head with defeat, she tried to keep her emotions in check. Yet her voice quivered when she finally answered, "I don't yet know, Jake. I've asked my mother to explain, but she's told me very little. She and Gertrude were twins. But at some point, after they became adults, they parted ways and lived totally separate lives."

"And she hasn't explained why?"

The dismay in his voice matched the disbelief she was still feeling. After years of believing her mother was a morally upright person, she now had to face the fact that Gwyn was deceptive. Not only deceptive, but unfeeling along with it.

"The only thing she says is that they were entirely different people and they simply chose to live different lives."

"Do you believe that's all there was to it?"

Rebecca let out an unladylike snort. "Of course I don't believe it! If it was all that simple, there would have been no need for my mother to keep Gertrude a secret from me."

"Hmm. Maybe she thought the woman would be a bad influence on you and didn't want you to be acquainted with her."

"Jake! Gertrude was the only other blood connection I could possibly have for most of my life. Even if she had been a bad person, that didn't give my mother the right to keep her existence from me! Every family has a misfit or two, but that doesn't make them any less a relative. Besides, I don't believe Gertrude was a bad person. Do you?"

He appeared surprised that she'd asked him such a thing.

"Why, no. I don't," he answered. "How could she have been bad? She kept to herself and as far as I know never caused anyone a problem. Did your mother try to paint her sister as a bad person?"

Rebecca grimaced. "Not really. She refused to say much at all. And that infuriates me. I can hardly bring myself to speak to my mother. Most days I don't bother answering her calls. It's always the same. Begging me to come home, but refusing to explain anything."

His hold tightened slightly on her hand. "The Cantrells noticed you were the only relative attending Gertie's funeral. They wondered why and frankly I did, too," he admitted. "Your mother didn't want to see her own sister laid to rest?"

Anger, frustration and an enormous sense of loss swept over Rebecca and for a moment she closed her eyes. "Mother refused to come out here. Said she wanted to remember Gertrude in her own way." Opening her eyes, she looked at him with all the pain and betrayal she was feeling. "I'm ashamed to tell you this, Jake, but I honestly believe the death of a stranger living down the street would have affected her more. She doesn't want to remember her sister in any way. Much less talk about her."

His head swung back and forth in contemplation. "You being her daughter, I'm sure you know more about that than anyone else. What I'm wondering is why Gertrude never tried to contact you. You say she told the lawyer not to contact you before her death, only afterward?"

Rebecca nodded, then stared at him as her thoughts took his direction. "That's right. And I've been so busy wondering about my mother's motives, that I've not stopped to think about Gertrude's. Why didn't she try to contact me? Why did she live here in New Mexico, when I know for certain that my mother was born and raised in Houston? So that means Gertrude once lived there, too." Wiping a hand over her face, she said in a strained voice, "Oh, Jake, maybe my aunt didn't want to know me. After all, she knew where I lived—where I worked. I can only believe that she wasn't that interested in spending time with her niece."

His expression full of empathy, he curled his arm around her shoulder and snuggled her close to his side. "Rebecca, you're agonizing over things that might not even be true. I didn't know Gertie, but I can't imagine her keeping you out of her life on purpose."

It felt wonderful to have his strong shoulder supporting her, to have the heat of his body seeping into hers, warming the empty chill inside her.

"You're just being kind, Jake."

"I'm being sensible."

She sighed. "I'm afraid I'll never get the answers I need to know about my aunt—my family."

He didn't say anything for a long time, so long in fact that Rebecca finally tipped her head back to glance up at him. She barely had time to catch the faint smile on his face when he tucked her head beneath his chin.

"Don't feel badly, Rebecca. I've wanted answers about my own family for years."

As he stroked fingers through her hair, Rebecca realized she was probably allowing herself to get too close to the man. She also realized she couldn't resist him. At this moment, she didn't want to move. Didn't want to break the sweetness of his touch.

"What sort of answers?" she asked quietly.

"Do you remember me telling you that I don't have a father?"

Her mind whirled back to the day of the funeral. As he'd driven her back to her car, she'd asked him about his father and the answer he'd given her had been curt and evasive. At the time, she'd been too upset with her own problems to think much about it. Now she was wondering and wanting to discover more about this man who'd quickly stepped into her life.

"Yes. I remember."

She felt his body move slightly as he let out a heavy breath and the idea that this man could be troubled about anything took her by surprise. From the moment she'd first met him, he'd seemed like a happy, carefree guy.

"Well, the reason I don't have a father is not because he died in an accident, like yours."

He turned his gaze on the open meadow, but Rebecca knew he wasn't looking at the waning twilight or the busy nighthawks. His thoughts were somewhere far away.

"Oh. Are you trying to tell me that you've never had a father? That your mother raised you single-handedly?"

"No. I had a father up until I was thirteen years old. Then he packed up and left us," he said flatly.

Pulling her head from beneath his chin, she stared up at him. "Oh, Jake, why?"

His arm dropped from her shoulder and he rose restlessly to his feet. Unwittingly, Rebecca also stood as she waited for him to answer.

"He found another woman that he wanted to make a life with—more than he did my mother."

"So your mother and father divorced?"

"Yeah, they broke up," he said, his voice heavy with cynicism. "Just like thousands of marriages break up every year."

Puzzled, she watched him lean a hand against a porch post. "I don't understand, Jake. What sort of answers don't you have about your family? Your father cheated on your mother and they ended their marriage."

"It's not that cut-and-dried. Maybe for them. But not for me." He looked at her and for the first time since she'd met him, she saw cold hardness in his eyes. The emotion didn't match the man she'd come to know and the sight of it left her chilled.

"What do you mean?" she asked softly.

"Before Lee—that was my dad's name—left home we had a long talk. He told me that he loved me and that I had nothing to do with the reason he and my mother were getting a divorce. He promised that I would always remain his son and he would call and come back to visit as often as he could."

"So what happened?"

"That was eighteen years ago and I never heard from him since."

When he answered his voice was flat, yet in spite of that Rebecca could pick up on his pain, the sense of betrayal he'd been living with for so long now.

"So you see, you and I have something in common, Rebecca. Neither of us knows why our parents lied to us. Or why they made the choices that they did."

Moving forward, she placed a hand against his back. "I'm sorry about your father, Jake. But I'll tell you like you told me a few minutes ago. I can't imagine the man keeping you out of his life on purpose."

He turned toward her and this time there was a rueful twist to his lips, a sad acceptance in his eyes. The idea that he'd been hurt as she'd been, that he'd lived with it for so many years, touched her deeply, drew her to him in a way she hadn't expected.

He said, "Well, I tell myself it doesn't matter anymore."

"But it does," she added softly.

"Yeah. Deep down, I guess it does. Just like this thing with your aunt matters to you."

Her eyes met his and it seemed like the natural thing to reach for his hands and move closer to him.

"Thank you, Jake."

His brows lifted ever so slightly. "For what?"

"Just for...being here."

She squeezed his hands and for long moments they simply looked at each other. And then Rebecca realized his head was bending down to hers and she was rising up on her tiptoes to meet him.

When their lips finally made contact, the jolt was electric. As his hard lips gently moved against hers, she lost her breath and a rushing noise sounded in her ears. She was wilting, she thought wildly, drowning in a wave of heat.

A tiny moan sounded in her throat and then she felt his hands moving to her back, anchoring a supportive hold just beneath her shoulder blades.

He thinks I'm going to faint! And maybe I will if he doesn't stop soon!

The thoughts sent her hands crawling up his chest and curling desperate holds on both shoulders. The movement pressed the fronts of their bodies even closer and, as it did, his mouth turned urgent, hungry.

She clung to him, her heart pounding fast, her lips a throbbing prisoner to his.

And then, just as her senses began to reel off into some heady place, he tore his mouth from hers and stepped backward.

"I—I'd better go, Rebecca. Now."

Before she could catch her breath to utter a word, he was already down the steps and rounding the back of the house.

Dazed, Rebecca stared after him. What had happened? Why was he leaving?

She didn't stop to think about the answers. Instead, she leaped off the porch and raced after him.

Chapter 6

"Jake! Wait!"

When Rebecca's voice sounded behind him, Jake was reaching for the door handle on his truck.

Pausing, he glanced over his shoulder to see her hurrying toward him. He'd not expected her to follow him out here and the fact that she had both stunned and frustrated him.

As he watched her come to a stop a few steps away from him, he braced himself as best he could and turned to face her head-on.

"Rebecca, you shouldn't have followed me," he said hoarsely. "I told you I had to leave."

Her head swung back and forth. "I don't understand, Jake. I thought we were having a lovely evening."

Something in the middle of his chest squeezed into a tight knot. It was a pain like he'd never felt before and the sensation scared him, almost as much as her kiss had scared him.

"We were. It has been...nice. Real nice. But—" He broke off, amazed that he was at a loss for words. He'd always been able to communicate with women. If words didn't work, then there were always physical ways to express his feelings. But he'd already expressed too much of himself to Rebecca in that way, he thought ruefully.

She stepped closer and for one ridiculous moment, he considered jumping into his truck. At least that way he wouldn't be tempted to jerk her into his arms and smother those luscious lips with more kisses. Instead, he stood his ground and tried not to think about the way she'd made him feel. The way he was still feeling.

Confusion filled her blue eyes. "But what, Jake? You didn't like kissing me?"

He couldn't stop a groan from slipping past his lips. "Of course I liked it!"

"Then why are you running from me?"

Why was he? he wondered. He'd never run from any woman. In fact, he was always happy to let himself be caught—for a little while. "Because what happened between us back there on the porch—I...never planned for that to happen."

No, but he sure as hell had thought about it, he thought grimly.

She said, "I didn't think you had."

He let out a heavy breath. "I don't want you to think—" He stopped, then started again. "Look, Rebecca, you're a lady and before I came out here tonight, I assured Quint that I knew how to be a gentleman."

A smile lifted the corners of her lips and Jake found himself staring at them, wondering why her kiss had

His Texas Wildflower

felt so different. After all, they were just another pair of plump, pretty lips. They shouldn't have the power to rocket his senses to the moon. But they had.

"Ladies kiss, too, Jake. Especially when they're with a gentleman they like."

Shaking his head, he tried to laugh, but the sound was more like a helpless groan. "And you think I'm one of those? You're misguided, Rebecca. I'm just a regular Joe, who's good at pretending to be something he isn't. I'm not like the men you go out with. The men you want to kiss."

Her expression turned serious as she moved another step closer. "How do you know what sort of man I want to kiss?"

He tried to be cool and shrug his shoulder, but inside he was trembling. It was crazy. Laughable. What was the matter with him? Having a woman close to him was a pleasure. One that he often sought.

"I don't. I just know that it isn't a guy like me."

"Maybe I should have made myself clearer."

If she'd made herself any clearer, he thought, his self-control would have snapped like a fragile twig between her soft little fingers. It still amazed him that he'd found the wherewithal to pull away from her and end the kiss.

"It's clear enough, Rebecca. We're completely different people. Right now I suspect I'm a novelty to you. City girl meets rough-and-tumble cowboy. That's why the only thing you and I need to be to each other is... friends."

Sighing, she stepped forward and curled a hand over his forearm. He swiftly realized the touch of her fingers felt just as sweet, or perhaps even sweeter, now that he'd experienced the yielding softness of her lips.

"Jake, why are you doing this?"

He swallowed. "Doing what?"

"Making a big issue over one little kiss. I promise I wasn't trying to tie a string to you while you weren't looking."

Any other time, Jake would have laughed at her remark. Especially when it was ludicrous for her to think he was worried about her trying to tie him up. After about thirty minutes she'd want to untie him, kick him in the rear, and send him on back to the rest of the herd. But nothing felt particularly funny to him at the moment.

"I wasn't thinking you were trying to do anything. And I'm not making a big issue."

"Really? Do you always just jump up and abruptly leave your female guests?"

"You're not my guest tonight. I'm yours."

Exasperation twisted her lips and then as she continued to study his face, her expression softened and her fingers gently squeezed his arm. "Jake, I don't want you to leave angry. I like you. And tonight has been very special for me."

The wall of resistance he'd been trying to throw between them suddenly crumbled like old adobe. "Rebecca, I'm not angry. Far from it. I'm just—" Trying to hang on to his sanity, he thought as he searched helplessly for the right words. When none came, he decided plain ole honesty would have to do. "Look, Rebecca, back there on the porch—if I hadn't pulled away from you I—well, if that kiss had went on much longer, I'm not sure I could have stopped."

"Would that have been so bad?"

Her question tied his gut into a hard knot. Which

didn't make sense. She was intimating that his making love to her wouldn't have been out of bounds. Normally that was just the sort of green light he wanted to get from a woman. But he wasn't at all sure it was what he needed to hear from Rebecca.

"A moment ago you said that you liked me," he replied. "Well, I like you, too, Rebecca. And I don't want something happening to mess that up."

She searched his face for what felt like an eternity and then she nodded thoughtfully and dropped her hold on his arm. "I understand."

Did she really? he wondered. Because he sure as hell didn't. Liking a woman had never interfered with him having sex with her. Liking had nothing to do with a roll between the sheets. Until now.

Turning toward the door, he momentarily closed his eyes. "I'd better be going, Rebecca."

"Will you—will I see you soon?" she asked.

He dared not look at her, otherwise his pretense of being a gentleman might fall apart.

"Sure. I'll come by one evening and take you over to the Rafter R. If you still want to go."

"Of course I want to go," she replied. "And before you leave, there's something else I wanted to ask you."

This caught his attention and forced him to glance over his shoulder at her. "Oh. What's that?"

"The woman at my aunt's funeral—her friend, the one you called Bess. If you think she wouldn't mind I'd like to talk with her. Could you tell me how to find her?"

He angled his shoulders back toward her. "Sure. When you go through Alto there's a little grocery store called Frank's off to your right on 532. She works there in the mornings."

"Thank you. I'm hoping she can give me a few answers about my aunt."

"Maybe so," he said, then jerked open the truck door and climbed beneath the steering wheel, before letting himself look at her. "Goodbye, Rebecca."

She didn't speak as she lifted a hand in farewell.

With a shaking hand, Jake started the engine and drove away before he could change his mind.

The next morning after Rebecca had eaten a small breakfast and fed all the animals, she whistled for Beau and the two of them climbed into the old red Ford and set off for Alto.

Traveling down to the little community to see Bess this morning had been a last-minute decision. Mainly as a reason to get out of the house and away from her thoughts. She'd had a restless night and sunrise hadn't done a thing to improve her mood.

Over and over, she'd been asking herself what had happened last night between her and Jake. They'd talked. A lot. And then they'd kissed. Passionately. She wasn't exactly certain which one of them had initiated their embrace, or if that even mattered. What mattered was that she couldn't get it out of her mind. Nor could she understand his reaction to it.

Forget it, Rebecca. The man doesn't want to get tangled up with you. You're not his type. He practically spelled it out in big bold letters. What more do you want him to do? Say go away?

Rebecca huffed out a heavy breath and glanced over at Beau. The dog was hanging his head out the window, oblivious to her miserable state of mind.

"You're no help at all, Beau. Give you an open window and a little wind in your face and you think you're in heaven," she muttered.

At the sound of his name, the dog glanced around at her, then just as swiftly turned his attention back to the passing landscape.

Rebecca swiped her blowing hair away from her forehead, while wishing she could just as easily swipe Jake from her mind. If he didn't want to get tangled up with her, then why would she want to get involved with him? She'd never had to plead or finagle for a man's attention. She had no intentions of starting now.

And yet, there was something about Jake that touched her, made her crave his company, made her dream about kissing him again.

The cell phone lying next to her on the bench seat rang and her foot eased on the accelerator as she glanced down at the illuminated number. Not surprisingly it was her mother ready to make another pitch for her daughter to return to Houston.

Rebecca didn't bother picking up the phone. She wasn't in the mood to have a go-around with Gwyn this morning. Besides that, she wanted her mind clear when she spoke to Gertie's friend, Bess.

In the small community of Alto, she turned right at the highway junction and immediately spotted Frank's, a small brick building with a plate-glass front and a wide dirt parking lot to one side. At the back of the parking area, two huge blue spruce trees shaded a handful of vehicles. She parked next to a dusty Jeep and, before she climbed out, rolled the windows down so that Beau would be cool.

"You stay here, boy, and be nice. I'll be back in a few

minutes." Patting his head, she added, "And maybe I'll bring you a treat."

The dog grinned and pounded his tail with happy anticipation. As Rebecca left the truck and started toward the store, she thought about her mother and the many times she'd scoffed at Rebecca's wishes to have a pet of her own.

An animal of any kind would be a nasty nuisance, Rebecca. You're going to have to get over such adolescent fancies. You have a telephone, stereo and television. Just how much more company do you need?

Even after she'd grown up and moved out, Gwyn had reminded her about how hard she worked, how much she traveled and how it wouldn't be fair to have an animal. Rebecca had been unable to make her mother understand that a pet would have been her own special confidant, something she could share her private joys and sorrows with. Gwyn hadn't understood because she was the sort of aloof person that didn't know how to share herself with anything or anyone. And sadly, that had included her twin sister.

Oh, God, don't let me think about my mother now, she prayed, as she stepped through the open door of the small grocery store. She didn't want to get all angry and stirred up. Not while she talked with the only friend that Gertrude appeared to have had.

After the bright sunlight outside, the interior of the store was dim. The scent of fried food immediately met her nostrils and as her gaze swung toward the one checkout counter to her left, she noticed it was connected to a small deli offering hot food.

Behind the counter, a plump woman wearing a pair of black slacks and a red blouse with the word *Frank's* embroidered on the left breast was counting change back to a young man purchasing bottled sodas. Her hair was a mixture of gray and chestnut and her skin was lined with wrinkles in spite of the fact that she'd probably not yet reached the age of sixty. Those minutes at the cemetery were sketchy for Rebecca, but she did recognize this woman's kind face.

Rebecca waited to one side until the customer had left the building, then stepped up to the counter.

"Can I help you, miss?"

"I think so. Your name is Bess, isn't it?"

The woman used her hip to shove the drawer on the cash register closed. "Why, yes. Do I know you?"

"I'm Rebecca Hardaway. Gertrude O'Dell's niece."

The woman stared at Rebecca as if she'd just announced she was from Mars.

"You're kiddin' me! You're the same young woman I saw at her funeral?"

Nodding, Rebecca unconsciously glanced down at her casual attire. For this trip, she'd made a point to wear her most faded jeans and a simple T-shirt. Her face was bare of makeup and her hair pulled back into a ponytail. No doubt she looked very different from the "Houston" Rebecca.

"That's right," she told the woman. "I'm sorry I didn't get a chance to talk with you that day. I wanted to thank you for taking the time to come to my aunt's funeral."

Bess studied her thoughtfully for a moment or two, then suddenly turned her head and yelled to someone at the back of the store.

"Sadie! Come here and watch the counter for me. It's time for my break."

"Hold on!" a voice shouted from somewhere in the back of the store. "I'll be there in a minute."

To Rebecca, Bess said, "There's a place we can sit outside and I got a few minutes if you'd like to talk."

Behind her, a very young woman with pink-and-black hair and a pierced lip trotted up. "Okay, Grannyma. I'm here. Take your time. It's not like we got a boatload of customers today." She glanced at Rebecca. "You been helped, sweetie?"

"She's here to see me," Bess said to the coworker, then grabbed Rebecca by the arm and quickly ushered her out the open door. "Sadie's a sweet girl, but she loves to gossip. If you know what I mean."

"Yes. I do," Rebecca agreed, while wondering if this woman intended to tell her something about her aunt that she didn't want other people to hear.

On the west side of the building, two aspen trees shaded a long wooden picnic table. Rebecca took a seat on one side, while on the opposite Bess plopped wearily onto the wooden bench.

"Oh, my," she said with a contented sigh. "That feels good to the ole feet. Been standing on them since five this morning."

Amazed, Rebecca glanced at her watch. It was nearly eleven. "You've been at work since five this morning?"

"If the truth be known it was a little before. 'Course the boss don't count that. I have to start the biscuits and breakfast tacos. The working men want something they can eat on the go. Guess they don't have wives to cook for 'em." She glanced at Rebecca and laughed. "I'm showing my age now, ain't I, honey? Wives don't cook nowadays."

A vague smile crossed Rebecca's face. "I wouldn't

know about that. I've never been a wife," she admitted to Bess. And neither had her closest friends. Like her, they'd all been career women. As for her mother, Gwyn stayed as far away from the kitchen as possible.

"Well, you're not missing much. I know from experience. I had me a man once, but he was a no-account. Didn't like to work and didn't much like me when I tried to make him work. One day he lit out for richer pastures and never came back."

The woman appeared completely casual about the whole incident and Rebecca could only presume it had all happened way back in Bess's younger years.

"Oh. Did the two of you have children?"

"Two. A boy and a girl. After that I raised them myself." She leveled a pointed look at Rebecca. "A woman has to do what she has to do, you know."

Yes, Rebecca did know. Even though it had been through no choice of his own, her father had left her. And without him her world had changed. After his death, she'd decided to never cling to any man or depend on him for her happiness. And so far that pledge had kept her from a broken heart. But it had also prevented her from obtaining a lasting relationship. A man wanted to be clung to. A man liked to be needed. But so far she'd never met a man that could make her shake her independence.

Jerking her thoughts back to the present, she said to Bess, "You must be a very strong woman."

Bess snorted. "Strong hell," she muttered. "Half the time I was scared to death. But that's another story and you didn't come here to talk about me."

"Actually, Jake Rollins told me where to find you. He said that you and my aunt were friends."

Bess's eyes squinted a curious glance at Rebecca. "Jake, eh? You know Jake?"

To Rebecca's amazement she could feel her cheeks fill with a heated blush. Just saying the man's name was more than enough to conjure the memory of his kiss, the taste of it, and the wild, reckless urgings it had elicited in her.

"We...we've gotten acquainted."

"You be careful of that one, honey. He's hell on wheels with the ladies."

Unwittingly, her fingertips fluttered to her lips as unaccustomed heat burned somewhere deep within her. As far as she was concerned the man was a potent elixir and the dose she'd taken last night still hadn't worn off.

"I'd already assumed as much," Rebecca admitted, then attempted to steer Bess in a different direction. "Had you known my aunt very long?"

Bess took a few moments to mentally calculate. "Probably twenty years or more. That's when I first came to work here at Frank's. You see, she'd come in once a week and buy supplies. We never exchanged more than a few words until she happened to have a deck of cards in with her grocery items. I asked her what she was going to do with them. 'Cause it seemed out of character, her buying a deck of cards. She was a quiet, meek little thing always going around with her head down. She mostly dressed like a man. To keep from drawing attention to herself, I think. But then you probably already know all about that."

Rebecca's head swung regretfully from side to side. "No. I'm sorry to say I know nothing about my aunt. I didn't even know I had an aunt until I learned that she'd passed away."

"The hell you say!"

"It's true. And now I'd like to find out as much about her as I can. Did she ever speak of her family? Mention me?"

Bess's head swung grimly back and forth. "Gertie told me that she had family in Texas but she never talked about anyone in particular. I knew that her parents were dead and that she'd never been married. I asked her once why she never went back for a visit and she explained that she hated to travel and hated the city. Many a time, especially when Gertie wasn't feeling well, I wanted to ask her why none of her family ever showed up here in New Mexico. But I didn't. I could tell she didn't want to talk about that kind of stuff and I respected her feelings. There's a hell of a lot of things I don't want to spill my guts about, either."

Bending her head, Rebecca wiped a hand over her face. "Gertrude—Gertie was my mother's twin sister. I've only just learned this in the past three weeks. I don't know what happened between the two women, but my mother has kept these facts hidden from me. I was hoping that my aunt had confided in you and that you might be able to give me some answers about our family."

In contrast to her gruff appearance, Bess reached over and gently patted Rebecca's forearm. "I'm real sorry, honey. I wish I could tell you more. Gertie and me were good friends for many years. We played cards every week together—just me and her. She didn't like to get out much, so I'd drive to her place. She was a lonely woman and for a long time—back when she was a lot younger—I urged her to get herself a man." She paused and let out a mocking snort. "But I couldn't make much headway there. She could see what kind of shape Jim had left me in. So I wasn't exactly in the right position to argue the good points of the male race."

"Was there ever anyone special in her life?"

Once again Bess shook her head. "Not that I know of. But there were times, from some of the sad sort of things she said, that I got the feeling there was a man in her life at one time. 'Course that could just be comin' from my imagination."

"You never asked her outright?"

"Oh, yeah. Years ago, after she first came here I asked her if she'd ever had a husband or anything like that.

"She told me that men and her didn't mix. And all the time she lived out by Apache Wells, it's just been her and her critters. She might not have got along with men, but she surely loved animals. By the way, is anyone taking care of the ones she left behind? I figured whoever was taking care of her estate would find homes for them."

"I'm taking care of them," Rebecca told her. "At least for now, while I'm here."

"Guess you'll be selling out," Bess pondered out loud. "I can't picture a girl like you livin' way out there in the boondocks the way Gertie did."

Selling the property had been Rebecca's intentions all along. But it seemed like the longer she stayed here in New Mexico, the less she warmed to the idea. In a small way, she felt she was beginning to know her aunt and that made everything about the place more important and special to Rebecca.

"I'm living there for now. I'm not sure for how long, though," Rebecca told her, then added, "There is something you can tell me, if you would. What did my aunt look like? Was she petite and dark-haired?"

Bess frowned. "Why, no. Just the opposite. In fact, she looked a lot like you. Tall with blue eyes. Her hair was blond, too, only that darker kind—dishwater blond is what we used to call it. Why? That's not the way her twin sister looks?"

"No. My mother is a brunette and smaller in stature. That could only mean the two of them weren't identical twins."

Bess tapped a thoughtful finger against her chin. "Gertie having a twin," she mused aloud. "I still can't get over it." She leveled a meaningful look at Rebecca. "If your mother couldn't bother to see her own sister laid in the ground, then there must have been some pretty bad blood between them."

Rebecca couldn't argue with that. Not when she'd been thinking the very same thing. It had been bad enough to learn that her mother had kept Gertrude a secret, but when Gwyn had refused to attend her sister's funeral, Rebecca's eyes had popped wide open. From that moment forward, her mother had taken on an entirely different image and in Rebecca's eyes it wasn't a nice one.

"You're probably right. But I—well, my mother doesn't want to talk about Gertrude." With a helpless shrug, she gave Bess a grateful smile. "Thank you for telling me about her."

Bess gave Rebecca's arm another pat. "Glad to do it, honey. If you get to hankering to talk again I live about a mile from here. Anybody can tell you how to find me." She rose to her feet. "I'd better get back before Sadie gets restless and leaves the register to come looking for me."

Rebecca thanked the woman again then bade her goodbye. As Bess walked back inside the building and Rebecca returned to the truck, her mind was spinning with the bits of information Bess had given her.

What did it all mean? Maybe they hadn't been twins after all, she thought. Maybe the two women had not really been sisters and that was why it had been so easy for them to go their separate ways? One or both of them could have been adopted. But why had her mother told her that she and Gertrude were twins?

None of it made sense and short of confronting Gwyn and demanding answers, she didn't know how she could ever get to the truth.

Three days later, Jake spent the morning and part of the afternoon branding calves that he and his two ranch hands, Trace and Jet, had rounded up from the river bottom. Quint, being the friend that he was, had driven over to help and other than a few kicked shins and a burned thumb on Jet's right hand, the work had gone smoothly.

Once the calves had been returned to their mamas, Jake had insisted the two hands take the rest of the day off. Being young and single, and looking for any extra time for fun, neither man had argued and the two had hightailed it to town.

As for Quint, he'd lingered long enough to help Jake unsaddle the horses and put away their equipment. After sharing a cold beer, the other man had left for home, where Maura was making a special meal for her parents, Fiona and Doyle Donovan.

As soon as Quint was gone, silence fell around Jake and with the solitude along came Rebecca's memory. Not that it took a silent moment to think about her, he reflected, as he stared pensively out at the grazing horses from his front porch chair. For the past three days, he'd thought of little else.

That kiss. Never had one little mouth-to-mouth moment affected him in such a way. He couldn't forget it. Couldn't stop wanting to repeat it. Kissing her had probably been a mistake. The whole incident had certainly been messing with his mind. Yet he had to admit he'd never tasted a sweeter mistake.

With an inward groan, he reached for his cell phone and flipped the instrument open. The other night, while he'd been helping Rebecca clean her kitchen, she'd given him her cell phone number. The fact that he'd been carrying it around had been tormenting him, tempting him, while at the same time he'd been trying like hell to forget he had the precious combination of numbers. It had only been three days since he'd spent the evening with Rebecca and he didn't want her to get the idea that he was desperate for her company. He'd never been desperate for any woman. Not when there was always another woman willing and waiting to give him a bit of company.

Hell, who are you trying to kid, Jake? You're problem isn't what Rebecca might be thinking about you. The problem is what you're thinking about yourself. The urge to see the woman, hold her, kiss her again is clawing at your insides, tormenting your every waking moment. And just any other woman won't do.

Muttering a curse under his breath, Jake snapped the

phone shut, closed his eyes and sucked in a harsh breath. What was coming over him? Was he turning into a sap?

With that thought he opened the phone and punched Rebecca's number before he could change his mind.

She answered on the third ring and from the faint swooshing noise in the background he could tell she was outside in the wind.

"Jake, how nice to hear from you," she greeted him.

Like a cool drink of water after a long thirst, pleasure poured through him and curved the corners of his lips. "Have I caught you at a bad time?"

"Not at all. I'm painting the yard fence so I welcome the interruption."

Painting the yard fence? That didn't sound like a woman with leaving on her mind. But then she could just be sprucing up the place and getting it ready to put on the market.

Hell, Jake, it doesn't matter one way or the other. Eventually she'll go back to Houston and you'll go back to your old roving ways.

Shoving that thought away, he said, "Well, I've wound up my work for the rest of the afternoon and wondered if you'd like to come over to the ranch?"

She paused, but only for a second. "I was thinking you'd probably forgotten about the invitation."

Forgotten? He could forget nothing about her or the words that had passed between them. If that was a romantic sap, then he'd fallen into that category.

"No. Just waiting for the right time. If you'd like to come I can be over to pick you up in about forty-five minutes."

"If you'd give me directions I can drive it, Jake.

There's no need for you to make such a long trip to pick me up."

Rising from his chair, he started into the house. As he walked through the living room, he said, "I realize your old truck is fairly dependable, but I wouldn't like to think of you driving it through the mountains after dark."

"Oh. I'm going to be at your place for that long?"

Pausing near an armchair, he chuckled, then said in a husky tone, "It's a big ranch, Rebecca. And I want you to see everything. Everything that matters, that is. Still want to come?"

There was another short pause and at that moment, Jake wished he could see her face and read what she was thinking. Maybe she was biting her lip, trying to decide whether he was worth the effort at all.

"I'll be ready," she answered.

"Forty-five minutes," he reminded her, then after a quick goodbye, tossed the phone onto the cushion of the chair and hurried to the shower.

She'd be ready, but would he? Jake asked himself, as he peeled off his sweaty shirt and kicked off his dirty boots. For the first time in his life, he had a real home and a real lady to show it to. And the idea shook him.

He'd never cared much about other people's opinion of him or his way of life. He was an unpretentious man and as far as he was concerned, they all could take him or leave him.

But it was different with Rebecca. He wanted her admiration and respect. He wanted to hear her say he was doing things right and good.

Did that mean he was falling in love? No. He couldn't fall in love. He had too much of Lee Rollins's genes running through his veins. He wasn't a one-woman man. He was a man for every woman. And when he looked into Rebecca's pretty blue eyes again, he couldn't let himself forget that.

Chapter 7

Rebecca had just finished changing into a cool sundress and dabbing perfume on her neck and wrist, when she heard Beau bark and a door slam.

Hurrying from the bedroom and through the house, she walked out onto the front porch just as Jake was climbing the steps. He was carrying a small potted cactus with a single yellow bloom adorning one of the branches.

Her gaze vacillated between the plant and the lazy smile on his face while her heart leaped into a higher gear. Three days had passed since she'd last seen him and although he'd never left her thoughts, the actual sight of him was like a delicious jolt of pleasure.

"Hello, Rebecca."

She smiled back at him. "Hello," she said, then inclined her head toward the plant he was carrying. "Is that for me?"

A dimple carved deep into his left cheek as one shoulder gave a casual shrug. "I thought you could set it on your kitchen windowsill. Or something like that. It'll brighten up the place."

Touched by his thoughtfulness, she reached to take the plant from him. "It's beautiful, Jake. Thank you."

"It's also very prickly," he warned. "Better let me carry it in for you. We wouldn't want to spend the evening picking spines from your fingers."

"All right." She opened the wooden screen door and followed him through the small living room and into the even tinier kitchen.

He placed the blooming cactus in the middle of the windowsill and glanced around for her approval.

"Very nice. The pot even matches the curtains," she said.

A few days ago, she'd replaced the faded fabric at the window with those woven of blue buffalo checks. The curtains had been one of many small improvements around the place and she was still asking herself why she was making them. For herself? Or for the aunt she'd never known?

"Sometimes a man gets lucky," he said, slanting her a wry grin.

Her heart, which was already thumping in a rhythm that was way too fast, somehow sped up even more. Clasping her hands together, she cleared her throat. "W-would you like something to drink before we go?"

Moving away from the window, he walked over to where she stood by the small dinette table. "No, thanks. We don't have a whole lot of daylight hours left and I don't want to waste them." His brown gaze slipped down the length of her tan-and-white-striped dress and the sandals strapped on her feet. "Are you ready?"

His inspection of her appearance made her hesitate. "Am I dressed appropriately for this tour? If you'd like I can change into jeans and boots."

His gaze settled back on her face and in spite of her weak-willed efforts, Rebecca focused directly on his mouth with its square, chiseled corners and the faint sheen to the curve of his lower lip. Since that kiss they'd shared on the porch, she'd thought of those lips, dreamed about them, hungered for them. And tried her best to forget them. All to no avail.

"I'm not going to put you to work in the branding pen," he said with an amused grunt, then added huskily, "I like you just as you are."

She drew in a deep breath and said, "I'll go get my purse and wrap and we can be on our way."

For a moment there was something in his eyes that made her think he was going to reach out and touch her, but if he was harboring those intentions, something must have waylaid them. Like common sense, Rebecca thought. Because she had the feeling if he touched her now, they'd never make it off the place.

"I'll wait on the porch," he told her, then quickly turned and left the room.

Minutes later, they were headed northward through mountainous countryside that Rebecca had never seen before. Traffic was light to nonexistent on the narrow highway and before long they were far away from any sort of settlement or civilization.

As Jake focused on his driving, Rebecca decided to speak the thoughts that had been racing through her mind. "I was surprised when you called me this afternoon."

Beneath the brim of his gray hat, she could see his brow arch faintly. "Oh. Why was that?" he asked.

She looked away from him and out toward the swiftly changing scenery. In the past couple of minutes the mountains were giving way to flat desert surrounded by low, balding hills.

"Because the other night when you left my place I couldn't help but think that—" She didn't know how to put her feelings into words and she groaned inwardly as she tried to fumble her way through it. "Well, that something about me had put you off. I figured you probably intended to avoid me. Because you considered me trouble."

He kept his eyes on the highway. "You are trouble, Rebecca."

Frowning, she stared at him. "So what am I doing here? With you?"

This time he chuckled and the sound released some of the tension inside of her.

With his eyes crinkled at the corners, he glanced at her. "Haven't you guessed by now that I'm a man who likes to flirt with danger?"

Oh, yes, he flirted without even realizing he was flirting. That was part of his charm, she thought. He didn't even know just how potent he was to a woman, how just a simple little expression on his face was enough to melt her heart.

She started to tell him that there was nothing dangerous about her, but instead she decided it would be best all around to let the matter drop and try to forget everything about that kiss.

"I talked to Bess the other day," she told him. "She wasn't exactly what I expected. But she appeared to have cared a great deal for Gertrude."

"Bess is a little rough around the edges, but that's understandable. Life hasn't been easy for the woman. Still, she's a good ole gal. The kind that would be the first to offer help if you needed it." He glanced curiously her way. "Was she able to give you any helpful information about your aunt?"

"Actually, she told me something that still has me puzzled. My aunt's physical appearance looked nothing like my mother's. She said that Gertrude was tall and blonde. Like me. Is that true? Did you ever see her up close?"

"Not what you'd call close. But she was a tall woman and her hair was light-colored. I used to see her out in the yard, watering the shrubs and flowers. At one time she had a lot of them that bloomed, but that was years ago, back when Quint and I were just young boys. Later on, well, she must have lost interest in the yard and the house. It all started looking run-down." He grimaced, then shook his head. "Sorry. I shouldn't have said that."

She looked at him with speculation. "Why? The place being run-down is an understatement. It needs plenty of home improvements."

"Well, yes. But that bit about her losing interest. That's just a guess on my part. Bad health is probably what made her let things go undone," he said flatly. "I've seen the very same things going on with my own mother."

Interest peaked her brows. "You've never spoken much about your mother. Does she live around here?"

"In Ruidoso. After her and my dad divorced she sold

the ranch where I grew up and bought herself a place 'among the living' as she calls it."

The thread of sarcasm she heard in his voice was probably wound around all sorts of family incidents, she decided, and none of them good. "And you didn't want her to sell?"

"Hell, no! She let the property go for less than half of what it was worth. The two of us could have made a good go of it, but she wasn't willing to try."

"I thought you said you were only thirteen when your father left?"

"I was. But I was a big strapping boy. I could do the manual work of a man. And Dad had already taught me all about caring for the livestock."

"Yes. But still it would have been only you and your mother to see after things. Keeping up a ranch of any size would have been a big job for the two of you."

"We would've had to hire day hands from time to time and a vet whenever one was needed. But—" He let out a long breath and shook his head once. "Sorry. Again. None of that matters anymore."

"But it still fires you up," she quietly deduced.

He smiled wanly. "You could tell?"

She chuckled. "Just a little." Squaring her knees around so that she was facing him, she asked, "Do you and your mother get along?"

He shrugged. "If you're asking me if I love her, then I do. Very much. God knows she worked hard to raise me—without any help from my dad. But there are times I get so frustrated with her. It's like she's given up on life. She only sees the negative side of everything."

"That's not good."

The corners of his mouth turned downward. "No.

But then she has her reasons for being like she is. First she lost her husband to another woman. And then about ten years ago she had cancer and went through months of grueling treatment. That wiped the cancer out, but it weakened her heart."

"Poor woman," Rebecca murmured, while thinking what Jake must have gone through while his mother was ill. She didn't have to ask to know that he'd been at her side whenever she needed him, which had probably been a lot. "Is she disabled now?"

"No. And her heart problem wouldn't be that serious if she would only do what the doctors tell her to do. But she doesn't. I think—well, I think she's like your aunt Gertie was these past years. She's lost all interest."

Rebecca gazed thoughtfully out the windshield. "Do you think she's still pining for your father? That she can't get over losing him?"

He muttered a curse under his breath. "I've tried to tell her that the man isn't worth losing sleep over. And she agrees. She knew he was no good. Even before he left, she knew he had a string of women, but she loved him." He looked at her and shook his head with dismay. "Like love means more than anything—even living."

The tiny ache that settled in her chest confused her. It shouldn't matter to her that Jake had a cynical outlook about love. But it did and she couldn't quite understand why. Except that she was beginning to see him as a gallant knight in spurs and blue jeans and knights believed in love. Didn't they?

"I asked Bess if Gertrude had a man in her life," Rebecca told him. "She says she thinks there might have been someone a long time ago, but that's only speculation on her part."

"What do you think?"

That the right man could make a fool out of most any woman, Rebecca thought. Aloud she said, "Since I never met her I can't say. I'm thinking that I might be able to glean some things about her whenever I start going through her personal papers. The spare bedroom is piled with boxes of old correspondence. When I sort through them, I might find old letters to friends or someone that mattered to her."

"You've not dug into that stuff yet?"

Rebecca shook her head. "I've taken a quick glance at some of the things lying on top, but they all seemed to be bills and receipts. The past couple of weeks I've been focused on the animals, clearing the yard of junk and making the house livable." Bending her head, she absently plucked at a tiny wrinkle in her skirt. "To be honest, Jake, I'm a little reluctant to dig into the correspondence."

Surprised by her remark, he darted a glance her way. "Why?"

She shrugged. "Fear of the unknown, I suppose."

He looked even more confused. "I don't understand, Rebecca. I thought you wanted to learn more about your aunt."

"I do. When I first found out about Aunt Gertrude I wanted to find out anything and everything—all at once. But I—" She stopped and let out a long sigh. "Now, the more I dwell on it—well, sometimes I get the feeling that I might be better off not knowing. My mother has certainly made it clear that she wants to keep the past hidden. Maybe she's trying to protect me in some way."

"From what? Gertrude wasn't a criminal."

Sighing, Rebecca swiped a hand through her blond hair. "No. But, Jake, whenever you think about your father—maybe about searching for him—don't you get the feeling that you might not like what you find?"

"Hell yes. I think that most all the time," he admitted. "I guess that's why I've never gone on a real search for the man. I'd like to know why he turned his back on me. But finding the answer might tell me more than I want to know."

"That's exactly what I'm thinking about Gertrude's correspondence." She cast him a helpless glance. "Are we being cowardly, Jake?"

He grimaced. "I like to think we're simply being human," he said.

Just being human. Jake's words continued to linger in her thoughts as the truck carried them toward a low rise of mountains. When she was near Jake she felt very human. And so much a woman. Whether that was good or bad, she didn't know. She only knew that Jake was the first man she'd ever allowed to see all sides of her, to view the woman she'd always kept curtained and private.

What did that mean? That he was simply a man that was easy to be with, talk to? Or was she falling in love with him?

Pondering that question, she looked over at his dark profile just as he pointed a finger toward the windshield.

"See that cedar post? You are now entering Rafter R land," he announced.

There was pride in his voice and the sound made her happy. "Abe tells me you've worked very hard on this place. That it's turning into a 'damned good ranch' I think were his exact words."

"You've been talking to Abe again?"

"Yesterday. He came over with two of his ranch hands to haul away the junk I'd gathered together in the yard."

"Well, I think I should warn you that you can't believe everything that Abe tells you. The man likes to exaggerate."

She watched a dimple come and go in his cheek. "I got the feeling that he enjoys telling a tall tale now and then, but in your case, I think I can believe him."

He chuckled. "You're about to find out for yourself."

Five minutes later, Jake steered the truck off the highway and passed beneath an arched entrance made of iron pipe. Sheet metal, cut in the shape of the ranch's brand, hung from the center of the arch and swung slightly in the dusty breeze.

They traveled at least a half a mile on down the red dirt road when a sprawling log house with a green tin roof appeared beyond a stand of aspen and willow trees. As they grew closer she could see the structure was surrounded with a wooden fence painted brown, while massive blue spruce trees shaded a long, ground level portico.

"How lovely!" she exclaimed, then when he failed to pull into the short drive, her head whipped around in surprise. "Aren't we going to stop? Or is this someone else's home?"

A wry grin slanted his lips. "It's mine. I thought I'd show you some of the other parts of the ranch while we still had daylight. You can always see the house later," he reasoned. "Unless you need to make a restroom stop before we go on?"

"No. I'm fine," she assured him. "I was just confused. For a moment I thought that perhaps other people lived on your property. Do they?"

"No. My hired hands live on their own places near Ruidoso and my nearest neighbor is about six miles from here. The closest town, Capitan, is about twenty minutes away. "

"Do you go there often?" she asked.

"I go over there on occasions, to see a few friends. It's more of a village than a town. So if I need supplies for the ranch, I drive into Ruidoso."

"I see," she murmured, as he turned right, onto what appeared to be little more than a two-rutted track with short, stubby grass growing down the middle.

Straightening the steering wheel, Jake glanced at her from the corner of his eye. Did she actually see and understand just how isolated his home really was? he wondered. It was true that Rebecca's place wasn't exactly in the middle of a metropolis, but at least Ruidoso was a heck of a lot closer to her place than to his. And compared to Houston, even Ruidoso was a little tadpole of a city.

"There's not much out here except the wildlife and my cattle and horses," he told her.

"Yes. But it's very beautiful. I wasn't expecting to see this many trees." She gestured toward a band of trees lining the riverbanks. "I thought it was going to look like the desert area we passed through. And those mountains to our left! Does your property include part of them?"

"No. It runs right up to the foothills. Next to me on that side is protected national forestland. And on the right I butt up to Fort Stanton, which was turned into a museum several years ago. So I have a little strip of property running between federal lands. But the strip crosses the river. And best of all, it's mine," he added.

She smiled at him and Jake found it damned hard to keep his eyes on the bumpy track. In that simple little dress she looked every inch a woman and every inch of him wanted her.

"Where are the cows?" she asked, her gaze scanning the horizon.

"All over the place. But I'm sure we'll probably find some down by the river. The grazing is better there."

Five minutes later, a few yards away from the river, Jake parked the truck in a flat, shady spot and helped Rebecca to the ground. Then with his hand wrapped firmly around hers, he led her through a tangle of waist-high sage and drooping willow limbs until they were standing at the water's edge.

"Oh, my! There's a little waterfall. How perfectly beautiful!" She turned a grateful smile on him. "And how sweet of you to show it to me."

Sweet? Hell, he'd never been called sweet before. And though it should have made him feel like a sap, it somehow made him feel warm and wanted. Quint would definitely get a laugh out of that, he thought.

Hoping he didn't look as goofy as he felt, he grinned at her. "I thought you might like it. Want to get a closer look?"

"I'd love to."

They walked several yards upstream to where a ledge of boulders had created a tiny dam. The crystal-clear water rushed over the rocky rim and fell at least ten feet before joining the rest of the river.

"Is the water always this clear and deep?" she asked as they stopped just short of the bank's edge.

"No. Later on in the summer, the level will drop considerably. It's always clear then. But in the spring, the snow runoff sometimes makes it muddy."

She turned her head to look at him and as their eyes met he felt as though something had punched him in the stomach. She was so fresh and pretty. Like a bright bird flying through a blue, blue sky. He wanted to touch her. Desperately.

"Do you fish for trout?" she asked.

"Once in a while. But I go to the lake to do that."

"Is the lake far from here?"

He didn't know why he couldn't quit looking at her lips. Why he kept remembering the taste of her kiss. After all, she was just another woman, he tried to tell himself.

He said, "A few miles. Quint and I used to camp there together from time to time. But that was—before he got married."

"Does that bother you? That Quint got married? You two probably spent lots of time together before he became a family man."

"Yeah, we did," he admitted. "But Maura and the babies make him happy. That's what counts."

She sighed. "I don't have any married friends. Most of them are like me, I suppose. Too busy to have a family."

Jake's gaze lingered on her face as he tried to read what was behind her pensive expression. "That's too bad. I'd bet you'd make a good wife and mother."

Her short laugh was threaded with cynicism. "No one has ever told me that before."

She gave him a faint smile and Jake was surprised at the sadness he saw in her eyes. "That's hard to believe. Surely there've been men in your life that have mentioned marriage to you before."

Shaking her head, she looked away from him and across the river to where a herd of black cattle were idly grazing. "Not really. With me and men—well, things never get that far. It's hard to have a relationship when I'm packing up every two or three weeks to travel to some far-off city."

For some reason, Jake wanted to wrap his hands over her shoulders and pull her back against his chest. He wanted to press his lips against the curve of her neck and tell her that she was a woman meant for loving, not packing. But that would be insinuating that he wanted to keep her at his side, wanted her to consider him more important than her job. And he was in no position to do that now. Maybe he never would be.

Worry is all a man ever does when he loves a beautiful woman. First he frets about catching her. And then when he does get his hands on her, he worries himself silly wondering if he'll be able to keep her.

Jake had told Quint those very words more than once. And he'd meant them. Having a taste of a smart, beautiful woman like Rebecca could only cause problems. But with her standing so close that he could see the fine pores of her soft skin, smell her flowery scent and gaze upon the moist curves of her lips, he could only think she'd almost be worth the risk.

"Well, your job is important to you. Isn't it?"

From the corner of her eye, she darted a dubious glance at him. "More important than what, Jake? Right now my job is all I have."

Why did he want to tell her that she—that the two of them—could have so much more if they were together? What was the matter with him, anyway? When it came to women he didn't think in terms of "together." And he damned sure never let the word *forever* enter his mind.

Clearing away an uncomfortable knot in his throat, he said, "I see what you mean."

She didn't reply and after a moment he reached for her arm. "We're losing daylight," he told her. "We'd better be on our way."

For the next hour, he drove to random spots on the ranch where he'd made vast improvements in the fences and grazing land. Jake tried to keep the conversation light, yet something between them had changed while they were standing at the river. He didn't know exactly what or why, except that there was a strained sort of tension between them. As though both of them were trying hard to avoid making eye contact or say anything that could be construed as personal.

By the time they arrived back at the ranch yard and entered the huge barn, Jake was ready to give in and say to hell with being a gentleman and worrying about tomorrow.

"Did you have to do much repair work to the barn?" she asked as the two of them meandered slowly down the alleyway.

On the left side of the structure, ten tons of alfalfa hay were stacked to the rafters. On the right, horse stalls were standing empty. Jake stopped at one of the huge posts that supported the roof and gently thumped the heel of his palm against the creosoted wood.

"Shoring up the support and a new roof. I've spent

more money on this barn than I have everything else put together."

She was standing next to him now and in the dim lighting, the angles of her face were softened, the curve of her lips even more inviting. The aching tension deep inside him coiled even tighter.

"You don't have any horses in the stalls. Why is that?"

"When the weather is nice and I don't need to use them the next day, I turn them out. They like being free—to do whatever they want," he added lowly.

She slanted him a glance and he watched her lips suddenly begin to quiver. "And you do, too, don't you?" she asked softly.

Jake didn't bother trying to summon up any resistance. His hands reached for her so quickly they were a blur.

With her breasts crushed against his chest, he bent her head back over one arm. "Hell yes," he muttered, his lips poised over hers. "And right now I'm damned tired of not doing what I want to do. And I want to do this more than I want to breathe."

He heard her suck in a sharp little breath just as his lips were settling over hers and then his mind went blank as his arms tightened around her and he deepened the kiss.

She tasted just as good or better than Jake remembered and when her arms slipped around his neck and drew her body closer to his, he realized this was something she wanted as much as he. It was a heady notion, one that fueled his rampant hunger.

Long seconds ticked by as their mouths fed upon each other's, their hands began to roam and seek, clench and cling. Jake's senses began to slip to some foggy place he'd never been before where there were no sights or sounds, just warm, velvety heat.

If not for the fiery pain in his lungs, he would have kept kissing her forever. But the need for oxygen finally tore his lips from hers. Yet even then he couldn't quit touching her. Between ragged breaths, he kissed a trail down the side of her neck, then onto the fragile bones of her shoulder.

Her skin was like the petal of a flower. Satiny and soft and so precious beneath his lips. And the more they explored and tasted, the more he wanted. At the back of his neck, he could feel her fingers digging into his flesh while at the same time her body was arching forward, pressing her breasts and the juncture of her thighs tightly against him. The silent invitation, one that he'd never dreamed he'd be getting from this woman, sent blood roaring to his head, making him almost forget where they were and why. She wanted to make love to him and there was no way he could disappoint her or himself.

"Jake," she whispered hoarsely. "I want you. Really want you."

Her words were enough to lift his head and as his heart continued to pound wildly, he looked into her eyes. Desire wrapped around his voice, strangling his question. "Are you sure?"

One hand lifted to trace the pads of her fingers across his cheek. The tender gesture was like nothing any woman had ever given him before and he felt an odd swelling in his chest, the urge to simply hold her and worship having her close.

"Very sure," she answered in a breathy rush.

"Then not here," he said brusquely and reached for her hand.

As he led her out of the barn and across the ranch yard toward the house, sundown arrived, sending slivers of pink across the lengthening shadows. The air was cool and quiet and he half expected the serenity of the evening to dash her ardor and make her think twice about becoming intimate with him.

But her fingers remained curled tightly around his and when they reached the porch and entered the house, she turned to him and smiled. And if Jake lived to be a hundred, he knew he would never forget the tenderness, the utter longing on her face.

If she'd looked at him with lust, Jake would have understood and felt at ease with her and himself. But this was something different, something deeper and sweeter. The realization shook him right down to the heels of his boots and for one wild second he considered telling her that he couldn't go through with it.

Jake Rollins couldn't make love to a woman! What a hell of a note that would be!

"Jake," she murmured softly. "Is something wrong?"

She stepped closer and as she placed her palm against his chest, his doubts slipped and the aching heat he'd been feeling in the barn returned twofold.

"Not one thing," he said with a growl of pleasure, then swinging her up into his arms, he carried her to the bedroom.

Chapter 8

When Jake eased Rebecca onto a queen-size bed covered with a smooth blue spread, she wondered how things between them had escalated so quickly. One moment she'd been kissing him and the next she'd felt certain her whole body would go up in flames if he didn't make love to her.

Had she gone crazy? Or just now come to her senses?

He didn't give her the opportunity to answer those questions as he followed her down onto the mattress and gathered her into his arms. And when his mouth latched onto hers in a deep, mindless kiss, she realized the answers didn't matter. All that mattered was the moment and the pleasure of being close to him, of tasting his lips, feeling the hard band of his arms holding her tight against him.

Eventually, he ended the contact of their lips and

nuzzled his cheek against hers. "Oh, Rebecca," he whispered rawly, "I never thought I'd have you here. Like this."

The wonder in his voice surprised her. Didn't he know his own sex appeal? Didn't he realize from the first time she'd met him, she'd thought of this very moment, of how it would be to make love to him?

"I never truly thought I'd be here like this. With you," she replied.

His shoulders were broad and the muscles surrounding them corded and hard. She ran her fingers along the strong slopes then down his arms until she reached the bulge of his biceps. There her fingers curled inward, until she was hanging on tightly.

He eased his head back just far enough to look at her. "Why?" he asked with a hint of wry acceptance. "Because you never dreamed you'd lie in a cowboy's bed?"

She smiled as her eyes dreamily scanned his dark features. "You say that like there's something wrong with cowboys."

"Only some of us."

"Meaning you have faults?"

He grunted with cynical amusement. "Faults? Look, Rebecca, I can't pretend. I like women."

She sighed with the sheer contentment of having his body next to hers. "That's good. Otherwise, you might not have ever looked at me."

He rolled his eyes. "That's only a part of my flaws, pretty lady. I like beer. And loafing. And I don't like being serious. And—"

"You talk way too much," she interrupted.

Bringing one hand to the back of his neck, she drew his mouth down to hers and that was all it took to end his litany. After that, she went to work showing him just how much she wanted to be in his arms and his bed.

Almost immediately the contact of their lips turned desperate and rough as they both tried to give and take more and more. As their tongues mated, Rebecca's hands wedged between them and began to fumble with the buttons on his shirt. By the time she'd reached the last one, her lungs were on fire, forcing her to drag her lips from his and draw in long, ragged breaths.

As she resupplied her oxygen, she shoved the fronts of his shirt aside and planted whisper-light kisses across his collarbone, down the middle of his chest and on to his flat stomach. His skin was hot and its masculine scent sparked the heat that was simmering low in her belly. Above her head, she could hear his breathing turn to quick, sharp intakes. Beneath the search of her hands, she could feel his heartbeat and the rapid rhythm matched the pounding in her own ears.

Ever since he'd first kissed her that night on the porch, she'd wanted him. Yet she'd not understood just how deep that wanting was until this moment. It was more than having the unbridled privilege to touch and taste him. It was being connected to him in any and every way.

When her tongue traced a wet circle around his navel, he gasped and thrust his hands in her hair and lifted her face up and away from him.

"Come here," he whispered.

She brought her face back to his and this time as their lips met his fingers left her hair to splay across her cheeks, his thumbs anchored beneath her jawline. He kissed her until she was moaning with need and then he went to work lowering the zipper at the back of her dress and pulling the fabric over her shoulders until it fell to a bunched heap around her waist.

Drunk with desire, her head fell limply back as she savored the sensation of his open mouth sliding slowly, deliciously down the front of her throat, then lower to where pink lace barely covered the tips of her breasts. With his tongue, he laved the open valley between them, then moved on to a peak, where he bit gently through the fabric and around one hard nipple.

Crying out, Rebecca arched toward the pleasure and tangled her legs through his. By now her breaths were coming in rapid pants and she almost screamed with relief when he finally lifted his head and began to remove the remainder of her clothing.

Once he'd tossed the garments out of the way, he quickly shrugged out of his shirt and kicked off his boots. Her gaze followed his every movement until he reached to unbutton his jeans and then their gazes met. And clung.

She could see a last-minute question in his eyes, as though he felt it was only right to give her one last chance to change her mind about this and him. The idea that he was thinking solely of her wants filled her heart with a wave of warm emotions.

Her lips parted to speak, to assure him she had no doubts or desire to end the path they were racing down. But her throat was too tight to utter a word. All she could do to convey her feelings was rise from the bed and wrap her arms around him.

As she buried her face against his chest, she heard him groan. But whether it was a sound of delight or reluctant surrender, she didn't know. Nor did it matter. At this moment he was hers and only hers.

His arms came around her and they stood like that until the heat between them became unbearable and the need to be connected on a deeper level took over their actions. Jake removed his jeans in hurried jerks and pressed Rebecca back onto the bed.

When he left her long enough to fish a packet from the nightstand and start to tear it open, she finally found her voice. "You don't need that, Jake," she said softly. "I'm protected with oral birth control. Unless—there's something else we should be extrasafe about?"

Extrasafe? With her? He would make love to her even if there was the possibility of a pregnancy hanging over his head. That was how much he wanted her. Needed her. And he'd never taken that chance with another woman. Even as a randy teenager he'd always had the forethought to wear his own protection. Thankfully, she didn't realize how reckless she made him, he thought. Thankfully she hadn't figured out that the mere thought of making love to her was making him tremble in places where he wasn't supposed to be feeling anything.

He tossed the unopened condom back onto the nightstand and joined her on the bed. Then dragging her naked body close to his, he buried his face in the curve of her neck. The scent of wildflowers and woman met his nostrils and swirled around in his head like the drunken whirl of a carnival ride.

He gripped her waist to steady his senses. "Nothing about this—about you and me—is safe. But I can't help myself. I've wanted you from the first moment I saw you."

"And I want you," she whispered. "That's all that matters."

The urgency in her voice was his undoing. He'd passed the point of taking things slowly, of being a gentleman even with her naked and in his arms. Passion had taken over and now all he could do was love her.

Rolling her onto her back, he parted her legs, then entered her with one smooth thrust. The sensation of being inside her was so potent, so new, it snapped his head back and snatched the air from his lungs.

Struggling to hang on to his control, he sucked in several deep breaths and began to move against her. She was soft. Oh, so soft. And the moist heat of her was searing his body, his mind. He'd never wanted a woman like this before. Desire was blinding him, threatening to send him flying into the dark sky.

Beneath him, he could hear her soft whimpers, feel her long, smooth legs wrapping around his, her hands racing over his chest and belly. Sensations were rushing at him at such an incredible speed he couldn't take them in fast enough. And though he wanted to slow everything down, to make the pleasure last forever, the frantic ache inside him made it impossible.

And then suddenly she was crying out his name, her whole body arching desperately toward his and all he wanted to do was give to her. Anything and everything she wanted. Bending his head, he latched his lips over hers and the link of their mouths was the last sweet nudge that pushed them both to a high-flying cloud. Clutching her tightly, he thrust deeply, mindlessly into her.

"Becca. Becca."

Her name slipped from his throat just as he felt himself pouring into her and his body shuddered uncon-

trollably as he rode out wave after wave of incredible
ecstasy.

By the time his body slumped to a depleted sprawl
over hers, his heart was hammering out of control and
sweat had slicked his skin. The roar in his ears made
it impossible to hear his own labored breathing, much
less hers.

He wasn't certain how long it took him to come back
to earth, but eventually he became aware of her shift-
ing beneath him and though she felt soft and warm and
totally luscious, he forced himself to roll to one side to
give her breathing space.

When he finally turned his head in her direction, he
saw that her eyes were closed, her blond hair tousled in
wild disarray around her head. The quick rise and fall
of her breasts told him her breathing hadn't yet returned
to normal. But then nothing about him had returned to
normal, either. He wasn't sure if it ever would.

Leaning toward her, he reached out and gently lifted
a heavy tendril of hair from her cheek. The movement
caused her eyes to flutter open and when she saw him
looking down at her, the corners of her lips slowly lifted
in a weak smile.

"Jake."

The murmur of his name was all she said, but that
one word was more than enough to thicken his throat
with emotions he didn't quite understand, or even
wished to acknowledge.

Giggles. Dirty pillow talk. Silly platitudes. Down
through the years he'd heard plenty of responses from
women after a round of sex with him. None of it had
meant anything more than empty noises to fill an awkward moment. But that had been sex. This thing that

had just happened with Rebecca was something else, something that had, quite honestly, blindsided him.

Lifting her hand to his lips, he kissed her fingers, while wondering how such small, fragile things could have such a potent effect on his body.

"Do you have any idea of how beautiful you are to me?"

For a moment he thought he saw a glaze of moisture fill her eyes. But the room had grown dusky dark and he couldn't be sure. Or maybe he didn't want to believe anything he did or said could touch her that much. It wasn't as though he was trying to ingrain himself in her heart. Oh, no. He didn't want her to love him. Like him, yes. But not love. She needed to save that for a worthy man. Yet to imagine her lying with another man, giving him the most intimate part of her was so repulsive to Jake that his mind refused to form the image.

Sighing, she shifted to her side so that she was facing him head-on. "I've never thought about it," she replied. "But I'm nothing special to look at. Especially like this."

"*Especially* like this, you are."

She closed her eyes and he leaned forward and placed his lips upon her forehead. It was damp and salty and her hair tickled his nose. With one hand, he pushed the long strands away from her face and onto the blue pillowcase. Her eyes fluttered open and this time they were dark and hesitant.

"Jake, I—"

She didn't go on and though he was almost afraid to hear the thoughts she had yet to put into words, he knew he had to hear them. Otherwise, he would always wonder.

"Go on, Rebecca," he said softly. "I'm listening."

A smile slanted her lips. "A few minutes ago you called me Becca. Did you know that?"

Barely, Jake thought. He'd been drunk on her and the shortened name had just slipped out, like a breath he could no longer hold on to.

"Yes. I remember. That's how I think of you," he admitted.

The smile fell from her face and her palm came to rest alongside his cheek. "Before I was only going to say that I'm so glad that I'm here with you. So glad that I came to New Mexico."

Suddenly there was an ache in his chest, as though two hands were reaching in and wringing his heart.

Closing his eyes against the unexpected pain, he murmured, "I'm glad you're here, too."

Two days later, Rebecca decided she could no longer put off going through Gertrude's correspondence. The task was slow and meticulous and with the phone ringing several times this afternoon her progress had been reduced to a snail's pace.

A few times throughout the day she'd been tempted to ignore the intrusive ring and let whoever was calling leave a message on her voice mail. But each time she'd snatched up the phone, hoping she would see Jake's number illuminated on the face of the instrument.

Instead the callers had been friends and coworkers from Houston and so far Rebecca had forced herself to talk with each of them. But she'd not given them any concrete reasons or hinted at a date when she might be returning to Texas. She didn't want to explain to any of them that she was presently living from day to day as she tried to come to terms, not only with Gertrude and her death, but also her newfound relationship with Jake.

Lincoln County was beginning to feel like home to her. And now that she and Jake had become intimate, she didn't want to think about leaving. If anything real and solid could develop between them, she wanted to give it a chance and the time to grow. Maybe that was foolish of her. After all, he'd told her that he was not the sort of man who wanted to get serious about her or any woman. And he'd not said a word to her to imply otherwise.

But he'd touched you like he loved you. He'd kissed you as though you were precious to him. More precious than anything.

Rebecca was trying to push that tormenting little voice out of her head when the phone rang again.

With a skeptical frown, she glanced over at the black instrument she'd left lying on the corner of a small wooden desk. "Beau, if that's Jake," she told the dog who was lying at her feet, "I'm going to shout hallelujah. If it's someone else I'm going to throw the thing out the window."

Only vaguely interested, Beau lifted his head and watched her walk over to retrieve the ringing phone, then decided to dismiss her threat and rest his chin back on his front paws.

Unfortunately, the number illuminated on the front wasn't Jake's. It belonged to her mother and for a moment Rebecca considered ignoring the call. There wasn't really anything she wanted to say to Gwyn. Unless the woman had finally decided to call and do some much-needed explaining.

It was that last hopeful thought that had Rebecca flipping open the phone and pressing it to her ear.

"Hello, Mother."

"Rebecca! Thank God you answered! Do you realize how many times I've tried to reach you? Why haven't you returned my calls?"

"Because I really don't have anything new to say. Two can play your game, Mother."

Gwyn let out an indignant huff. "That's not any way to talk to me, Rebecca. And I don't understand. You were always such a respectful daughter. Now you're like a stranger to me."

At one time, Rebecca would have agreed with her. She would have been ashamed to use any sort of sarcastic tone with her mother. But since she'd learned that Gwyn had been so deliberately deceptive, she'd lost all respect. Rebecca hated feeling that way. She desperately wished that Gwyn could give her a good explanation for her behavior. But so far she'd given her nothing but more frustration.

"It's funny that you should say that, Mother. Because you certainly seem like a stranger to me. I find myself questioning everything you say and wondering what else you're keeping from me."

There was a long silence and then Gwyn countered in a husky voice, "When are you coming home, Rebecca?"

Rebecca groaned inwardly. How many times was that question going to be thrown at her today? "We went over this the last time we talked. And I'll tell you the same thing as I told you then. I don't know." She stared across the cluttered room at Beau and then another thought struck her. "Have you been talking to my friends?"

"Why would you ask that question?"

She didn't sound indignant, Rebecca decided. More like cautious. "Because I've gotten several calls today and all of them were pressing me for a time when I'd be returning to Houston. You put them up to it, didn't you?"

"Has it ever occurred to you, Rebecca, that your friends are asking that question because they're concerned about you?"

Rebecca grimaced. "My friends normally don't pry into my private affairs. They show their concern by offering their ear, and that's it."

"All right." Gwyn suddenly spat out the admission. "I did talk to a few of your coworkers. Only because I love you."

"If you loved me—really loved me—you'd want to answer my questions about Aunt Gertrude. You'd want to explain and help me understand why you didn't want her in my life. Don't you understand this is all very hurtful and confusing to me?"

Awkward silence stretched between them.

"I didn't call to talk about Gertrude," Gwyn said brusquely. "I want to know if you're all right and what you've been doing. I want to hear your intentions about your job and—"

How could she begin to describe how she'd been spending her time here in New Mexico? Gwyn wouldn't understand any of it. Especially not Jake. She'd think he was far too rough around the edges for her daughter. Funny how it was those very rough edges that drew Rebecca to him even more, she thought. "I'm fine, Mother, just keeping busy with chores around the place and taking care of the animals. As for my intentions I've not made any plans yet."

"Rebecca! Arlene has been calling me every day to see if I've gotten any news from you. Sooner or later she's going to have to fill the void you've left behind. And from the frustration I'm getting from her it's going to be a lot sooner than you think."

Rebecca was amazed at how unaffected she was by this news. Her job at Bordeaux's had once meant everything to her. It had been her whole life. Now she couldn't imagine herself jumping back into that frantic pace, the stressful demands. Or most of all, leaving Jake.

"If Arlene feels she needs to replace me, then that's her prerogative."

To Rebecca's surprise her mother released several curse words. Gwyn had always striven to present herself to everyone as a first-class lady, especially to her daughter. She could only remember one other time she'd heard her mother cuss and that had been when Rebecca had announced she was traveling out here to New Mexico for Gertrude's funeral.

"Don't you even care?" Gwyn blasted at her. "All those years of college? All the long hours you've spent traveling, working to prove yourself? I'm not getting any of this, Rebecca. This thing with Gertrude is ruining you! And for what? You didn't even know the woman!"

"Thanks to you," Rebecca countered sharply, then forcing herself to breathe deeply and calm herself, she added, "This is not all about Gertrude, Mother. And right now I have to go."

"Rebecca, don't hang up! You're going to listen to me and get home—"

Rebecca dropped the phone from her ear and clicked the instrument together. Her hands were shaking as she placed the phone back on the desktop. She should have never confronted her mother, she thought with disgust. The only thing it achieved was making the both of them upset.

With a heavy sigh she walked back over to Beau and the box of correspondence she'd been sifting through. "Guess you could tell it wasn't Jake," she mumbled to the dog, then picked up a handful of papers and envelopes.

Thirty minutes later, Rebecca stopped the sorting long enough to make herself coffee. She carried the cup back to the spare bedroom and worked between sips. Eventually she finished one whole box and, after marking it, stacked it to one side. As she picked up a plastic container filled with more correspondence and placed it on the bed, a flash of midnight-blue velvet caught her eye.

On second glance, Rebecca noticed a jewelry box sitting on a cluttered nightstand. Expecting it to be full of costume pieces, she ignored the correspondence, and reached curiously for the rectangular box covered in blue velvet. The jewelry would certainly give her an insight into the fashion taste of her aunt, she thought.

At first she thought the tiny lock on the front was locked tight, but on second glance she could see the latch wasn't completely together. Easing onto the edge of the bed, she gathered the dusty box onto her lap and opened the lid.

Rebecca was instantly deflated. There were no pieces

of jewelry, only more correspondence. The only other thing in the box was a newspaper clipping with Rebecca opening a fashion show at Bordeaux's—that must have been how Gertie knew where she worked.

Letters bundled with faded blue ribbon. She started to shut the lid, but then paused in midtask as she noticed the return address on the top envelope.

The letter was from Vance Hardaway, a post office box number, then Houston, Texas.

Her father had written to Gertrude? But why?

Her thoughts suddenly spinning, Rebecca untied the ribbon and quickly shuffled through the different-shaped envelopes. Each one had come from Vance Hardaway and from the same post office box in Houston. Until she reached the last five. Those had been sent from Dubai City, the area where he'd been working before he'd lost his life.

Carefully sitting the box to one side, she picked out the envelope with the earliest posted date and opened it.

When she unfolded the two handwritten pages, a photo fluttered facedown onto her lap. Deciding to look at it before she began to read, she turned it upright, and gasped with shock.

The last thing she'd expected to see was an image of herself. Pulling the dog-eared pic closer, she scanned it closely and, as she did, faded memories rushed to life. Even though she'd only been seven or eight at the time, she remembered the day her father had taken the photo. They'd gone to the zoo. Just the two of them. When they'd stopped in front of the monkey enclosure he'd had her pose for the camera, saying he wanted a picture of his own little monkey. They'd had a fun-filled day; one of the most memorable occasions she'd had with her father.

But why had he mailed the photo to Gertrude?

Laying the faded image aside, she opened the letter and began to read:

Dearest Gerta,

I'm sorry so much time has passed since my last letter. But things have been hectic here. The company is expanding and they want to send me to a city on the Persian Gulf. I'm not keen on leaving the States, but the money would be good. And Rebecca's welfare is my main concern. I want to give her all the things I never had as a child and make sure doors open for her at the right time. And I know you want those same things for her, too. You're living so modestly, Gerta, just so you can save and help me provide for her future. I don't want you to have to sacrifice that way. But if that makes you happy—makes you feel more like her mother—then I can hardly deny you.

As it stands, I'm scheduled to leave Houston in three weeks. My fondest hope is that you will allow me to see you before I leave for overseas. I could take two extra days and spend them with you. I understand that you don't want me to come out there, but I miss you, Gerta. And there's not a day goes by without my wishing that things could be different for you and me and our daughter.

Our daughter! Did her father's words mean what she thought they meant? Rebecca wondered wildly.

Her heart suddenly pounding with a strange mixture of fear and excitement, she scanned the last paragraph of the letter.

I'm sending these photos of Rebecca that I took at the zoo last week. Gwyn didn't go—said it was too nasty an outing for her. But as you can see Rebecca loves the animals. She's like you, dear Gerta, in so many ways. And as I watch her grow, I only love you more.

Dazed, Rebecca quickly read the last few lines of the letter and then as she lifted her head and stared unseeingly at the bedroom wall, the aged slips of paper fell to her lap.

Dear God, had Gertrude O'Dell been her mother? Everything about her father's words had said so! And there was no doubt in her mind that the letter was from Vance Hardaway. Rebecca had recognized his handwriting instantly. She still had letters that, as a child, she'd received from him.

What did it all mean? That a few weeks ago she'd watched her real mother being lowered into the earth? And never had the chance to know her? Love her?

Pain and confusion cut into her so suddenly and deeply that she clutched a hand to her stomach and choked out a sob.

Her life, as she knew it, had been one big deception! Lies on top of lies!

With tears sliding down her cheeks, she reached for the telephone and punched her mother's—no, she couldn't even use that title for the woman anymore, she thought bitterly. Now she was simply Gwyn Hardaway, a woman who owed her answers. Answers that had been twenty-eight years overdue.

Chapter 9

Later that afternoon, Jake pulled his truck and horse trailer to a stop in front of his mother's modest house, which was located on the eastern edge of Ruidoso. He found Clara sitting on the front porch and as he climbed the steps, she rose to her feet to greet him.

Today she looked somewhat perkier and Jake was relieved that he'd not found her lying on the couch, bemoaning the state of her health.

"This is a nice surprise," she said, turning her cheek up for his kiss. "What brings you to town? On your way to Apache Wells?"

"Not exactly," he hedged. "I'm going to see...a woman. Gertie O'Dell's niece."

Clara peeped around his shoulder at the rig he'd parked in the driveway. "And you're taking a horse?"

She returned to the wicker seat she'd been sitting

in and gestured for him to take the one nearest to her. Jake eased his long frame into the chair and stretched his legs out in front of him.

"That's right. I thought Rebecca might enjoy taking a ride. She has a horse that I need to check out."

The skeptical look on Clara's face disappeared. "Oh. For shoes, you mean."

"No. I need to make sure the mare is broke to ride."

"I didn't know you were hiring out as a horse trainer anymore, Jake. You're so busy now you hardly have time to draw a good breath."

It was true that on a good day his time was limited, but the past few days had been worse than hectic. A sick bull had been discovered in a back pasture and it had taken him and his two hired hands several hours just to get him loaded and back to the ranch. Added to that, a broken pump had left the barns and feed lots without a drop of water for the livestock, then one of his best horses had cut his foot and required surgery at the vet's clinic in Ruidoso. And to make matters worse, he had no land telephone line at his house, so when he'd lost his cell phone signal it had been impossible to call Rebecca. He'd never planned for three days to go by without contacting her and now it felt like weeks since she'd been at his ranch.

"I know, Mom, but Rebecca is—well, I'm not hiring out as a horse trainer for her. I'm doing this as a favor."

Rolling her eyes, Clara groaned with misgivings. "Oh, son, don't tell me you've gone and gotten yourself involved with this girl from Texas. Don't you have enough women around here without adding her to your string?"

Jake didn't bother to stop the grimace on his face.

Linking Rebecca to the other women he'd known over the years seemed downright disrespectful. She wasn't like those women and neither was their relationship.

Who are you kidding, Jake? You've already taken her to your bed. And you can't wait to get her back in it. What makes this thing with Rebecca any different than the last woman you bedded?

Dammit, now was hardly the time for his conscience to start talking to him. His mother's voiced opinion was bad enough.

"I'm not—this is not what you're thinking, Mom."

She shot him a look of disgust. One that Jake had seen a hundred times before. "The woman doesn't even belong around here. Sooner or later, she'll be going back to wherever she came from. That tells me you're not serious about her. But then you're never serious about any of them, are you?" Shaking her head, she lifted her gaze to the roof of the porch and sighed. "You'll be like your father until the day you die."

Over the years Clara had said some demeaning things to Jake, all of them pointing back to Lee's failings as a father and a husband, and how Jake had inherited the man's shortcomings. But she'd never spoken to him in such a sarcastic tone before and Jake didn't know whether he was angry or hurt or simply weary of being linked to Lee's mistakes.

Leaning forward in his chair, he studied her sad face. "Why are you doing this to me? I'm not Lee Rollins. I've not left a wife and child behind."

She flinched, then turned her gaze away from him. "No," she said bitterly. "That's one thing I won't have to worry about. You'll make damned sure you don't have either one of those."

Disgusted now, Jake muttered a few choice words under his breath. "I don't know what in hell you want or expect from me, Mom. You say I'm just like Lee and not fit to be a husband or father. And then in the next breath, you ridicule me for not having a family. I guess it would be too much of a strain for you to find anything worthwhile in your son, yourself or your life."

Her head whipped around and she gaped at him in shock. "That's a horrible thing to say to me!"

"Is it? I'm thinking I should have said it a long time ago."

"Jake—"

"Look, Mom, just because you want to be alone and miserable doesn't mean I want to be."

She looked at him in stunned disbelief and Jake suddenly realized that he was partly to blame for his mother's cynical attitude toward life. All these years of coddling had only fed into her self-pity.

"What are you talking about? You are alone, Jake," she shot back at him. "And that's the way the both of us are always gonna be. Your father ruined us."

His jaw tight, Jake rose to his feet. "Only because we've let him."

He started off the porch and Clara called after him. "Come back here, Jake. I'm not finished."

Stepping onto the ground, he glanced over his shoulder at her. "But I am finished, Mom. Finished with the whole rotten mess of Lee Rollins."

Minutes later, as Jake drove north of Ruidoso to Rebecca's place, he tried to forget the exchange he'd had with his mother. It wasn't like him to lose his temper with her. She was basically the only family he had and after his father had left, she'd worked hard and sacri-

ficed to raise Jake. He respected her for that and he
loved her. But that didn't mean he had to abide her attitude toward him or herself.

You are alone, Jake.

Of all the things Clara had said to him that had cut
the worst. Although, he didn't understand exactly why.
A few weeks ago, he probably would have agreed with
his mother's observation. He'd always been a man alone.
Until Rebecca had come into his life. Now he felt different. Now he felt a connection.

Was it love?

Hell, how could he know the answer to that? He'd
never been in love. And maybe this thing with Rebecca
was just lust, he mentally argued. God only knew how
much he'd wanted her the other night. He'd not been
satisfied to make love to her once and then take her
home. No, he'd had to make love to her a second time
and then a third. And to make the matter even more
worrisome, he'd wanted to keep her with him all night.
He'd wanted to wrap his arms around her and hold her
until morning filled the sky. Something he'd never done
with any woman.

But somehow, in the wee hours of the morning, he'd
found the strength, or maybe it had been fear that had finally pushed him, to drive her home and kiss her good-
night. Since that night his thoughts had been besieged
with the woman and now he was beginning to wonder
what tomorrow was going to bring to him. Once she
returned to Texas, how would he go back to being the
old Jake, the man who flitted from one woman to the
next, the man who never thought about a wife, children
or the future?

A half hour later, he rolled to a stop behind Rebecca's

old truck. The sight of the vehicle assured him that she was home, so he climbed to the ground and went to work unloading his horse.

By the time he'd taken Banjo to the barn and turned him loose in a small catch pen, Rebecca still hadn't appeared, so he quickly returned to the house and knocked on the front door.

There was no sound coming from inside and he was beginning to think that maybe Abe or Maura might have picked her up and taken her to Apache Wells for a neighborly visit, when he finally heard footsteps rushing through the house.

After a moment, she appeared behind the screen door and he smiled with relief. "Rebecca, for a minute I thought you were gone."

She pushed the door wide and without a word fell sobbing into his arms.

"Rebecca! Honey, what's wrong? Are you hurt? Sick?"

Lifting her head from his chest, she tried to speak, but only more sobs passed her parted lips. Jake urgently wrapped an arm around her waist and ushered her into the house.

Once he had her sitting on the couch, he sank down beside her and pressed both her hands tightly between his. "Take a deep breath, Becca. Calm down and tell me what has you so upset."

Nodding jerkily, she drew in several bracing breaths. "I—I'm so sorry, Jake. I didn't mean to—to break down like this. But when I saw you—oh, Jake—I don't know where to begin."

Fresh tears rolled down her cheeks and he quickly pulled a bandanna from the back pocket of his jeans and wiped them away. Once he was finished, her trembling lips tried to form a grateful smile.

"Are you ill, Becca?"

She shook her head. "No. I guess you could call it... shock." She pulled her hands from his and swiped at the tumble of blond hair hanging near her eyes. "This afternoon I was going through Gertrude's correspondence and I found out—quite by accident that—she was...my mother."

Stunned, Jake stared at her. "Did I hear you right? Did you say mother?"

Rebecca nodded, then released a long, shuddering sigh. "That's right. I said that Gertrude was my mother."

"But how? Are you sure?"

Jumping to her feet, she began to pace around the tiny living room. "I found letters from my father written to Gertrude. He called her Gerta and talked about how much he regretted the fact that they couldn't be together." Her woeful gaze lifted from the floor and over to him. "Oh, Jake, the things he wrote—he clearly loved her. And—"

His heart aching for her, he watched her cover her face with both hands. "Are you sure about this, Rebecca? Just because he loved Gertrude, that doesn't make the woman your mother. And even if she was actually your mother, why didn't she raise you?"

Dropping her hands from her face, she stared helplessly at him. "I'm going crazy trying to figure that out, Jake. None of it makes sense."

"Does your mother—the mother who raised you— know that you've uncovered these letters?"

She nodded stiffly. "Right after I found the letters I called my—I called Gwyn and confronted her with the contents. She didn't try to deny any of it. She simply said she'd catch a plane to Ruidoso tomorrow and I'm to meet her there so that we can talk. Apparently she's decided she can't hide the truth any longer. But what that truth is—well, I can't imagine what I'll hear from her. All I know is that my real mother is dead. And I never had the chance to see her, touch her or hear her voice. It's killing me, Jake."

The agony in her voice pushed Jake to his feet and he quickly pulled her into his arms and cradled her head against his chest. "I don't know what to say. To say I'm sorry wouldn't be right. Because this might be a good thing, Becca. You've been confused and wanting answers about Gertrude. Now you have them."

Her hands gripped the front of his denim shirt as though he was her lifeline. The idea that she needed to be close to him, that she was even sharing this most private part of her life with him, left Jake overwhelmed with emotions.

"Yes. But I've lost so much," she said in a tear-ravaged voice. "And why?"

"Oh, Becca, I can't give you the answers. But please don't cry anymore." Gently, he stroked a hand down the back of her head. "No matter what the truth is, it's not going to change the wonderful person that you are. And trust me, this will all get better with time."

Tilting her head back, she focused her watery gaze upon his face. "Oh, Jake, I'm so glad you're here," she whispered hoarsely. "I need you. You can't imagine how much."

Need. Not want. Need. The notion that this woman needed him, in any capacity, amazed Jake, filled his heart with a kind of warmth he'd never experienced before. And as he watched the dark agony in her eyes turn to something soft and sweet, he couldn't stop his head from bending or his lips from finding hers.

A faint groan sounded deep in her throat. Or was it a whimper of surrender? Either way, the sound stirred him, made him forget that he was supposed to be consoling her. Heat flashed through him as he tightened his arms and crushed her closer against him.

The taste of her mouth was like sipping a favorite wine, one that he could never get enough of. As his lips plundered hers, his tongue slipped between her teeth and rubbed a bumpy track along the roof of her mouth. At the same time he could feel her hips arching toward his, her fingers crawling up his chest and linking at the back of his neck.

His body had forgotten none of the pleasures she'd given him the other night and the memories melded with the erotic sensations zipping hot and wild along his veins. The search of his lips turned rough and urgent and she matched each desperate movement with a frantic need that left his whole body aching to be inside her once again.

Eventually the need for air and the desire to take the embrace to a deeper level forced their mouths apart. His breathing heavy, he gripped her shoulders and looked ruefully down at her.

"I must be a bastard, Becca, for wanting you like this—now. You need—"

"I need you. Only you," she interrupted in a desperate whisper. "Make love to me, Jake. Make me forget everything. Everything but you."

He kissed her again. More gently this time and once

their lips parted, she took him by the hand and led him down the short hallway to her bedroom.

The small space was equipped with only one window facing the backyard. It was bare of curtains and opened to the cool breeze. Now as she pulled Jake down on the bed beside her, the sage-scented air wafted across their heated skin and ruffled the blond tendrils of hair lying upon her shoulders.

For long moments as they lay with their faces mere inches apart, Jake could only wonder how much longer he would have her to himself like this. She was at a crossroads in her life. That much was obvious to Jake. And the road she eventually chose to take would more than likely be away from Lincoln County, away from him. The notion chilled him and he fought to push it away at the same time he reached to draw her close to his heart.

The next afternoon, Rebecca drove to the Ruidoso airport and waited for Gwyn Hardaway's small commuter jet to land. Their initial meeting in the lobby was worse than stiff and, though Rebecca allowed the woman to give her a brief hug, there was little warmth between them as they exited the building and walked to the parking lot.

When they reached Rebecca's old Ford, it was clear that Gwyn was disgusted by the mode of transportation and even more embarrassed to be seen in it, but Rebecca didn't make any apologies. The truck had belonged to her mother and that alone made it special.

Rebecca drove them to the hotel where Gwyn had booked a room for the night, then waited in the spacious lobby while the other woman checked in and dealt with her luggage. So far only a handful of words had passed between the two of them and the strained silence reminded Rebecca how drastically her life had changed since she'd come to New Mexico. She watched her real mother be laid to rest and the woman who'd raised her had become a distant stranger. And then there was Jake. The man she'd fallen in love with. Would he want to be a part of her scattered life?

Her mind was replaying last night and how Jake had made love to her so tenderly and completely when Gwyn's voice abruptly sounded behind her.

"Would you like to go up to my room to talk?"

For some reason Rebecca had no desire to closet herself in a private room with Gwyn. She already felt as though the woman had isolated her. As far as Rebecca was concerned, it was time for everything to be out in the open.

"Let's find a restaurant," Rebecca suggested. "I need a cup of coffee."

Thankfully, there was an eating place connected to the hotel and after a short walk, they seated themselves in a booth looking out a wide plate-glass window. After the waitress left to fetch their drinks, Gwyn stared out the window.

"I wonder what Gertrude saw in this place," she mused aloud. "I admit it has a quaint charm, but it's so Western."

And Gwyn was so big-city, Rebecca thought. She loved the hustle and bustle, the shops, the arts and social life attached to them. On the other hand, from what Rebecca could gather from her home place, Gertrude had been just the opposite. A quiet loner who was content to live with her animals.

"Do you know why she chose to live here?" Rebecca asked.

Gwyn's gaze remained on the window. "No idea. In fact, after we parted ways, I never knew where she'd gone to. I didn't want to know," she added bitterly.

As the two of them had walked to the restaurant, Rebecca kept reminding herself to keep an open mind and not allow her temper to rise to the angry point. After all, she didn't yet know what had gone on between the twin sisters. So now she quietly studied Gwyn's stiff expression and wondered how the woman could've turned her back on her sister and deceived her own child.

"Why?"

Gwyn turned her gaze on Rebecca and this time she could see dark shadows of pure hatred in their depths. The sight shocked Rebecca and made her realize there were sides to this woman that she could have never imagined.

"Do we really have to get into all of this, Rebecca? Isn't it enough to know that she was your biological mother? The rest is…unimportant."

Unimportant? Rebecca wanted to scream. Before Jake had shown up at her door yesterday evening, she'd read all the letters that had been stashed in the jewelry box and they'd given her bittersweet glimpses to her parents' relationship. The words her father had written to Gertrude were full of anguish, love, sorrow and regret. His life had been torn between two women and a child. How could Gwyn have the gall to say none of it was important?

"I'm not a child, Mother. And don't insult my intelligence. I didn't come here to meet with you just so you could hem and haw. If you don't want to give me the truth, I'll be on my way."

Gwyn's nostrils flared with anger, but any retort she might have said at that moment was interrupted by the waitress returning to their table. After the woman had served them and gone on her way, Rebecca stirred cream into her coffee and waited with patience that was wearing thinner and thinner with each passing moment.

"If you walk away now, Rebecca," Gwyn finally said, "you'll never know the truth."

She made it sound almost like a threat, as though she wouldn't think twice about withholding the answers that Rebecca so desperately needed. The realization stunned her. Gwyn had always been a temperamental person and spoiled by having her own way, but Rebecca had never seen this sort of cruelty in the woman.

"That's where you're wrong. I have Daddy's letters. They explain a lot."

Gwyn had ordered iced tea. Now, after a long sip, she plopped the glass down with a loud thud and quickly reached for the sugar shaker. "Damn people! Don't have the slightest idea of how to serve sweet tea!" She dumped a small mountain of white granules into the drink and as she absently stirred the tea, she turned an unseeing gaze toward the window. "Oh, yes," she said bitterly. "Those letters you found. I wasn't expecting you to stumble across anything like...that."

"Why not? You knew I was staying in Gertrude's house. Surely you figured I would run across them at some point."

Gwyn's head jerked around and Rebecca could see her face was now mottled with red splotches. "I didn't— I never knew Vance had been corresponding with Gertrude. I didn't know my husband had been speaking to the woman in any form or fashion!"

Oh, God, this was worse than anything Rebecca had anticipated. She wanted answers, but unlike Gwyn, she wasn't a hurtful person. She didn't want to cause her mother more pain than she was already going through. But neither could she avoid the truth. "You never suspected that he was harboring feelings for Gertrude?"

Gwyn's gaze dropped shamefully to the tabletop. "No," she said hoarsely. "I thought all of that was over—after—"

When she didn't go on, Rebecca pressed her. "After what? After I was conceived? For both of our sakes, I think you need to go back to the beginning, Mother."

With a long weary sigh, she lifted her head and looked straight at Rebecca. By now her face had gone very pale, making her red lipstick stand out garishly against her white skin.

"All right. From the beginning my sister and I were always very different people. Even our looks were nothing alike. Gertrude was tall and blonde while I was dark and petite."

"Was she pretty?"

Gwyn shrugged one shoulder, an expression she'd always reprimanded Rebecca for using. "I suppose you could've called her pretty. She was the outdoorsy, girl-next-door type. And so quiet and reserved that I often wanted to scream at her. Yet as children we—well, we loved each other and were actually quite close."

"I find that hard to believe."

"Well, we were. Even though we did have our differences at times. As teenagers I was always pushing her to be more outgoing. I wanted her to have dates and fun—I wanted her to be someone I could be proud of. Instead, she chose to be a bookworm and for the most part shunned any advances the boys made toward her. She said they made her uncomfortable and that she would have a relationship whenever it felt right and not before. At that time neither one of us had met Vance. That didn't come until much later when we were in our twenties and our parents—your grandparents—had already passed on."

"You told me that you met Daddy at a dinner party. Is that where Gertrude met him, too?"

Gwyn grimaced. "Yes. At the time I thought she hardly noticed him. But that could have been because I was too busy trying to catch his eye," she added thoughtfully. "Anyway, after that we began to date. When he asked me to marry him, I was over the moon. Your father was killer handsome and though he wasn't rich by any means, he was a man with prospects and all of that put together made him one of the most eligible bachelors in our social circle. After he proposed, I immediately began to plan a big wedding and with Mother already gone, I needed Gertrude to help me with the details."

"And did she?"

Gwyn's expression turned hard. "Oh, yes. She even seemed happy for me. Little did I know that she had her eyes set on my fiancé."

"When did you find out about the two of them?"

"Not until a couple of months after Vance and I were married. Gertrude came to me and told me that she was carrying Vance's child and that their…indiscretion had happened before the wedding. She'd planned to keep their tryst a secret, but that the pregnancy forced her to come out with the truth. I was completely devastated. I'd been betrayed by both my husband and my sister."

Rebecca clutched the coffee cup as she watched pain slip across Gwyn's face. "I understand this isn't easy for you to say. It's not particularly easy for me to hear. And I realize that you were wronged. Terribly so. But that hardly justified you living a lie."

Gwyn's mouth fell open. "A lie? Why, what do you mean? I'm not the one who cheated!"

"You cheated me out of knowing my own mother. As far as I'm concerned you cheated in the worst kind of way. What I can't understand is why Gertrude and my father allowed it."

Her eyes lit with vengeful fire, Gwyn leaned forward. "They allowed it because I held the cards, that's why! She was nothing but a backstabbing slut and I was ready to smear her reputation into the dirt. She'd always gone around acting so meek and mild and holier-than-thou when all along she was a nothing, a nobody! I was the social flower, not her! And I damned sure wasn't going to let our friends and acquaintances learn what she and Vance had done to me!"

Revenge. Nothing good could ever come from it. But apparently Gwyn had yet to realize that lesson.

"How were you going to smear her reputation without dragging Daddy into it?"

"I wasn't above making up a sordid story about her. That wouldn't have been nearly as bad as what she'd actually done to me. So when I threatened, she caved. And believe me, it didn't take much threatening. Gertrude was the type who always did have too much conscience. She felt as guilty as hell and wanted to make it up to me. And most of all, she wanted what was best for her baby. She didn't want you raised up under a cloud of nasty gossip and illegitimacy. So I immediately spread the news that I was pregnant and then a few weeks later, I made up a cock-and-bull story that Gertrude and I had a widowed aunt in California who had taken ill and we were going out to care for her until she could get back on her feet. The two of us did go to California, a little town on the southern coast where no acquaintances would likely run into us. Once you were born, I came back with you as a new mother. Gertrude went her own way and I never spoke to her after that."

"And Daddy? What did he have to say about all this? About getting Gertrude pregnant? About this plan of yours?"

"He was contrite, of course. He assured me that he'd only made love to Gertrude one time and that it hadn't meant anything. He'd just had a last-minute panic about losing his bachelorhood and Gertrude had been handy and willing. He wanted to raise his child and once Gertrude agreed to turn the baby over to me, he had to stick by my side. He didn't have any other choice. And in the long run, I don't think he wanted anyone to think badly of Gertrude. He didn't want her hurt in that way. And he didn't want you to be raised up under a shroud of ugly gossip, either."

It was all Rebecca could do to keep from rolling her eyes toward the ceiling. The more Gwyn talked the more psychotic she sounded. "And why do you think that was, Mother? If it was just a physical thing between them, why would he care if Gertrude was hurt? Do you think it might have been because he loved her?"

The anger on Gwyn's face suddenly disappeared and in its place came a look of weary defeat. "For years I never believed Vance had ever cared for Gertrude. I believed his heart was truly mine. But I didn't know about the letters—that he'd stayed in contact with her until he died. Now I can only think that they probably continued to see each other—until Vance was killed."

Bitter nausea swam in the pit of Rebecca's stomach. So many people had lied and loved and lost. "I was an innocent baby and you used me as a pawn—to get what you wanted. You didn't care that you took me away from my mother or that I might have needed her. You didn't even care about me, did you?"

If possible, Gwyn's face turned even paler. She took a nervous gulp of tea and answered in a flat voice, "All right, you asked for honesty so I'm going to give it to you. In the beginning I didn't want you. Each time I looked at you it killed me. You were a constant reminder of my husband's infidelity, my sister's betrayal. But then—" Her eyes suddenly filled with tears as she reached an imploring hand toward Rebecca. "You were such a lovely baby and after a while I couldn't help but fall in love with you. And then it was easy for me to pretend that none of it had ever happened. That I had actually given birth to you."

Rebecca didn't allow Gwyn to clasp her hand. There was too much hurt and confusion going on inside Rebecca to summon up any tender emotions for this woman who'd turned a bad choice into a lifelong nightmare. "Why did you never speak to Gertrude again? Why couldn't you find it in your heart to attend her funeral?"

Gwyn was dumbfounded. "Rebecca! Do you actually have to ask those questions? The woman wronged me!"

"And what did you do to her? Extorted her child from

her! Hid the identity of my real mother from me! That's not a little wrong, that's a massive one."

Refusing to acknowledge her own faults, Gwyn said through clenched teeth, "Sister or not, I could never forgive her. And I don't know how you could possibly pitch a defense for the woman!"

Sadness fell like a heavy cloak around Rebecca's shoulders and filled her heart with silent tears. "Yes, she made a bad mistake. But you retaliated and made even more. The way I see it, if a person doesn't have the capacity to forgive then they hardly have the ability to love."

As Gwyn stared at her, a flicker of hope lit her eyes. "Does that mean—you're willing to forgive me?"

Grabbing up her handbag, Rebecca rose to her feet. "It's way too early for me to answer that. And who knows, maybe being raised by you has influenced me more than you think."

Bewildered, Gwyn frowned. "What does that mean?"

"That I might just hold a grudge against you for the rest of my life."

Gwyn gasped. "Rebecca!"

"I've got to go," Rebecca said abruptly. "Goodbye."

The other woman rose to her feet as though she was prepared to grab on to Rebecca and prevent her from walking out of the restaurant. "But you can't leave now—like this! When are you coming home?"

Rebecca swallowed as a cold, hard lump threatened to choke her. *Home.* The one she'd grown up in had been built upon a foundation of lies. Where was her home now? She didn't know anymore. At this moment all she could think about was Jake, the comfort of his strong arms, the steadying sound of his rich voice. He was the only real thing left in her life. But even he was a temporary component.

"I don't know the answer to that. Maybe soon. Maybe never."

"Rebecca, I—"

Rebecca didn't wait to hear more. She'd already heard more than enough to break her heart.

Chapter 10

Later that evening, when she arrived back at her little ranch, she was surprised to see Jake's truck parked in the driveway. When he'd left early this morning, he'd not mentioned when he'd be back and today while she'd been in Ruidoso, he'd not rung her cell. But then she was learning he didn't necessarily believe in notices or plans. He was a man who simply acted upon whatever he was feeling at the moment.

She found him sitting on the front porch waiting for her to arrive and as she climbed the steps he must have noticed the weary sag of her shoulders, because he stood immediately and held out his arms.

Wordlessly, she dropped her handbag onto the floor of the porch and rushed to him. As she nestled her cheek against his chest, she felt his chin rest atop her head.

"You saw your mother."

It wasn't a question, it was a statement spoken in a flat voice, as though he already understood she was miserable. The fact that he could read her so well, that he was here at the moment she needed him most, filled her with bittersweet emotions. He might not think of himself as a permanent fixture in a woman's life, but he'd already found a permanent place in her heart.

But it wouldn't be right to tell him how she felt. He'd not asked for her love. He'd even warned her that he wasn't the loving kind. And she wasn't going to weigh his conscience down with declarations and demands. The last thing she wanted to be was like Gwyn, who'd demanded that Vance love her, or else.

"Yes," she said with a weary sigh. "And it was worse than I imagined."

He stroked a hand down her back. "I figured it might be. That's why I showed up. I thought you might need a little distraction this evening."

Tilting her head back, she looked at him with a mixture of curiosity and provocative surmise. "What sort of distraction?"

His grin was warm and sexy and just what she needed to make her feel as though she was actually going to survive.

"Since we—uh—got sidetracked last night and Banjo was already here, I thought we might try again. So I've saddled him and Starr. I thought we might ride across your land and check the fences. Do you feel up to it?"

Even though he was sounding like the quintessential rancher, she realized the invitation had nothing to do with fences or making sure livestock remained on the proper property. He was trying to take her mind off her problems and on to something simple and pleasant.

Touched by his thoughtfulness, she blinked at the moisture gathering at the back of her eyes. "I wouldn't miss the chance for anything. Just let me change into some jeans and boots," she told him.

A few minutes later, after assuring her that he'd already ridden Starr and found the mare to be extremely gentle, he helped her into the saddle and swung himself up on the gelding he called Banjo.

Even though it had been years since she'd been on a horse, it took her only a few minutes to get the hang of handling the reins and giving the horse the right cues to follow her directions. As the house and barn receded in the distance behind them, the sage-dotted land opened, making the trek easy for horse and rider.

"This is nice," she told him. "Being on Starr almost makes me forget about this afternoon."

His expression full of concern, he studied her closely. "I was hoping you found the answers you wanted."

She released a sharp, bitter laugh. "Oh, I got plenty of answers. They were just nothing like I'd expected them to be."

"Want to tell me about it?"

To her amazement, she did want to tell him about it. Of all the people she knew, he would be the one who would understand the most. And that idea told her more about herself and the life she'd been leading than anything yet.

"If you want to listen," she told him.

"I do."

Rebecca told him the whole unfortunate story, ending with Gwyn's attitude. "Her sister is dead, yet she's still harboring hatred toward the woman. You'd think after all these years she could forgive and forget."

Thoughtfully, Jake lifted his gray hat from his head and ran a hand over his thick waves. "You telling her about those letters probably threw her for a loop. She learned her husband really did love another woman and that she'd been hanging on to something she'd never really had in the first place. Including you. That would be a heck of a pill for most people to swallow."

Hanging on to something she'd never really had. Jake's observation struck her like a thunderbolt. Was that what Rebecca was trying to do? Hang on to regrets of a mother she never knew and resentment for a mother who had pushed her to always do more and be better? Maybe even hang on to a life here in New Mexico even though her home had always been in Houston? No! She didn't want to think about that now. If she did she might break apart completely.

"You're probably right," she murmured glumly.

Sage snapped against the horses' legs and filled the evening air with the pungent scent. Behind them the sun began to sink and the desert around them became washed in hues of gold and purple. For a long stretch, they rode in silence, but every now and then their mounts drifted together and Rebecca's leg would brush against Jake's. The connection comforted her. And each time she glanced over at his dark profile, her heart filled to the brim and ached with a longing she'd never felt before.

Her love for Jake was growing and so was this new life she'd found with him. But he wasn't going to hang around forever. He simply wasn't that type. And when he moved on to the next woman, where was that going to leave her? Without him would there be any reason for her to stay here?

For the next few minutes, she did her best to push those questions from her mind and soak in her surroundings. After all, this land belonged to her and, other than a few short walks in the pasture, this was the first chance she'd had to look it over.

Eventually the landscape began to change to low rolling hills and washed-out gullies. As they topped one particular rise, a windmill and water tank came into view.

Jake tilted his head in that direction. "You probably need a break," he said. "Let's ride over there and give the horses a drink."

"Sounds good," she agreed.

It took them another ten minutes to reach the windmill and by then Rebecca was feeling the effects of being in the saddle. When Jake helped her to the ground her legs were trembling with fatigue and for a moment, she clutched his arm.

"Sorry," she said with a self-deprecating laugh. "I guess when it comes to riding I'm a bit of a wimp."

He smiled down at her and as their eyes met, Rebecca had to fight back the urge to slip her arms around him, to tell him that she loved him, that she would always need and want him in her life. If he knew how she felt, would it change anything? Or would she simply be making a fool of herself? Oh, God, she didn't know what to do about him, herself or anything.

"I wouldn't say that. It's something you have to get conditioned to," he told her, then reached for the reins of both horses. "I'll lead them over to the tank for a drink while you find a place to sit down."

As Jake saw to the horses, the thought came to mind that this was the first time he'd ever taken a woman horseback riding. The pleasure was one of those things he'd never wanted to share with a female. For the most part they were too chatty to appreciate the bond a man had with his horse and too soft to deal with the heat and the flies and the grime that went with it. Besides all that, when a cowboy acquired a saddle pal he kept him for life. That was a code he didn't break.

So what was he doing here with Rebecca? he asked himself. He wasn't planning on keeping her for life. He couldn't. She wasn't the keeper type. Not for a man like him, a man who changed women more often than he changed the oil in his truck. And even if he was the family type with dreams and hopes for a wife and kids, he could see she wasn't ready to deal with such plans. This thing with Gertie and her parents had turned her world upside down and he figured it was going to take Rebecca a long time to get things figured out. Or she might never come to terms with it. He'd spent the past eighteen years trying to figure out why his father had deserted him and he still didn't have the answers.

Yet in spite of all this, he wanted to be with her. He wanted to take away the confusion and hurt in her heart. He didn't know what that meant or why he was feeling this way. But he was beginning to understand what Quint had been trying to tell him. It was going to hurt and hurt bad whenever he had to let her go.

After the horses had their fill of water, he tied them loosely to the wooden frame of the windmill. While he'd been dealing with their mounts, Rebecca had taken a seat on a grassy slope a few feet away. Now he walked over and sank down next to her.

"Feeling better?" he asked.

She looked away from him and he could see her throat work as she swallowed hard.

"A little."

He rubbed the back of his fingers against her upper arm, while wishing he could wipe away the pain inside her just as easily. "It's hell learning that your parents are something different than what you always believed them to be. I know."

She looked back at him and the misty glaze in her blue eyes very nearly tore a hole in his chest.

"Yes, you would understand, Jake." With a wan smile, she touched her fingers to his cheek. "I'm sorry I'm not very good company this evening."

"I didn't come here for company. I came because—" He stopped and cleared his throat. "I thought you might need me."

The glaze in her eyes swelled to full-blown tears and with a choked groan she flung her arms around his neck and pressed her cheek against his. "Oh, Jake, I do need you! I—" Pausing, she eased her head back far enough to look into his eyes. "I want you to make love to me. Now. Please."

Jake didn't know what he'd been expecting her to say, but that was all he needed to hear. Galvanized by her plea, he circled his arms around her and found her mouth with his.

The moment their lips met, Jake knew she was not in a gentle mood. Her tongue plunged between his teeth, while her fingers dug into his shoulders and pulled him tight against her. A groan rumbled deep in his throat as hot desire slammed into him and sent his head reeling from the force of it.

If she was using him to wipe her mind of her troubles, Jake didn't care. The taste, the very scent of her, wrapped around his senses and cloaked him from the whys or what-ifs of tomorrow. He was connected to her and her to him. That was more than he could ask for.

In a matter of moments, the wild demands of their kiss caused them to tumble sideways and onto the pad of cool grass. Something hard and sharp jabbed him in the side, but Jake ignored the pain, which was an easy thing to do given the fact that his whole body was already humming, throbbing with the need to be inside her.

When their mouths finally ripped apart, Jake rolled onto his back and pulled her atop him. In a thick, raspy voice, he explained, "The ground is too rough for you."

Propping her forearms against his chest, she lifted her head to look at him. "For you, too," she pointed out.

The sound he made was something between a chuckle and a groan. "The only thing I feel is you, little darlin'. Now, come here."

Tunneling his hand beneath her hair, he cupped it around the back of her neck and drew her face down to his. She didn't resist. In fact, her lips made such a slow delicious feast of his that his whole body began to burn and ache. And when she unsnapped his shirt and planted little wet kisses down the middle of his chest and onto his abdomen, he could do nothing but surrender to her sweet ministrations.

But eventually that pleasure was not nearly enough for either of them. Clothes and boots were quickly removed and tossed aside. Then she was pushing him onto his back and straddling his hips.

Jake was vaguely aware of the dusky sky above, while a few feet behind them the horses swished their tails and gently stomped away the pestering insects. Water trickled in the tank and the windmill slowly creaked in the cool evening breeze. Somehow his mind managed to register all those things.Until she positioned herself over him and thrust downward.

The moment he slid into her, sensations rushed wildly through him and didn't stop until they'd whammed the top of his skull and sent his whole head reeling back against the ground.

Trying to catch his breath and hang on to what little self-control he had left, he anchored both hands at the sides of her waist and attempted to slow the pace of her thrust. But that was like stopping the wind. He couldn't brake a wild gale down to a gentle breeze. All he could do was ride it out and let the frantic motion of her body carry him to a mindless place he could only call ecstasy.

When Jake finally returned to his surroundings, Rebecca was draped over him with her cheek pressed against the middle of his chest and her hands curled over the top of his shoulders. Except for the rise and fall of her lungs, she was motionless, but her soft breath caressed his skin like a gentle finger. Her golden hair spilled over his ribs and in the process hid her face from his view.

Sliding his fingers into the silky strands, he lifted them away from her cheek. She stirred and tilted her head just enough to be able to meet his gaze. As Jake looked into her blue eyes he was stunned at how replete she made him feel. In the past week he'd lost count of how many times they'd made love and by now he would have expected the familiarity of her to bore him. Instead, it thrilled him. Each curve, each texture and scent of her body was a treasure to experience over and over. Each whispered word and touch, every kiss from her lips was the most precious thing he'd ever been given. Loving her was like coming home. And each time grew sweeter.

That was a scary realization for Jake; one that he didn't know how to deal with. A part of him wanted to tell her what he was feeling, but the other, bigger part of him wanted to hide those tender emotions, bury the thoughts of longing going on in his heart. He didn't want her to know just how vulnerable she made him feel. That would only make it more clumsy and uncomfortable when she did finally say goodbye.

"It's getting dark," he murmured huskily. "We'd better mount up and get back."

She gazed at him for long moments, then with a wistful sigh, she placed a kiss on his cheek. "Give me just a few minutes longer, Jake. Please."

How could he deny her, he asked himself, when all he wanted to do was hold her forever?

"All right," he murmured. "We'll go in a little while."

He held her quietly in his arms until dusk faded into darkness and a crescent moon appeared above the jagged line of mountains to the east. After that they dressed quickly, mounted their horses and headed them homeward.

The ride back to the house was done mainly in silence, while they carefully maneuvered the horses through sagebrush and clumps of cacti. Rebecca seemed lost in thought and Jake could hardly resent her quietness. Especially when his own mind was absorbed with questions and doubts. Something had changed her or the both of them on that grassy bed. And once they'd left it to dress and return to the real world, he'd felt certain he would never be the same man. As for Rebecca he could only guess what was going on inside her.

She'd clung to him as though she loved him. Yet he told himself that couldn't be the reason why she'd wanted to stay in his arms with her cheek pressed against the beat of his heart. That idea—that she could possibly love him—was too incredible for Jake to wrap his mind around.

When they reached the barn, Jake unsaddled both horses and while Rebecca poured a bucket of feed into Starr's trough, he loaded the tack and Banjo into his trailer for the trip back to the Rafter R.

Once the animals had been dealt with, Rebecca invited him into the house for a light supper of cold-cut sandwiches and iced tea. Throughout the simple meal, their conversation came and went in brief, awkward spurts. Until finally, Jake reached across the little table and brought her chin up with his forefinger.

"What's wrong, Rebecca? And don't tell me it's all this stuff about Gertrude and your parents. I already know you're upset about that. There's something else. Tell me."

She closed her eyes and swallowed. "I can't explain what's wrong, Jake. I guess today, after talking with my mother—" She broke off and with a shake of her head, let out a humorless laugh. "Dear God, I can't call Gwyn my mother anymore, can I? Because she isn't or wasn't. She's my aunt. Gertrude was my mother."

"Rebecca—"

"I'm sorry, Jake. I'm not going to say any more about her or what happened. I just—well, I guess the whole thing has confused me. And I realize that these past few weeks that I've been here in New Mexico I—I've been living in limbo."

An ominous chill crept down Jake's spine. "What does that mean?"

She gave him a long, searching look, one that made Jake feel cowardly and worthless. Two things he'd never felt in his life.

You'll be like your father until the day you die. Oh, God, why were his mother's words haunting him now? Jake wondered. Because she was right about him? Because he lacked what it took to be a man who could faithfully love one woman?

She reached for his hand and clung to it tightly.

"It means that I've been going through the motions of living without really knowing who I am or where I belong. I wanted to think I belonged here. But I'm beginning to see I—well, that I'm deluding myself."

"I thought you liked it here."

Her gaze swung away from him as she pulled her hand back to her side of the table. "I was. I do," she said. "But I need to do more than just exist. And I—well, I have nothing to hold me here."

That cut him deep. So deep that he could feel the blood drain from his face. Did she think of him as nothing?

Whoa, Jake. Before you go getting all hurt and bothered, you'd better stop and take a good look at this situation—at yourself. You've had some incredible sex with this woman, but you never told her what it's meant to you. What she means to you. How can you expect her to see you as anything more than a passing affair?

The voice traipsing through Jake's thoughts brought him up short. For a minute there he'd almost forgotten that Rebecca was only a temporary pleasure in his life. That was all he'd set out to have and he couldn't expect to have more with her now.

"You have this place and the animals."

Avoiding his gaze, she rose from the table and carried her plate over to the sink. With her back to him, she said, "Yes. But I have to have a means to live. Gert—my mother left me a nice sum of money and I do have some of my own saved. But all of that will go quickly if I'm not working."

"And your job is in Houston." He knew his voice sounded flat, maybe even accusing. But dammit, he didn't want her to go. He wasn't ready to give her up. Not just yet.

"Well, I really doubt there's any need for a fashion buyer around these parts." With a wry smile, she turned to face him. "And I'm not trained to do anything else."

In spite of the warmth of the kitchen, he felt cold, his face stiff. "I'm sure it's a very good job and that you do it well."

She drew in a long breath and let it out as though she was exhausted. Jake stared at her and wondered how things had quickly moved from making love to this?

"I've put in years of college and long, hard hours of work to get to the coveted position I have. I'm putting it all in jeopardy by hanging on here."

With a shake of his head, he rose from the table and walked over to her. "You didn't seem all that concerned about your job before. I don't understand this sudden change in you, Rebecca. Earlier—out by the windmill—were you already thinking this?"

Her gaze dropped to her feet as a blush washed her cheeks with pink. "Not exactly, Jake. I— To be honest, there's nothing sudden about it. I've been thinking about this every day. And tonight, as we rode home, I realized I couldn't put it off any longer. I—I'm going back to Houston."

She might as well have slapped him, Jake thought. And then it dawned on him. For the first time in his life, he was getting exactly what he'd dished out to his lady friends over the years. A few romps between the sheets and then a quick goodbye. He'd just learned how it felt to be on the receiving end.

But in his defense, he'd never given any of those women rosy promises or pledges of love, he thought.

And Rebecca never gave them to you, either.

Wiping a hand over his face, he turned and walked to the middle of the room. Beau was lying just inside the screen door and the sight of the dog made it somehow even harder to deal with her decision. He'd thought she loved the dog. But then, he'd begun to think that she might love him. What a fool thought that had been.

"I see. So what about Beau and the rest of the animals?"

She didn't answer immediately and he glanced over his shoulder to see her wiping her eyes. And suddenly he was angry. Angrier than he'd ever felt in his life. Why hadn't she packed up and left a long time ago? he wondered. Why in hell had she stuck around and made him and the animals fall in love with her?

"I want Starr to have acreage to roam over instead of taking her back to Houston and confining her in a stable. And since I live in an apartment that doesn't allow pets, I'll have to find homes for the cats and Beau with someone around here."

"They already have a home," he said gruffly. "They'll be lost anywhere else."

Lifting her head, she looked at him with an anger that matched his own. "Don't make this any harder for me than it already is, Jake."

Turning, he walked back to her and gestured around the small kitchen. "What about this place? What are you going to do with it? Sell it?"

Her nostrils flared at his accusing tone. He made it sound like she was a criminal for leaving. "This was my mother's home. I'll never sell it for any reason."

"You just won't live here."

She shot him a daring stare. "Why should I?"

"Why should you?" Earlier he'd laid his hat on top of the refrigerator. Now he pulled down the stained gray Stetson and levered it onto his head. "If you have to ask, Rebecca, then I sure can't tell you."

She took a halting step in his direction. "You have no right to be judgmental with me, Jake."

That was true enough, he thought ruefully. Where she was concerned, he had no right to feel anything, think anything. And the less he did, the better off he'd be.

Closing the space between them, he touched a hand to her cheek. "I'm sorry, Rebecca. I don't want our time together to be marred by these last words between us. That's why… I'm going to say goodbye. And if you do decide to come back, you know where to find me."

So they could have another casual affair? Rebecca was tempted to fling the loaded question at him. But he robbed her of the chance by quickly turning and walking out the door.

Seconds later she heard the engine of his truck fire to

life and then the rattle of the trailer as he pulled away. In the far distance she heard Starr nicker loudly and the sound of the mare calling out for Banjo to come back to her brought a wall of tears to Rebecca's eyes.

She wanted Jake to come back, too. She ached for him to walk back into the kitchen, take her into his arms and tell her that he loved her. That the only place she belonged was with him.

But she'd given him all kinds of chances to speak the words, to ask her not to go. Instead, he'd said goodbye and now she had to deal with a breaking heart.

As she tried to fight back her tears, she felt something cold and wet nudge against her hand. Glancing down, she saw Beau's sad eyes staring up at her, as though he knew their time together was over.

It was more than Rebecca could bear and she dropped to her knees and hugged the dog close to her breast.

Chapter 11

Three weeks later, Jake was walking from the barn to his house when the sound of a vehicle had him looking over his shoulder to see Quint's truck coming up the driveway.

The sight of his friend at this late hour was a bit surprising. Once Quint had gotten a family, he didn't roam from the Golden Spur after working hours, unless he had to deal with some sort of business outside of the ranch.

Jake waited for his friend to park and climb to the ground before he walked over to join him at the side of the truck.

"Hey, bud, what are you doing over here at this hour? It's nearly dark."

"Maura sent me on a mission," Quint explained, then reached inside the back door and pulled out a long casserole dish covered with aluminum foil. "She thinks you're starving to death so she made something to tempt you."

With a wry shake of his head, Jake asked, "What makes her think I'm in need of food?"

Quint shoved the glass dish at him, forcing Jake to accept it before it fell to the ground. "When you came by the Golden Spur yesterday, she said you looked thin and terrible. Her words. Not mine."

"Well, I should have known my good looks would start to go sooner or later," Jake tried to joke, then inclined his head toward the house. "Let's go inside and have a beer."

"You finished with the evening chores?" Quint asked as they walked through a gate and across the front lawn.

Unlike Quint, who had a roster of hands to deal with the mundane chores of feeding, watering and spreading hay, Jake only had two men to help with the everyday tasks. Sometimes it was long after dark before they were finished and the men headed for home. "Yeah. Before you drove up I was down at the cow lot. I got a problem."

"What's wrong?"

"A hell of a lot!"

At the house, the two men entered a side door that led them directly in the kitchen. While Jake set the casserole on the cabinet counter, Quint straddled one of the tall stools at a breakfast bar.

"I'm waiting," Quint prodded. "What's happened?"

"Nothing. That's what's happened. This morning me and the guys pregnancy tested the herd on the east range. Ten of the cows are empty. And you know what that means—ten less calves this spring!" Jake went to the refrigerator and pulled out two long-necked beers. After shoving one in Quint's direction, he twisted the top off the one he was holding and downed a third of the contents.

Quint eyed him closely. "So how many cows did you have in that herd? Two hundred? Two-fifty?"

Jake grimaced. "Two hundred and thirty."

"Well, ten out of that many is not a big enough percentage to raise a ruckus over. This kind of thing happens to every rancher."

"Yeah, I know. But that doesn't make it any easier to take," Jake muttered.

"Have you had the bull tested?"

Jake shook his head. "I don't see any need for that. The rest of the cows in his herd are all carrying calves. That's what makes it so bad. I'll have to sell and replace them. And with the cows being open, I'll hardly get a decent market price."

"I doubt it. But that's part of ranching, too. There will always be ups and downs in the business. This is just one of those downs and if I were you, I'd call it a very minor one."

Jake shot him a cynical glare. "You would. Ten cows wouldn't count much to you."

Quint plopped the beer bottle down on the bar with a heavy thud. "Dammit, Jake, don't talk to me that way! Every cow on my ranch is important to me. Right now I have twenty that are too old to calve anymore. They've not produced in two years and they never will again. But I don't have the heart to send them to slaughter. So I feed and care for them just like the others. It's not good business sense, but it makes Maura happy. And I guess, to be honest, it makes me happy, too."

Heaving a weary breath, Jake walked over to a pine farm table and sank into a chair at one end. He felt awful and spouting off to the man who'd been like a brother since they were very small boys, only made him feel worse.

"Sorry, Quint. I didn't mean that like it sounded. But you can absorb the loss much easier than I can."

Quint mouthed a curse word. "You're not exactly poor, Jake. Not anymore."

They both knew he was referring to the dividends he received from shares of the Golden Spur Mine. And Quint was basically right in saying Jake wasn't poor anymore. He owned more valuable assets now than he'd ever dreamed possible. Yet he still couldn't think of himself as solvent. Maybe that was because he'd never felt confident that he could hang on to all he'd acquired.

"I believe you ought to have the bull checked," Quint went on. "I don't see ten cows having a fertility problem. But that's just my opinion."

Jake stared at him. "If the bull is the problem that's even worse! Replacing him would take a hunk of money!"

Quint frowned. "Look, Jake, if you're so worried about taking losses, then you might as well pack up and sell this place, because every good rancher knows he's going to take some hammering at times!"

Jake's gaze slipped to the beer bottle he was gripping with both hands. "I'm thinking about doing just that!"

"What?"

The incredulous tone in Quint's voice had Jake looking up at his longtime buddy. "You heard me right," he muttered. "I'm thinking about…doing something else."

With slow, purposeful movements, Quint climbed

down from the stool and walked over to the table. "What are you talking about?"

The censure in Quint's voice made Jake feel even worse. Like it was possible to feel worse, he thought grimly. His mind, his whole body felt as if he'd been whipped, beaten down by a hand that he couldn't see or defend himself against.

"I was at the track a couple of days ago and—"

"I should have known," Quint interrupted with disgust. "You just can't stay away from that place, can you?"

Angry now, Jake glared at him. "And why the hell should I? Shoeing racehorses, managing the stables, those jobs made me a living for many years, Quint. And I have good friends there. Friends that don't preach to me because I'm not perfect," he added hotly.

The caustic remark didn't send Quint packing out the door. Instead, he eased down in the seat across from Jake and gave his friend a long, troubled look. "All right, Jake," he said quietly. "I'm sorry. I was out of line and I shouldn't have said anything about you visiting the track. I understand that place will always be a part of you."

"Damn right it will. And they've offered me a huge salary to come back to work."

Quint stiffened. "Are you considering taking it?"

Jake couldn't look him square in the face. "Maybe."

Shaking his head, Quint mouthed a curse word under his breath. "So you're just going to throw all this away? All you've worked for?"

"Look, Quint, I'm not cut out for this. In the end, I'll probably lose it all, anyway. Better to sell out and get what I can while the getting is good."

"That's a hell of a thing to say!" Quint spat. "And I don't know where this thinking of yours is coming from. You were my ranch foreman for a few years—*you know everything* about ranching. Your dad—"

"My dad is gone!" Jake interrupted flatly. "So don't go trying to bring him into this!"

Unfazed by Jake's anger, Quint said, "The man taught you a lot about horses and cattle."

And women, Jake thought bitterly. Oh, yes, Lee Rollins had charmed them, loved them and left them. Just like Jake. Until one important woman had come along. Until Rebecca had taught him that giving up his heart was something entirely different.

When Jake didn't reply, Quint leaned back in his chair and folded his arms across his chest. "All right, Jake, my father is gone, too. So what do you think we ought to do? Sit here and cry in our beer? Convince ourselves that we're losers?"

Jake glared at him. "Sometimes you can be a real bastard, Quint, and if we were eight years old again, I'd knock your head off. Or at least try."

Quint shrugged a shoulder. "If that would make you feel any better, we can go outside and pretend we're eight years old again."

Realizing the absurdity of that notion, Jake scrubbed his face with both hands and let out a long, weary breath. "Things were simple back then, weren't they?" he asked softly. "We both had fathers and I had no idea that mine was going to leave me behind."

Quint leaned forward and laid a hand on Jake's shoulder. "I thought you weren't going to let that—him—hurt you anymore."

"I believed I'd put it all behind me," he admitted, "until Rebecca came."

"Ah."

The one knowing word from Quint put a rueful twist to Jake's lips. "Yeah. I guess she reminded me all over again what it's like to lose someone you care about."

Quint studied him for long moments. "The racetrack, this ranch, the land, you're not agonizing over any of those things, Jake. You're just learning that none of it means a damn thing without someone to love. And someone to love you back."

Pain smacked the middle of Jake's chest and he fixed his gaze on the tabletop in hopes that his friend wouldn't be able to spot the misery.

"Well, she doesn't. Love me back, that is," Jake muttered.

"How do you know?" Quint countered. "I doubt you asked her."

"I didn't have to. She left. That was the answer she gave me."

"Did you give her any reason to stay?"

Jake looked dismally up at him. "No. I don't guess I did."

A week later, Rebecca lifted the stainless steel lid covering the main course of her dinner and gave the piece of glazed salmon a disinterested glance. It might have whetted her appetite if she'd gone down to the hotel restaurant instead of ordering room service, she thought. At least she could have sat among the other diners and pretended she wanted to eat. Now the food was growing cold and she had little desire to fork any of it to her mouth.

Across the opulent hotel room, piled upon the bed, were a countless number of flowing ruffled dresses, lightweight spring jackets, handbags, shoes and chunky pieces of jewelry. All of which she'd collected at today's fashion bazaar. None of those things interested her, either.

With a heavy sigh, she walked over to the outer wall of plate glass and stared out at the dark night. The twinkling lights of the Chicago skyline stretched endlessly in all directions and directly below on the well-lit street, people were entering and exiting cabs as they made their way to some of the nearby nightspots.

There were times when an assistant traveled with Rebecca, but this time she'd made the trip alone to the Midwest Fashion Fair. Yet even if a friend had accompanied her, she wouldn't have had any desire to go out for a night on the town.

Face it, Rebecca, you're confused, miserable and missing Jake Rollins something fierce.

The voice going off in her head was suddenly interrupted by the ring of her cell phone.

Turning away from the untouched meal, she walked over to the nightstand where she'd left the phone and immediately frowned. She'd expected the caller to be her boss, Arlene, but the number illuminated on the front of the instrument was totally unfamiliar.

And then it dawned on Rebecca that the area code she was seeing was from New Mexico! Dear God, could it be Jake?

Snatching up the instrument, she fumbled it open and finally managed to slap it next to her ear. "Hello," she answered in a rush.

"Rebecca? That you?"

Stunned to hear Abe Cantrell's voice, she sank weakly onto the edge of the bed. Had something happened to Jake and the older man had called to let her know? The mere idea left her hands trembling.

"Yes, this is Rebecca. How are you, Abe?"

"Fine and dandy. Been sittin' outside watchin' the sunset and it was mighty pretty. Made me think of you. So I gave you a call to see how you're doin'."

A hot, painful lump filled her throat. While she'd lived on her mother's place, she'd not spent a great deal of time with her elderly neighbor, but enough to get to know and love him. Before she'd left for Houston, she'd told Abe about Gertrude being her mother and how confused and hurt the whole thing had left her. Surprisingly, Abe had understood her distress more than any of her friends in Houston. Perhaps that was because he was much older and wiser. Or maybe she'd simply opened up to him more. Either way, his thoughtful support had bonded her to him in a way she'd not expected.

"Well, right now I'm sitting in a hotel room in Chicago," she told him.

"You on a vacation?"

Rebecca closed her eyes as images of everything she'd come to love in New Mexico swam to the forefront of her thoughts. "Nothing that pleasant. I'm on a business trip. My job requires a lot of traveling."

"Went right back to work, did you? Guess that means you haven't had time to miss much about this place back here."

"Actually, I—I've been missing everything out there."

He said, "Your mother's place looks deserted now. I don't like seeing it that way."

Before she'd left for Houston, Abe had taken her animals and given them a nice home on Apache Wells. Another reason she was very grateful to the man.

She said, "It would be better if I could find a nice little family to live there and keep the place maintained. Maybe you know of someone?"

"I'd rather see you there."

She swallowed hard as she struggled to blink back a wall of tears. "Well, you know how it is, Abe, a person has to work to keep their head afloat." She cleared her throat, then asked, "How is Beau?"

"After you left he moped around for a few days. But he's okay now. I never was one to have a dog for a buddy, but he can't seem to shake me and I can't seem to shake him, so we're stuck together. The cats are in mouse heaven down at the barn and Starr has made a few friends in the remuda. And I know you didn't ask me to, but I sent someone to mow your grass. Just in case you decide to come back."

Beyond the door to her suite, Rebecca could hear a group of people passing in the hallway. From the sound of their laughter, they sounded happy and young. Had she ever been that way? Yes, she'd been happy, but that had been eons ago. Long before she'd grown dissatisfied with her job, before she'd learned Gertrude was her mother, that Gwyn had been harboring secrets, and her father had been unfaithful. And definitely long before she'd met Jake and fallen in love with him.

Tugging her attention back to Abe, she said, "Unfortunately, that won't be anytime soon. But thank you for the lawn work. It makes me feel better to know the place doesn't look raggedy."

"You haven't asked about Jake," he said pointedly.

The old man was crafty, Rebecca would give him that much. She breathed deeply, then asked, "How is Jake?"

"He ain't good. That's about all I can say."

Rebecca instantly gripped the phone. "Why? What's wrong with him?"

"You'd have to ask him to get the answer. All I know is what Quint tells me. And he tells me that Jake is considering taking a job at the track and selling the Rafter R."

"Selling his ranch?" She was stunned. "But, Abe, that doesn't make sense! He's worked so hard on it! And he seemed so proud of the place."

"Well, Jake never was one to want a pile of material things. To a certain point, Quint's the same way. Guess that's why the two boys have always been such good friends. Frankly, I think he needs to get rid of every damn cow on the place and focus on raisin' his horses. That's what he loves to do and that's what he ought to do."

"Then you should tell him so, Abe! You're his friend and I know he respects your opinion."

Abe chuckled. "He wouldn't appreciate me tellin' him what to do. Now you, that's another matter—if you was to tell him that might carry some weight."

A tear slipped from Rebecca's eye and fell onto her cheek. At one point during her stay in New Mexico, she'd believed that Jake might actually grow to care for her, maybe even love her. But once she'd met Gwyn in Ruidoso and learned the truth about how she was conceived, something had happened to her. She'd felt sick and desperate and lost.

And when she and Jake had ridden out to the windmill and made love under the open sky it had been so beautiful, so bittersweet, that her heart had ached. She'd desperately longed to hear him say that he loved her. Or at the very least, he wanted her to remain in New Mexico. But while he'd held her for those long minutes, he'd not said anything and his silence had opened her eyes. Suddenly, she could see she was deluding herself in thinking he would ever love her and the longer she stayed, the more her heart was going to break.

Then later, at the house, Rebecca had once again attempted to draw out his feelings, to get any sort of sign from him that he wanted her in a permanent way. When she'd told him she no longer knew where she belonged, she'd done so while hoping and praying he would open his mouth and tell her that she belonged with him. For always. But he'd failed to say anything meaningful, except goodbye.

"I don't think so, Abe. I've not even heard from Jake and I don't expect to."

"There ain't no law written that says you can't call him, is there?"

Call Jake? What good would that do, except tear her heart wide open again? she wondered miserably. "Jake doesn't want to hear from me."

Abe snorted. "And grass don't grow in the spring."

Closing her eyes, Rebecca rubbed fingertips against her furrowed brow. "In order for grass to grow it has to be fed sun and rain," she reminded the old man.

There was a long pause and while she waited for Abe to reply, in the far background she could hear a horse neigh softly. Was it Starr still calling out for Banjo? The notion put a hard lump in Rebecca's throat.

"Jake is like a son to me," Abe finally said. "I don't

want to see him mess up. Think about calling him, Rebecca. That's all I ask."

"I'll do that much," Rebecca conceded.

Abe thanked her and after a quick good-night ended the call.

Rebecca placed the phone back on the nightstand, then dropped her face in her hands and sobbed.

The next morning Jake was on his way to the Downs to shoe three racehorses when Clara rang his cell phone and asked that he stop by her place before going on about his business.

Jake had agreed to see his mother, although he'd been surprised by her request. Only last night he'd dropped by for a visit, the first one he'd had with her since the day he'd raked her over the coals about his father and how she'd allowed the man to dictate her life. Taking all that in account, Jake had expected to find Clara more than a little frosty, but she'd met him at the door with a welcoming hug. And when he'd told her about Rebecca going back to Texas, he'd braced himself to hear a bunch of I-told-you-sos. Instead, she'd appeared truly sorry for him. He'd been inwardly shocked by the pleasant change in her and though he'd wondered what had brought it about, he'd decided it best not to ask and simply be thankful for it.

Now this morning as he walked onto the porch of his mother's house, he could only wonder what was going on with her and hope that she'd not had another health setback.

Rapping his knuckles slightly on the storm door, he opened it and stepped inside. "Mom? I'm here."

Clara immediately hurried through a doorway leading to the back of the house. She smiled at him with a measure of relief.

"Jake, I'm so glad you took the time to come by. I know you're busy, but I have something important to give you. At least, I think it will be important."

Walking over to his mother, Jake dropped a kiss on the top of her head. "What is it? You sent plenty of baked things home with me last night. I don't need any more food."

She let out a short laugh that sounded strangely nervous to Jake. Which only confused him more. In the past Clara had often complained and whined and accused him of being like his father, but one thing she'd never been with him was nervous.

"It's nothing like that." She took him by the hand and led him over to a short couch. "I—uh—I didn't tell you last night, but I talked to Quint the other day."

"That's nothing new. You two have always been friends."

A sheepish expression stole over her face. "We talked about you."

Jake grimaced. "Oh. You shouldn't have done that, Mom."

"I didn't. He's the one who approached me. And frankly, I'm glad that he did. I didn't know—well, that day we argued—I didn't understand about Rebecca, not really. I thought she was just another one of your women. I think—well, I've been so wrapped up in feeling sorry for myself that I couldn't really see what was going on with you and the girl from Texas."

Jake stiffened. "What makes you think she's any different?"

"Oh, son, don't try to pretend with me," she said gently, then attempted to laugh and lighten the moment. "I mean, your mother has finally opened her eyes, don't try to hide from me now."

Dropping his head, Jake stared at the scuffed toes of his boots, but all he was really seeing was Rebecca's face, her sweet smile, the warm shine in her blue eyes. "I miss her," he mumbled. "So much."

He felt his mother's hand rest upon his back and then she said softly, "That's how it is when you love someone."

Lifting his head, he looked at her with remorse. "I'm sorry, Mom. I've been hard on you at times. I said things to you that I didn't know about or understand."

Smiling faintly, she shook her head. "You had every right to say what you did. I've been wallowing in self-pity for far too long. I lost Lee and let the hurt ruin a big chunk of my life. I don't want that to happen to you."

She pulled a small piece of paper from a pocket on her blouse and thrust it at him. "Here. I think you need to use this."

He glanced down to see a phone number scratched across a torn piece of notebook paper. "I don't need that. I already have Rebecca's number. Besides, I wouldn't know what to say to her."

With a smile of encouragement, Clara pressed the paper into Jake's hand and folded his fingers around it. "When the time is right you'll know what to say to her. But before you talk to Rebecca I think you should make this call."

Bewildered, he asked, "Why?"

"Because it's a link to your father."

* * *

Less than a week later, Rebecca was sitting at her desk, sifting through a stack of fashion sketches, when Arlene's voice came over the intercom.

"Rebecca, I need you on the second floor. We're having a disagreement that only you can settle."

"I'll be right there."

She walked out of her sumptuous office and took the elevator up to the second floor, a space used exclusively to display Bordeaux's formal evening wear. At the front entrance of the department, she found Arlene and her young assistant, a guy named Nigel, trying to put the finishing touches to a mannequin dressed in a designer frock fashioned from yards and yards of shiny faille. She considered the dress far too flamboyant for the store, but this was one time Arlene had dismissed Rebecca's opinion and purchased the garment in several sizes anyway.

Now as she approached the bickering coworkers, Arlene split away from the young man and grabbed Rebecca by the arm. "It's about time I had some help," she said with a flustered wave at her assistant. "Please tell Nigel that I'm right and he's wrong. This dress needs more than a single strand of pearls."

The young man cast an imploring look at Rebecca. "Arlene thinks the chunky gold and ruby thing would look better. I think it's too much for all that dress. But what do I know? I only work here."

Rebecca took the tiny pearls from his hand and draped them around the mannequin's neck. "He's right, Arlene. The pearls."

The other woman gasped, then spluttered, "But, Rebecca, pearls are so—so retro and ho-hum!"

"They're also classy," Rebecca pointed out. "And this dress definitely needs something to give it a little elegance."

Nigel smiled with smug triumph while Arlene jerked on Rebecca's arm until the two women were standing some distance away from the display.

"Rebecca, I realize you're still angry with me, but you don't have to carry it over to our work," Arlene said under her breath so the women browsing nearby couldn't overhear.

Arlene had always been a bit of a drama queen, but she'd never taken this sort of tone with Rebecca. "You wanted my opinion and I gave it. That's what I'm paid to do. Besides, I've never been angry with you. Impatient at times, but never angry."

Arlene's lips pressed to a thin line. "Well, you were all out of sorts with me when you decided to take that vacation in New Mexico. And from what I can see you're still not behaving like yourself."

It had been more than a vacation and they both knew it. The truth was that Arlene had never quite gotten over Rebecca's challenge for a leave of indefinite absence, but she wasn't in the mood to have an out-and-out confrontation with the woman. "I have a lot to deal with, Arlene."

The other woman let out a disgusted huff. "Don't we all."

Rebecca stared at her. "Are you finished?"

"No! I just want to say that you need to wake up and look around you. There are other employees here at Bordeaux's who've had a family member die, but they don't go around taking out their grief on others. They handle it with maturity."

In other words, they don't go against your wishes, Rebecca thought. She should have been angry with the other woman for behaving so childishly, but she couldn't summon up that much energy.

"I've lost more than a family member, Arlene."

The woman frowned. "What does that mean?"

"It means that everything that ever mattered to me is gone. That's what it means."

She walked away from Arlene and, after an encouraging word to Nigel, took the stairs down to the first floor where the street clothes were displayed, along with fragrance, jewelry, and makeup counters, the facial area and countless dressing rooms. This was the store's hot spot and since it was a Friday afternoon and shoppers were readying themselves for the weekend, every area was busy.

At one time Rebecca would have been excited to see the throngs of clientele. But that was back when she'd considered Bordeaux's her second home. Back when she'd been excited about her job and determined to be a success at it. For years now she'd made it her life and along the way, she'd convinced herself that she was happy. She'd even quit dreaming that a man and a family could be in her future. She'd told herself those things were for other women, not her.

Until she met Jake. Dear God, he'd shaken the very depths of her. And try as she might she couldn't go back to being the old Rebecca, the fashion buyer, the career woman. Arlene had been right on one count. Rebecca hadn't been behaving like herself. Because she was a different woman now and she needed more than a position at Bordeaux's. She needed Jake.

Gwyn and Gertrude had wasted their lives trying to

hide the truth from each other, Vance, their friends and even Rebecca. She couldn't allow herself to go down that same path. She had to let Jake know how much she loved him, how much she wanted him in her life.

If he still wasn't interested, then at least she could tell herself she'd gone down trying rather than hiding.

The decision quickened her steps as she turned toward an exit that would take her back to her office. Once she reached the private spot, she was going to call Jake and tell him they still had things to talk about and she would be flying out to Lincoln County as soon as she could arrange it. And then from somewhere behind her she heard a salesclerk say, "There's Ms. Hardaway now. If you hurry you might catch her."

At the sound of her name, Rebecca paused and turned to see who wanted a word with her. And then she saw the object of her thoughts. Jake was standing there as big as life in his boots and Stetson and staring straight at her.

In a daze, she wondered what *he* was doing here and then she noticed the women customers around him were apparently wondering the same thing. All eyes were on him as he began walking toward Rebecca and the closer he got to her, the faster her heart pounded.

By the time he came to a stop only a few inches separated them and as Rebecca looked into his familiar brown eyes, she feared her knees were going to buckle.

"Jake. What— Why are you here in Houston?" she asked in a voice faint with shock.

The half grin on his lips was a bit sheepish and completely endearing. "Isn't it obvious? You."

Rebecca didn't realize she'd been holding her breath

until a long gush of air rushed past her parted lips. "I don't understand. You haven't called."

"Neither have you."

She swallowed as hope tried to bubble up inside her. Surely he was here because he cared, she thought. Why else would he travel all the way to Texas? "I decided today—a few moments ago, to be exact—to call you. But—"

He moved close enough for her to smell the sunshine on his cowboy shirt, see the faint lines at the corners of his eyes. Since they'd been apart, his skin had browned even more from the summer sun, giving him a swarthy appearance and as she looked at him everything inside her melted with longing.

"I was going to call you, too," he said. "But then I decided that what I had to say needed to be said in person."

Suddenly the store, the customers and salesclerks all faded into oblivion. The only thing she could see was him.

"And what was that?"

Stepping forward, he wrapped his hands around her upper arms. "Before you left, you told me you didn't know where you belonged. Well, I'm here to tell you exactly where you belong. With me. Forever."

Stunned with joy, she tried to find her voice to respond. And then it didn't matter because he lifted her completely off her feet and planted a long, thorough kiss upon her lips.

Behind them she could hear several oohs and awws and then a spattering of applause. By the time their heads came apart, they'd garnered a gawking audience.

Laughing, Rebecca grabbed him by the hand and hurried him out of sight and down a large corridor to her office. When she shut the door behind them, she turned to see Jake inspecting the room.

"This is where you work?"

She came up behind him. "This is my office."

He whistled under his breath. "It's really something."

Now that they were completely alone Rebecca's first inclination was to throw herself into his arms and cling with all her might. She was hungry for the taste, the touch, the very scent of him. But she also needed explanations.

"Jake, I've got to know why—"

Before she could finish her broken question, he turned and put his arms around her.

"I came to my senses and realized that I love you?" he finished for her.

To hear him say the word *love* very nearly wilted her and she snatched holds on the front of his shirt to steady herself. "You love me?"

"With all my heart," he answered. "But I was afraid to admit it to myself and especially to you. I'm not exactly molded out of family-man material, Becca. And I always believed the greatest favor I could do for a woman was walk away from her before I caused her the same sort of pain my father caused my mother. But I can't walk away from you. So here I am asking you to give me a chance to be something I never thought I could be. A husband. A father."

Her heart brimming with love, she reached up and brushed her fingers against his dark cheek. "You're not Lee Rollins. You're your own man. The man I love."

His hands splayed against her back and tugged her close against him. "Since you left, I've spoken to my stepmother and learned that my father died a couple of years ago. And that I have a half brother and sister," he told her.

"Oh, my. And how did she react to you contacting her?"

"Surprisingly, she was very warm and understanding. She even insists that my half siblings want to meet me."

"That's wonderful. But what about your father— did she have any explanations as to why he left you totally behind?"

"His widow told me that Lee believed I'd be better off without him in my life. He realized he wasn't exactly the best of role models for a son to follow. Plus, there was so much anger and fighting between him and Mom that he figured the constant warfare would only hurt me more. His way of loving me was to stay away so I'd look to others to learn how a real man should conduct his life, rather than patterning myself after him."

She carefully studied his face. "And how did that make you feel?"

He let out a long breath. "Very sad. But strangely free. For years I'd thought about searching for him. I had this idea that it would give me some sort of satisfaction to tell him face-to-face just how much he'd hurt me and Mom and what a sorry human being he'd been. But, you know, when his widow told me that he'd passed away, none of that really mattered anymore. I realized there were so many more important things in my life. Mainly you."

With a sob of relief, she pressed her cheek against his chest. "Oh, Jake, I'm so glad. You and I might not have come from the best of homes, but we're going to make a good home together."

Tilting up her chin, Jake motioned to her luxurious office. "Can you give all of this up for me?"

Her eyes shining with love, she smiled at him. "Can you love me for the rest of our lives?"

"Easy," he whispered.

She slipped her arms around him. "You took the word right out of my mouth. Easy."

Epilogue

Fourteen months later, Jake stepped down from the chestnut colt he'd been breaking to the saddle and tethered him to a nearby fence post. The sun had shown its face only a half hour ago, but long before daylight the ranch hands had arrived to tend to the early-morning barn chores.

"That was real fine, Smarty Cat." He gave the horse an affectionate pat on the neck. "You're going to be ready to gallop on the track soon and by this time next year you might be ready for the Sunland Derby."

"That's a big prediction."

At the sound of Rebecca's voice, Jake turned to see his wife walking up with their three-month-old daughter cradled in her arms and Beau trotting happily at their heels. The morning was sunny, but there was still a definite chill to the early March day. Rebecca had the baby bundled in a thick yellow blanket and a pink sock cap.

Jake couldn't resist pulling the blanket away from his daughter's cheek and smacking a kiss on her cherub face. Having a child filled him with indescribable joy and the moment he'd first held her in his arms, he'd understood what Quint had meant when he'd talked about Jake having a real home.

"Hi, Jacklyn," he crooned to the baby. "Did you come to see Daddy work?"

"You call that work?" Rebecca teased. "I thought you were playing."

Chuckling, Jake leaned forward and planted a soft kiss on his wife's mouth. "I can't fool you, can I? Riding Smarty Cat is play for me."

Since he and Rebecca had married more than a year ago, many changes had taken place at the Rafter R. With Rebecca's encouragement, he'd taken Abe's advice and sold every cow on the place. Broodmares now filled the pastures and race prospects were stabled in a huge horse barn equipped with heated stalls and a foaling area. A galloping track had been built and horse walkers erected. Jake was doing what he loved and thriving at it.

"Do you really think Smarty Cat might become that good? To race in the Sunland Derby? That's only a step away from the Kentucky Derby," she reminded him.

Chuckling, Jake curled his arm around her shoulder and gathered her and the baby close to his side. "I know it's a big dream, Becca. And if I sound confident, you can take the blame for that. I'm not settling for just existing—just hoping to keep the ranch in the black. I want our horses to be champions."

"And they will be if you have anything to do with it," she assured him.

"So what are you and Jacklyn doing down here at

the barns so early this morning?" he asked. "Getting your exercise?"

"Well, I could have called you on the cell, but I wanted to see you."

The half grin on his face was a sensual reminder of the lusty lovemaking he'd given her last night. "Just can't get enough of me, can you?"

She wrinkled her nose playfully at him. "I don't want to burst your bubble, but I'm down here for a different reason. I wanted to ask if you'd mind quitting work a little early this evening. I just talked to your mother about having her over for dinner tonight. She's coming and bringing a friend."

Jake arched a quizzical brow at her. "A friend? Are you talking about a man? A date?"

Rebecca laughed softly. "That's exactly what I mean. Believe me, I'm just as surprised as you."

"Hmm." He stroked his thumb and forefinger thoughtfully over his chin. "Did she tell you his name?"

"No. Does it matter?"

A slow grin spread across his face. "Not really. I'm just thrilled that Mom is starting to live again. Her health has improved by leaps and bounds. And she seems actually happy now. Thanks to you."

"Me? I can't take the credit for your mother's turn-around. I think when she made the choice to help you find Lee Rollins it freed the demons she'd been carrying for so long."

"You may be right. But I know for a fact that seeing how happy you've made me has inspired her."

"Her son makes me very happy, too," she said, then lifting her gaze to the distant mountains, added, "I only wish things with me and Gwyn could be fixed so easily. I've been thinking about inviting her out here for a little visit. Would you mind?"

"Now why would I mind? You were such a great hostess when my brother and sister came a few weeks ago."

"That was fun—they're both just as charming as you, my dear husband. But this thing with Gwyn could get awkward," she warned him.

"Maybe. But you've got to start somewhere, Becca. And the invitation would let her see that you're willing to forgive and begin working past the problems between you. But do you think she'll come?"

"Who knows? She doesn't like the big outdoors. But if she wants to understand me, she needs to see what I'm all about. She also needs to see where her sister lived and where she's now buried."

"Gwyn might not go for that idea."

Rebecca shrugged. "She might not. But I'm hoping she's had time to think about doing some forgiving and letting go. And I think she'll jump at any chance to be with Jacklyn. I believe if there's anything that can help heal the wounds of the past, it will be our daughter."

Glancing down at the dark-haired baby, Rebecca adjusted Jacklyn's warm cap, then handed her over to Jake. While he cooed and talked to the baby Rebecca stepped over to stroke Smarty Cat's blazed face. The horse immediately nudged her hand for a treat and she pulled a piece of apple from her jacket pocket and fed it to him.

From behind her, Jake teased, "Just what I thought. You didn't come down here to see me. You came to spoil the horses."

"I can't help it. I love them."

A smile bent the corners of her lips as she felt Jake's hand come to rest upon her shoulder.

"You miss working at Dr. Adams's, don't you?"

A few months after she and Jake had married, a vet with a clinic near the racetrack had offered her a job as an assistant in training. And up until Jacklyn was born, she'd worked full-time for him. The learning experience had taught her much more than how to deal with animals, she'd come to realize her long-ago dreams as a young girl hadn't been a foolish aspiration.

"I loved the job. But I also love being a mother. Besides, taking maternity leave has given me the opportunity to start some online classes toward that animal husbandry degree I always wanted."

"It's going to take you a long time to get that degree with just a handful of classes at a time," he pointed out.

Twisting her head around, she gave him a provocative smile. "I'll have plenty of time in between babies to get a degree."

Both of his brows shot up. "Babies? As in plural?"

She chuckled. "Why, yes. You wouldn't want to have just one horse in your racing stable, would you?"

"No. But you can rest assured—" His eyes full of promises, he bent his head and rested his cheek alongside hers. "I only want one woman in my bed and in my life."

"That's good to know," she said with a contented sigh, "because you're going to have me around for the rest of our lives."

* * * * *

SPECIAL EXCERPT FROM

H HARLEQUIN®

SPECIAL EDITION

*Arizona park ranger Vivian Hollister is not having
a holiday fling with Sawyer Whitehorse—no matter
how attracted she is to her irresistible new partner.
So why is she starting to feel that Sawyer is the one
to help carry on her family legacy? A man to have
and to hold forever…*

Read on for a sneak preview of
A Ranger for Christmas,
the next book in the Men of the West miniseries
by USA TODAY bestselling author Stella Bagwell.

She rose from her seat of slab rock. "We'd probably better
be going. We still have one more hiking trail to cover before
we hit another set of campgrounds."

While she gathered up her partially eaten lunch, Sawyer
left his seat and walked over to the edge of the bluff.

"This is an incredible view," he said. "From this distance,
the saguaros look like green needles stuck in a sandpile."

She looked over to see the strong north wind was hitting
him in the face and molding his uniform against his muscled
body. The sight of his imposing figure etched against the
blue sky and desert valley caused her breath to hang in her
throat.

She walked over to where he stood, then took a cautious
step closer to the ledge in order to peer down at the view
directly below.

"I never get tired of it," she admitted. "There are a few
Native American ruins not far from here. We'll hike by
those before we finish our route."

A hard gust of wind suddenly whipped across the ledge and caused Vivian to sway on her feet. Sawyer swiftly caught her by the arm and pulled her back to his side.

"Careful," he warned. "I wouldn't want you to topple over the edge."

With his hand on her arm and his sturdy body shielding her from the wind, she felt very warm and protected. And for one reckless moment, she wondered how it would feel to slip her arms around his lean waist, to rise up on the tips of her toes and press her mouth to his. Would his lips taste as good as she imagined?

Shaken by the direction of her runaway thoughts, she tried to make light of the moment. "That would be awful," she agreed. "Mort would have to find you another partner."

"Yeah, and she might not be as cute as you."

With a little laugh of disbelief, she stepped away from his side. "Cute? I haven't been called that since I was in high school. I'm beginning to think you're nineteen instead of twenty-nine."

He pulled a playful frown at her. "You prefer your men to be old and somber?"

"I prefer them to keep their minds on their jobs," she said staunchly. "And you are not *my* man."

His laugh was more like a sexy promise.

"Not yet."

Don't miss
A Ranger for Christmas *by Stella Bagwell,*
available December 2018 wherever
Harlequin® Special Edition *books and ebooks are sold.*

www.Harlequin.com

HSEEXP1118

HARLEQUIN®

SPECIAL EDITION

Life, Love and Family

Save **$1.00**

on the purchase of **ANY**

Harlequin® Special Edition book.

Available whever books are sold,
including most bookstores, supermarkets,
drugstores and discount stores.

Save **$1.00**

on the purchase of any Harlequin® Special Edition book.

Coupon valid until February 28, 2019.
Redeemable at participating outlets in the U.S. and Canada only.
Limit one coupon per customer.

52616105

5 65373 00076 2   (8100)0 12397

HSECOUP04506

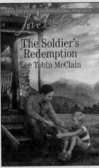

Love Harlequin romance?

DISCOVER.

Be the first to find out about promotions, news and exclusive content!

Facebook.com/HarlequinBooks

Twitter.com/HarlequinBooks

Instagram.com/HarlequinBooks

Pinterest.com/HarlequinBooks

ReaderService.com

EXPLORE.

Sign up for the Harlequin e-newsletter and download a free book from any series at **TryHarlequin.com.**

CONNECT.

Join our Harlequin community to share your thoughts and connect with other romance readers!
Facebook.com/groups/HarlequinConnection

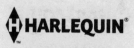

ROMANCE WHEN YOU NEED IT